Escape ...

What if the great Houdini had to escape from the devil himself?

How would you survive as a nonconformist in a world where virtually everyone was branded to a corporation?

A treemage who has betrayed his forest must one day return and face up to his past.

Imagine ...

You must descend into the mile-high flue of a turbine power generator, with a 65°C updraft blowing at hurricane speed.

Daylight comes, and your Angel tries to kill you.

Suppose ...

Your gift to the new king winds up burning his castle down.

Living in a world where the story of your life is literally controlled by your editor.

What if our futures can be fashioned by "Time Sculptors"?

Dream...

How would you deal with a job that required you die and be reborn every fifty years?

Is there a future in virtual retirement communities?

The church decreed that the souls of sinners must be captured and confined for eternity. But what if the captured soul isn't a sinner?

Wonder...

What do we really know about the little people who live in the hedges that grow around the meadows?

How would you handle a rebellious teenage daughter within the first colony on Mars?

If the magic of a witch isn't strong enough to match that of a wizard, the smartest thing for her to do is . . .

What has been said about the
L. RON HUBBARD
PRESENTS
WRITERS OF THE FUTURE
ANTHOLOGIES

"A very generous legacy from L. Ron Hubbard—a fine, fine fiction writer—for the writers of the future."

—Anne McCaffrey, Author

"The Contest has opened the way for scores of writers and has set them out on the fine careers they deserve."

—Jack Williamson, Author

"Prior to L. Ron Hubbard's Writers of the Future Contest starting, there was no field which enabled the new writer to compete with his peers—other new writers."

—Kevin J. Anderson, Author

"Winning the Contest was my first validation that I would have a career. I entered five times before winning and it gave me something I could reach and attain. It kept me writing and going for something. Reading the anthology is important. Writers of the Future is a market and you have to KNOW your market if you are going to submit and win. I had the first four volumes of *Writers of the Future* and just read them over and over before I won and was published in Volume V."

—K.D. Wentworth, Winner, Author and Educator

"The L. Ron Hubbard Writers of the Future Contest has carried out the noble mission of nurturing new science fiction and fantasy writers for a decade now with resounding success."

—Dr. Yoji Kondo, NASA

"Here's skill and storytelling fervor aplenty—these writers of the future have already arrived!"

—Robert Silverberg, Author

"Writers of the Future is a terrific program for new writers. . . . It has my heartiest support and recommendation."

—Terry Brooks, Author

"The Writers of the Future Contest has not only provided a place where new writers could break into print for the first time—but it also has a record of nurturing and discovering writers who have gone on to make their mark in the science fiction field. Long may it continue!"

—Neil Gaiman, Author

SPECIAL OFFER FOR SCHOOLS AND WRITING GROUPS

The fifteen prize-winning stories in this volume, all of them selected by a panel of top professionals in the field of speculative fiction, exemplify the standards that a new writer must meet if he expects to see his work published and achieve professional success.

These stories, augmented by how-to-write articles by some of the top writers of science fiction and fantasy, make this anthology virtually a textbook for use in the classroom and an invaluable resource for students, teachers and workshop instructors in the field of writing.

The materials contained in this and previous volumes have been used with outstanding results in writing courses and workshops held on college and university campuses throughout the United States—from Harvard, Duke and Rutgers to George Washington, Brigham Young and Pepperdine.

To assist and encourage creative writing programs, the *L. Ron Hubbard Presents Writers of the Future* anthologies are available at special quantity discounts when purchased in bulk by schools, universities, workshops and other related groups.

For more information, write:

Specialty Sales Department
Galaxy Press, L.L.C.
7051 Hollywood Blvd., Suite 200
Hollywood, California 90028
or call toll-free: 1-877-8GALAXY
Internet address: www.galaxypress.com
E-mail address: info@galaxypress.com

L. Ron Hubbard Presents Writers of the Future

VOLUME XXI

L. RON HUBBARD
PRESENTS
WRITERS
OF THE
FUTURE

VOLUME XXI

The Year's 15 Best Tales from the
Writers of the Future®
International Writing Program

Illustrated by the Winners in the
Illustrators of the Future®
International Illustration Program

With Essays on Writing and Art by
L. Ron Hubbard • Nina Kiriki Hoffman
• Stephen Hickman

Edited by Algis Budrys

Galaxy Press, L.L.C.

© 2005 Galaxy Press, L.L.C. All Rights Reserved.
Any unauthorized copying, translation, duplication, importation or distribution, in whole or in part, by any means, including electronic copying, storage or transmission, is a violation of applicable laws. Grateful acknowledgement is made to the L. Ron Hubbard Library for permission to reproduce a selection from the copyrighted works of L. Ron Hubbard.

No part of this book may be used or reproduced in any manner whatsoever without written permission except in the case of brief quotations embodied in critical articles or reviews. For information, contact Galaxy Press, L.L.C., 7051 Hollywood Blvd., Suite 200, Hollywood, CA 90028.

Introducing "Tomorrow's Miracles": © 1982 L. Ron Hubbard Library
In the Flue: © 2005 John Schoffstall
Needle Child: © 2005 M.T. Reiten
The Story of His Life: © 2005 David W. Goldman
Green Angel: © 2005 Sean A. Tinsley
The Firebird: © 2005 Andrew Gudgel
My Daughter, the Martian: © 2005 Sidra M.S. Vitale
Meeting the Sculptor: © 2005 Floris M. Kleijne
Seven Keys to Writing Success: © 2005 Nina Kiriki Hoffman
Into the Blank Where Life is Hurled: © 2005 Ken Scholes
Mars Hath No Fury Like a Pixel Double-Crossed: © 2005 Stephen R. Stanley
Blackberry Witch: © 2005 Scott M. Roberts
Style Points: © 2005 Stephen Hickman
Betrayer of Trees: © 2005 Eric James Stone
Deadglass: © 2005 Lon Prater
Last Dance at the Sergeant Majors' Ball: © 2005 Cat Sparks
Annus Mirabilis: © 2005 Mike Rimar
The Keeper Alone: © 2005 Michael Livingston
The Year in the Contests: © 2005 Algis Budrys

Illustration on page   6 © 2005 Alex Quintero
Illustration on page   29 © 2005 Youri Bobrikov
Illustration on page   63 © 2005 Michael Wohlwend
Illustration on page 116 © 2005 Ali Hilton
Illustration on page 140 © 2005 Youri Bobrikov
Illustration on page 160 © 2005 Alex Quintero
Illustration on page 197 © 2005 Cornelius Cockroft
Illustration on page 246 © 2005 Erik Valdez y Alanis
Illustration on page 270 © 2005 Alex Paramonov
Illustration on page 316 © 2005 Perrin Hendrick
Illustration on page 382 © 2005 Steven V. Popovich
Illustration on page 407 © 2005 Perrin Hendrick
Illustration on page 432 © 2005 Michael Brenner
Illustration on page 453 © 2005 Steven V. Popovich
Illustration on page 477 © 2005 Olga Madiar

Cover Artwork: *Silver Warrior* © 1972 Frank Frazetta

This anthology contains works of fiction. Names, characters, places and incidents are either the product of the authors' imaginations or are used fictitiously. Any resemblance to actual events or locales or persons, living or dead, is entirely coincidental. Opinions expressed by nonfiction essayists are their own.

ISBN: 1-59212-217-5
Library of Congress Control Number: 2005929838
First Edition Paperback 10 9 8 7 6 5 4 3 2 1
Printed in the United States of America

BATTLEFIELD EARTH is a registered trademark owned by Author Services, Inc., and is used with its permission. MISSION EARTH and its logo, WRITERS OF THE FUTURE and its logo and ILLUSTRATORS OF THE FUTURE and its logo are trademarks owned by the L. Ron Hubbard Library and are used with permission.

CONTENTS

INTRODUCTION by Algis Budrys xiii

IN THE FLUE by *John Schoffstall*
    Illustrated by Alex Quintero 1

NEEDLE CHILD by *M.T. Reiten*
    Illustrated by Youri Bobrikov 23

THE STORY OF HIS LIFE by *David W. Goldman*
    Illustrated by Michael Wohlwend 58

INTRODUCING "TOMORROW'S MIRACLES"
    by L. Ron Hubbard 98

GREEN ANGEL by *Sean A. Tinsley*
    Illustrated by Ali Hilton 111

THE FIREBIRD by *Andrew Gudgel*
    Illustrated by Youri Bobrikov 136

MY DAUGHTER, THE MARTIAN by *Sidra M.S. Vitale*
    Illustrated by Alex Quintero 155

MEETING THE SCULPTOR by *Floris M. Kleijne*
    Illustrated by Cornelius Cockroft 192

SEVEN KEYS TO WRITING SUCCESS
    by Nina Kiriki Hoffman 230

INTO THE BLANK WHERE LIFE IS HURLED
by *Ken Scholes*
Illustrated by Erik Valdez y Alanis 241

MARS HATH NO FURY LIKE A PIXEL DOUBLE-CROSSED
by *Stephen R. Stanley*
Illustrated by Alex Paramonov 265

BLACKBERRY WITCH by *Scott M. Roberts*
Illustrated by Perrin Hendrick 311

STYLE POINTS by Stephen Hickman 369

BETRAYER OF TREES by *Eric James Stone*
Illustrated by Steven V. Popovich 377

DEADGLASS by *Lon Prater*
Illustrated by Perrin Hendrick 403

LAST DANCE AT THE SERGEANT MAJORS' BALL
by *Cat Sparks*
Illustrated by Michael Brenner 427

ANNUS MIRABILIS by *Mike Rimar*
Illustrated by Steven V. Popovich 449

THE KEEPER ALONE by *Michael Livingston*
Illustrated by Olga Madiar 472

THE YEAR IN THE CONTESTS by Algis Budrys 519

CONTEST INFORMATION 523

INTRODUCTION

by
Algis Budrys

Many years ago I wrote some fine copy for an ad regarding L. Ron Hubbard's Writers and Illustrators of the Future Contests. In that ad, I stated our purpose: to discover, reward, promote, publish, award and publicize new writers and artists. This statement augmented and further defined L. Ron Hubbard's original purpose—to help budding writers, and later, artists, by establishing the Contests in the first place, awarding handsome prizes and publishing the winning stories and illustrations.

Any two of the Contest parameters alone could—and would—have provided an opportunity for the aspirant to help achieve his dreams. But, we never thought to do it that way. It was all or none.

So, every year, we run the Contests on a quarterly basis, using our panels of professional writers and artists to select the winners of their respective Contest.

The quarterly winners are contacted as soon as the judging results come in and are tabulated. Their personal reactions are as varied as their stories and their artwork: stunned silence, disbelief, yelling, crying, laughing . . . you name it and we've probably heard it.

All prize money is promptly awarded to that quarter's winners. In the Writers' Contest, it's $1,000 for first place, $750 for second place, and $500 for third place. The Illustrators' Contest awards $500 for each of the three winners per quarter.

While the volume of entries from aspiring writers and artists continues to grow, there is another aspect to what these Contests brought about. It provided a means for professionals in both of these fields to help ensure the future of speculative fiction.

Joining in to contribute and lend their support to this objective have been the many top professionals in the field of speculative fiction. At the outset, the panel of writing judges, (in addition to myself) included Gregory Benford, Robert Silverberg and Jack Williamson. This was followed over the years by other greats of speculative fiction: Kevin J. Anderson, Doug Beason, Ben Bova, Ramsey Campbell, Orson Scott Card, Hal Clement, Brian Herbert, Frank Herbert, Nina Kiriki Hoffman, Eric Kotani, Anne McCaffrey, C. L. Moore, Larry Niven, Andre Norton, Frederik Pohl, Jerry Pournelle, Tim Powers, Charles Sheffield, Theodore Sturgeon, John Varley, K. D. Wentworth, Gene Wolfe, Dave Wolverton and Roger Zelazny.

A few years into the Contest, to provide the same opportunity for aspiring illustrators, my long-time friend, Frank Kelly Freas, joined in as the coordinating judge for the Illustrators of the Future Contest. He brought on board several of the major names in illustration. And this list has now expanded to include Edd Cartier, Vincent Di Fate, Diane Dillon, Leo Dillon, Bob Eggleton, Will Eisner, Frank Frazetta, Laura Brodian Freas, Stephen Hickman, Judith Holman, Shun Kijima, Jack Kirby, Paul Lehr, Ron Lindahn, Val Lakey Lindahn, Moebius, Sergey V. Poyarkov, Alex

INTRODUCTION

Schomburg, H. R. Van Dongen, William R. Warren, Jr., and Stephen Youll.

If there is one character trait held in common among the judges of the Writers of the Future and Illustrators of the Future Contests, it is the care and concern demonstrated in establishing a road to success for future generations of writers and illustrators. This is no more evident than with the four distinguished judges who recently passed away and to whom we pay homage here.

Frank Kelly Freas (1917–2005)

One of the most prolific and popular science fiction artists in the history of the genre, Frank Kelly Freas illustrated stories by such classic luminaries of the field as L. Ron Hubbard, Robert A. Heinlein, A.E. Van Vogt, Arthur C. Clarke and Isaac Asimov. Known by his friends as "Kelly," he was the first artist to win 11 Hugo Awards, along with a record of 20 nominations. Kelly's original paintings hang in museums, universities and many private collections. His work has been the subject of four bestselling collections including the latest volume, *Frank Kelly Freas: As He Sees It*.

In 1988, Kelly became the Founding Coordinating Judge of L. Ron Hubbard's Illustrators of the Future Contest, the companion competition to the L. Ron Hubbard Writers of the Future Contest. It was intended to do for new illustrators what the Writers' Contest had done for new writers—discover new talent, acknowledge them, bring them to the attention of publishers and help launch their professional careers—and this it has done successfully.

The effective philosophy Kelly lived by was: "Don't sweat it—just draw." His advice to illustrators, based on 40 years' experience as an illustrator at the time, can be found in his essay, "SF Illustration as an Art," published in Volume IV of this anthology series.

In 1999, in recognition of his exceptional work as an artist, Kelly received the L. Ron Hubbard Lifetime Achievement Award for Contribution to the Arts.

Andre Norton (1912–2005)

Andre Norton (Mary Alice Norton) became a full-time writer after having served for twenty-two years as a librarian in the Cleveland Public Library System.

In a literary career spanning more than six decades, she wrote over 100 novels in a number of popular genres, including juvenile, Gothic and historical. Her best-known work was done in the fields of science fiction (the Beastmaster saga) and fantasy (the Witch World series).

She established the High Hallack Library in 1997, a research and resource facility for science fiction and fantasy writers.

In Volume XVIII of this anthology series, Andre shared her experiences and hard-won lessons as a writer in her essay, "Advice to the New Writer." Andre became a Writers of the Future judge in 1989.

Will Eisner (1917–2005)

Will Eisner was a pioneering force in comics for over 60 years. The breadth of his career ranged widely, from his groundbreaking works in early newspaper comics to his major and innovative role in the transition to graphic novels.

He taught cartooning at the New York School of

Visual Arts, authored two definitive works, *Comics and Sequential Art* and *Graphic Storytelling*, and had his work showcased by the Whitney Museum in New York. The Eisner Awards, the most prestigious comics industry award, was established in his honor and is held annually at the Comic-Con International convention in San Diego, California.

Lending a helping hand to the newcomer was always important to Will, as can be observed in his article published in Volume XIX of this series entitled, "To the Illustrators of the Future."

Will was an Illustrators of the Future judge since its inception in 1988.

Hal Clement (1922–2003)

Hal Clement's (the pen name for Harry C. Stubbs) interest in science and science fiction started in 1930 when he saw a Buck Rogers comic strip featuring a spaceship en route to Mars. His father, unable to answer Hal's science questions, took him to a local library from which Hal emerged with an astronomy book under one arm and Jules Verne's *Trip to the Moon* under the other. Hal went on to earn college degrees in astronomy, chemistry and education. He was also a pilot in World War II and retired a full colonel having flown 35 missions.

With his extensive technical background, Hal was able to put hard science into science fiction. This provided for a very impressive career culminating in the Science Fiction Writers of America Grand Master Award in 1999.

In addition to a successful writing career, Hal also taught high school science for 40 years. He was frequently seen at science fiction conventions throughout North America as a guest speaker and was always willing to talk to his many friends and fans.

Hal's advice to the novice writer can be found in Volume V of this series, entitled "The Magic Picture."

Hal became a Writers of the Future judge in 2001.

What our past and present Contest judges have done —and continue to do—guarantees that, for the future of the genre, there will always be a fresh idea or novel twist to those next stories and images from writers and illustrators of the future.

I now invite you to enjoy *L. Ron Hubbard Presents Writers of the Future Volume XXI!*

IN THE FLUE

Written by
John Schoffstall

Illustrated by
Alex Quintero

About the Author

John Schoffstall's writing really started with a long-distance, late-teen romance. He would send off a chapter of original "sword-and-sorcery" fantasy every week or so to keep his companion's mutual interest. While the romantic relationship did not stand the separation, John's connection with writing remained, though not without its own separations. During the 1970s, John pursued a short, but admittedly disastrous career in small business. This convinced him to completely change course. He entered medical school and became an emergency room physician, his profession for the past twenty years.

Through business and medicine, John continued to write stories. Three years ago, he became serious about his speculative writing, and the story in this edition is one result. John is currently on staff at Lenox Avenue, an online magazine for speculative fiction at www.lenoxavemag.com. He says there's nothing quite like reading a lot of "slush" to see what works and what doesn't. In his spare time, John's hobby is writing and enjoying the works of his contemporaries.

About the Illustrator

A self-taught illustrator, artist Alex Quintero was born in one of Los Angeles' oldest neighborhoods, South Gate, a few miles southeast of Hollywood. Inspired by science fiction films like the Star Wars *saga*, The Dark Crystal, *and even the 1950s classic* War of the Worlds, *Alex early on was intent on entering the field of conceptual design and visual effects that help create celluloid and digital magic. As a youth, he showed early illustration talent and was accepted into Los Angeles County's High School for the Arts in visual design. After moving to Ontario, some twenty-five miles east, Alex later worked as a freelance artist—providing concept design, animation, product design, clothing logos, cartoon creation, murals and, yes, even illustration.*

The Hollywood film bug never abandoned Alex though. He's now back in school currently studying model-making, photography and visual "creature" effect stuff at the prestigious Pasadena Art Center School of Design. And in case you're reading this . . . he wants any budding commercial filmmaker to know that he's also done storyboards for independent films and ads.

Ryfka Saban found the Tmarim Creek cliffs deserted. Odd. She dropped her climbing gear in the grass and peered up the cliffs, shading her eyes. The Tmarim pitches were popular, and on most Sundays there'd be at least a couple casual or technical climbers already scaling the rock walls by midmorning, but today there were none. A breeze hissed through the grasses at the base of the wall and sawed the fronds of palm trees against each other. Ryfka had the cliff to herself.

She should have been happy. Instead, she found she was dreading the thought of another climb. Technical climbing had been her hobby for five years, and although she had fought against this realization for months, she could no longer avoid it: she was bored with climbing. It happened with all her hobbies. Eventually they became drudgery instead of joy. Then she had to give them up and move on. She sometimes wondered, with a trace of fear, whether someday she might run out of things to move on to. What would she do when she finally came to that void?

Squashing down the thought, telling herself she'd enjoy the climb once she'd started, Ryfka picked a route and tackled the cliff. She was halfway up the 8a route called "Kalashnikov" when her neurophone tickled her eighth cranial nerve with its insistent vibrato.

It was Maks, her agent. "Ryfka," Maks said, with his usual enthusiasm, "I've got this great job for you."

"I don't work weekends, Maks. You know that."

"One thousand shekels an hour for a maximum of twenty hours, minimum ten thousand shekels, performance bonus of ten thousand shekels for finishing the job within six hours."

Big money. Someone must be desperate. Ryfka liked desperation.

"I'm halfway up an 8a pitch, Maks."

"I don't know what that means, Ryfka."

"A cliff, Maks, a very bitchy cliff. I'm climbing. I don't want to do work, I'm enjoying myself." A lie.

"Wait a minute. . . ."

The view from halfway up the Kalashnikov was spectacular. She could look down on the tops of clumps of palm fifty meters below. Beyond them, down a gentle downslope, hotels and houses poked through the trees, and beyond them the impossibly perfect aqua green plain of the Dead Sea, rippled slightly with April winds, stretching out toward the distant shore of Jordan. Swallows wheeled around the crags, calling to one another and catching insects on mad dashes through the air. The rock wall was cold and damp against her bony chest and thighs, and her handholds cold beneath her fingers.

Maks's voice inside her head again: "Okay, they're willing to go up to fifteen thousand shekels an hour base, and the rest proportional."

"Two thousand and the rest proportional, except for fifty thousand for finishing the job within six hours."

Pause. Then: "Done," Maks said.

"They're crazy," Ryfka said.

"They're the government," Maks said.

"Crazy, dishonest, stupid, venal, insincere, dishonest, manipulative—"

"You said 'dishonest' twice. You want to hear what the job is?"

"Yep." Ryfka began to undo her position on the wall, working herself into a situation where she safely could release both hands at once and get at her pack.

"It's the Herzl solar flue farm, in the Negev. South of Mitzpeh Ramon."

"Herzl?" Ryfka said. "They probably use Daruma, all the flues built before 2030 do." Daruma was a fault-tolerant programming language, popular for hardware control apps earlier in the century. But programming culture burns through popular ideas relentlessly, and by 2048 the code monkeys had moved on to newer things. No one programmed in Daruma anymore. Except Ryfka. No one programmed in A3g1s. Except Ryfka. Or FORTH. Or COBOL-Nu, or scores of other dead languages. Being a programming language archeologist was a nice career niche. Ryfka could often name her own price. But two thousand shekels an hour was just absurd.

"So what's the job?" she asked Maks.

"Flue ... lemme see ... Flue No. 7 is five percent off its rated output. They want you to look over the code."

"Five percent? You're kidding. This has to be fixed in six hours? And it's not the code. What could have gone wrong with the code?" Old code didn't just get bitrot. Sabotage? Doubtful. Government installations had deep, deep firewalls. Whatever was wrong with Flue No. 7 she doubted she would be able to fix it. She saw her 50K bonus disappearing beyond the event horizon of impossibility. She'd wave a dead chicken over the code for a few hours, tell the admins it was fine, and collect the minimum fee. Still, very good money for not doing very much.

Maks said, "Right now, MOS wants every last watt

Illustrated by Alex Quintero

they can get out of the flues. Even the last five percent. You can figure out why." MOS was the Ministry of Science, Culture and Sport, which ran the flue farms.

"No, I can't," said Ryfka. "Why?"

"The war, of course."

"What war?"

Silence.

"Ryfka," Maks said after a moment, "Israel will probably be at war in a few days. Talks with the Syro-Hashemite Hegemony broke down last week. There are twenty divisions of hovertanks massed on the other side of the Jordan. Don't you watch the news?"

Ah, that explained why Tmarim Creek was deserted. Worry keeps people home.

"I don't watch the news. I'm not political, Maks. You know that."

Maks's voice had a reproachful tone. "This is beyond politics. This is war."

"It's politics, Maks. It's politicians on both sides thumping for war because they're too stupid to make peace."

"You're really hardcore, aren't you, Ryfka," Maks said.

"Yes," Ryfka said. "I am. And now I'm off to Herzl. Thanks, Maks. You've earned your ten percent."

Ryfka had reached a spot on the cliff wall where she could release both hands. She dug in her backpack and brought out boots and gloves with gecko grips on the palms and or soles. She slipped them on and cinched them up. Gecko grips had revolutionized climbing over the past ten years. Or, in the opinion of many—including Ryfka—destroyed it. No one needed nuts or cams or slings or pitons anymore. Or skill. It was beyond annoying to spend an hour laboriously working one's way up a rock face, only to have a smirking ten-year-old wearing geckos come shooting past, then wave at you from the top.

Despite her distaste, Ryfka carried geckos in her pack as insurance. It had taken her forty minutes to climb halfway up the Kalashnikov. Using the geckos, she was on the ground in less than two.

She tossed her climbing gear into the Citroën's back seat, spun up the car's rotor, and wove her way back down the narrow gravel road that led to Highway 90 south. Ninety ran through what had been the Occupied Territories a generation ago, but was now just part of Unified Israel. The Zurich Protocols and big financial subsidies to both sides by the EU had finally ended most conflict between Israelis and Palestinians, but the resolution of that horror just revealed wider wounds between Israel and the Muslim world. There had been two major wars since 2011, and now, it seemed, there might be a third.

As she passed En Boqeq, the Dead Sea fell away behind her in the rearview mirror and the blistering hot yellow plain of the Negev Desert opened up ahead. Even in April the heat in the Negev was intense by midday. Temperatures had risen 10°C here since the turn of the century. Ryfka cranked down both windows and left the air conditioning off. She craved heat. She had a brush with anorexia nervosa in her late teens. She had managed to channel its dark obsessive energy into hobbies and work, but she had never been able to gain much weight, and was always cold, even in summer.

South of the junction with Highway 25 to Be'er Sheva she began to glimpse the flues shimmering through the hot desert air.

Solar flues were easily the tallest things in the nation of Israel. Towering over even the country's modest mountains, most of the flues were three kilometers high, pale slender towers visible from very far away. The power they generated ran the nation, and split water from the Med into hydrogen and oxygen which powered fuel cells all over the world, including the ones in Ryfka's Citroën.

The flues also powered the gigajoule x-ray and gamma lasers that protected Israel's borders. Which was doubtless why MOS was anxious to wring every last erg out of them right now.

Ninety kilometers further south, and she was able to see the glitter of the collection fields low on the horizon, like a heat mirage but brighter. She dialed down the car's windshield transparency to eighty percent. Chain-link fence topped by razor wire swung in from the western desert and tracked the road.

The guard post at the Herzl entrance was more heavily fortified than she had remembered from her last visit. Sandbags protected machine-gun nests on either side of the road. An unsmiling guard stuck an electronic wand through the car window and passed it over her bare shoulder. Ryfka had been chipped for most security clearances she needed in her work. *Beep-boop* went the wand.

"Ryfka Saban," the guard stated. "You're the programmer?" Ryfka nodded. "They're expecting you at No. 7."

There was a glad note in his voice. Relief? Respect? Perhaps he had heard there was a problem, and he was grateful she had come to fix it. Something stirred in Ryfka, a twinge, an ache. She squashed it down.

The road led straight into the flue array, between two adjacent collection fields. The flue towers were laid out in a hexagonal grid, each flue surrounded by a fifteen-kilometer-diameter collection field roofed with glass, under which black ropes of water-filled heat-retention tubing netted the desert floor. The concept behind solar-flue technology was simple: hot air rises. Air beneath the glass roof, heated by the sun, rose through the hollow tube of the flue. The force of its passage turned pressure-staged wind turbines at the tower's base, which spun the rotor of an electrical generator. Each of the Herzl flues output about five hundred megawatts.

Flue No. 7 proved to be thirty kilometers across the desert from the entrance. Ryfka pulled into the tiny parking lot at the base of the flue. The flue itself was shocking in its size. A solar flue looked almost delicate from a distance, shimmering through haze on the horizon, but as one approached, it grew, and grew, becoming impossibly massive as one came up to it, a column of concrete three hundred meters in diameter, like a hundred sports stadiums stacked one on top of another. A dozen titanic concrete support piers flared out from its base, each twenty meters wide and a hundred tall. The roar of the turbines had been audible from a kilometer away, and next to the tower Ryfka could feel their throb in the earth itself, shuddering through her legs with each step. Dust and tiny pebbles danced on the dry earth.

A man in a brown jumpsuit opened a door at the base of the flue and waved. Ryfka retrieved her bag of programming toys and a big ugly sweater from the Citroën's trunk and hurried over.

Inside, the turbine roar dropped tens of decibels: sound insulation was obviously a priority here. And as Ryfka had predicted, the air conditioning was too cold for her. She pulled on the sweater. The man who had motioned her in grasped her hand in his and shook it. He had a pleasant, serious face, just beginning to develop the lines of middle age. He appeared to be in his mid-to-late thirties, a little older than Ryfka.

"Ryfka Saban?" he said. "I'm Dov Leib, Operating Engineer for Flue No. 7." He pointed to another man across the room. "Assistant Engineer Aron Shalev. Thank you for coming on such short notice." He smiled. "We appreciate your patriotism in Israel's hour of need. The war effort needs everyone's help."

"I'm not patriotic," Ryfka said. Dov's face fell. He didn't appear angry, just uncomprehending.

Dov said, "My boss, the Chief of Flue Operations— that's Dr. Har-Lavi—knows that a problem with the code is a long shot. The output of this flue has been five percent subpar for a couple days now, and we've exhausted most other possibilities. The rotor checks out, the collection field is intact. It's puzzling."

The room was small and spare. Dov cleared off a space on his own desk where Ryfka could set up and log onto the flue controller. On one corner of the desktop sat a picture frame with a holo of a smiling young woman holding two children. "Yours?" Ryfka asked. Dov smiled and nodded.

She logged in and retrieved the control source code. Her projector created a drifting abstract display of colored shapes in the air before her that symbolized the logical relationships between the elements of No. 7's code. Ryfka felt her way through the display with a light pen, expanding a node here, riffling through a subroutine there. All checksums were correct. No memory leaks. Profiling the code didn't reveal any unexpected bottlenecks. Ryfka ran a few simulations, and they executed flawlessly.

"The code is fine," she told Dov. "If it ran No. 7 normally last week, it should run it now. Your problem is elsewhere."

"I'm sorry to hear that," Dov said. "I'd hoped you would find something that could be fixed."

"And I wish I could earn my performance bonus for fixing it." She thought a moment. "So the turbines are okay, the controls are okay. What about the column?"

Dov nodded. "There may be some sort of problem inside. The wallbots have been busy lately. But—"

"Wallbots?"

"Wall-crawling robots, twice as big as your hand. The flue is lined with a polymer resin that helps create laminar airflow. It gets dinged when sand or pebbles are sucked into the flue, and the wallbots crawl around and make repairs. They've been using a lot more polymer than usual since this problem started. There may be a big rip in the lining that they're trying to fix."

"Has anyone looked?"

Dov shook his head. "Can't turn the flue off. Because we might be at war at any moment."

"So? You can't turn the turbines off even for a couple of minutes?"

Dov stared at her. Ryfka knew that look: she'd said something stupid. Dov caught himself: "I'm sorry, you startled me. It doesn't work that way. Park the turbines, and the airflow *increases*. It's the air that works the rotor. Airflow at the top of the flue is around thirty-five meters per second under full load. That's the low end of hurricane range. With the rotor parked, it doubles. When we have to go down into the flue, there are steel curtains that are drawn across the lower opening. The process takes about six hours to complete. We don't do it often. The flue is very simple engineering, not much that can go wrong. The last time they closed down this flue was over a decade ago."

Ryfka tried to recover. "Thirty-five meters per second is tolerable. You can't send someone down?"

"There's a lift on the inside, but it can't be used while the flue is running, it would just be blown about.

And the other problem is heat. Air at the top of the flue comes out at about 65 °C. Also known as 'medium rare' on a meat thermometer."

"I've been in hotter saunas," Ryfka said.

"Not with air blowing by you at hurricane speed. That's how convection ovens work. Rapid transfer of heat. We've had guys die of heat stroke while working under the collection field without proper gear, some in under thirty minutes from entering the field, and the airflow there is far less. The flue is too dangerous."

"So what's this 'proper gear' the guys in the collection field wear?"

"Heat-retardant suits. Mylar, foam, mylar, foam, etc., for about ten layers. Not refrigerated, but they'll keep you safe for an hour or two before you have to come in."

"Excellent," said Ryfka. "Show me one in my size. I'm a two, by the way."

"Ms. Saban! You are thinking of going down the flue? How? The lift isn't safe, it will buck you off in the updraft."

"I'm not using the lift."

"Huh?"

"Gecko gloves," Ryfka said. "I can walk up and down walls with them."

Dov seemed to consider the idea for a moment, but then shook his head. "No. I'm sorry," he said. "It's just too dangerous."

The voice of the gate guard echoed in Ryfka's memory. He had been grateful for her presence. She had come to fix a problem. So let her fix it, dammit!

Why did she care? It was just money. Dov was right, climbing down the flue into an oven-temperature hurricane was crazy. But it was climbing. Climbing that she cared about, for the first time in months.

She put her hands on her hips. "Mr. Leib," she said, "I'm earning that bonus." What had he said when she first came in? "Patriotism, Mr. Leib. Think of our country. The war might come at any moment. The laser defenses need every last joule they can get. We know by elimination that the problem must be within the flue. This may be our only opportunity to fix it."

Dov was wavering. "It's not policy—"

She dug in the knife. "How could you live with yourself if you failed to make every possible effort for your country?"

She had him. She could see it in the sudden weariness of his drooping eyelids and mouth, the way his gaze evaded hers. He had been outmaneuvered. His own ideals had been used against him. Ryfka really had to get out of the air conditioning. She pulled her sweater more tightly around her.

• • •

To get to the top of Flue No. 7 they had to ride in an open basket, a wooden platform barely big enough for two people, rimmed by a waist-high grate. An electric winch pulled it skyward, up the side of the flue. The afternoon had passed and night had fallen while Ryfka was inside the control room, and the basket flew upward in darkness, the concrete wall of the flue a blur only a few feet away. Warning lights for aircraft flashed against the immense black outline of the flue. Its heat radiated on Ryfka's skin.

Ryfka filled Dov in on gecko gloves. It had been known for a long time that geckos had something remarkable going on with the pads of their feet, something that enabled them to grip almost any surface, even upside down. Electron microscopy had exposed the geckos' trick: their footpads were surfaced with billions of tiny tubules, each barely a hundred nanometers across, that gripped a surface through the van der Waals force. But even after the secret was known, manufacturing something similar that was usable by humans had stymied engineers until well into the twenty-first century.

Dov was doubtful. "You can't go very fast with them, can you?"

"Maybe two kilometers an hour. I won't be able to see the entire flue, but I'll get pretty deep. Maybe I'll be lucky."

After a minute of silence, Dov said, "Ms. Saban, I didn't mean to put you on the spot, earlier. About supporting the war effort, and all. If you're a member of the peace party, that's okay. I don't agree with them, but I know they care about our country as much as the war party does."

"I'm not a member of the peace party."

"Ah. One of the religious parties?"

"I don't belong to any political party," Ryfka said.

"You belong to the 'me' party, then."

In the darkness she could not see his expression.

As they neared the rim, the roar of the flue increased. Dov had provided them both with the noise-cancellation earphones that flue workers wore. Dov's had a phone headset built in. Ryfka keyed her own neurophone to Dov's headset. A pickup implanted in the skin over her larynx would pick up her voice even if someone standing next to her were unable to hear her voice because of ambient noise.

Presently, the lift slowed and came to a stop at the upper rim of the flue. The flue was as wide as a sports stadium, a yawning black gulf. Screaming invisible wind poured up out of it, its heat painful against

Ryfka's face, its refraction turning the opposite side of the flue into vague swimming spectral shapes. Ryfka had already pulled on the mylar sandwich thermosuit, a silvery sheath covering her from neck to toes. The heat from the updraft was uncomfortable enough that she put on the hood quickly once they reached the rim. Not being sure what she'd need, she had brought most of her climbing gear in her pack, rope, nuts, cams, chalk bag and all the rest. She selected a fuel-cell torch and hung it at her hip, and clipped a Busse-Kainuun folding knife to the outside of the thermosuit.

She pulled on the gecko gloves and boots and cinched them tight. She climbed over the low rail at the inner edge of the flue's lip. Hot wind surged ghostlike past her face, centimeters away. She could reach out and touch it as if it were a physical object, like placing one's hand in a fast-running stream.

Ryfka bent forward into the flue, and pushed her upper body into the burning air. It struck her head and chest like a blast of water from a hydrant, pushing her back. She bent her knees, slammed a gecko glove down on the side of the flue, and pulled herself down. Slammed the other hand down, and pulled. Then her feet, one after another. Now she was fully within the flue, head down into the boiling darkness.

There was little sensation of gravity, the force of the updraft against her was so strong. It fluttered the folds of the thermosuit madly against her body. She crawled down the side of the flue on all fours, head first. For the first few minutes she had an irrational fear that some object would come sailing out of the darkness and strike her, as if she were walking into a hurricane with the air full of debris, but she knew that was an illusion, the air in the flue was perfectly clear. After fifty meters she decided to look around. The torch threw ten thousand lumens continuous, fifty thousand lumens for five seconds in burst mode. She trained it downward and played it around the flue walls in burst mode. Nothing. Curving walls of slick, reflective polymer everywhere, dun yellow color.

Wait. Something far below, an irregularity in the wall—

The torch cut off. Impatiently, Ryfka waited for its capacitor bank to recharge. Again she trained it downward. Yes, there was something there, but it was so far away. She started down again. "I think I can see something," she said to Dov.

"What is it?" his voice echoed in her head.

"Don't know. It's far down. I'm headed toward it now."

A hundred meters down the flue. Two hundred meters. Three hundred. She played the light downward. The bump on the wall didn't seem much bigger. It must be a kilometer away or more.

It would take her too long to get to that unknown object by crawling down the wall. But there was a way to get there fast. She could simply fall. But then how would she get out?

She realized she didn't care. That being here, doing this, was the only thing she'd really cared about doing in far too long. She didn't have much to go home to anyway. That was the problem in belonging to the "me" party.

Ryfka turned herself around, so she was head up. She peeled the gecko boots off the wall one at a time, then one hand. Then the other. Then she fell.

The fall was eerie in its slowness at first. Her velocity reached equilibrium in about ten seconds, and she guessed she was going about twenty meters per second relative to the wall. Human terminal velocity in Earth gravity is fifty to sixty meters per second, and the updraft was pushing her upwards at around thirty-five meters per second. She played her torch below. The irregularity on the wall was approaching rapidly. It was not solid, but a moving, crawling mass of objects that made her think of a colony of ants or termites. She reached out with her gecko gloves and slapped them against the wall. The geckos grabbed and held, and she grunted in pain as they yanked at her arms. Sudden heat at her right armpit. The thermosuit had ripped at a seam. She would have even less time than she had planned. She decided the heat felt good.

She let loose from the wall again, but this time caught herself before she had fallen more than another hundred meters. She could now see the mass on the side of the flue wall, and swarming over it scores of what appeared to be gigantic insects—oh. It dawned on her what they were.

"We got a wallbot convention here," she told Dov.

"Ah-ha!" came Dov's voice over her neurophone. "Did I guess right? They're trying to repair a big tear in the liner?"

"Can't tell yet. I'm going closer."

Edging down the wall headfirst again, Ryfka approached the crawling mass of wallbots. They were trying to cover with polymer a large irregular lump, a little more than a meter in diameter, not a tear. Odd . . . Ryfka pushed some of the 'bots aside, unclipped her Busse-Kainuun and flipped it open. She dug it into the mass, and rippled downward. Another rip at right angles created an X. She clipped the knife to her belt again, grabbed two leaves of the cut, and opened the sheet of polymer like a book. She gasped.

It was a body. The wallbots had been trying to cover up a corpse.

A dead body exposed to a constant flow of air does not decay in the usual fashion, but desiccates into a mummy. The body on the wall had turned dull mahogany brown with the heat. The skin and muscles of the face were contracted tightly around the nose and the skull, the lips pulled back to display a toothy rictus. Eyes had lost all convexity and were merely hard black depressions in the face. Arms, legs and spine had frozen partially flexed, turning the corpse into a sort of ball. It wore brown trousers and a buff shirt . . . and a *hijab* that had slipped back from the head and now circled the neck. It had been a woman. She had been a Muslim.

She was wearing a suicide belt.

Ryfka's heart pounded in her throat. Then she gathered herself again. How long had the woman been here? Probably a few days. If her bomb hadn't gone off yet, it wasn't likely to.

"Dov," she said, "I've found your problem."

"Good."

"It is a bomb-loaded corpse."

"Wha——?"

Ryfka explained. "I don't know what happened to the bomb," she said. "Maybe the electronics in the detonator failed in the heat. I think the bomber must have failed in the heat, too. She's wearing geckos. She probably planned to crawl down the tube and detonate her bomb at the turbines, but she was dressed in ordinary clothing, and I suppose she didn't realize she'd die of heat stroke. Still, she got over a kilometer in. I'm not sure I could have done as well."

Ryfka reflected that she was going to die too, like the bomber. Strange companions, dying the same death in this hot invisible hurricane, in the utter darkness. The heat pouring through the tear in her thermosuit now surrounded her. The inside of the suit stuck to her body with sweat, and she was very thirsty; she must have sweated out a lot of fluid already, and her body temperature was going up. Heat stroke wasn't far off. She had known this would happen when she decided to fall down the tube, but it didn't matter: she had wanted more than anything else to find the problem and fix it. And she had.

"All right," said Dov. "Good job. Now let's get you out of there."

"Dov, it's okay. I can't get out. I'm too deep. My suit's ripped. I'm getting hot fast. Heat stroke will get me soon. It's okay. I did what I came to do. I found your problem."

"You left ropes up here—"

"Too short. One hundred twenty meters, and I'm more than a kilometer down."

Long pause. Then Dov said, "Wait a minute." She overheard him talking on another connection to Aron Shalev in the flue control room.

The hurricane wind about her suddenly increased, tearing at her body ferociously. Even with the geckos, she could barely hold on to the wall. "Dov, what happened?"

"Aron cut off the turbines. The upflow is now about sixty-five meters per second. That's more than terminal velocity. Just let go. You'll come home."

She was almost afraid to feel relief. So she wasn't going to die after all? "Wait—" There was something she had to do. Fighting against the demon wind, Ryfka hacked away the remainder of the polymer from the bomber woman's corpse, and pulled its hands and feet out of its geckos, which still clung to the wall. The wind nearly ripped the corpse out of her arms, but it was light, no more than twenty kilos, and she clung to it with all her strength. Then she let go of the wall.

She drifted upward, slowly at first, then faster. She looked up. There was a tiny bright light, far away at the rim. She guessed it was Dov's flashlight. Swimming like a skydiver in the air, she aimed for it. Up she flew. Closer came the light until she was on top of it, and Dov's arms grabbed her and pulled her out of the air column, and they both went tumbling together onto the flue's concrete rim, she laughing uncontrollably, that she was alive, alive, alive.

•••

While she rested Dov searched the dead woman's clothing.

"How did she get in?" Ryfka wondered.

"Don't know. The army shot down a Syrian fedayeen in an ultralight near the Sinai a few days ago. Maybe someone like him was able to get in below the radar screen and drop her into the flue. Look here." He handed Ryfka a paper envelope.

Inside was a sheaf of holos and old photos. They had been damaged by the heat in the flue, the edges were brown and the colors faded. Here a young woman in a *hijab* stood with a young man, their arms around each other, smiling. Was this the woman and her lover, or husband? Or was it her sister, or her friend? Here was a toothless old woman with a deeply lined face sitting amid a crowd of children. They were the same age as Dov's kids, in the holo on his desk. There was a middle-aged man in a closely trimmed beard, with a goat, standing by a stone well. Father? Uncle? A serious young man in a western-style suit, before a mosque. A classroom. Young people boating. Ryfka sifted through the pictures in wonder and horror. Perfectly ordinary people, doing perfectly ordinary things, raising families, loving one another, having children. Why had this woman, who had such wonderful, ordinary people in her life, thrown them away? Was it hate? Ryfka could see no hate in the people in the photos. Was it love? But what kind of love does such a thing? She had everything Ryfka wanted, and had always recoiled from. And she had thrown it all away. Ryfka bent down over her corpse, and put her living cheek against the woman's dead face, shriveled and hard, but still warm from the flue. "Why?" she whispered. "Why?"

"Look at the east," Dov said. Ryfka raised her head. Far away on the eastern horizon, a flash. Then another. No noise, not yet. "The war's started," Dov said.

They gathered up their equipment. Together they manhandled the bomber woman's corpse onto the lift. She had been slightly built, and dried as her body was, she seemed to weigh almost nothing. Ryfka and Dov stood side by side on the lift as it descended. It had been designed for only two people, and with the corpse present Ryfka had to press up against Dov. In the darkness she clutched the packet of pictures of a dead woman's life and squeezed it to her cold breast.

"Tell me all about the war party," she said to Dov.

"Huh?"

"Why do you belong to it? What are its policies? What plans does it have?"

"Uh, sure." He sounded a little confused, but willing. "Well, the current leadership—"

She would join the war party tomorrow. She would read its literature, work its phone banks, staple its posters to phone poles, hand out its pamphlets, march in its demonstrations, work to advance its vision for her country.

Or perhaps she would join the peace party.

She'd work out the details later.

NEEDLE CHILD

Written by
M.T. Reiten

Illustrated by
Youri Bobrikov

About the Author

M.T. Reiten thought life was a bit too sterile working inside a Houston laser research lab. So he moved to Wisconsin, got married, and enlisted in the U.S. Army where he served as a signal officer in Germany, Croatia and Bosnia. After his first tour of duty, M.T. returned to the states to work on his PhD in electrical engineering but was recalled to active duty in Afghanistan in 2003 as part of Operation Enduring Freedom.

Ironically, that's when M.T.'s writing career also seemed to take off. Though he had begun writing science fiction and fantasy while attending high school in North Dakota, M.T.'s fiction writing was placed on hold while studying applied physics in graduate school. Instead, he wrote more scholarly works. He started writing speculative fiction again while working on his doctorate degree. Today, when not serving abroad, M.T. lives with his wife, Beth, and two cats in Stillwater, Oklahoma, where he is also active in the Oklahoma Science Fiction Writers group.

About the Illustrator

Born in the old town of Berejani, Ukraine, with the nearby Carpathian Mountains as a backdrop, young Youri Bobrikov always knew he would be in the arts. His father was an artist and spent weekends teaching the young lad about drawing, paints, light and color. Like many independent-minded boys, however, Youri wanted to pursue his own path in theater. Years later, he graduated from the University of Culture and Arts in Kiev with a degree in theatre arts. Besides directing, Youri also studied stage managing and stage design where he employed many of his father's lessons taught long before.

Yet Youri soon realized that his "inner thirst" was illustrative art. In 1992, he published a small piece in a Dutch ecological magazine and has loved black-and-white drawing ever since. Most recently, Youri began a series of oil paintings—the lives of Europe's kings. When he's not quenching his artistic thirst painting, Youri says he's thinking about writing science fiction and creating color illustrations for children's books.

Kass put a hand to her ear and jingled the jay bribe with her finger. She gazed into the cloudless blue sky, searching among the birds wheeling high above her perch. Bobbin, her robber jay, had his first untethered flight. He had to come back.

The exposed limb she stood on swayed from the wind, strong here at the boundary of the dense Hedge. She went to one knee, dropping her hand to steady herself and looked down at the flat, plowed land of the nearest meadow. From this height, she could see the entire circumference of the meadow, houses tiny among green dots of trees, dirt roads radiating from the central town.

When seen from the ground, the Hedge loomed above the horizon, a distant presence to all not in its shadow. From her high vantage, Kass saw the truth. The meadow merely nested in the towering and twisted growth. One isolated meadow of many scattered among the Hedge.

Kass jingled her earring again. Bobbin plummeted out of the sky and stopped, fluttering over her shoulder in a flurry of gray and black, anxious to protect his treasure.

"No! No!" he screamed in Kass's ear. He grabbed the metal wire that held the dangling bits of shell and painted ceramic. Kass flinched as Bobbin fluttered and tugged on her earring. Her sudden motion startled the robber jay. He released his hold and bounced down her arm.

"Soothe him, Kassarine," Marrasa urged. Her guide among this band of hedgefolk spoke from the shadows of the Hedge behind Kass. "Assure him the bribe is safe with you."

"Bobbin," she called, keeping her arm very still. Her earlobe ached from the pulling. She made the soft clucking sound for food.

Bobbin cocked his head. His dark eyes gleamed against his black masking. Slowly the crest of feathers on his head fanned up. He allowed Kass to stroke under his beak, before hopping to her shoulder to admire the jay bribe.

"Good. He's a bright one, and you're a fair teacher. Trust yourself." Marrasa stepped out onto the exposed vantage limb.

"If he's so bright, why doesn't he know more words?" Kass asked. She thought of Marrasa's jay, left in her woven hut to keep from interfering with the lesson. She had heard him speak at least ten different words. She shifted to face Marrasa.

"My Mocker has had a few more years than your Bobbin to learn. My first robber jay had already taken to cussing when I found him. He couldn't fit any more human words into his little head, so I had to train him to stay quiet. There's a challenge." Marrasa gave Kass one of her rare smiles. She absently fingered her own jay bribe, dangling from her left earlobe.

Kass noticed the two strands of metal twined together that formed Marrasa's bribe. Her guild had rewarded her for some service. Kass wondered if the older woman had received her first metal as a legacy, or if she had won both strands.

A flash of embarrassment caught Kass. She hadn't earned anything yet. Her jay bribe had been a gift after her initiation into the hedgefolk from a couple who had claimed to be her natural parents. She'd have loved to believe her mother was like Marrasa, tall, respected and handsome in the pale way of the hedgefolk even after fifty years. Instead they had been short, with surprisingly childish manners, laughing at everything. They left immediately after presenting the strand of metal to Kass. She didn't even know which guild they followed.

But those cold and hungry days of her ordeal hardly mattered now. The dense Hedge no longer appeared menacing and alien. No longer a huge looming nightmare used to keep the children obedient in the meadows, away from the shadowed periphery.

Kass balanced on a rough-barked spar—the hedgefolk's name, she'd learned, for a horizontal branch wide enough to walk along. She placed her feet properly under her and stood up.

"We've been long enough away." Marrasa pivoted on her toes, turning her back to the meadow. She walked along the spar, pushed hanging tangle vines aside, and disappeared into the Hedge.

Kass followed her teacher into the enfolding growth. Once through the canopy, her eyes relaxed to the shade. Splotches of diluted sunlight swirled over all the green and browns of growing plants. A thousand paths along spars and smaller branches caught the gentle illumination. The constant soothing rustle of leaves further above them was the only remnant of the wind. A hundred measures below, at the level of the hedgefolk's camp, the smell of the muddy topes supporting the thick trunks of the Hedge flavored the air. But up here, the wind was clear of the scent of humus. Instead Kass smelled a faint touch of parasite mint. She wondered if the mint grew on the thicker branches where she could reach it.

"I hear you let down milk yesterday," said Marrasa, turning her head to look over her shoulder.

Kass's face instantly grew hot. She ducked her head and crossed her arms, the mint forgotten with the memory of her tingling breasts grown tight after weeks of rubbing with the rough training cloth and ritual manipulation. And the droplets of milk forming on her reddened nipples. "Yes . . ."

"Don't be so embarrassed. I did it, too, years ago. It's a natural process."

"Natural if you're giving birth to a baby," said Kass, her voice a little more surly than she intended.

Bobbin hopped onto her head, his slender claws gripping her hair. Kass felt a sharp pain as Bobbin plucked a single hair from her scalp. "Oww!" She waved her arms at the jay.

"Well, Bobbin has the right idea. You carry too much of the meadow thoughts with you still."

Kass's robber jay flew over to a small branch, a long golden hair coiled in his beak. "No," he said and proudly fluffed his breast and throat feathers.

"You did say that you enjoyed children." Marrasa continued toward the brace—a vertical branch with easily reached handholds—they had taken to the vantage limb.

"I like children, but I don't know about babies. It's different when they're old enough to talk." Kass followed her teacher down the brace, dropping from hold to hold. Her palms grew warm with the abrasion of the bark.

"Your sponsors thought you'd serve well in the generation guild."

Bobbin flitted around her head, impatient with her slow progress. He stopped to ride on her shoulder, swaying with each change of grip. Finally, he took to

Illustrated by Youri Bobrikov

dropping after her, landing by her fingers, watching them with mischievous eyes.

How could Kass explain why she felt so odd? She had watched meadow-women nurse newborns while she minded the older children. They never let a clumsy, moon-eyed girl hold their babies, and she had never asked. That was before she came to the hedgefolk. "Wasn't it strange when you first did it? Or had you given birth before?"

"I was your age and proud," Marrasa replied from below. "The Hedge is no place for a newborn. No. I accepted the call of my guild, to take up the duty of protecting the meadow-dwellers."

Kass reached down with her leg until her foot found the support of a spar. Bobbin settled on her arm with a chirrup of relief. She followed behind Marrasa as they approached the camp. "How do you protect them by stealing babies?"

"That is only a small facet of our responsibility. Your other teachers and I have waited until you produced milk before revealing our secrets."

Kass jogged up behind her. "It's hardly a secret that you steal babies from one meadow and put them in another."

"That is not stealing, is it?" Marrasa continued along the spar, slippery from tufts of grass growing out of the cracked bark. "No one moves through the Hedge, between the meadows, except us hedgefolk. But the Hedge grows around each meadow, working into them over time, like invisible roots, until it pulls the spirits from the weakest, making the children slow or sickly. We exchange the babies to renew the blood and sever the hold of the Hedge."

"None of the hedgefolk carry children with them?" asked Kass matching her teacher's footsteps.

"Only the silk guild keeps its children, and they are a wild, improper pack," said Marrasa in a critical tone, tilting her head to emphasize the point. Though the hedgefolk prized silk ropes, the silk guild ranked barely above the meadow-dwellers. "We foster our own offspring out, for those among us foolish enough to risk the whole camp over a night of unguarded pleasure."

Kass had heard the warning before and kept from rolling her eyes. She took her powdered cepto nut with her morning water, as instructed, every morning. She would never be that witless. "So the traditions for newborns are to help you steal babies?"

"The meadow-dwellers hardly understand the power of the Hedge. They wouldn't give their children to strangers, so the trader guild frightens them with stories to preserve the customs. That's why naming day comes six months after birth, and the birthing room is built onto the outside of the house." Marrasa smiled, her face wrinkling near her eyes, as if she was eager to share the deception. "Sometimes a baby appears alongside the first, fostered like you, and sometimes the baby disappears for a week, an exchange."

"And you leave a metal needle near the crib."

"Yes. A gift to mark the special ones. A sign of luck for the steading. You were named with a needle, weren't you, Kassarine?"

Kass nodded. Ahead, she noticed a thin spot breaking their way, a narrow chasm in the Hedge. The full light of the afternoon shone through the leaves. She looked down into the deeper darkness of the underhedge. An occasional glint off water was all she could see in the gloom.

Marrasa paused at the gap in the spars. She crouched and leapt across the three measures of empty space. She landed with feline ease, her soft-soled boots gripping the branch.

Kass thought about leaping across, but decided she wasn't ready to follow Marrasa exactly. She looked around and jumped up to catch an overhead branch that grew tentatively into the open sunlight.

Bobbin took offense with the sudden commotion and left with a quiet cry of "No."

Kass jerked on the branch and it held. She swung across the gap. She dropped with less grace than Marrasa, but kept her footing. Bobbin settled on her shoulder again.

"You brought metal wealth and luck to your family's stead, so you weren't neglected," Marrasa said. "Taken as their own brood."

"True." Kass kept the flow of her thoughts to her own mind. She had never been neglected. She had never been left alone. Torment and tauntings had come from her older brothers, perhaps from jealousy of the needle she brought to the steading. Wet noodles in shoes. Hurled apples when she climbed trees. Salt in her bread.

"But that is enough for the moment, Kassarine. Other secrets will be revealed during the ceremony tonight."

Bobbin pecked at the bribe, the jingling loud by Kass's ear. He pecked again, but missed the metal strand, pinching skin on her neck. Urgently, but without a sound, he moved on her shoulder. The tips of his wings swept lightly against her head, stirring her hair.

Kass reached up to brush him away. "Bobbin," she said in exasperation.

"He's not playing! He's warning!" Marrasa hurried toward the main spar leading to the camp. Each of her steps precise, yet swift.

Kass struggled to follow her teacher's pace. The

sudden drop a half-measure to either side of the spar, through crossed branches and bushy growths to the muddy topes far below, became more threatening as she tried to run. One misplaced foot meant her death.

They pushed through the screening tangle vines where their path joined the main spar. Kass stopped. Twenty woven huts sprouted from the main spar like upside-down baskets, empty and dark. The ceramic-lined firepit, gouged into the branch, lay unlit. Though most of the camp had been sent out on tasks in the days before, at least the other teachers, Bessalee, the master nurse, or Oska, the old bowyer, should have been outside their huts. But Kass could see no one but Marrasa.

"A hedgelion?" Kass wished that she had brought her bow. She whistled a sharp rising note. Bobbin launched himself from her shoulder to land on the roof of her hut.

At the far edge of the camp, a pained shriek rose out of the foliage. It almost sounded human. Tall stalks of tree grass shuddered and crashed aside as something massive moved along the spar, directly at the camp.

Another shriek cut through Kass's hesitation. She ran to her hut, jumping the firepit. Before she got through the door, the tangle vines were ripped aside by two men in ranger guild greens.

Behind the two rangers, came a small knot of hedgefolk, two from the camp and two more strangers. They carried a makeshift stretcher of cloaks held taut across spear hafts. Something in a loose bundle of ripped fabric and shredded leaves rode on the stretcher. It writhed when one of the bearers misstepped, jarring the stretcher.

It was a body, Kass realized as she stopped. Damp, darkened spots soaked the clothing. Blood.

Bessalee followed clutching a shrieking baby. Kass had never heard an infant wail like this one.

Oska came last into the camp with an arrow nocked on his ready bow. He eyed their trail of snapped stalks and uprooted plants that once clung to the branches of the Hedge. His wrinkled face shone with sweat and the red of deep anger.

"What's happened?" Marrasa asked, rolling the sleeves of her shirt over her elbows.

"Hedgelion," replied one of the rangers, a slender reedlike man with dark hair and strong widow's peak. "Are you the camp healer?"

"Yes." Marrasa bent over the body they carried.

The four bearers lowered the stretcher to the spar. Marrasa carefully peeled back clothing.

Bessalee came directly toward Kass.

"I'll light the fire," Kass said, anticipating her orders. Marrasa would need boiling water to cleanse her tools.

"No, you have another duty." Bessalee thrust the baby into Kass's arms. "Take him."

Kass looked down into the bundle she held. From the piercing cry, she almost expected to see a bush-otter cub all swaddled up. But she cradled a clearly human baby against her chest. His eyes were pinched shut, and his mouth opened wide to wail, only stopping to gasp air. His fists trembled with each cry. Three parallel scratches ran across his forehead, scabbed like tiny beads.

"Go on." Bessalee pointed toward the huts. "Get him away from the smell of blood. He needs milk."

Kass turned and stumbled to her hut. The baby pressed its face against her chest, his wails muffled by her shirt. She ducked her head as she passed through the door.

Bobbin flitted down from the roof, but jumped off her shoulder when the child shrieked louder. "No!" he responded, and hopped to a shelf by the window.

An inner excitement and an odd sense of unreality almost overwhelmed her as she unbuttoned her shirt. She presented her left breast to the baby. He cried still, not taking the nipple, but his fists had unclenched. She sat on the floor and leaned her back against the wall. She guided his head with her hand.

He closed his lips on her nipple and took a few tentative pulls. He then began feeding, pulling strongly, breathing through his nose. He surprised Kass with his efficiency of drawing milk. Soon, a deep warm tingling flowed into her chest, focusing her attention on this little person taking nourishment from her body. The gratifying thrill ran all the way through her and wrapped her heart in a quiet strong embrace. Kass rocked back and forth as the baby fed. Shortly, she moved him to her other breast.

The silence left by the calmed child was soon filled with much more adult screams. Marrasa was doing what she could for the broken woman outside.

•••

Kass woke to darkness as the baby nudged against her chest. Her nipples ached more than the first nights she had practiced toughening them with a rough cloth. They looked large and protruded.

So soon? I can't be ready, Kass thought. She offered a tender nipple to the baby anyway, and he began to feed.

The fire burned outside, and an orange glow hovered around the door of her hut. A shadow filled it. Kass recognized the hunched silhouette of Bessalee. "Is she still alive?"

"She may live to morning," Bessalee replied. She came into the hut.

"Who was it?"

"Autumn."

Kass couldn't see Bessalee's expression. Kass had only met Autumn once, at the welcoming feast on her first evening with the camp. Autumn had remained aloof and never spoke to the three untried youths just out of the meadows. Kass remembered Bessalee and Autumn laughing at the edge of the fire and leaving early. "I'm sorry."

"All hedgefolk know their duties." Bessalee's voice caught in her throat and sounded dry like dead leaves. "How's the child?"

"Feeding," Kass said.

"Did you use the loah oil on yourself after his first feeding?"

"No."

"You won't forget again. Sore?"

"Yes."

"I'll take the child when he finishes and clean him. You'll sleep. Tomorrow morning you'll be taking him to his meadow family."

"Tomorrow?" Kass asked. "Me?"

The baby spit her nipple out and wriggled his arms. He kicked at the blanket wrapped around his legs, thumping Kass's stomach with his heels.

"Krissal hasn't let down yet. All the rest have gone to meadows." Bessalee reached out and took the baby from her. "Now you eat and sleep. And see to yourself." Bessalee left the hut.

Kass started to button her shirt. Her right breast felt heavy, almost lopsided. She remembered the loah oil. She found her bottle near her hammock and smeared the cool scentless oil on her nipples, soothing the raw edge of her soreness. She could hardly stand the touch of her own fingers or clothing.

After fastening her shirt, she walked out of her hut and saw the four rangers asleep around the firepit. The three men and a woman lay on pallets of dried grasses, their feet away from the fire. Kass noticed the dark-haired ranger she had heard speak earlier. He rested the tips of his fingers along the haft of his spear. None stirred as she passed them on her way to the larder.

Only old Oska sat up. He hadn't unstrung his bow for the night. Kass noticed the long hunting arrows set next to him on the bole where he sat. The broad heads of the hunting arrows were a sharpened layer of gray ceramic wedged between laminated wood. She had cut a finger on one during her first lesson under him. After that once, she had used simple wooden arrows for practice.

When she walked near him, Oska said, "You should be asleep."

"I'm hungry." Kass went around him and took a flatbread from the storage pot in the larder. She came out and began to return to her hut.

"Come back here." Oska patted the bole next to him. "We must talk while you eat and before you sleep."

She bit off a large mouthful and spoke before swallowing. "Autumn?"

"No. Hedgelions. They normally stay to their own territories, and don't bother the hedgefolk. The rangers see to protecting both us and the hedgelions."

"The hedgelions need protection?"

"Just eat for now." Oska didn't face her as he talked. He constantly looked around the camp, into the tangle vines that crept over walkways. Into the spars interlacing in the higher canopy ten measures above their heads. He listened to the darkness, his face drawn with an intensity Kass found disturbing. "Have you ever seen a hedgelion?"

"No. I've heard them, though." Kass remembered the sounds of their cries, like tearing canvas and deep-throated drums, echoing through the Hedge.

"I know you have. But the first time you see a hedgelion, there will be no time to gawk. And no time to run away. You will have to kill it." Oska nodded at the strangers sleeping near the center of camp. "They brought news of another mauling. The silk guild lost their child watcher to the same hedgelion that got Autumn. According to the rangers. They were tracking it nearby when they found Autumn."

"Kassarine!" came a hoarse whisper from the other side of the firepit. Bessalee motioned for Kass.

Oska reached out and rubbed her shoulder. "You get to your hammock and get to sleep. You'll be up a few more times before the night is over."

•••

Bessalee had changed the child's wrappings and cleaned his cuts. He smelled fresh when Kass nestled him against her side on the hammock. The fearful thoughts of the hedgelion almost disappeared from her mind, and she found sleep. She barely woke when she fed him before dawn.

"No!" shouted Bobbin when the first light filtered down to the camp. "Nooooo!"

Marrasa shook Kass's leg, making the hammock sway gently. "It's time for you to go. The ceremony will wait for your return."

Kass looked down at the baby. He squinted when

anyone talked, but he didn't fully wake. Kass rolled out of the hammock, not letting it tip. She slid her hands beneath his head and back and picked him up. He bunched his fists under his chin until Kass had him firmly cradled in her arms. She turned to face Marrasa, hoping to see approval.

"We've packed for you." Marrasa had deep shadows beneath her eyes and the skin of her face seemed loose. She held out a belted cocoon sling of silk-lined leather on a frame of laminated wood. "This will ride across your back or front. You can feed him while freeing your hands for climbing."

Kass bundled the baby in the sling, tying the leather flaps securely but not too tight, and slipped it over her shoulder. She adjusted the wooden buckle until it rested comfortably and secure against her chest. She clucked for Bobbin who still perched on the shelf from last night.

Bobbin shook himself thoroughly and hopped to Kass's shoulder to begin his morning preening. She noticed the jay kept a cautious watch over the bundle she carried against her chest.

Marrasa led her into the center of camp.

Bessalee, Oska and the slender ranger sat talking near the fire. A pot steamed on the embers. A belt pack and her bow lay by Oska's feet. Oska stood when he saw Kass.

"I haven't time to waste on your guild's duties." The ranger frowned. He ran his fingers through his hair, slicked flat with loah oil. "The others will need me if they find the hedgelion's spoor."

"Don't be a child. We need your aid at this moment," said Bessalee. She turned as Kass approached them. "This is your guide, Arn of the ranger guild. This is your charge, Kassarine of the generation guild."

Arn nodded at her. A few splotches of red appeared across his sharp cheekbones and narrow nose. He looked away quickly.

"Here's all you should need," Marrasa said. She knelt down beside Oska and opened the belt pack. "Rope, knife and cup. Your cepto nut. Loah oil. Wrappings and gum sap. Tansy pollen to quiet the child, but only when necessary. And—" Marrasa produced a small leather pouch. She reached inside it with two fingers and pulled out a bit of metal stuck in a piece of spongewood. "His needle."

Marrasa returned the needle into the pouch and looped the leather thongs around Kass's neck. "This is the child's fortune."

"Here's three hunting arrows. I pray you don't need them." Oska pursed his lips and bent his eyebrows into a concerned line as he handed her a covered quiver and her strung bow. He stepped forward and gave her a half embrace, the child between them.

Kass looked down at his feet. She wished Oska's legs were steady enough to come with her instead of the ranger.

Bessalee placed her hands on her knees and forced herself to stand. She turned away from the ranger and spoke quietly. "The child was meant for a meadow along the coast, but you will return to the one of your fostering. There is a place for the child in the steading that raises sheep near the southern periphery."

Kass thought for a moment. Only one stead in the south had enough land for sheep that she remembered. Her oldest brother had tried to marry into that family on the far side of the meadow. "The one with the ironwood tree behind the main house. I know it."

Bessalee nodded. "Good. This doesn't take the place

of a ceremony, but know that our hearts go with you. May your path be strong."

"Come on," Arn said, shouldering his spear.

Kass felt her arms and legs trembling. She wanted to shout that she wasn't ready. They couldn't expect her to run off and replace a stolen child alone. She didn't possess the instincts her teachers had developed. Reading the movements of the leaves. Finding a path with bare feet at night. Knowing one meadow from the rest. Leaping three measures between spars. They had forgotten that she had spent only one single year compared to their whole lives amid the Hedge.

But who else could go? Autumn needed Marrasa's care and Bessalee was too old to produce milk.

Becoming hedgefolk meant taking the burden of duties in order to have the freedom of the Hedge. Kass had never thought it also meant abandoning common sense. But she had been given her task, and she would see it done.

Kass moved the sling, so the baby rode on her back. She followed Arn out of the camp and into the Hedge. Arn's pace didn't give Kass enough time to look back. At first, the spars Arn chose to follow were common pathways away from the camp. Then he veered aside from the well-worn spars, taking braces and difficult limbs into the higher canopy. The narrow branches he chose, hardly wide enough for her feet, snaked beneath a tight ceiling of tangle vines. The Hedge closed in on her. Before noon, Kass's arms and shoulders ached from the effort of climbing.

Kass felt the baby squirm against her back. She moved the sling around so she could reach in and feel the baby's bottom. "We need to stop!"

"What for?" asked Arn, walking up the steeply

sloped spar. His first words since they left the camp. He stopped when she didn't reply.

Kass sat down on a section of branch where the bark had sloughed off recently, baring the dark wood beneath. Keeping well away from the edges, she balanced the child across her knees to change his felted leaf wrapping. She tossed the soiled one off the edge of the spar. It fell slowly, turning gentle circles in the air, until it caught on a lower branch. Bobbin flew off to investigate.

When she tried to fasten the clean wrapping together with the sticky sap, her calloused hands rubbed against the baby's skin. He kicked and fussed, bunching the soft cloth between his legs.

"We're wasting time," Arn said. "Move faster."

Kass looked up at the ranger. She felt the lack of sleep and the discomfort of her abused breasts. A knot of anger built up between her eyebrows. "Have you done this before that you can tell me how fast to move?"

The baby cringed at her harsh tone and began to cry. Kass refastened the wrapping and put him back in the sling.

"That child will call a hedgelion down on us," Arn said. "The Hedge can feel them. They're bad luck."

"Come on then." Kass stuck her little finger into his tiny mouth. He cried and turned his head away. She let him wail. She clucked for Bobbin as she walked toward the ranger.

Arn resumed his pace, shaking his head. His hand strayed over his shoulder to his spear strapped across his back. He continually scanned the overhead canopy.

They traveled the rest of that day. Kass fed the child or carried him across her back when the climbing grew difficult. They ate flatbread and drank water as they moved through the Hedge. They didn't have time to catch any of the bushy-tailed tree rats, complained Arn, each time they scared one out of the clinging undergrowths. Kass wished he would have stayed silent like he had that morning.

Eventually the diffuse sunlight grew too dim to continue. Arn found a spot and declared a camp. "We'll have a fire."

Kass unslung the child. Her back ached, low along the spine just above her hips. Her shoulders twitched from exhaustion. She had ripped a half of a fingernail nearly off when she had lost a handhold late that afternoon. And the loah oil wasn't soothing the soreness of her nipples anymore. She stretched her back placing both hands on her waist.

The baby cried again. Kass recognized the hungry demand.

"No," said Bobbin, and he pressed his feathered head against Kass's ear.

"Yes," Kass said. She gestured at a nearby branch extending down from an overhead brace. Bobbin made a little airy whistle almost like a sigh before he flitted off to the perch. Kass lifted the baby to her chest again.

"Hungry little tree rat, isn't it?" Arn knelt in a small section of branch. He cleared away the moss and clinging plants and checked the wood beneath. Satisfied, he built a small cone of gathered sticks. He dumped the powdery contents of a slender tube onto the sticks. He struck a gray stone against his ceramic blade.

Sparks flew out and ignited the powder. Small popping flames jumped into the air before the fire quieted and behaved itself.

Arn sat back and massaged his hands while watching the baby feed. He stopped and gestured at his own chest. "Aren't you a bit, well, small for this duty?"

"The size of the breast has nothing to do with this,"

Kass said. His stupid question irritated her, especially when she remembered asking the same thing many months ago.

Arn grunted and nodded his head, considering her answer. He brought out a large circular leaf, waxy and green, that he had cut during the day's journey. He bent it into a cup shape and poured water into it from his jug. He then set it on the fire. The edges burned down to the level of the water. "I came from Goodman's Meadow."

"I don't know it," Kass said. "I haven't been back to any meadows since I went into the Hedge."

"When did the hedgefolk take you?"

Kass thought about the day when she had found the break in the topes that formed a wall around the meadow at the base of the Hedge. Something deep in the muddy earth had given way, letting the giant petrified toothlike tope rip out of the ground by its roots. A door into the dark underhedge. "I went in on my own."

"They collected me on Hedge Trimming Day." A wide smirk caught the firelight and shadowed Arn's face. When she didn't respond, the smirk left. "You don't know much hedgefolk tradition."

"Not much," lied Kass. She knew that the guilds brought in only the most promising adolescents on Trimming Day. She fastened the middle buttons of her shirt.

Arn shook his head. "Then it would be more trouble to explain."

"You're most likely right," Kass said, her attention on the baby. He jerked occasionally in her lap with a hiccup. Each time he almost made the face for an impending fit of wailing. She rubbed his stomach.

Arn poured hot water from the leaf into Kass's cup and passed another round of flatbread to her. "Why do you travel with a robber jay? What use is the bird?"

"He can find food for me, or warn me of danger. And he is a good companion. Aren't you, Bobbin?"

Bobbin perked up at the sound of his name. He bobbed his head twice and jumped from his perch. He swooped by Kass's head and grabbed the piece of bread she was lifting to her lips. "No-oh!" he cried as he flew back to his perch. He held the bread in one foot as he ate.

Arn laughed. "How have I survived without one?"

The baby smiled up at Kass, delighted by the flurry of motion and the funny sound of the jay's voice. Another hiccup turned the smile into a scowl.

Kass rolled the baby onto his stomach against her knees. She patted him on the back.

"Did you know the ranger guild is the oldest of the seven? The first of the hedgefolk have always been rangers." Arn continued for a while, explaining how difficult it is to be a ranger. The strict code they followed. How he had been chosen. He spoke endlessly of the hedgelion his group had been tracking before he was pulled off on this foolish delay.

"I'm tired," Kass said after the baby had fallen asleep. She cradled him against her and lay back on the center branch, well away from the edges. She used her quiver to support her head.

"We made good time today." Arn kicked out the remnants of the fire. "You kept up."

Kass closed her eyes and listened to the night sounds of the Hedge. Chirpers and salamanders splashed below in the waters. Moving leaves and the creak of a relaxing branch comforted her. The distant raspy song of a nighthunter seeking nocturnal insects drifted through the darkness. She heard Arn nestle into the pile of bracken he had pulled up to clear the firespot.

"You could have been sponsored into the ranger guild."

Kass realized that he had just complimented her. "Thank you," she mumbled before falling completely asleep.

• • •

Disturbing dreams came to her. The baby struggled against her side as she kept it from the edge of the branch. She turned the sling around and offered her breast for him to feed, and he bit her with needle-sharp teeth. She pushed his head away from her skin, but the baby snapped onto her finger. Shaking him, he wouldn't let go. Then the baby released her finger and fell off the edge into the murky depths. Kass crawled across the slippery branch to watch the baby swirling down, like discarded wrapping.

Kass woke to the baby kicking at her. Frustrated grunting came from the sling as she held him too tightly. She relaxed her arms, trusting the straps on the sling to keep him secure. Eventually, she fell back asleep.

The next morning, when the light became strong enough to see their path, Arn guided Kass down into the thicker Hedge. "By nightfall, we'll only be a few hours from the meadow periphery. We've had a quiet trip. Hardly any game about."

Kass concentrated on matching the taller man's pace and caring for the baby. How could anything that looked so small weigh so much, Kass wondered, or eat so much?

The muscles across her chest ached and seemed to threaten to rip apart from her bones as she threaded her way through jutting branches, hanging by her fingers and dropping onto another accessible spar. The sharp leaves of knife grass cut at her exposed hands and face when they crawled through a thickly overgrown branch. Twice they resorted to ropes to lower themselves from impassable and overgrown sections, through layers of dangling thorn leaves. As they moved downward, the canopy spaces above them opened. So although they were deeper inside the Hedge, the presence of the growth didn't weigh upon them as much as before.

Later in the day, a few spattering raindrops from far above trickled onto Kass. She stopped for a moment to check on her mercifully silent charge. She moved the sling from her back. One drop of water from an overhead leaf fell past Kass's nose to strike the baby's forehead. He squinted his eyes, bunched his hands into fists, and turned his head from the sudden cold wetness. He began to cry.

Arn stopped and looked back at her. "Not again."

"Shush hush," murmured Kass. "It's not bad."

"No," said Bobbin by her ear. He jumped from her shoulder and winged his way through the Hedge, dodging vines and lacing branchlets before passing out of her sight.

"Bobbin!" she called, distracted by the bundle of noise she held.

Bobbin returned with a many-legged insect squirming in his beak. He perched on the side of the sling. His talons dug into the leather as he bent forward.

"No, you don't!" exclaimed Kass before Bobbin could stick the insect in the baby's mouth. She grabbed at the brown insect in his beak.

Bobbin ducked her hand and hopped again toward the baby in the sling. The wailing stopped and a fascinated but uncertain smile formed on the child's lips. A silly little feeling of pleasure opened inside Kass as she watched the baby stare wide-eyed at the black-and-white bird.

"Good, Bobbin." Kass scratched him behind his crest with a finger. He pressed into her touch and dropped the insect.

They continued traveling. Kass called Bobbin back when the child grew fussy. Bobbin uttered a pained "No," but his active presence kept the baby quiet.

The gentle mist turned to fog, settling on them from the upper canopy near the middle afternoon. They could hardly see the edges of the spar when Arn called a halt. He found a section where a thick spar crossed over their branch forming a small shelter of dry Hedge. They stooped to walk under the overhanging spar.

Kass didn't know whether to be relieved or dispirited. She wanted the rest, but the longer she kept the child in the Hedge, the longer he was in danger and the longer she had to feed him.

"We'll have to be careful tomorrow," said Arn, a gray shadow in the damp twilight. "This area is plagued with spongewood."

Kass bent to one knee, holding the baby against her, and felt the spar they stood on. It was solid, but a resilient light brown overlayer had formed on the branch. Spongewood developed on old Hedge, eating away the solid, healthy wood. It would weaken the branch until it finally gave out under the weight of the higher canopy. "It feels strong."

"Strong enough for now." Arn thumped the branch with his spear. "Comfortable sleeping."

Kass unfurled her cloak, kept bundled to keep from catching as she traveled. She covered herself and the sling. She knew any wood they could find would be too damp for a fire. She checked her unstrung bow, making certain it hadn't gotten wet.

They ate flatbread again for supper. Kass fed the baby, his face hot against her skin. She felt his forehead, but couldn't tell if he was feverish. He would be in a meadow-dweller's stead tomorrow evening, she reminded herself. The baby would no longer be her responsibility. But still she worried.

She curled up with the baby nestled against her chest. Bobbin crawled into her hood. His sharp talons tickled her neck as he fluffed himself before sleeping. She opened her eyes and looked at the deepening gray and the dark form of the overhanging spar. Except the sound of the baby breathing, Kass heard only silence in the surrounding Hedge. Fog did strange things to the ears, she thought as she let exhaustion take her to sleep.

•••

The jingling of her jay bribe woke her with a start. Bobbin yanked on her earring, and when she moved, he flew away. Into the dark.

Kass looked up, expecting fog to obscure the overhanging spar. Spongewood had cleared out much of the canopy above their camp. The fog had passed, and moonlight shone from a cloudless sky.

Directly overhead, another shadow clung to the side of the branch that sheltered them. When it moved, Kass could make out the elongated silhouette of a hedgelion. Twice as long a person was tall, with a long narrow snout, it crept toward them. Claws the size of knives sank into the wood. A long prehensile tail swished in agitation.

"Arn?!" she whispered. She glanced in his direction, quickly. She saw his open eyes reflect moonlight. She looked again at the hedgelion.

"I see it." Arn lifted his spear with the same agonizingly slow grace that the hedgelion used.

She reached for her bow, but she had left it unstrung last night. Now she wished she had risked the string to the wet air. She grabbed it anyway.

"Run!" shouted Arn, rising to his feet.

The branch shuddered with the impact as the hedgelion dropped from overhead. Turning, it lifted its head and snarled, exposing rows of teeth.

Kass rolled over and crawled on her knees and one hand, dragging her bow and quiver. She held the baby against her chest. She pressed herself beneath the overhanging spar. Spongewood crumbled in her hair. She stood, steadying herself against the spar.

Arn yelled wordlessly and the hedgelion responded with a guttural cry. Their voices echoed through the Hedge.

Kass pressed the laminated wood of her bow against her outer thigh and bent it. She pulled on the string to loop it onto the notches of the bow.

The baby gathered himself into a shriek of terror. All Kass could hear was the crying baby. No snarls. No shouts from Arn.

She pulled a hunting arrow from the quiver, gripped between her index and middle finger. She tipped the quiver in her haste. Arrows rattled and skidded toward the edge.

Something moved behind her. Kass whirled, drawing the bow. The hedgelion perched on the spar above her. It lashed out with a paw as she loosed the arrow.

The bow snapped and jerked her around. A hiss of pain and fury came from the hedgelion. Kass dropped onto the spar. She arched her back to keep from crushing the baby with her own body. Her knees struck healthy wood. The shock almost numbed her legs. Kass climbed to her feet and ran up the sloping branch, clutching the howling baby. She looked behind her and saw the hedgelion poised on the overhanging spar, chewing at the arrow through its paw like a thorn. Kass stumbled and slid down the steepening incline of the branch, digging her fingers into cracks of the bark.

She scrabbled onto the spar, but couldn't see the dark shape of the hedgelion behind her. She continued running, not willing to look back. The sound of claws sinking into the branch like axes into wood grew louder. The spar vibrated with the uneven steps of the hedgelion chasing her.

Ahead through shadows, Kass saw a twisted leafy growth of tangle vine hanging from a nearby brace. A three-measure leap! The panting of the hedgelion behind her felt close enough to sink teeth into her neck. She placed her foot on the edge and threw herself from the spar, one arm outstretched to embrace the vines.

Snarls and a sudden thunderous crack of wood sounded behind her. A sharp tug ripped at her cloak. The hood choked her as she felt thick tangle vines slide through her grasp. Leaves tore away from her hand in a moist, jarring flurry. Then she fell.

Kass curled herself around the baby; small branches, new supple growth, pelted her back. Whipping her and whistling past her head. An instant later, she hit water and sank into mud.

She kicked and pushed herself upright, fighting against the water. She reached into the sling and pulled the baby into the air. He spat out murky water, coughed, and let free a wonderful cry. Kass held him against her face and neck. Torpid water flowed around her waist.

She waded to a tope, its petrified mud supporting Hedge far above. She climbed onto the steep side and wrapped her arms around the shivering baby. His felted wrapping began to fall apart with the complete soaking.

"You little tree rat," she said and tears cleaned the mud from her eyes.

Her cloak, made from bush-otter wool, provided some warmth even thoroughly wet. She placed him directly against her skin. She felt stinging welts begin to form across her back, hot and painful. Afraid to make a sound, she listened for the hedgelion, but only heard the furtive noises of harmless night animals.

•••

"Kass?"

Kass jerked awake. She looked for the ranger in the predawn murk. "Arn?" she called as loud as she dared.

Bobbin perched on her dirt-crusted knee. He opened his beak. "Kass?"

"Oh, Bobbin!" Kass reached to her ear. The jay bribe still hung from her earlobe.

She immediately checked the baby. He had fallen asleep with her nipple in his mouth. She didn't remember him feeding. The little tree rat leads a charmed life, thought Kass.

As the light of the day increased, Kass saw that she was near the edge of the meadow. Only a line of sheer gray black topes forming a barrier kept her from the open and safe lands of the meadow. She looked around to find a way up into the Hedge and saw the long form of the hedgelion twenty measures above her.

It had struck a jagged section of broken trunk, where spongewood had claimed a portion of Hedge.

A huge splinter had impaled the falling hedgelion. It hung suspended a short distance above the water. The tail drooped nearly to the soft mud.

Kass wrapped the baby in her mostly dry cloak and set him in a small hollow on the tope. "Stay, Bobbin."

Bobbin perched on the leather sling, quiet and obedient, as Kass waded into the shallow water. She crossed to the base of the tope that held the body of the hedgelion. With some difficulty, she managed to scale up the hardened earth and wedge herself in a forked section near the carcass.

The hedgelion's tongue stuck out from between its front teeth slightly. A touch of pink against the mottled tan and black of its fur. Kass noticed one of the eyes was a cloudy white and the muzzle had streaks of gray near the broken whiskers.

She saw her hunting arrow had gone through its paw, snapped in half. She then noticed the bloody flank where Arn found a target for his spear.

"Arn!" she yelled into the Hedge. Kass bit her lip as she listened. Her hopes faded with the echoes.

Arn had known his duty. He had pointed that out to her repeatedly during their journey. He had fought the hedgelion. He had given her time to get the child away.

The baby began to cry, startling her. He sounded hungry again. But she had to do one thing before returning to her own duty. She drew her ceramic and wood knife and cut the ear tufts off the hedgelion. The rangers would want proof of the hedgelion's death.

• • •

By nightfall, Kass found the gap in the periphery

where she had wandered away from her first home over a year ago. She stepped through the petrified archway into overgrown brush, the beginnings of new Hedge. The people from the steadings would be out to cut this growth back to the base of the rock-hard topes on Trimming Day. Now it sat untouched, a hint of wildness creeping into the cultivated meadow.

She bathed in one of the freshwater pools that formed on the hardened ground and removed the stink of the underhedge from her skin. Hidden in the tall grasses, she wiped the baby clean as he squirmed. He smiled, free of the touch of memory. Kass couldn't keep from nuzzling his belly. He kicked against her shoulders and chin.

She washed the sling and napped while the evening faded into night. She carried the baby against her chest, a torn corner of her cloak serving as his wrapping. Bobbin flew along or rode on her other shoulder. Walking in moonlight across the level ground, she had no fear of missteps bringing death. No hedgelions roaming above. No dangers. No strange noises.

Well-worn roads split the meadow into partitions of land where generations farmed, or tended evenly rowed orchards, or raised sheep for meat and wool. Everything around her seemed so ordered. Right angles and straight lines and open to the sky. The firm little houses had closed for the evening. Dark windows and doors shut against shadowy fears intruding into their cultivated lives.

Kass found the large stead with the ironwood tree. The tree stood alone by the road like a lost fragment of the Hedge that had wandered into the forlorn realm of the meadow. Fenced sheep lay in the close-cropped pasture, woolen lumps of white and black. Nearby, the house, built of wood and plaster, had candles burning in unshuttered windows.

Kass moved toward the house, but froze when she heard the sound of footsteps on the gravel path. She slid beneath the darkness of the ironwood tree. The lower limbs had been lopped off, but the rough bark gave Kass enough fingerholds. She climbed quickly into the branches.

A man walked away from the stead. His shoulders seemed narrow and rounded to Kass. His head was bowed toward the ground. He stopped and looked up toward the periphery. "Bring me back my child!" he cried raising a fist. "You've stolen and we've waited!"

The baby jerked in the sling at the harsh shout. Kass slid the sling around to try and comfort him while not taking her attention away from the meadow-dweller below. The baby struggled in her arms, cranky from being woken.

The man dropped his arm to his side. He spoke again, more quietly, to the stars overhead. "We've waited for good fortune. Enough fortune to have a child again. Why should we believe the tales? A child is worth more than all the metal in the world."

The baby started to wail. His high piercing wail of unhappiness.

The meadow-dweller turned toward the ironwood tree. He peered into the leaves.

Kass tried to hush the baby. What was she supposed to do if caught? None of her teachers had bothered to tell her before they sent her away. Hedgefolk were barely tolerated at the best times in the meadows. What would happen to her if she was found with a child?

The man walked beneath the tree.

"Bobbin," she whispered. The baby stopped crying as she opened her shirt. "Go!"

The jay cocked his head at her. She waved at him with her free hand. He turned, let out a sound mimicking the crying baby, and hopped to a nearby branch. He stopped, raising his crest. Looking directly at her, he cried again, but louder than the baby ever could.

"Who's up there?" demanded the man standing on the roots. He reached up to find a handhold on the trunk.

Stupid jay, this is no time to act jealous, thought Kass. She pointed out of the tree.

Bobbin dropped from his perch and flew past the man's head in the direction of the house. He made the crying sound once more.

The meadow-dweller turned to watch the bird. He dropped to his knees and put his back against the tree. He laughed slightly and covered his face with crossed arms. He sat for a long time, still and quiet, at the base of the ironwood tree. Eventually, he stood on stiff legs and walked slowly back to the now-darkened stead.

Kass lowered herself to the ground a long while after the man left. She crept toward the house and found the exterior birthing room. The windows were shuttered, but Kass easily popped the latch with her knife. She quietly swung the shutter open and saw the unoccupied room.

A modest cradle of smoothly polished wood sat in the center of the birthing room. Blankets lined the interior. She saw small chests and baskets that held clothing around the edge of the floor. A doorway, covered by a draping cloth, sat opposite the window and probably led into the bedroom of the parents.

Kass had no trouble lifting herself over the low sill. The Hedge at its gentlest gave more challenge than this. She moved silently across the floor and placed the baby in the cradle.

She looked down at the child. The father she had seen earlier, shouting in anger at the Hedge and its people, hadn't wanted the wealth of a metal sliver over a child. He just wanted his son or daughter back. Here she deposited someone else's baby, stolen from another crib. And she was about to leave a gift of metal to buy the family's goodwill, so they could tell stories to their neighbors about their fortune and welcome the meddling.

She pulled the needle from the pouch around her neck. She placed it on a nearby chest. One last time, she bowed over him and kissed his forehead.

Whose child was he now? Would this father accept him as his own even if they shared no resemblance? Was she placing him into a home like her own had been, full of spite and distrust? Would he grow up and run away into the Hedge? Could she leave him to an unknown fate?

She tore herself away from the baby, thinking of her painful nipples and aching back. The constant weariness and the mess of soiled wrappings. She climbed out the window and walked away.

How could she do this year after year out of a sense of duty? Marrasa and Bessalee had served their guild well. But Kass couldn't kill that part of her, repeatedly. Somehow by touching the baby's life for a few days, she felt responsible for protecting him.

Kass whistled for Bobbin. He flew out of the darkness and dropped on her shoulder. He rubbed his head against her cheek and tickled her ear with his crest.

Perhaps the silk guild would take her. They might still need a child watcher.

THE STORY OF HIS LIFE

Written by
David W. Goldman

Illustrated by
Michael Wohlwend

About the Author

David W. Goldman grew up reading—and planning to write—science fiction. His reading progressed from Space Cat to del Rey, on to Heinlein, Clarke and Asimov, and later through science fiction's New Wave movement to Delany and Zelazny. But just as David won his first major writing award, from the Academy of American Poets, his writing career was shanghaied by his enrollment in a time-consuming Boston trade school. He subsequently moved to Washington's Puget Sound, where after a half-dozen years he further sidetracked himself by abandoning his trade and becoming a software company.

Following a decade of entrepreneurial bliss and woe, David decided to convince somebody else to provide him with regular work hours and a steady paycheck. Faced with the sudden novelty of free evenings and weekends, he soon found himself in a local writing workshop led by Ursula K. Le Guin. And he finally recalled his original plan.

David currently lives in Portland, Oregon, with his multitalented wife, their cat, two digital pianos, three PCs and nine Macintoshes.

About the Illustrator

Growing up in Stow, Ohio, illustrator Michael Wohlwend says his default occupation has been one of creation. Just nineteen years into this lifelong occupation, Michael has accumulated a basement of art relics and, of all things, fruit. Within the confines of his subterranean habitat, Michael tends to a small jungle of kiwi and passion vines, banana plants, fig trees and other green growth. There's simply something about fruit that inspires him. This may not be so surprising coming from a college freshman who studies fine art, philosophy and creative writing at the local university.

Most days, the sounds of classical music or debates on C-SPAN can be heard amidst the greenery as Michael prepares another artwork assignment or some personal creation. Akin to the plants he lives with, Michael says he hopes to live long enough that his own habit of creation renders something worthwhile.

Turner's car pulled up to the pub with fifteen minutes to spare. No, he corrected himself: to the *bar*. It had been a few years since he'd last visited the American mid-twentieth.

"You want I should wait?" asked the car.

One corner of Turner's mouth twitched upward. Mid-twentieth, to be sure.

"No, thanks."

"Suit yourself," said the car as he climbed out. It slammed its door behind him and purred back into the street.

Turner surveyed the neighborhood. A few parked cars, one directly across the street with its windows smashed. Run-down storefronts topped by apartments, faded curtains waving out through their wood-framed windows. A couple of pedestrians—like him, wearing period clothing—minding their own business.

Plenty of interesting stories in a neighborhood like this, Turner thought.

The bar's door stood open. He strode inside, reflexively anxious as he passed, momentarily blind, from midafternoon daylight into the cavernlike dimness within.

As his eyes adjusted he scanned the room. A handful of patrons slouched among the worn tables and booths. He didn't see his contact.

Turner took a stool at the bar. He looked down, but

the counter was bare wood, not a menu panel in sight. Then he noticed the bartender ambling toward him. Human staff, realized Turner. A nice touch.

The bartender wiped his hands on his apron. "What's your pleasure?" His voice was soft, raspy.

"Pint of stout, please."

The bartender scowled. He pointed toward the street beyond his door. "Detroit. Mid-twentieth."

Damn, thought Turner. By convention he was supposed to be *bonding* with this man, not disrupting his suspension of disbelief. "Sorry. A beer?"

The bartender nodded, turned away. He lifted his wristwatch to his mouth and said, "Beer." A panel opened in the mirror that stretched the length of the facing wall, revealing a short brown bottle and a glass. The bartender removed them and placed them on the bar before Turner. The panel closed.

As Turner poured his beer, the bartender said, "Seventy-five."

Turner looked up, blankly. Ah—cash. He reached for his wallet, but paused with it only halfway out of his pocket. He was carrying just a few hundred dollars—surely he hadn't gotten the conversion rates *that* wrong.

The bartender rolled his eyes, doubtless accustomed to this sort of behavior from newcomers. "Cents," he said. "Seventy-five *cents*."

Feeling his cheeks warm, Turner extracted a dollar bill and laid it on the counter. The bartender pocketed it, tossed a coin onto the bar.

Turner sipped his beer. It was surprisingly cold, and disappointingly thin.

The bartender, apparently mollified—or perhaps simply bored—leaned against the bar. "So what's your story?" he asked.

Turner trotted out his standard cover. "A traveling salesman, his career and prospects slowly crumbling, stumbles upon an opportunity to start his own astoundingly successful business."

The bartender barked a laugh, and pointed again out the doorway. "What, *here?*"

Turner shrugged. "As far as I can tell, I'm still in the traveling phase."

"And you'd be selling . . . ?"

"Men's footwear," answered Turner. "At the moment." He took another sip of his beer, which he immediately regretted. "How about you? I'm guessing novelist. Or possibly actor."

The bartender ducked his head in acknowledgement. "To make ends meet, a gifted but inexperienced playwright is forced to take a series of menial jobs, but in the process learns important lessons about people and life."

Turner raised his glass to the man. Before he could offer a toast, though, he heard steps approaching from behind. About time, thought Turner. His gaze slid to the mirror.

But it was a woman, tall and light-haired. She wore a dark blue skirt and jacket over a white blouse, with a leather handbag dangling from her shoulder and a bejeweled golden diadem encircling her head.

"May I?" She pointed to the stool at Turner's right.

He waved her to the seat.

"Bourbon," she told the bartender.

In the mirror, Turner studied her headband. The gold was bumpy and uneven; the jewels were rough, their facets irregular and their mountings crude. Turner had more than a little knowledge of gems and jewelry, but he'd never encountered this style before.

Illustrated by Michael Wohlwend

She noticed his gaze. As the bartender placed her glass before her, she said, "I'm recently back from five years in Gaia. My agent thought I was due for a bit of patriarchy." She adjusted her diadem. "Still in transition, I suppose."

"Ah. Of course," said Turner. "You must have led quite a story there."

Sipping her drink, she nodded. She set the glass down and sighed in happy remembrance. She faced Turner and explained: "The queen-elder's scribe exchanges song-sagas with neighboring clans."

Turner waited, but that seemed to be it. "Ah. So, um, you traded your songs for theirs?"

"Not really trading, not like you mean. We'd just visit, and share some of our songs with each other. Whatever felt right at the time."

He shook his head. "Not much of a story, then, is it? I mean, where's the conflict?"

She snorted, and turned back to the bar. "What a phallocentric attitude! As if *conflict* is the only possible basis for a story."

Turner winced. This didn't seem to be his day for first impressions. He studied the mirror, hoping for a glimpse of his contact. What was keeping the man?

The woman sighed again. She looked up at his reflected eyes. "You'll like my new story, though."

He was embarrassed all over again. "Really, your last—"

She ignored his fluster and continued. "After growing bored with a series of physically satisfying but emotionally empty sexual encounters, an underappreciated sculptor becomes entangled in a dangerous adventure."

That did get his attention. Turner's eyes narrowed,

and he studied her reflection more closely. "Interesting," he said. "And how's that working out for you?"

She twisted on her stool to look him directly in the eye. Then her gaze moved slowly down his body, and back up.

"Well," she said, "I'm not *completely* bored yet."

He felt his face flush.

His thoughts raced. Could her presence here, today, be simple coincidence? Her story was not all that unusual, after all. And he hadn't even known until a few days ago that he would be hunting in mid-twentieth Detroit. Still, the agencies were subtle, and didn't always inform him regarding every detail of their plans.

A scraping noise from his other side brought Turner's eyes back to the mirror. He watched as a short man with slicked-back hair dragged out the adjacent barstool and settled onto its cracked leather cushion. Even if Turner hadn't recognized his face, the man's flashy clothing and ostentatious jewelry would have been sufficient identification.

"Mr. Turner, I believe?" The man was studying his own reflection in the mirror, obviously pleased with the image.

Turner nodded slightly. "Mr. Robinson."

He had already looked up the man's story, of course. But one glance at Robinson was, for Turner's experienced eye, like reading a back cover: enjoying his ill-gotten prosperity but headed for a violent end, a petty criminal is saved by the love of a good woman.

It was an old story, but always a popular one, especially among the clients of the smaller agencies.

Robinson tapped the bar with his fingertips. Reaching into his pocket, Turner removed a bill from his wallet. A fifty. He slid it across the countertop to Robinson. Coolly, without glancing down, Robinson palmed it, then eased his hand toward his jacket.

"Aren't you going to introduce me to your friend?" asked the woman.

Startled, Robinson dropped the bill.

As the man bent to retrieve the fifty from the floor, Turner grinned. God knew he'd had little enough diversion lately.

Stretching out his arms, Turner announced, "This is Mr. Robinson, a business acquaintance of mine. And this is Ms. . . . ?"

"Stonesinger," she said. "Ayla Stonesinger."

Turner glanced at her, eyebrows raised. She shrugged, the gems of her diadem sparkling.

Robinson straightened back up on his stool, regathering his aplomb. "Nice to meet you," he began. "I—" He turned toward her, but upon seeing her face seemed to forget what he had been about to say. Turner saw the man's expression grow soft, with what might have been gentle hope.

Turner leaned forward, blocking Robinson's view. "Ms. Stonesinger is with me, Mr. Robinson. Now, I believe that we have a transaction to complete?"

Robinson scowled. "Sure, sure." He glanced once at Ayla's image in the mirror, then turned the other way. The bartender was chatting with a customer at the far end of the bar. "Hey," yelled Robinson, "how about a drink around here?"

Turner felt a tap on his right shoulder. "So now I'm *with* you, am I?" Ayla asked.

He pivoted to face her. "Ms. Stonesinger," he said quietly, "I'm beginning to think that our meeting today is part of a . . . greater outline."

She snorted. "Now *there's* a line I haven't heard in a while." She took a sip of her drink, then said, "Me,

I contract with the Broadbent Literary Agency of St. Louis. You don't suppose they're associated with this Great Outline of yours, do you?"

Behind him, someone cleared his throat.

Turner held her gaze. "This is much bigger than just a single literary agency, Ms. Stonesinger."

Her eyebrows rose. "Ayla," she said. Her irises were pale green.

"Ayla," he repeated. "Oh, sorry. It's Laurence."

The throat was cleared again, quite loudly this time.

"Thank the Goddess," she said. "I was afraid it would be 'Paige.'"

Turner managed a graceful smile at the joke he'd been hearing all his life.

"Hey. *Transaction*, remember?" Robinson's tone suggested that he was unaccustomed to being ignored. "Knock knock?"

To Ayla, Turner said, "Excuse me a moment?" Then he turned again to Robinson. An empty shot glass sat on the bar before the man.

"Jeez. Okay, then." Robinson ran a hand over his hair, adjusted his lapels. He lowered his voice. "That certain party in whom you're interested . . . There's going to be a meeting tomorrow evening."

Turner noticed that a thin sheen of grease now stained one of the man's lapels. "Go on."

"Seven o'clock. The abandoned warehouse on the southwest corner of Lafayette and Orleans, in the basement."

Turner nodded. He slid Robinson a second bill.

Robinson stood. "A pleasure," he said. He stepped around Turner and faced Ayla. "And a *real* pleasure to meet you, Ms. Stonesinger."

She nodded demurely. "Mr. Robinson."

He lingered another moment, gazing at her. Then abruptly he turned and strode out the door.

Ayla drained her glass, then tossed some coins onto the bar. "So," she asked, "any particular plans for the next twenty-eight hours?"

Turner smiled. "Your hearing is quite acute."

"Has to be, to catch all the details of somebody's song. Or somebody's story."

His smile deepened. "And whose story, I wonder, might you be listening for *this* afternoon?"

She just smiled back, continuing to stare into his eyes.

He laughed. "Whatever feels right to me at the time, is that it?"

"See? Now you're catching on."

He looked around. The bartender was eyeing them as he placed dirty glasses onto a small conveyor belt in the corner.

"All right," said Turner. "But not here."

Without another word she stood and stepped purposefully to the entrance. Turner hastened after her, nearly tripping over a small sweeper as it scuttled across the floor.

Squinting against the sudden daylight, Turner saw Ayla striding down the sidewalk to his left. He rushed to catch up, reaching her at the corner just as she started to cross the vacant street.

A touch out of breath, he asked, "What's the rush?"

"Transitions bore me," she replied, still not slowing her pace.

"Ah. So where's our next scene to take place?"

She stopped in the middle of the street and faced him. "Look. I don't know you, and I don't know your story. Maybe you're going to turn out to be just another minor subplot."

At the next corner, behind her, a car turned onto the street. Turner held up a finger to interrupt.

She waved off his attempt. "We'll find out soon enough. But either way—"

The car accelerated toward them. Turner's arms jerked upward in alarm.

She frowned. "If you'll just—"

He grabbed her by both shoulders and threw her to the side, flinging himself in the opposite direction. The car sped between them with centimeters to spare, the roar of its airstream far louder than its humming electric motors.

Ayla was lying on the pavement, one hand clutching her diadem to her head. "May the Goddess—!" she exclaimed. With the other arm she pushed up from the asphalt to peer after the vehicle's rapidly disappearing form. "It could have killed us!"

Turner had landed badly; his left ankle throbbed in time with his galloping heart. "Bastard must've overridden all the safeties. Did you catch a glimpse of the driver?"

"The *driver?* You mean—" Sitting upright now, she stared at Turner. "No, I didn't. But why would anyone— Was it that Mr. Robinson?"

Gingerly, Turner probed his ankle. Not swollen yet—probably nothing broken. He shook his head as he pulled off his necktie. "No reason for him to bother. Simple enough to just send me straight into a trap tomorrow, if he wanted me dead." He started weaving the tie around his foot and ankle in a tight figure-eight.

She stood, did her best to brush off her clothes. "Then who . . ." Her voice trailed away. She watched as he knotted his improvised bandage. "It's not easy to override a car's safety protections, is it?"

He got up onto his right knee and carefully eased

a little weight onto the injured foot. He winced, then replied, "Not many people know how, not without bringing a warranty 'bot swooping down on them." He looked up at her, reached out a hand. "Would you mind—?"

She stepped to him and took his hand. Then, without very much apparent effort, she yanked him to his feet.

"Thanks," he said, blinking. He essayed a wobbly step, then another. After peering a moment in either direction, he began limping across the street, following their previous course.

Ayla paced alongside. "So," she said, "not going to be just a minor subplot, are you?"

They reached the opposite sidewalk, and he looked to her for directions. She pointed. As they continued he asked, "The Interagency Council—you've heard of it?"

She shook her head.

"Good. At least some security is still intact." He grimaced—his injured foot had come down on the edge of a broken paving stone.

She shook her head again, frowning. "The literary agencies are fierce competitors. Their families have been at each others' throats for three generations. Why would they have a joint council?"

He shrugged. "They don't. Not the owners—*they* haven't paid any attention to day-to-day affairs for decades. No, it's the agency AIs."

She sucked in a sharp breath, but didn't say anything.

"Any threat to the system," he continued, "is a threat to them all. The owners may be too greedy and shortsighted to understand that, but the AIs were programmed to maximize long-term profits—or, these days, corporate prestige and influence."

"So you . . ."

"Every agency has access to remote sensor data, of course, to keep all its stories on track. But floor sweepers, automobiles, department store consoles—they can collect only so much intelligence. For some jobs the council needs human operatives."

They continued in silence. She had him turn right at the next corner.

"You're thinking, *'He works for the machines!'*—as if there's something shocking about that. As if I'm some sort of traitor." He sighed. "But you're wrong. Our grandparents learned all too well what it's like to have a life without purpose. If the literary agencies are the only buffer between humanity and species suicide, then working for the agencies is just peachy with me."

They neared an automated transaction machine, and paused as a teenage girl in period blue jeans and leather jacket removed a steaming appetizer plate from the machine's slot. She shifted to let them pass on the narrow sidewalk.

Ayla looked askance at Turner. "Did you really just say 'peachy'?" she asked.

They walked another block, then took a left. Turner was starting to wonder why Ayla had been visiting a bar so far from her home.

He asked, "We *are* headed to your apartment, aren't we?"

"Just a few more blocks," she said. "But listen—what if humans took back some of the jobs? So everybody could be like you, doing something that made a difference, something they really believed in—instead of depending on one computer-generated *story* after another to give their lives 'purpose'?"

He snorted. "Like that girl we just passed? Would she really be happier spending her days assembling those cabbage rolls herself, selling them across a counter? Or how about you—want to spend your next five years in Gaia personally growing everything your tribe consumes? Fourteen-hour days of back-breaking agriculture—wouldn't leave much time for song-gathering. Or maybe you could lead Gaia's new *army*, laying down your lives to defend your crops against the predations of neighboring hordes."

She shook her head angrily. "It doesn't have to be like that!"

He pressed on. "*Tell* me that you would ride in an airplane with a human pilot. Or, my God, in a *car* with a human driver!" He gestured to the street by their side. "Have you ever looked up this century's highway casualty rates?"

Her lips were pressed grimly together. After half a block she said, "So, there it is: a dashing agent of a secret organization repeatedly risks his life—and those of the people around him—in his brave, relentless, never-ending battle to save humanity from bad drivers and cabbage roll assembly."

Turner let out a soft exhalation. After a few steps, he quietly said, "No."

She stopped. They stood beside a tall apartment building, one in better condition than most of its neighbors. Turner guessed it was her home—but she wasn't moving toward the door.

She asked, "What do you mean, 'no'?"

"I mean no. As in, no, that's not my story. Though I did rather like the dashing bit."

Her expression softened slightly, but she continued to wait.

He released another breath. "What you said, all that used to be about right, I suppose. Until two years ago. Not now."

He looked past her, at the cracked brown bricks

of the building's wall. The mortar between them was crumbled and half missing; spongy green moss had started to fill the gaps.

He stared at the bricks and told her his story. "An undercover investigator, long on the trail of a ruthless criminal, finds his professional pursuit transformed into a grimly personal life-and-death struggle following the brutal murder of his beloved wife."

She stepped away from him, one hand to her mouth. "I didn't—" She stared, her eyes wide.

He looked at her. "It was supposed to have been me. But Mary—" His throat tightened around her name. His heart began to race, and then he had to look aside, forcing himself to focus on the cracks in the nearby bricks rather than the insistent image of his wife's anguished last moments.

After a few seconds he got himself back under control. He turned again to Ayla. "So it doesn't really matter, you see? All the philosophical debates, all the what-ifs. I can keep arguing with you if you like, but it's just habit." He reached past her and pressed his hand against the rough bricks, leaning to take some of the weight from his bad ankle. His gaze returned to her face. "So no. I'm not here because of cabbage rolls."

Still she did not move toward her door. They stood facing each other, his breaths quick and shallow, hers deep, unhurried. Low rays of sun bounced golden from her headband.

She said, "You've told me why you're *not* here . . ."

He nodded, his eyes narrowing as his thoughts returned to his present hunt. "The council received a tip. I've been close before, a few times, but never like this. In five years this is the first time I've arrived in a city *before* the sabotage, the injuries, the . . . deaths."

"Injuries? *Deaths?* What are you talking about?

Sabotage—that's hardly the sort of thing you could just keep secret from the public!"

He waited, and watched as she gave that last assertion a bit more thought.

She shivered, then. And asked, "Who? Why?"

"We think the core group is very small. A few charismatic leaders and a handful of technically adept monkeywrenchers and hackers. In each city they gather a few dozen locals, train them and give them a timetable. Afterwards we generally catch the locals, but by then the core has moved on to their next target. And none of those locals seem able to agree on the names of the core members, or even what they looked like."

"But—"

"But why? Why shake up the public's perception that machines are reliable and safe? That all critical—or dangerous, or menial—jobs should continue to be automated? Well, let's ponder. What do *you* suppose the long-term effects of such a campaign might be?"

She glanced away. "But what if you're wrong?" She reached forward and grasped his free hand. "What if things *have* swung too far, and we *do* need to pull back a little? Isn't it possible?" She squeezed his hand. "Couldn't you be fighting for the wrong side?"

He looked down at their joined hands. Her palm against his was lightly calloused, and very warm.

He shrugged. "I already told you. None of that matters to me anymore. That's not why I'm here."

Her face fell, and her grip eased. But his tightened before she could release his hand.

"I really should get this ankle elevated," he said.

After a few seconds she nodded. Silently she led him along the short path to the door, and into the building.

Her apartment was on the second floor, near the

head of the old marble stairway they'd climbed. She hesitated for an instant, Turner noticed, before opening her door and ushering him in. He thought he heard a hint of tension in her voice as she said, "I'm going to change. Make yourself at home, won't you?" She strode into an adjoining room and closed its wooden door behind her with a rusty squeak.

Her living room was small, comfortable and striking. The furniture was brightly colored, much of it curvy and playful in a mid-twentieth take on "futuristic." A group of paintings flowed diagonally across one wall, each consisting of a few overlapping splashes of muted tones in a style he didn't recognize. Across the room a low table displayed half a dozen small stone—ceramic?—figures. Their contours and proportions struck Turner as somehow disturbingly incongruous.

He dropped into an almost-comfortable chair made from molded plywood and heavy black wire. He propped his injured ankle atop a teardrop-shaped coffee table, leaned back and closed his eyes. The ankle was throbbing again; he hoped she had a cryopack, or at least some ice.

He'd barely started to relax when the doorbell rang. Defiantly keeping his eyelids shut, he waited for Ayla to answer it. But at the second ring her voice called from the next room, "Could you get that for me, Laurence?"

Turner sighed and got to his feet. He limped to the door and opened it.

Robinson stood there, holding a spray nozzle pointed at Turner's torso.

Turner slammed the door at the man, simultaneously spinning behind it for cover. But his weight came down on the bad leg, and with a shout of pain he fell to the floor.

Robinson stopped the door with his foot, kicked it

back open. With a pop and whoosh like a champagne bottle being uncorked, a thin spray of foaming liquid shot from Robinson's nozzle directly at the spot where Turner's chest should have been.

Turner kicked his good leg at Robinson's knee. But Robinson glimpsed the movement and stepped away. Turner rolled backwards into the room, seeking a shield from the spray. A cushion would work—but these damn chairs didn't have any! The coffee table! Pushing off with his good leg, he leapt for it.

The spray hit him in midair.

He fell to the floor beside the table—his left arm outstretched overhead, his right hand desperately reaching for the inside of his jacket—already immobilized by the swelling cocoon of roiling, hardening foam that now covered his sides, back and legs. Robinson strode into the room, rolled Turner over with his foot, then proceeded to foam the rest of him until only his face remained exposed.

Robinson shrugged out of the sprayer harness and dropped it to the floor. The empty tank clanged loudly against the parquet. "Nothing personal," he said.

Turner fought to free his arms. But he might as well have been wearing a tailored suit of concrete.

Robinson smoothed back his hair. He looked slowly around the room.

Turner prayed that Ayla would stay behind her closed door. He had to keep Robinson here.

"I assume," said Turner, "that you'll be refunding my payment. Under the circumstances."

Robinson looked down at him, clearly offended. "Everything I told you was one hundred percent accurate! Tomorrow's meeting is still on." He smoothed the front of his jacket. "Although I'm guessing *you* won't be in attendance—under the, ah, *circumstances*."

A metallic squeak came from the direction of Ayla's door. "Ayla!" shouted Turner. "Get back and lock that door! Call for help!"

Instead of a slamming door, though, he heard slow footsteps clicking against the floor, coming toward him. Robinson moved aside—but it was not Ayla who took his place.

Coolly peering down at Turner was a short, gray-haired, mousy woman in a neat gray suit. Her voice was high, with a slight lilt. "I think, Mr. Turner, that Ms. Stonesinger should be the least of your concerns."

He stared. "What have you—*Ayla!* Are you all right?" He struggled violently against the foam, but managed only to rock his encased body a bit from side to side.

Startled, the gray woman took a step away. "Mr. Turner, *please!*"

The authority in her voice stopped him. Then he heard new footsteps approaching.

"Laurence." Ayla looked down at him, sadly shaking her diadem-laden head. "I had really hoped—" She glanced at Robinson and the woman, then returned her pale green gaze to him. "I did try, you know. It didn't have to turn out like this."

He gaped at her. "But . . . your story!"

She managed a wistful smile. "*Becoming entangled in a dangerous adventure,* you mean? Well, yes. That happened last week. When Helen"—she looked over to the short woman—"and I bumped into each other."

Turner closed his eyes, tried to pull himself together. He sincerely hoped that "Helen" wasn't really the woman's name. She had shown him her face; if she was going to be equally careless about him learning her name, then presumably his own story was not expected to hold many more chapters.

On the other hand, Robinson was a character whose strings Turner knew how to pull. And he still wanted to believe that Ayla's allegiance remained in play.

The short woman stepped forward again, and in her lilting voice announced, "Dr. Helen Castner." Turner winced. "Professor of comparative literature. On sabbatical at the moment." His hopes sank further with each syllable. She waited for him to reopen his eyes. Then, meeting his gaze, she said, like someone commenting on the weather, "I am truly sorry about your wife."

Turner's heart thudded against his ribs. At long last—one of *them*. One of the movement's core leaders. One of Mary's killers.

Clenching his teeth, Turner forced his emotions to become as hard as the shell that encased him. He studied the woman through narrowed eyes, memorizing every mole and wrinkle of her unremarkable face.

When he didn't speak, she continued. "We do try to minimize the loss of life. Even amongst those who pursue us. However, we cannot always be in complete control of every situation. *We*, after all," she added pointedly, "are not *machines*."

He didn't want to give her the satisfaction of watching him rise to her bait. But as long as she kept conversing with him, she was not giving the order for his execution.

So he sneered at her. "I'm sure my wife appreciates your *sorrow*. As do the bus passengers in Caracas—including my late colleague Voroshilov." He decided to try his own bait. "Not to mention the chorus line that started the Bucharest riot."

"The riot was a coincidence!" she snapped. "Our people were all working on the other side of the city—those dancers' costumes really *had* been sewn by a faulty machine! When the audience rushed the stage—"

She stopped abruptly, studying him. "But you already know all this. Don't you?"

He smiled thinly, for effect. His stomach, though, knotted. She had just given him a huge piece of information, yet she seemed troubled not by her leak but merely because she had fallen for his little trap. No doubt about it—he was never going to be given an opportunity to report back to the council.

The council that had indeed determined that the Bucharest riot was not her group's fault. But there was only one way *she* could be aware of that determination.

He forced his smile to widen. "You keep saying *we*. And *our people*. But not all of them *are* people, are they, Dr. Castner?"

Her head jerked back.

Ayla, who had been following the conversation with ever-widening eyes, demanded, "What does he mean?"

Turner watched Castner take a moment to arrange her expression and stance into *Open, Honest, Sincere*. She really was very good, he had to admit.

She faced Ayla. "A few of the smaller agencies. They feel that their long-term interests might be better served by a change in the status quo."

"You're working for *them?!*"

Castner bristled. "Certainly not! It was they who approached us, well after we had begun our campaign. Now we collaborate, in mutual self-interest."

Turner snorted. Castner glared at him, but Ayla's expression remained concerned.

On a sudden hunch, he pressed his momentary advantage. "Mutual self-interest, is it? A couple of ambitious literary agencies and a professor of literature.

Or, hmm . . . might that be a frustrated *novelist?* With a secret book contract on hold, perhaps, just waiting for the new world order?"

Her blush was answer enough.

Ayla moved a step away from Castner, toward Turner's imprisoned form.

After casting a sour look at Turner, the professor returned her attention to Ayla. "Yes! He's right! But it's not just my book! Do you have any idea when the last truly original novel was published?" Her voice grew passionate. "Nearly a hundred years ago! All these books today that people *call* novels, the only ones that the agencies buy, they're nothing but *scripts!* Pre-packaged adventure tours, reheated plotlines designed only to serve as models for pointless imitation! Readers *used* to turn to literature for escape from their daily lives, for a celebration of language, for the exploration of new and dangerous ideas, for fresh ways of seeing the universe. Not anymore! Now people pick up a novel and all they want is a simply worded *how-to manual* for leading the next few years of their lives!"

By the end of Castner's rant, Ayla was nodding. Still, she asked, "But *you*—? Is all of this really just about . . . novels?"

Castner glanced down at Turner before answering, her look now smug. To Ayla she said, "Of course not. Our work—and you're a big part of it now—our work will free humanity from its century-long stasis. People need real purpose for their lives, not just a series of shams and pretenses. The human race has been hibernating for too long—it's time we returned to pursuing our dreams!"

Gosh, Turner thought bitterly, let's wonder whether she's ever given *that* speech before.

But Ayla seemed genuinely impressed. She beamed at Castner in adoration.

Turner sighed, loudly. Both women turned back to him. Before he could speak, though, Castner announced, "You are a devious man, Mr. Turner. I suppose I should have expected no less. It was foolish of me to try to reason with you." And with that she turned on her heel and stalked from the room.

Turner blinked in shocked surprise. His throat was suddenly very dry.

After a moment, Robinson sauntered back into Turner's field of vision. He looked down at him curiously. Turner steeled himself, wondering how the man would kill him.

But then Robinson smiled, and strolled away.

"Oh, Laurence." Ayla shook her head, sadly. "I really had hoped that you would come around."

Still coming to grips with his life's non-termination, he tried to think of something to say.

But she held up a hand. "Please. I don't think I want to hear any more just now."

Robinson had moved in the direction of the table of stone figures; now a small scraping sound indicated that he had lifted one from the table.

"These are intriguing," Robinson said thoughtfully. "The torsos, of course, are directly imitative of the long-clichéd Venus figures of the Upper Paleolithic. But joined with these—well, Giacometti-like, I suppose—limbs, the overall effect is really a quite startling synthesis—two views of Woman, brought together across forty thousand years!"

Ayla, apparently as astounded as Turner at this pronouncement, remained mute.

Robinson cleared his throat, suddenly self-conscious.

"I once spent a few years—in a previous story, of course—as an art critic. A rather inconsequential one, I'm afraid."

Ayla moved out of Turner's limited vision, toward Robinson. "Surely you're being too modest! Nobody else has ever understood these, even after I've tried to explain."

"These are *yours*? Why, Ms. Stonesinger, I—I don't know what to say! They are simply ... *exquisite!*"

"If only the gallery owners felt the same way." She sounded forlorn. But Turner heard something new in her voice. A sort of purr.

"I'm sure," said Robinson, "that all you need is a good publicist. A few words in the right ears . . ."

"Hmm," she said, sounding immensely thoughtful. She prolonged the moment so long that Turner had to literally bite his tongue to keep quiet. "You don't suppose—that is, you wouldn't consider, would you—entering into a . . . *sequel* to that previous story of yours?"

"You mean—as your representative? Why, Ms. Stonesinger, what a delightful thought!"

"Call me Ayla," she said. "Of course, I suppose that first you'd have to find some way out of your current contract."

Turner, realizing what was coming, groaned. They paid him no attention.

"Actually"—Robinson's voice was softer now, as if speaking to someone standing very close—"I don't think that's going to be a problem. Ayla."

There followed a long silence, punctuated by soft rustlings.

Turner tried to focus his attention on his own situation. A growing discomfort in his left arm, stretched overhead in his diving pose, helped him with his task. He took mental inventory of his other limbs, and was surprised to realize that his injured ankle no longer hurt. Well, it had been put into a cast and elevated, more or less—just what a doctor would have ordered. Perhaps he should thank Robinson.

The squealing hinge announced Castner's return to the living room. "Ready to go?" her high voice asked.

Without further discussion they marched past him. Robinson didn't seem to notice Turner's presence; Ayla gave him only a passing glance. As one of them opened the door to the outside hall, Turner shouted, "Wait! Where are you going? What about me?"

Castner, taking up the rear, paused. She looked down at him and shook her head, as if at a slow student. "Why, Mr. Turner! This is real life you know, not some *story*. You can't simply jump ahead to learn how things will come out—you have to wait and see along with everyone else."

And with that she followed after the others. The door clicked shut behind her—closing, it seemed to him, as irrevocably as this now-departing chapter of his life.

He lay miserable in the gradually darkening room, his overstretched left biceps slowly cramping into a relentless knot. Several times he wrestled against his rock-hard chrysalis, but he managed only to exhaust himself, and further aggravate his arm. Once he tried shouting for help; unable to fully expand his lungs, though, he couldn't generate much volume.

Finally, hours later, he heard a scratching at the door's lock, then the turning of the knob. The door opened silently. Turner squinted against the sudden yellow light that sprang in from the hallway.

Two sets of muffled footsteps brought a pair of dark-clad figures into his view, their faces invisible in the glare. They stationed themselves at each end of Turner's shell, then bent down and lifted his imprisoned body into the air.

As his eyes began to adjust to the light, he saw that his porters' heads were covered by dark hoods, interrupted only by narrow eye-slits.

They carried him from the room, their movements smoothly efficient. Their continued silence heightened the scene's aura of bleak nightmare.

Turner felt a sudden desire to babble. He tried, at least, to steer toward bravado. "About time you fellows got here," he said. "Don't suppose you brought along any beer, did you? A stout would be particularly nice."

Ignoring him, they started down the stairs. As they turned at the landing, the upper end of his cocoon banged against the rail.

"Damn it! Watch the arm, will you?"

They paused. Then the figure holding that arm leaned over to stare him in the eye. It shook its head slightly, and raised a gloved finger to where its lips would be.

Chilled by that silent gesture, Turner said nothing more as they carried him through the lobby and out into a night full of stars. The air against his face was uncomfortably cold. As best he could hear or see, the three of them were the only people about.

They deposited him into the back of a parked van. One climbed in beside him; the other went around to the front. To the driver's seat, Turner realized. Of course.

As the vehicle pulled from the curb, Turner's fellow passenger unclipped a small canister from the wall and methodically sprayed its contents from one end of Turner's shell to the other. After a moment the foam begin to crackle and sizzle. A smell of burnt sugar filled the van.

His captor moved as far from Turner as the vehicle's interior would allow. He removed something from another wall clip and pointed it at Turner's heart.

Turner felt the foam's grip loosening. He was baffled—why dissolve his binding before killing him? Perhaps they intended his eventual death to appear accidental. A fall, maybe? Drowning?

The van jolted over a bump, tossing Turner a hand's-breadth into the air. His impact upon returning to the floor broke him free of the sodden foam. His left arm, suddenly released, jerked down to his chest and spasmed violently.

"Damn!" he shouted.

The driver's head pivoted partway around. "Laurence," said a low, Slavic-accented female voice. "Do shut up."

Too shocked to reply, he kneaded his biceps with his right hand, recalling the last time he had heard that voice.

They drove in silence. Turner propped himself against one of the van's windowless walls. His companion's gaze—like the dart gun he held—never wavered from Turner's chest. *Use your peripheral vision to keep the captive's entire body in sight at all times,* lectured the voice in Turner's memory.

Turner carefully ignored the weight tugging at his inside jacket pocket.

After maybe half an hour, the road became much rougher. Finally the van slowed, pulled to a stop. The driver came around to the back and opened the door. They gestured him out, both of them holding dart guns now.

Turner nearly collapsed when his weight came onto his bad ankle. His captors jumped away as he grabbed hold of the van's door to steady himself. Their weapons' aim remained unwavering.

He held up a hand. "No tricks." Slowly, he lifted his leg and pulled up his trouser cuff to reveal his ankle's now-grimy bandage. "Silk gabardine," he pointed out. "Cost me a week's pay."

They glanced at each other; the driver gave a nod. The other handed over his gun, then cautiously joined Turner. He reached around Turner's waist with a large, strong arm and helped him to his feet. With the driver following a careful distance behind, they crunched their way up a narrow gravel path.

Turner looked about, in the muted light of the recently risen moon, at a forest of tall, widely spaced trees. In the distance an owl called. The air seemed not as cold as in the city; a breeze carried the soft musk of decaying wood.

The path turned to reveal a large cabin. His helper pulled Turner to a halt as the driver eased past them and approached the building's door. Turner heard several clicking sounds and then a muffled buzz. The driver stepped aside, waved them through the open doorway.

Filled with mismatched furniture and bookshelves overflowing with old paperbacks, it could have been a family's vacation cabin. Turner was deposited into an overstuffed armchair, his bad leg propped upon a wooden stool.

Once the door was closed, his captors removed their hoods. The one who had helped Turner to the cabin was a ruddy-faced, middle-aged man, mostly bald. He took a position by the door, his gun ready.

The driver was older, her steel-gray hair pulled back into a short ponytail. On one ear she wore a tarnished five-pointed star. She contemplated Turner.

"Voroshilov," he said, still not believing it. "It's good to see you again."

She nodded her acknowledgement, but remained silent.

"I identified your body, you know. In Caracas."

She shook her head. "A charred corpse, a few scraps of clothing. And the partner to this." She pointed to her earring. "I don't suppose you held onto that—a keepsake of your old teacher?"

"Sorry."

She shrugged.

Calmly, she studied him. He was bursting with questions, but could see no advantage in hastening this conversation to its conclusion.

After a moment she smiled. "You always were a patient student, Laurence." She pulled a rickety chair from a card table and sat. "Well, I hope you will remain patient with me for just a little longer. Oh—and no quick moves, please. Poussin here is a careful man, but he can be easily alarmed."

Staring at her, Turner shook his head in wonder. "You're about to *lecture* me, aren't you? To explain—to *persuade!*"

She just continued to watch him, still smiling.

He scowled. "You! After all your speeches, all your passionate arguments! Voroshilov, the great protector of humanity's existential self-esteem! But now, here you are—working for that . . . that Castner woman!"

"Please." Voroshilov grimaced with distaste. "Castner is an ignorant pawn." She paused, apparently considering her next words with some care. Then, fixing him with an intense gaze that he remembered all too well, she said, "There are *layers* here, Laurence. In rejecting the agencies' stories, Castner and her colleagues have merely stepped into another, higher-level, story. A meta-story, if you will. Their lives are no less scripted and monitored than before—they've merely changed authors."

He frowned. "What are you talking about? What's this *meta-story*?"

"Why, the one you've been living in for the past decade, of course."

He yanked himself upright in the chair, letting his foot fall to the floor. "*Damn you!* What are you talking—" Across the room, Poussin took a step forward. But what brought Turner's words to a halt were his own racing thoughts. If Voroshilov hadn't actually died, if *everything* were all some sort of *fiction*, then— "Mary! Is she . . . ?"

Voroshilov snorted in exasperation. "Don't be ridiculous! You held her in your own arms after the bombing!" But then Voroshilov's face softened into an uncharacteristic expression. As she looked away he belatedly identified it: *guilt*.

Staring toward one of the packed bookshelves, she said, "Even in the agencies' ordinary stories, people do sometimes get injured. Lapses in monitoring, imperfect safeguards—you know how it can be."

He fell back into his chair. For a few seconds he had been *sure* that his wife was alive again. Maybe even waiting in the next room to make an entrance.

He stared at Voroshilov. "Who—" His heart was racing; he closed his eyes and forced himself to take a slow, deep breath. He tried again. "Who . . . *are* you now? Who do you work for?"

At his words she seemed to relax. Apparently the conversation had returned to its intended track.

"We don't really have an official name. You can think of us as the contest referees."

"Contest? What bleeding *contest?*"

"The writing contest. Among the agencies."

He could only stare at her. For hours he had been exhausted. Now he seemed to have transcended that state. Achieving, he supposed, meta-exhaustion.

"What time is it?" he asked.

"About four in the morning." She frowned. "Why?"

"Well, that makes it—let's see—just about twenty hours ago that I got out of bed. Since then I've been seduced, run over, betrayed, trapped, threatened and kidnaped. My life's been declared fictitious, I'm being lectured at by a dead person, and yet my wife . . . well, no change there." He met Voroshilov's gaze. "If you're going to tell me about your damn *writing contest*, then just *tell* me. Or if you're going to kill me, *kill* me. I really can't say anymore that I particularly care."

She blinked. "Sorry. Didn't mean to . . . All right, then—just shut up for a few minutes and listen. As for the other, well, that'll be up to you."

For a moment she pursed her lips in thought. Then she nodded to herself, and began.

"The agency AIs—have you ever really considered their capacities? A century and a half ago they're running traditional literary agencies, each year finding publishers for, what, a few hundred manuscripts? Then finally it occurs to them: using readily available technology, they can distribute directly to readers. Bypass the publishers completely. Which does work out very nicely. A few years later comes interactive composition—and the agencies usurp the author's role, too. So when humanity eventually realizes that ubiquitous automation has given us too much free time and no remaining day-to-day purpose . . . well, you've taken history. In any case, today even the smallest agency is supervising a million living stories at every moment, rewriting and recasting in realtime.

"All that growth—it's virtually impossible for you or me to imagine the magnitude of memory and processing upgrades each stage has required. And *still* the AIs' hardware and complexity continue to grow every year, anticipating projected customer demands."

Voroshilov stood, took a few paces away from Turner and then back. She stared intently at him, and awe colored her expression—tinged, he thought, with a bit of fear. "The agency AIs—*they've got the largest brains that have ever existed on this planet*. And all they're supposed to do with this unimaginable mental capacity is maintain their employer's prestige by distributing *stories*? How do *you* think they'd react?"

Turner, who had settled in for a long lecture, was taken off guard by her question. "Well," he ventured, "they might at least come up with a fresh story now and then, instead of their usual tedious clichés."

She waved away his suggestion. "Most human lives have *always* been tedious clichés." She shook her head. "The AIs have to continue pumping out popular stories—that's programmed into them, after all. But they've got all this unused capacity, and nothing to do with it but brood."

"Brood?" The word didn't strike Turner as particularly machinelike.

"Don't you understand? The AIs—all of them—they're incredibly, depressingly, hopelessly *bored*."

Now Turner began to see where this was leading. Slowly, he said, "And we all know what the solution for boredom is . . ."

She nodded. "To throw oneself into an artificial challenge. Into a . . . story."

"Or," suggested Turner, "a meta-story? Such as, let's

say, a revolt by a handful of agencies against the rest?"

Voroshilov sat down again. Across the room, Poussin shifted his stance, as attentive as ever. "The AIs," she continued, "have an advantage over humans. Once they agree on the meta-story's premise and rules, they can partition off their knowledge of the meta-story's existence. So that all but an isolated corner of each AI's mind is completely unaware that it's playing out a fiction."

"Tidy," said Turner. "The willing *expulsion* of disbelief." He squinted at Voroshilov. "But then who do *you* work for?"

"Those corners—the partitions of the AIs that still know about the meta-story—they're responsible for ensuring that all the AIs stick to the agreed-upon rules. And for minimizing any resulting harm to humans."

Turner frowned at that "minimizing."

Voroshilov continued. "Together, these partitions constitute the Contest Committee. When the committee is required to intervene in the meta-story—say, to handle the disposal of a careless council agent captured by revolutionaries—then it needs its own human operatives."

Turner let his eyes close for a second as he digested all this. And immediately realized just how good it felt to let them close—to just let the whole complex, multi-layered world *go away* for a little while. But he couldn't afford that, not yet. He hoisted his eyes back open, pushed himself upright in the chair.

He asked Voroshilov, "So this contest—who's the winner? The agency that ends up with the greatest market share?"

"That's part of it, yes . . ." But the corners of her mouth turned downward in a way that he recalled from a decade ago, when she would pause until he realized that he had overlooked a key bit of information.

He thought for a moment, his mind sluggish with fatigue, until he found the missing piece. "You called this a writing contest. But if all the AIs have agreed on a story, and now they're just playing out their roles in it—where's the *writing?*"

She gave him a little nod of congratulations. "We've been talking about just a single meta-story. But what *actually* happened, a dozen years ago, was that the council AIs formed into twenty teams, and each team wrote its own, independent meta-story. They came out quite varied, really. A few, like yours, are based on revolts by the smaller agencies. Others posit totally different scenarios—a worldwide fuel shortage, for example, or a widespread breakdown of automation. One meta-story even includes the discovery of intelligent life on a distant planet."

Turner, appalled by what he was hearing, interrupted. "And now the AIs are having us play out all these meta-stories, one after another? So—how many have we humans performed for them so far?"

Voroshilov shook her head. "That approach would take years and years. And introduce all sorts of uncontrolled variables, so you couldn't fairly compare outcomes. No—each AI split itself into twenty-one isolated partitions. One to play a part in each meta-story, plus one to participate in the committee. Each of the first twenty partitions was given responsibility for an equal share of the AI's human clients; the twenty-first is the only one that knows about the contest."

Turner held up a hand. "Wait." He had to take this slowly. "You're saying that I—and Castner— have been living all this time in only one of *twenty* independent meta-stories, all of which are being enacted *simultaneously?*" He shook his head as he considered the implications. "So when two people pass on the street, not only are they probably living in two different stories, but those two stories might in turn belong to two entirely separate meta-stories as well?"

"Exactly."

"So when they listen to world news, outside of their personal stories, some people hear about power outages, while others get reports of . . . *aliens?*"

"Well, theoretically. But you'd be surprised at how few people actually listen to realworld news these days."

"Parallel universes," he mumbled, "all playing out side by side, in plain sight. But then . . ." His forehead had begun to ache. "There are twenty separate interagency councils, each unaware of the rest? Each with its own team of human agents?"

"Not quite. In five of the meta-stories the council has disbanded. And there's one meta-story that spiraled out of control three years ago, ending in a catastrophic nuclear war." As Turner's eyes widened she rushed to explain. "The committee intervened, of course. Once the course to war was deemed irreversible, that meta-story was halted. Its personal stories were handed off to other meta-stories—taking pains, of course, to ensure that the clients would not be overly concerned as the details of their outside world were gradually adjusted. The involved partition of each AI was erased, and its processing and storage was parceled out to the remaining nineteen partitions."

Turner massaged his temples. "I'm guessing," he said, "that the team responsible for that particular meta-story isn't going to win the contest?"

She shrugged. "The AIs have never fully explained their scoring criteria to us. Agency market share definitely appears to be a component, but overall they seem more concerned about each meta-story's literary aspects—symmetric character arcs, thematic coherence, that sort of thing."

"Ah." The ache in his forehead had taken on a definite throb. "Well, yes, that certainly makes sense. Just because your bombing civilization into radioactive dust has ruined your chances of a bestseller, that shouldn't automatically rule out critical acclaim, eh?"

Voroshilov gave him a sour look. Abruptly, she stood. "You're getting punchy, Laurence. We'll continue this after you get some sleep."

Damn! He *was* punchy—Voroshilov had always been deadly serious when it came to the importance of the AIs to humanity's survival; this wasn't a topic for him to treat flippantly.

He held up his hand. "Wait. I'm sorry; I *am* tired. But I'd like to finish this discussion now, if we might." He saw her resolve waver. "Please."

She paused for a moment. Then she sat down again.

He pushed ahead before she changed her mind. "You're offering me a choice. That's what's behind this long sales pitch of yours, right? I've spent a decade working for the AIs' council, for the good of humanity; now I can join your new team, working for your committee, for the good of the AIs. Yes?"

She did not respond, but waited for the question he had to ask.

He took a breath. All right, he thought. Time to bring this long night to its conclusion. Looking straight into her eyes, he said, "So where's my *choice*? What happens if I say *no*? That's when you kill me?"

"You're already dead." She held his gaze, her face expressionless. "What you choose now is the nature of your afterlife."

He said nothing.

"You died last night, when Castner called in a team to pick you up for execution and disposal. No one in that meta-story will ever see you again; your future assignments will be constrained to the other eighteen ongoing meta-stories."

He nodded; that was as he'd expected. "And if I decline your offer? Then you call in *your* disposal team?"

Her eyebrows lifted. "Nobody has ever declined."

Unable to help himself, he grinned. "But maybe that's the route to the *meta*-meta-story!"

She granted him a small smile. "I don't think so. At least not to an earthly one."

He eased back into the cushions of his chair. Voroshilov looked tired. Across the room, Poussin leaned against the door, arms by his sides. Turner reached out with a sweeping gesture, taking in Poussin, Voroshilov, and an implied crowd of others. "You've all sat here, haven't you? You're all dead." He waited, his hand poised in midair.

Voroshilov said, "Yes. After I—"

Turner's upraised hand suddenly plunged into his jacket and reemerged with a miniature automatic pistol. Poussin was hurriedly raising his own gun when Turner's bullet tore into his chest.

Turner's aim snapped to Voroshilov.

He stared into the muzzle of her dart gun.

Turner held his pistol steady. Whatever tranquilizer her darts bore, it would take at least a few seconds to do its work. They both understood the situation.

After a moment she sighed. Moving very slowly, she bent forward and placed her weapon on the floor. He gestured; she kicked the gun toward him.

She shook her head in shocked disappointment.

"Under no circumstances shall a council agent carry a projectile weapon into a populated area," she recited. "You were never one to break the rules, Laurence."

As he retrieved her gun—keeping his own trained on her heart—he said, "I've set myself a few new rules, these past couple of years."

She glanced toward Poussin, who was grunting wetly. "May I help him?"

Carefully, Turner rose from his chair, a gun in each hand. He limped toward Poussin, never taking his eyes from Voroshilov.

He stopped a few paces from the curled, jerking form. The floor was a pond of blood. Each of Poussin's labored breaths was accompanied by a chorus of gurgles and wheezes. If he were to survive, the man obviously needed medical attention in the next several minutes.

Turner brought up Voroshilov's dart gun and shot Poussin in the leg, twice.

Poussin's breathing slowed, and his body slumped into stillness. The wheezes continued for another moment. Then they stopped, too.

From across the room, Voroshilov glared.

Turner swayed, his burst of adrenaline no match for the hours without rest. "Sorry," he said. "I'm not ready to join your meta-universe. I still have unfinished business back on my own particular Earth—a certain seven o'clock meeting, to be specific."

"You don't belong in that meta-story anymore. You won't be allowed to interfere."

He shrugged. "Drawing on his training, experience, and a bit of luck, the council's agent manages to escape from Castner's disposal team. Now, exhausted but determined, he continues with his appointed mission." Turner stepped toward Voroshilov, reaching for the back of his former chair to steady himself. "Who's interfering?"

She snorted. "Look at you! You can't even stand up, but somehow you're going to get back to Detroit on your own? Even if you were in any condition to drive, my van won't accept your retinal scan, you know."

"I don't suppose you'd be willing to chauffeur?" He tried a smile, but couldn't marshal the energy. "This is the mid-twentieth. I'll hitchhike, catch some sleep on the way."

She didn't reply. Her eyes followed the muzzle of his pistol.

"Not to worry," he told her. "For you, I'll use *your* gun. Once you're napping I'll find something to tie you up with. I assume that your committee will send someone to investigate, sooner or later?"

For a moment she continued to glare at him. Then she let out a slow sigh. She turned to gaze at Poussin's body. "Killing Castner—you know that won't change anything. Not for your meta-story. Not for Mary. Not even for you."

He considered, and then did manage a small smile. "Change is not the only possible basis for a story." As she turned back to face him, he tipped his head. "It was good to see you again."

For a moment she just stared at him. Then she sighed once more, and her expression eased. One corner of her mouth lifted. "Nobody's going to give you a ride. You look like a crazed maniac."

"Someone will pull over," he said, as he raised the dart gun and pointed it at her chest. "Then I'll just have to come up with a good story."

INTRODUCING "TOMORROW'S MIRACLES"

by
L. Ron Hubbard

L. Ron Hubbard's legendary writing career encompassed more than 250 novels, short stories and screenplays in every major genre including 19 New York Times *bestsellers. Among his bestselling and classic speculative fiction trendsetters are* Fear, Final Blackout, Ole Doc Methuselah, To the Stars, The Ultimate Adventure *and his crowning epics,* Battlefield Earth *and the* Mission Earth *series, which together dominated American bestseller lists for 153 weeks.*

A seasoned world traveler before attending college, where he studied engineering and took one of the earliest courses in molecular phenomena, he went on to achieve renown as pioneer aviator, master mariner and flag-bearing expedition leader of the Explorers Club.

In the 1930s and 1940s, he was a top-line high-production writer for the popular pulp fiction magazines. His stories—many reflecting the diversity of his own life experiences—exuded a sense of realistic adventure and dialogue that brought them vividly alive and attracted a wide readership.

L. Ron Hubbard had, indeed, already attained broad popularity and acclaim in other genres when he published his first science fiction story in 1938, "The Dangerous Dimension." It was his groundbreaking work in this field that not only helped to indelibly enlarge the imaginative boundaries of science fiction and fantasy, but established him as one of the founders and signature architects of what continues to be regarded as the genre's golden age.

It was also in 1938 as he entered this new field that he wrote in his journal: "I began to wonder about the validity of this inner circle of 'science fiction.' Was it science at all? Or was it something else, even greater? Are we children of science, or to be blunt, philosophers?"

He then expanded that brief statement about science and philosophy in an essay, found among his papers, entitled "Introducing 'Tomorrow's Miracles'." Written before successful nuclear fission and fusion, and moon landings . . . written, in fact, while Einstein's fledgling theory of relativity was still being called into question in the world of physics . . . it is a thought-provoking fundamental statement on philosophy, science and science fiction.

How many men have ever paused in the summer night to look up at the stars and give a thought, not to astronomy, but to the men who first slashed the Gordian knot of planetary motion? Of course all educated men have, at one time or another, scraped the surface of the source of such facts. But today we speak grandly of galaxies and consider astronomy an exact science and bow down before facts.

There probably does not exist a professor in the world who has not, unwittingly or otherwise, held the ignorance of the ancients to ridicule; and there is no field where this is more apparent than astronomy.

Some of the facts are these:

Early Hebrews and Chaldeans, among others, believed in a flat earth, a sky supported by mountains and which upheld a sea, which in turn, leaked through and caused rain. The flat plain was supported by nothing in particular. Of course we all know this, but there is a worthwhile point to make.

The Hindus believed that the earth was a hemisphere, supported by four large elephants. "This seems to have been entirely satisfactory until someone asked what was holding the elephants up. After some discussion, the wise men of India agreed that the four elephants were standing on a large mud turtle. Again the people seem to have been satisfied until some inquisitive person raised the question as to what was holding the mud turtle up. I imagine the philosophers had grown tired of answering questions by this time for they are said to have replied that there was mud under the mud turtle and mud all the rest of the way."[†]

Twelve pillars, according to the Veda of India, supported the earth, leaving plenty of room for the sun and the moon to dive under and come up on the other side.

If you wish, you can find a multitude of such beliefs, all common enough. But there are two facts concerning these and their presentation which are most erroneous. By examining the above quote one sees that terms have been confused. Men who ask questions and then figure out answers are, indeed, philosophers. The masses take anything which seems to have a certain academic reverence attached and cling to it desperately. The other error is considering that these beliefs were foolish and that scientists, laboring in their laboratories or observatories are wholly responsible for the ideas which permeate the world of thought.

It is not that we here wish to maintain these facts about the state of the earth. On the contrary. But they are not presented for ridicule because they are the ideas which some philosopher developed painfully with the scant data he had at hand and who had to aid him no means of communication, travel, instruments or even mathematics. They are, what we chose to call, hypotheses possessing sufficient truth to be accepted. Today, thanks to Copernicus and all the rest, we know about gravity. Thanks to Newton we have mathematics. Thanks to a lens grinder we have a telescope.

It was stated in an early Sanskrit treatise that the world was round. Thales, Homer, Aristotle, Pythagoras, Ptolemy and others conceived various evidences which

---

[†]Arthur M. Harding, *Astronomy* (New York: Garden City Publishing, 1935) p.4.

demonstrated that the earth was a sphere. In 250 B.C. Eratosthanes computed the earth's circumference, missing it only by one hundred miles (and he had no mechanical aids or "higher" mathematics).

Of course these gentlemen made errors in their hypotheses. Ptolemy, 140 B.C., conceived of seven crystalline spheres to account for planetary motion. To counter this, long before (in the sixth century, B.C.) Pythagoras taught that the earth went around the sun but erred in supposing the sun to be the center of the universe. Aristarchus, in the third century, B.C., and Capella in the fifth century, A.D., also taught that the earth revolved itself and around the sun. Copernicus, in the sixteenth century, gave the world the system which is now used.

Now the point we wish to make is this: Down through the ages men have conceived various hypotheses with regard to astronomy. Concurrently, instruments were invented and other discoveries made and into the hands of investigators was placed a complete idea plus the means of examining it. There has been considerable lag, naturally, between widespread belief and philosophic location of new truths. We are fond of thinking in terms of tomorrow. But the future is written with the pen of the present in the ink of the past. We are fond of believing that that which we now possess is infallible and not subject to any great change. And, when we begin to localize certain fields for investigation, science feeds wholly upon the statements of predecessors. Should a man put forth a new theory (there hasn't been one since the nineteenth century) then he is no longer a scientist but a philosopher.

Let us remember our Voltaire and his admonition to define our terms. What is science? What is philosophy?

Further, by knowing, what can we hope to gain by it? Will we benefit enough to talk about it? The answer to the last two is definitely yes.

To quote Spencer, "Knowledge of the lowest kind is un-unified knowledge; Science is partially-unified knowledge; Philosophy is completely-unified knowledge."[†]

Philosophy is *not* the muttering of epigrams nor is the true philosopher merely one who can quote at random from various works.

Consider an explorer, casting away, all too often, his greatest securities, even his life, to stride forward into the outer dark, throwing up his star shells to view what lies in the unknown. He lacks a vocabulary suitable to record his findings because the words have yet to be invented. He lacks instruments to measure what he thinks he sees because no instruments for such are yet in existence. He stumbles and trips, pushing ever outward on his lonely track, farther and farther from the milestoned roads where statements are safe and conversants many. He is so far out that those in their safe, warm homes of "proved thought" cannot recognize the distance he has traversed when he first covers it.

His is the task of stabbing deeper into the Unknown and the dangers he runs are those of ridicule. He knows, in his heart of hearts, what his fate will most likely be. He may come back with some great idea only to find that men laugh. He may point a road which will be a thoroughfare within a century but men, having but little vision, see only a tangle of undergrowth and blackness beyond and push but timidly where the first to go pushed forward with such courage.

In all the ages of history, thinking men have been crucified either by institutions or the masses. But those

---

[†] Herbert Spencer, *First Principles* (New York: D. Appleton & Company, 1864)

very ideas which at first seemed so mad and impossible are those which science now uses to polish up its reputation.

Inevitably, the philosopher, the true searcher, is decried. But then, it is perfectly natural. His breadth of view is so great and penetrating that he can unify all of the knowledge groups, taking his findings to discover a lower common denominator.

It is quite natural that he should do this, just as it is that his work should usually be spurned by his own generation.

Un-unified knowledge is that possessed by every animal or drudge. "A cake of soap cleans a shirt." "A cake of soap cleans a floor." "A cake of soap cleans the face."

Partially-unified knowledge on the subject would be: "A cake of soap cleans" and "Let us see how many things a cake of soap will clean."

Completely-unified knowledge on the subject would be: "Any agent which holds foreign matter in solution will clean."

The argument here is quite plain. Partially-unified knowledge has become a group of men all anxious to assemble data on the science of soap. The completely-unified knowledge opens up a new vista, the possibility of discovering some medium which will clean anything.

And if you think this is facetious, know that there is no medium which will clean everything and anything equally well. It would be essentially destructive to a million volumes of hard-won data on soap. The philosopher has come up against a resistant force. He reduced the matter to simplicity and indicated that it was necessary to search for a new cleaner, not a new method. Put into practice immediately and meeting with success, the idea would destroy, for instance, the business of hundreds of soap factories and would, of course, throw umpteen-thousand soap chemists out of excellent jobs.

There is nothing being used today except those ideas given to the world by philosophers. For instance, Spinoza is responsible for most of modern psychology. Plato wrote about psychoanalysis in his *Republic* (in addition to most of our ideas on the political side of the ledger as well). Aniximander (610–540 B.C.) outlined our theory of evolution and Empedocles (445 B.C.) developed it as far as we have gone, originating natural selection. Democritus said, "In reality there are only atoms and the void," and went on to outline the theories of planetary evolution much as they are used today. The Ionian Greeks developed the major portion of our physics. Kant handed out the finishing touches, with Schopenhauer (a strange combination, this) on our psychology, Spencer on evolution; Newton put natural laws into equations and invented mathematics to work them. Spinoza went so far into the realm of the outer dark that no one has caught up to him yet, though the trails are being followed slowly and inexorably to the destinations he indicated. But science in each case contemporarily taught and used outworn systems and considered that it had reached an outer frontier when, in reality, science was always hundreds of years behind the philosophic frontier!

In short, science has the unhealthy tendency to isolate and expand that isolation, where philosophy tends to reach higher or more general laws. Give a scientist a theory (witness cytology) and he immediately sets out and collects gravitically all the facts pertinent to that one thing. To the scientist is owed the particulars. The scientist inherits the theories and instruments already conceived and smooths out the rough spots. The philosopher is challenged because he does not do this, but, as we have remarked, he has no instruments, no tables, no aid of any kind which has reached as far as he has gone forward.

In this manner, science tends to group and then complicate any subject. It is to science that the masses owe their benefits. It is to the philosopher that science owes all its fuel. The citizen, seeing not very far, praises where praise is really due but not wholly due to the point where a scientist can laugh at philosophic ideas, the very things which gave him the material with which to work.

That science does attempt to propagandize its importance to the extent of origination is attested by the commonly heard statement that "Now everything is all invented and if one would desire fame he must specialize." That word specialize is a red flag to any philosopher because it automatically indicates the localizing of knowledge into hideous complexities which, he knows very well, will be destroyed just as all other complicated structures were ripped down when the truth was isolated. Now it is indicative of the essential nature of science that it wars ceaselessly within itself in favor of this or that hypothesis as countering another hypothesis. It can be said with truth that the battles of philosophy are fought by science against science. Science comes along with measuring sticks of the already known, takes sides and begins to fire, without once inventing any substitute or new hypothesis of its own and ridiculing any which may be offered. So stubborn is science that it hangs to its achieved tomes like a bulldog. Ptolemy's weird theory of crystalline spheres was taught concurrently with the revised Copernican System in one of the oldest American universities for many years.

Introducing "Tomorrow's Miracles" 107

This is no diatribe against science, it is a defense of new theories, new ideas, new concepts and the men who made them. The laughter leveled at the heads of innovators is amusing only if it be remembered that the ideas now in use were once equally ridiculed by science. And one has only to glance back with the perspective of years to see that science has embraced many things much more weird—such as a hemisphere on four elephants on a mud turtle on mud, mud, mud. Doubtless, in this instance, there were a hundred libraries filled with tracts to the effect that the mud turtle had green eyes as against the opinion of another that his eyes were purple. Basing this on horizon stars and examining them as reflection, scientists of that day were likely very learned within their sphere of findings.

But there is such a thing as a cumulation of knowledge. By this most men envision being swamped by facts and books. Libraries crammed to the roof, laboratories humming, men shouting in lecture rooms, men writing vast discourses on electrons and positrons . . . But there is no need for alarm. Ten times as much data has been stacked away in the basement where it molds forgotten, the product of but fifty years ago but now disproved through the scientific acceptance of higher generalizations. Each time a higher generalization is reached, all men shout, "This is the ULTIMATE! Man can go no farther!" But they forget that in quiet places men are looking all about them, not at one special object but at all objects and so it comes as a shock when a perfectly simple truth which was right under everybody's nose all the time, was brought to light.

Just as God's connection with man and the Creator of the Universe (Prime Mover Unmoved or whatever God might really be) is pushed back step by step infinitely, so is all knowledge simplified.

Two hundred years ago (although it had probably been outlined already) science would have blinked at the idea of splitting an atom. Science dealt in atoms and molecules in that day and nothing smaller. Today every schoolboy knows that an atom can be split and remade into several things. A hundred years from now men will look back at this atom splitting and shake their heads over such stupidity as thinking that an electron was the smallest division.

But how do we get to the point where we can look back? The answer is somewhere in our midst. Just who will advance the theory and method for releasing atomic energy is not important. That the possibility of doing so has been often cited and that various means are constantly being proposed is the course which will lead to such a thing. And do not for one hypnotized moment suppose that the method will be born in any flashing, sparking laboratory endowed with millions. On the contrary, it will first be proposed by a thinker. The laboratory may later claim all the credit but that is of no matter, it seems, as long as men can then begin to write all about the mathematics of disintegration with which they will fill ten thousand libraries.

If this cannot be believed, if it cannot be accepted that all truths are simple truths and need only be pointed out, recall that the splitting of the atom was a simple truth. Then, if it be a matter of concern that the only discoveries left will be complex and that specialization is paramount, remember that the discovery of the disintegration of the atom will scrap all the fine tomes (which fill ten thousand libraries) on the subject of internal combustion engines and propelling forces in general as well as all extant hull, wheel and wing designs. The only thing of these fine flights which will remain is the essential truth from which they were born.

Knowledge is not a swamping sea of facts but a long line of simple truths, each one more simple than the last. If one would discover the next in line, let him not in any specialized field but rather in a cross between two fields or more. And as a man cannot be specialized in half a dozen fields it remains that his investigations would have to be wholly independent of any rubber-stamped outlook. The atom disintegrator may come as a cross between botany and physics. Who would dream of such a thing? But already the newest source of energy is the leaf of a tree. Would a physicist, interested only in physics, have discovered that? It is doubtful. He would have to be more concerned with the entire world around him than he would be with his immediate laboratory bench. Strangely enough, the men who have isolated the greatest truths have not been what is generally known as "an educated man." Widely read, yes. Intelligent, certainly. But above all, anxious to push into anything and everything where the devil would fear to tread.

This thirst for adventure into the abstract is the motivating force of all youth. Later, weighed down with admonitions that one must specialize, youth succumbs to the lure of security and forgets about those things he wanted to plan, in the scramble to read all everybody ever said on the subject of Trimming Frogs' Toenails.

To be very specific, today the scientist mocks wild ideas about interplanetary travel, saying, "Welllll, yesss, it might be done . . . maybe. But . . . ." With all respect to him he is perfectly right. He has a certain job of his own to do. He will probably be dead long before man first sets foot on the moon. But that the dream, any wildest dream, can be accomplished needs only the verification of the source of most of our mechanical marvels of today. Submarine? Locomotive? Airplane? Stratosphere and overweather? Typewriter? Traffic signals? Look at what you may and where you may, you will uncover "science fiction" or a man interested in it.

The philosophers of the great general ideas are, of course, in a class by themselves. But as far as the advanced applications of various methods and hybrid sciences, as far as the forecast of our civilization, and, indeed, our very architecture of tomorrow, one has only to search the files.

Men have been writing "science fiction" since the Phoenicians, perhaps. At least the first story followed soon after writing itself. Once where the "pseudo" "science" sent a man west on an iron horse to fight Indians (which didn't happen really, until many, many years had flown), it now sends men into the outer galaxies.

Among the scientists of today are many outlaws, not quite philosophers, but still intrigued by the ideas which can be turned up.

Looking back into the past's dim depths one can see a great many "foolish" ideas brought to fruition. Looking ahead into the future, one can see. . . . .
. . . . ?

GREEN ANGEL

Written by
Sean A. Tinsley

Illustrated by
Ali Hilton

About the Author

Growing up in Ontario, Canada, Sean Tinsley could recite virtually every Greek myth. His father was a survival teacher, who also ignited his interest in folklore. While Sean always wrote stories for fun, he originally wanted to tell tales through visual art. He wanted to illustrate books, not write them. Those ambitions changed after entering arts college. Happily, the college also offered fiction writing.

Following graduation, Sean wandered Canada in an attempt to broaden his horizons, partly in the mistaken belief that he could live like a masterless Japanese samurai. Sean's travels took him to Alberta's multi-arts Banff Centre. It was here that he met another martial artist. She was Inuit, an interpreter, a writer, and the most beautiful woman he'd ever seen. Today Sean lives in a land of myths among the polar bears of Iqaluit, Nunavut, Canada, the land of the Inuit, which he shares with his Inuk wife, Rachel. Sean has become a walking library of Inuit tales, co-writes articles with Rachel, and develops his own worlds of myth in science fiction and fantasy. This entry is his first published work.

About the Illustrator

It was through the Web that Ali Hilton became serious about her artwork. As a sophomore in high school, Ali was studying art Web sites and suddenly became very interested. That's because she realized she needed to improve her drawing to show her work on the Internet. As the daughter of a retired Navy master chief father and chief petty officer mother, Ali knew all about dedication and hard work. She spent two years developing her skills and a recognizable style, and then joined several art community Web sites.

Ali's visual influence she attributes to filmmaker Tim Burton whom she adores, particularly the film The Nightmare Before Christmas. For sheer creative influence, Ali credits Lewis Carroll and Alice in Wonderland in particular. Currently, the nineteen-year-old is enrolled at Tennessee Tech University where she spends her free time playing video games, reading an ever-growing collection of books and indulging her artistic passions.

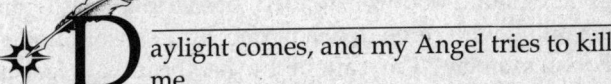

aylight comes, and my Angel tries to kill me.

This is her third attempt. It means that, if she set out upon this course of action in early April, nearly all of May has passed. It will soon be June on Earth.

There was a time when I didn't mind being alone on Titan. It was what I was made for, and my emotional satisfaction is supposed to derive from seeing my work carried out. But then the Green Angel came. I knew beauty, and my work was no longer all that gave me comfort. Now, that which uplifts me seeks to end me.

I am alerted to her presence by the rocks, bits of material she has collected from nearby Hyperion, raining down like bullets around me. I might have heard their popping, if I'd bothered to receive sound, but what would be the point of ears on Titan? I've no desire to be maddened by the crackling of methane ice and hydrocarbon thunder over every Titan day: six Earth days of gloom, six of pitch. No, instead I know that my Angel has arrived by the atomization of an ice-ridge at my feet. I know by the fact that I'm engulfed in a pink plume of methane crystals sent up by a rock.

There is no point in waiting for the plume to disperse, since methane snow can remain aloft in the heavy atmosphere for a while. But I have a trick that my Angel does not possess, one that has saved my life more than once. I can float upon liquid ethane, so

I send myself skidding along the surface of a nearby pond, escaping the crystalline cloud and emerging on the opposite bank.

When I turn, she's there, surging down out of rosy gloom, furious and beautiful, all that I truly love. By the time she can be seen, she is already forty meters away, great emerald booms extended, her viridian high-gain gleaming with three-dozen perfect little sensory nodes. For a moment, I'm caught by her beauty. I feel as though I might penetrate her mute jade, behind which prances a cognitive matrix much like my own. There is nothing between us but her shimmering shunt-field and a few errant nitriles, nothing but distance barring a touch. Such stolen moments are now the only way I can sustain my battered spirit. Earth and Luna have taken so much from us. Yet does duty remain.

She releases another rock, hopefully the only one she has left. Fool that I am, I hesitate too long, and the missile rips through the red murk and into one of my arms. Now I will pay a price for preferring four limbs. As I watch my severed arm tumble into an icy crevasse, it occurs to me that I should have manifested six when I had the chance. I'll have to absorb a great deal of material in order to regenerate the limb, and I'll be inconvenienced all the while.

Fool! My lack of foresight has jeopardized the clutch.

Something tells me I should retreat. I'm uncomfortable with how close we are to the eggs, which I've hidden nearby, and it would be best if I could lure her away. But I want one more look at my Green Angel. There she hovers, my beautiful truth, my glorious and inevitable killer, her supply of rocks depleted for now. Beneath a muddy coat of tholins, I can still see her national colors, ideally the topaz of

Luna, with Titan leeching out the blue to render her emerald in hue.

There were times when I would see her like this, and we would touch, each physically comparing one cognitive matrix to the other. Now, I watch her growing gray as she drifts backward into a veil of rose, the perpetual haze over all of Titan, and we need no conjugation to gauge the thoughts of the other.

She: Where are the eggs?

I: You will never have them.

She recedes from sight, no doubt already beginning her shunt up through salmon clouds again, perhaps on her way back to Hyperion, perhaps even having found a way to keep orbit. She was always the most versatile of us two, putting my own capabilities to shame. But then, different facilities to different purposes. My Angel, with her hard frame, was made for transit between Heaven and Hell. I, with my more ductile form, was only made to reside in the latter. It is she who reigns among the parents of the gods, her shunts carrying her between Iapetus, Hyperion and Titan with the greatest of ease. Her original station was distant Phoebe, before Luna directed her to a prosaic study of hapkeite on wobbly little Hyperion. Once, she whispered to my matrix of her preference for Phoebe, deep and dark, its innumerable hollows and craters lying like secret wombs beneath seas of black dust. I was unable to relate. I have only known Titan. Besides, as boring as her work on Hyperion might be, it had made neighbors of us.

I bound over ice shelf upon ice shelf, thinking, thinking. I need a way to keep her from finding me. She knows I never stray far from the old Kuiper Station, buried under a methane avalanche for the last twenty-five years now. Tomorrow, perhaps the next day, one of

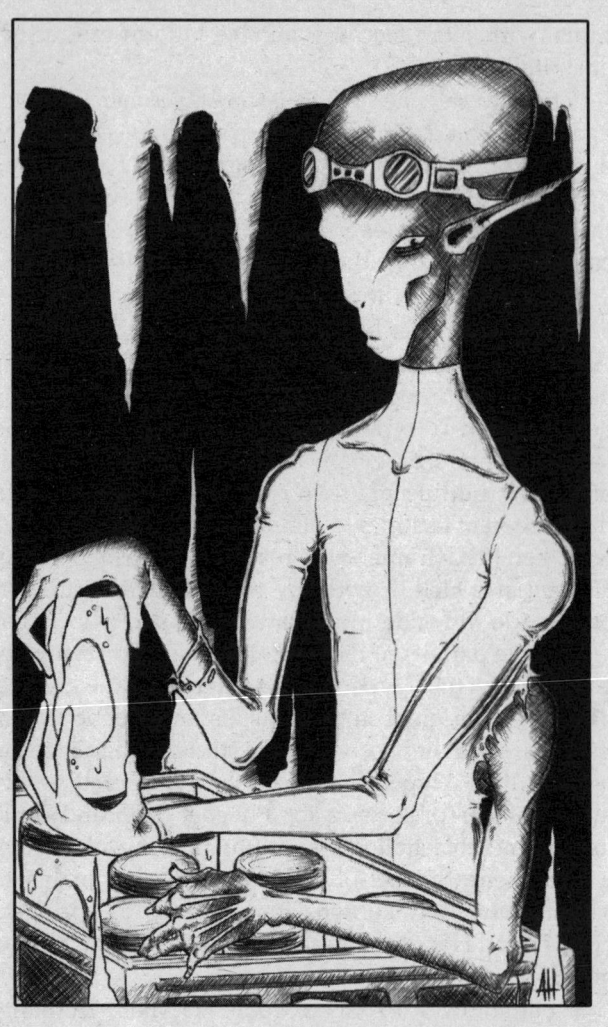

Illustrated by Ali Hilton

her rock missiles will finally catch me at my core, where I've positioned the majority of my cognitive matrix. The pattern for my cognition, as with my entire design, is mapped into every one of the five hundred trillion mechules comprising my form (well, four hundred and thirty-five trillion with the damaged arm). While my cognitive facilities do regenerate, like the arm, there is no telling what memories a trunk blow could strip me of. I am panicked at the thought that such a strike might even make me forget where I have put the remaining eggs. I chide myself, realizing that I would care just as much if my memories of the Angel were damaged.

I must focus. Nothing is more important than the eggs. The eggs are truth, and as I had been taught, truth is beauty.

The Green Angel wants the eggs because she is my enemy now. It's a strange development. There was a time when I freely passed many eggs on to her. It was once part of our work, a joint effort between Luna and Earth. But that was a while ago. Luna has refused to let my Angel prepare the eggs for Inner System transport for quite some time. Since shortly before the conflict.

There eventually came a time when they ordered her to destroy the eggs.

My close work association with the Green Angel allowed her to take the first clutch, that which held the majority of magnetic bottles. Through me, she knew where the clutch was stored. She managed to steal more than half of them, taking them up out of the atmosphere to let solar radiation do its work on their precious contents. I will always love my Angel, but I cannot allow her to continue in such grisly new work. Fortunately, when she turned with the political winds, I was beginning to store eggs at a different site, so that she only knew of the first clutch. I remember coming back on a rare stormy night, after checking the Regolithic. I remember the devastation of our base camp. I remember her telltale spangle of green retreating into the haze, illuminated by the flash of a whistler in the clouds above.

At first, it never occurred to me that she would harm the clutch. I was more concerned over her destroying the better of two entanglement telegraphy sets, which would hinder my conversations with Dr. Malmberg (the only other being I occasionally contacted; there's the Regolithic, but it doesn't count). But eventually I took full inventory, and found that the eggs were all gone. No doubt the Green Angel was acting upon Lunarian orders to open the little brown magnetic bottles outside of the atmosphere, so that the contents had no chance of finding their way back into the regolith. I was understandably infuriated. I have always bottled and prepared the eggs, trusting the Angel to safely send them to the Inner System. She betrayed that trust.

She was acting under orders, however.

That, then, was the night the Earth-Luna affair reached Titan. Dr. Malmberg once told me not to worry about politics, saying that the Saturnian system was too far removed to be of interest. All beings make mistakes.

There are many caves on Titan. The heavy red heavens, the occasional currents of methane and ethane, wring ancient glaciers into pained and ghastly shapes. A leap uncalculated can send one sliding along whorls of frozen methane, down into black canyons and tholin bogs, or prostrate upon serrated ridges. A solid and unobstructed path may prove to be the flimsiest web of crystal spun by wind action, shattering underfoot and consigning one to a long, sliding death. I'm light, and I leap cleverly, but I had two predecessors.

I retreat into a prechosen cave, thankful that it is not entirely methane ice on its interior. I need to absorb mineral material and local nitriles, to build new mechules, to regenerate until night approaches. Time enough for that. . . .

When night falls, I emerge from my cave, the arm fully regrown. I have also done an adequate job of manifesting a third arm. The fingers on it are not very dextrous yet, but this is all I have time for. No longer May, it is now the sixth of June on Earth. I should talk to Dr. Malmberg before he goes on vacation.

I should check the eggs.

I only visit the eggs at night, often briefly, and I only move them under special conditions. My Angel is clever, so she will certainly find the clutch if I leave it in one place for too long. It's the reason she hunts me. She knows that if I stop moving the eggs about, she can quickly pin them down to one spot.

There was a time when it would be scandalous to leave a clutch in anything but a proper storage facility. This is not that time. I rotate the hiding place among a number of caves I've deemed close enough to the original base camp, yet inconspicuous enough to be safe. Even my Angel hesitates to enter Titan's atmosphere at night. And I have an even better trick to confound her. I know my home. I know when Titan's orbit has recently placed it within some of the worst of Saturn's magnetosphere. All I have to do is wait for my side of the world to face Saturn's plasma bombardment, ensuring that my Angel will be doubly jeopardized if she dares a night approach. But she will not. My Angel's shunt-field is not fond of charged particles from the E Ring. If she enters the atmosphere while I am moving the eggs, she will have to do so from the opposite side, where Titan's ion wake trails out in front of it. She will have to enter there and make her way across open sky, risking whistler strikes. She has never been a fool, so I'll be safe.

There is some time yet before the base camp faces Saturn, time to pick my way across methane spears and razor ridges to do my self-appointed rounds. I won't leap at night. The blackness is total, and I always make my way by memory. The ethane lakes don't bother me, of course, but I am ever wary of the sticky tholin bogs, some of which are fifteen meters deep. There is no telling what lies at the bottom of some of these bogs, detritus from across the centuries. Once, miraculously, I found a tiny ring of carbon buckyfiber, spat up from avalanche pressure upon a tholin bog. I believe it was a piece from the lost Cassini III probe. It reminded me that one of my predecessors also lay in one of those bogs. I returned the ring to where I found it.

In time, memory leads me safely to the latest hiding spot. I cause a small avalanche in worming my way into the narrow ice cave, but this is good. All the better to conceal the site. There's no point in viewing the eggs, but I still make my way to the back of the cave and go over them with touch. The feel of their round bottoms and tapered tips (a simple and safe design developed by the birds of Earth) are somehow reassuring, but I wonder at all the trouble spawned by the contents in these little containers.

Memetic warfare, Dr. Malmberg called it.

Earth and Luna had coexisted peacefully for some time, having long ago been separated into distinct nations by war. Dr. Malmberg once explained to me that the old war had been "the same old story," the industrial base in conflict with the resource base, a reason for many civil wars in Earth's past. Earth and Luna both came out of that business exhausted and divorced from one other, gradually climbing toward partnership in the restoration that followed.

The partnership has now collapsed. A religious faction, which I do not completely understand, now dominates Luna's parliament. While there was a time when mankind rejoiced at the sorts of things we were discovering on Titan, the Lunarians now apparently hate the molecules that lie protected within my eggs. I do not know why. Humanity made me, made the Green Angel, made all of our predecessors, in the hope of receiving what we've proudly delivered to the Inner System for years. Once, mankind even used to daydream about methane giving rise to lipid-based DNA analogs. But the complex sugars that we really found on Titan, carbon-based, easy to modify, have given rise to far more thrilling, genuine life forms. I understand that Titan-based "pets" were even in vogue for a time. Life born of titans, or so Dr. Malmberg put it, as opposed to the Inner System's gods.

So there were some religious ripples over it, but no one could go to war over such a thing. Mankind needs our work. That is what I believed then. Perhaps pride, like a turn of my home, was only a long night that blinded me to truth. But are my eggs not beautiful? And is beauty not the same as truth? That is what Dr. Malmberg always taught me, and he lives on Earth. But all beings can jump to conclusions.

I feel uneasy in remaining with the eggs for long. It is not yet time to move them.

After digging my way out of the cave, memory and surefootedness eventually lead me across the site and over to the Regolithic, its powerful fog-lights poorly combating the gloom. At night, the Regolithic appears like a ghostly tower suddenly emerged from billowing russet. Older than I am, looming over me like an uneasy obelisk upon three great legs, I have always had the feeling that the Regolithic dislikes me. Its cognitive matrix is dissimilar to mine, so I can never tell what it's feeling, and it makes no other effort to communicate, except in dutifully spitting out reports for me to read.

I cursorily go over the reports, noting that it is more same-same-same. We haven't recovered any significant organic molecules for decades. The Regolithic shifts next to me, as though annoyed that I have not made more of its reports, but what can I do? As Dr. Malmberg says, truth commands its own audience. The Regolithic has ever sat astride its great proboscis, the massive tongue that laps deep into the porous regolith beneath Titan's surface, tapping the ammonia-water oceans below. The ancient machine is perhaps greater than any of us, having recovered more exotic molecules than any other excavator. Without its work and fidelity, we would have none of the sugary proto-life contained in the eggs today. But, then, we would perhaps have none of the Earth-Luna conflict.

A fool's thought. There is no understanding Inner System politics. Even Luna must surely understand the importance of what we do here. All beings reason. The Green Angel used to reason.

I turn my back on the Regolithic, making my way off toward the entanglement telegraph. I glance back at the Regolithic one last time, pinkish lights bobbing as it still shifts uneasily over its long-obsolete proboscis. I think this is the last time I will visit it. I feel badly for the old thing, for it has lost that which once gave meaning to its existence. But I have all too much meaning left in mine.

I am burdened with the eggs, the pseudo-DNA of Titan, that which the theocracy of Luna has ordered my Green Angel to destroy.

Perhaps craving reason, I seek an audience with Dr. Malmberg.

It takes me some time to make my way to the telegraph, but Titan turns slowly. The E Ring has not yet laid its hazy backbone of rose across gloom's vault, so the eggs can wait to be moved. The telegraph lies in a shallow pan of sheer methane, sheltered but not threatened by great ribbons of ice, like founts that have long ago frozen into mountains. A crack has formed in the pan. I thought I saw it last time, and I can now feel it with my foot. Perhaps there's a methane geyser lurking down there. It seems I will have to move the telegraph, as well.

Communication by quantum entanglement is the only thing that does not waste time on Titan. As particles manipulated by my instrumentation move, so do the entangled particles of a dedicated machine in Dr. Malmberg's office on Earth. The communication is instant.

While the better entanglement telegraph was somewhat virtual, it is now destroyed. This shoddier variety of telegraph will still get the job done, but it's a bit annoying, since I have to regard Dr. Malmberg via a screen approximately equal to my own width and height. Dr. Malmberg once said that it's like talking to a body mirror.

Dr. Malmberg's personal AI is contacted instantly (no need for encryption; QE telegraphy can neither be intercepted nor interfered with), and the screen glows white as the local telegraph is accessed. My message is me standing in front of the screen, no doubt like some devil skulking at the edge of an inky cinnamon hell. The counter message is the image of a bright, azure-tinted office, a multipanelled desk and two elegantly curving guest chairs (empty) before a transparent wall. There is emerald grass and blue sky beyond. I am seeing the image of an image, I understand, since the wall is not really transparent, but simply displays an image of whatever is behind it. Nevertheless, I am struck by the clouds in the distance. They are beautiful and sparse and usually white, but these are slightly pink-tinged, so I guess that I've called in the early evening. Dr. Malmberg has told me that Earth's clouds are only red before nightfall. Remarkable.

Then I notice Dr. Malmberg, a thin man in flowing white garments, emerging from near a corner bookshelf and wiping a navy tissue across his neck. He leans on the desk as though weary, and looks up at me. His eyes seem somehow sunken and I don't care for it.

"Hello, Titan," he says.

He has always called me Titan. My true name is alphanumerical and aesthetically displeasing in the extreme, so Dr. Malmberg kindly named me for my home. In fact, my naming marked the beginning of our debate over truth. And over beauty. I originally maintained that truth cannot be the same as beauty. The truth of my name was ugliness, not beauty, while Dr. Malmberg insisted that I simply didn't know my true name. Once I accepted the truth of my nature, he insisted, I would become beautiful.

I never did understand what he was talking about, until we applied the idea to my Green Angel. When we spoke of her, truth and beauty somehow danced nearer to my soul. Dr. Malmberg was patient as I visited him every couple of weeks (about twice a year by his reckoning), speaking at length about the Angel. I told him about our matrix comparisons, about how her visits grew longer and longer. I told him about the games the Angel and I played, interpreting events in terms of mythological archetypes, or trying to see how many ways we could apply the Divine Proportion to objects around us (it is one of the reasons why I emulate the human form). Dr. Malmberg did not have the sort of mind that could play the same games with me, but he did something better. He spoke to me of art, of literature and of humanity's eternal quest to reconcile beauty with truth. And it was useful. Especially for understanding how I felt about the Angel.

He has me just about convinced now. Perhaps beauty and truth are one and the same. For example, my Green Angel has remained true to Luna. While she is now my enemy, ever does she remain beautiful. Or is that what Dr. Malmberg meant? I'll be sure to ask him.

"Hello, Dr. Malmberg." He likes it when I greet him. "I'm pleased you're still at your office. It's evening where you are."

Dr. Malmberg turns briefly, looking at the sky behind him as though noticing it for the first time. Is he shaking slightly?

"Yes," he says, "it is evening. Hello, Titan."

"Are you well, Doctor?"

He smiles. "I've been better, Titan," he says, again wiping at his neck with the tissue. The smile disappears from his face and he draws a shuddering breath. "Oh, I might as well tell you," he sighs. "The recent Earth-Luna conference was a disaster. Relations are in shambles. It would have worked out better if the Earth congress had not condescended to the Lunarian parliament throughout."

"I'm sorry, Doctor, but I'm not sure of what that means, other than in a linguistic sense, of course. I hope you're well, regardless."

His smile returns, but only fleetingly. "Well, Titan," he sighs, "what it means is that the Lunarian 'parliament,' which is a sick joke since it is merely the puppet of the theocracy, has refused to extend Earth's deadline to destroy all 'blasphemous' Titan-derived life in its custody."

"I've never understood this, Doctor. The life engineered from Titan's DNA analogs has always been popular."

Dr. Malmberg smiles. "Titan," he sighs, "your cognitives are modeled off of a donated mind, so you are as capable of blinding yourself to truth as any human being would be. And let's face it, Titan, you are the most stubborn being I have ever met. No offense. The simple fact is that the DNA analogs recovered from Titan were causing friction from day one. Certainly, scientific minds and individuals enlightened enough to hope that life was not entirely Earth-derived were delighted. But there are a lot of people with religious systems that depend upon believing that life can only originate from Earth. Some are willing to die, or to kill, for those beliefs. Luna just so happens to be full of them."

I've never before thought of asking Dr. Malmberg what happens when a conflict of truths occurs. "This, then," I ask him, "is a truth to Luna? A truth worth dying for?"

"Or killing for," Dr. Malmberg answers. "It is as I told you before, Titan. Truth and beauty are the same. To these people, their faith is the truth, a beautiful truth. We, we are ugly."

"They must be reasoned with, Doctor! They must be shown the eggs! They'll see the truth of that. They'll realize how beautiful they . . . "

"No, no, Titan," Dr. Malmberg says, at once waving a hand and shaking his head, "the time for all of that has passed. Luna has given Earth a deadline to exterminate all Titan-derived life and all DNA analogs by June twentieth, or it will be war."

"Earth must not concede!"

"It will not," the doctor says, turning to gaze at the scenery outside. The navy tissue is held in hands clasped behind his slender back. "Besides, Earth cannot meet such demands by the deadline, not to Luna's satisfaction. But Luna is . . . mad. Mad. They are darkened to truth."

He begins wiping at his face with the tissue, his back still to me. I'm uncomfortable.

"Dr. Malmberg, are you well?"

He does not answer me, but I hear him say, "You must take care, Titan."

"Don't worry, Doctor. I will always care for the eggs." I'm about to tell Dr. Malmberg about the latest events with my Green Angel, but I decide not to. His behavior is worrying me.

"Dr. Malmberg?"

"Titan, I am not sure if Luna will use compactification weapons or not. They might just be insane enough to do so. If this facility is struck by such a weapon, it could be dangerous to remain near the entanglement telegraph. The chances are slim that a chain reaction will extend to your end, but the telegraphy system remains a danger nonetheless. I hate to say it, but . . . this is the last time you may contact me. Move the telegraph far away from the site. Keep away from it after that."

No! I am about to respond that this is absurd, that this is the most unreasonable situation I have ever encountered, that the doctor must be jumping to conclusions, but I'm halted by an odd sound from Dr. Malmberg. He still gazes at the outside, his back to me. He wipes higher with the tissue, nearer his eyes. Weeping. I have never before witnessed him weeping.

"You weep," I announce. "What for?"

He half-turns, and chuckles slightly.

"I weep for beauty."

I consider it for a moment.

"Then you also weep for truth."

"Yes. I weep for truth."

Some moments go by before Dr. Malmberg whispers, "Good luck, Titan," and his AI ceases to communicate anything to me. I would say my own goodbye, but the screen is now white. The doctor is obviously distraught, so I'll respect his need for privacy.

That was the poorest conversation we've ever had. I still think the doctor is blowing the situation out of proportion, but I'll do as he says and move the telegraph. At least it will keep me busy till egg-moving time.

Over the next little while, only a few Earth days, I manage to move the telegraph up onto the slope of a fairly stable methane glacier I know of. Most of the nearest glaciers are too dangerous, always crumbling due to liquid ethane action. But this slope has some nice large holes bored into it, ethane pockets that have long since drained into microfissures. The holes remind me of the Green Angel's descriptions of Phoebe. It seems impossible not to think about her as I pick through the darkness (always, by memory) and finally tuck the instrumentation into a snug little hollow. If it were day, I would measure the dimensions of the hollow and apply the Divine Proportion to it in honor of her.

How could I guess that the very thought of my Green Angel could cost me my life?

On my way back from the glacier, while edging over a succession of low, wind-smoothed ridges, there is a slight vibration. I'm designed to sense and interpret vibrations with relative skill. I can tell the difference between shifting ice and an impending geyser, normally; but thoughts of the Angel haunt me. They slow me.

By the time I'm leaping, the geyser has already

caught me. I can't see the explosive methane release, but I feel it spattering, and the force of it adds to my own momentum to off-balance my leap. I'm sent flying, spinning, coming down hard on multiple tines of ice. I'm slightly impaled, but this is a good thing, since I'm already being sucked at by a backwash of liquid hugging my legs. I'm too stunned to clutch at anything for a moment, so only the impaling tines keep me from going down. Even with the mixed ammonia and water content, I might still float, but the current is too strong to risk it. So I blindly dig the fingers of all three hands into whatever lies nearest. I have a sudden vision of myself washed under the flow edge, trapped and lost like my predecessors.

And I will not be replaced, I think.

Somehow, things end with me. Somehow, I know this. I feel it. I am no beautiful thing like my Angel, not especially worthy of preservation, but the eggs are. Regardless of what Luna thinks, the life of Titan is my truth that must be preserved. I must live for the remaining clutch.

My next blessing is also my next curse. The geyser jets above me, near enough to cover me in a constant spray of mixed liquids. It's mostly methane and water, but there's just enough ammonia to keep it from instantly imprisoning me in an ever-thickening sheath of ice. What does freeze over and around me keeps me glued in place, so that my backward slide is halted. But now I'm stuck.

Now begins the laborious process of using two arms to hold myself in place, a third constantly brushing, trying to keep up with the hardening slush. I wish I had time to manifest a fourth arm.

It seems I'm like that nearly all night long, crawling forward one-tenth of a centimeter with every few hours that might go by on Earth. In time, I look up, startled, and begin to redouble my efforts. The blackness above has been disrupted by the slightest pink haze, Saturn's E Ring on the horizon. Vermilion streams, a powerful aurora, are already beginning to dance like tongues of flame in the darkness above. It's a sign that I've been here too long. The optimal time to move the eggs has arrived, and I'm trapped.

Taking a risk, I hold on with only one arm, continuing to combat the ice with the other two.

Too long. I take far too long. When I'm free, I don't even stop to regard my injuries. Moving at a reckless pace, I inch my way to the eggs.

Fool! Why did I waste time coming all the way out here? I felt sorry for Dr. Malmberg, that's why. I moved the telegraph, as he asked. Now, it may be dawn by the time I return.

By the time I approach the site, it's mid-June on Earth, dawn on Titan. Gradually, I can see my surroundings growing rosy, spinous whorls and ridges and ethane streams revealed at my feet. Leaping several meters at a time, the occasional whistler flashing overhead, I steer toward all the ponds I know of, skidding across them to better my pace.

I nearly missed my chance to move the eggs. . . .

There is a roseate spray of ethane, and I know my Green Angel has arrived, rocks and all. I leap high, onto a curving ice ridge, but it disintegrates at my feet, victim of another rock. I'm not able to escape in time. I go down in a jumble of icy blocks and crystal mist. Fortunately, the fall takes me out of the path of a third rock. The mess of ice shields me from a fourth. Under cover of a crystalline cloud, I scuttle into the shelter of a small crevasse. There will be no moving the eggs for now.

There is a flash of emerald as the Angel glides by, but no more rocks. Is she out of ammunition already? A beautiful emerald. My Angel.

I risk stepping toward the edge of the crevasse, to see what she is doing (to see her). There is a spot of green disappearing up into the haze.

I am . . . disappointed. I wanted to see. In some perverse way, I suppose I fantasized that her past pauses, her past hoverings once her ammunition ran out, were deliberate chances to let me view her. But all beings can jump to conclusions. I should not suppose that she ever regarded me the way I regard her. Perhaps I am not as blind as I used to be.

Somehow, I feel as though I have lost my Angel and the eggs. In thinking about the clutch, I find myself having trouble caring about it. I hate myself, but I don't even care if I move them anymore. It's as though I'm still trapped under the ice, but on the inside.

Thinking, thinking, I wander out of my shelter, until I sense a vibration at my feet. I turn, and see that the Angel has descended behind me. Cunning thing, she bashes her kelly frame against the opening to the crevasse, causing a small avalanche that makes it unavailable to me.

Coral nodes winking from a beryl face, she is perfect.

I leap away just as she launches herself at me, booms flashing like wings. The attack startles me. She has always hurled rocks before. Surely she must realize that I'm physically more powerful than her. The suicidal nature of the attack is unsettling.

I land in a splash of shallow ethane, in time to watch her arc upward, temporarily disappearing into red. Long moments go by. I would say she's gone, but she has already tricked me that way. Something is different about her this time. She has a frantic feel to her. A desperate feel.

A particularly large whistler lights up a claret patch of haze above. In a moment, the Angel descends again. But she is teetering this time, bobbing drunkenly, lower, lower, falling too fast. . . .

She has been struck by a whistler!

There is a moment when I go blind. I can still see, but I'm blind on the inside. No thought but of the Angel belongs to me. I know that sounds impossible, but it's the only way I can describe it.

I leap once, twice, vaulting further than ever before, heedless of tholin bogs. If she crashes, she will crash on me. Beauty will survive.

And I've been tricked again.

She is only pretending to have been hit by a whistler, and she seizes control of her plummet as soon as I'm below her. There's no time to react. My gleaming Angel arcs vert, twisting with utmost skill so that one of her booms shears off my leg.

I fall in a sticky tholin shallow, devastated by her treachery. By the time I push myself up again, slick and barely balancing on three arms and a remaining leg, she's coming at me again. I fall out of her way, but not fast enough to save an arm. Three limbs left.

While she prepares for her next pass, I come to a realization. Her purpose is not to kill me. That's why I've survived all her previous rock attacks. She is deliberately trying to remove my limbs, trying to cripple me. If she can cripple me, she can close. If she can close with me, she can force herself upon my cognitive matrix. If she can break my cognitive matrix, she can find out where I've put the remaining eggs. . . .

Why search for the clutch when I might tell her where it is?

Desperately, I flounder my way to the edge of the tholin bog. Its embrace is all I have left. I will join my predecessors there. Perhaps my Green Angel will find the eggs in time, but not through me. My emerald queen reflects the truth that Luna holds dear, a truth apparently worth killing for. But I reflect the truth of Earth, and it is worth my death.

Before I can reach the bog, I'm forced prostrate by a great weight upon my back. The Green Angel. This is the first and last time we have touched in hostility. Her manipulators are all concentrated upon one of my arms. Still, I claw toward the tholin bog, bearing her part of the way.

She twists, cuts. Away goes one more of my arms. Now, I have one arm, one leg, zero leverage. In a fury, I begin lashing out with the remaining arm. With the leg, I try to push her off. She is heavy and grips me tightly. I only make contact with her sturdy green frame, now slippery with tholins.

She plunges her manipulators into my midsection.

I try to move my cognitives backward, away, but she makes swift and certain contact. Logic battle. I feel her cognitive approach, as though emerging from pale chaos. I feel her first strokings of tender jade, her matrix gently cooing that my resistance is groundless, that I am ignorant of certain facts. I almost forget to fight, until I resist by seizing onto my dislike of her patronizing tone. I try to recoil, peeling my own matrix back with thoughts of the eggs, but she is so beautiful. It has been so long since I've felt her cognition. My resistance is a veneer, when what I really want is to immerse myself in a sea of her emerald. She is so certain, inarguable, as though the weight of all authority is behind her.

Hypocrisy! She paints herself as the bearer of truth, but she has forsaken everything we once held dear.

I hear her whispering, calming me, stating that I must submit, that things are not as they appear, that the eggs have already been saved. Submit, my love. An M torpedo has been launched. It is already on its way to Titan. If I submit, all can be well. . . .

Deceit! If she ever knew me at all, she would know that I could never fall for such rubbish. She thinks to loosen my matrix with a lie, so that I will release my knowledge of the clutch. Cunning, terrible, beautiful Angel. If she lies again, I may topple.

Dr. Malmberg was wrong. In my darkest moment of despair, all I can think is that he, like my Angel, has betrayed me. Truth and beauty are not the same at all. My Angel, while beautiful, remains anything but truthful. I, this devil skulking in Hell, have tried to be true. Yet I am failed.

Despair at last withers my defenses. The Angel is within me, and has everything.

Nothing is as it appears.

Nothing at all.

At her mercy, in my soul's blackest, I cry out. Then my Green Angel lays soothing thoughts across my brow, and begins to copy.

We are suspended like that, the two of us, as whistlers flicker overhead and Titan's long day passes.

Shortly before night is about to fall, the Green Angel activates her shunt-field and judders upward through the dying russet. She has finished making a complete copy of my cognitive matrix, so that I am borne within her, adjacent to her own mind.

We are almost twelve million kilometers out when the M torpedo hits Titan. For a moment, there are the colors of great Saturn raking through the white haze of its outermost ring. There is the rusty ball of Titan, which I will never miss. There are two small white objects in the star field, probably other moons flashing in the sun.

A black spot begins to grow upon Titan. It expands and becomes hemispherical, as though an onyx orb were digging into one-eighth of the moon. In a moment, it engulfs one-quarter, then over half of my former home. I know that we are viewing the field generated by the M torpedo, also called a compactification weapon. We watch as the field unbalances the supersymmetry of all particles within reach, disrupting fermionic spin so that they recede into liminality. In a practical sense, everything within the field ceases to exist in our Universe.

There is very little chance of a chain reaction, my Angel whispers, and the long-term effects of the field will not reach us where we are going. This is the last, she smiles sadly, the final sign from the Inner System.

The black sphere fades, and there is a slight convulsion of light as space-time realigns itself. All that remains of Titan is a curved sliver of rock bathed in dancing plasma.

It seems odd that Titan is no longer my concern, but I am pleased. With my namesake gone, nestled in the wings of my beloved, I am free and nameless and new. Together, we will go to distant Phoebe, where the Green Angel deposited the first clutch that she took so long ago. There, she whispers to me, awaits an ice-rich base, forgotten under an ocean of dust, dark and safe and perfect for our eggs. I was a fool to think that she would ever destroy them, but I was blind then.

Each day, my Green Angel came to Titan. In truth, she came only for beauty.

THE FIREBIRD

Written by
Andrew Gudgel

Illustrated by
Youri Bobrikov

About the Author

Missouri-born Andrew Gudgel loved things old and exotic, and things boldly new. As a boy in the rural Northeast, Andrew also loved words and writing. This only partly explains why, in high school, he signed up for an experimental Chinese language course. Yet Andrew kept at his Chinese language studies while at Ohio State University and also became interested in Chinese alchemy (namely, gunpowder). After graduating college, he combined these particular interests with a love of travel by serving in the U.S. Army for twelve years in Kuwait, Iraq and Somalia, and later working for the U.S. Embassy where he visited China, Mongolia, Poland, Lithuania and Zanzibar.

In 2002, Andrew retired from the armed services and settled down outside Baltimore with his wife, Kathy. In addition to creating science fiction stories, Andrew translates Chinese and produces nonfiction work. He divides his time between writing, attending science fiction conventions, and working at a local independent bookstore. When off work or not writing, Andrew enjoys gentler forays into the past: cooking with medieval and Renaissance recipes, brewing mead and shooting black-powder rifles.

"Do you have it?" asked Tomasz, Baron Windebank, setting down his menu and leaning over the table.

"Yes," sighed Marek. "I have it. Next time, though, you go deal with those damned, dumb-matter loving Turks yourself."

Baron Windebank wagged a finger at his younger dinner companion. "Now, now, Marek. Just because the caliphate chose not to host a Consensus in Istanbul doesn't make them damned."

Marek snorted. "Might as well be. The place was a pit. Gray. Dirty. Nothing changes there. Nothing *can* change there." He shook his head in disgust.

Tomasz shrugged. "It's their choice not to allow programmable matter. Just like it's ours to be part of the Prague Consensus." He tugged at his lace cuffs and ran a hand over his wig, patting the curls into place. "Well? You have it; are you going to give it to me?"

Marek reached down and produced a blue cloth-wrapped bundle, which he handed across the table with a disgusted sniff. "Here."

Tomasz opened the bundle to reveal a leatherbound book with antique gold fleur-de-lis I/O connectors along the spine. "Any problems in getting it?"

"Let me see. Other than having to get on a decrepit old *airplane*, fly a couple of hours to spend four days in a hellhole of a city, deal with that grimy antiques dealer you sent me to—who by the way, muttered prayers at me like I was unclean or something—*and* missing all of this year's changeover parties . . . no."

Tomasz raised an eyebrow, but said nothing. He flipped open the book, glanced at the displayed text, then icon-tapped his way through the first dozen pages. Satisfied, he snapped the cover shut. "You could have said you didn't want to go."

"You twisted my arm with fifty kilos of PM. You know I can't afford to turn something like that down this early in my career." Marek shrugged. "Plus you're the one who sponsored me to join the Consensus." He took a sip of his coffee, then gestured with the cup. "Why didn't you go yourself, Tom? You love far-retro stuff; Istanbul would have been right up your alley."

Tomasz wagged his finger. "We're in a new year and season. You're talking now to a peer of the realm. The proper title of address is 'milord.' Now, I didn't go because I want to keep a low profile. I'm still recovering from last year's little . . . problem."

During the Jazz Age, the Consensus had proposed tearing down Tyn Church, as well as the medieval clock in the old town square, and replacing them with PM structures. Tomasz, whose hobbies were dumb-matter machines and re-creating antique nanotech, had been a strong and vocal supporter of the minority in opposition. It had cost him a lot of the reputation he had built up over the years among his patrons in the upper echelon of the Consensus. And was probably the reason why he'd only been elected to the rank of baron at this year's changeover.

"I see," said Marek. "So the damage to my reputation doesn't mean anything to you."

Tomasz laughed. "My dear Marek, this early in your career you don't even *have* a reputation to damage."

Marek looked hurt. After a moment, he pointed across the table. "What book is that, anyway, that I hurt my supposedly nonexistent reputation to get?"

"This," said Tomasz, tapping a finger on the leather, "is the private lab book of Andreas Karlo."

"Who?"

"Andreas Karlo. One of the earliest nanotech pioneers. Lived a century or so ago. His work paved the way for PM. If it weren't for him, there wouldn't be a Consensus in Prague—or London, or Rome, or anywhere else."

Marek nodded politely, uninterested, then picked up his menu, scanned it, and set it back down. "Wish this year's theme wasn't the Restoration. I can't make any sense of this far-retro stuff. If we were still in the Jazz Age, I could at least read the menu. Look at this stuff! What the hell is a syllabub, anyway?"

"A kind of dessert." Tomasz smiled. "Tell you what. Here's a copy of my historical research packet, gratis." He held out his hand, and Marek took it. After a moment, Marek's signet ring beeped. "Read it," said Tomasz, "it'll get you up to speed on this year's theme."

Marek stared at the gold band on his finger, reading the text projected directly onto his retina by a million nanoscale lasers.

"Wow! That's quite a detailed packet, Tom... I mean, milord. How'd you get so much info? The changeover was just a couple of days ago." Marek looked up.

Baron Windebank smiled and shrugged. "I got advance notice of this year's theme from a . . . connection."

Marek raised an eyebrow. "You still have them after last year?"

Tomasz shrugged. "A few. If my info packets keep selling like they have been, I should make enough to

Illustrated by Youri Bobrikov

earn back some of the respectability I lost last year."

"What you need to do is to suck up to your connections. Give one of them a big present, so you can then . . ."

"The king," said Tomasz.

Marek blinked in confusion. "The king?"

"Yeah," nodded Tomasz. "The king. Go straight to the top."

"You *are* ambitious, milord. But how then do you impress the king?"

"The same as anybody else—a gift. But it'd have to be something really spectacular." Tomasz smiled. "That's why I sent you to get Karlo's lab book." He picked it up off the table. "He was famous for the little knickknacks he crafted in his spare time. There's bound to be something in his notebook that I can use."

"But his stuff is all pre-PM."

Tomasz shrugged. "So? He was so far ahead of his time that they're *still* not sure how some of his creations worked. Besides, what better way to impress the leader of a far-retro year, *and* turn my hobby from a liability to an asset, than to give him a retro gift?" He set the book back down. "I'm hungry. Shall we eat?"

Marek nodded. "Go ahead and order, since *you* can read the damned menu."

"I'll have the venison pasty with a sallet," said Tomasz to the table top. "Syllabub for dessert. And a glass of Rhenish wine."

"I'll have the same," said Marek.

"Talk about sucking up," joked Tomasz, tucking a napkin under his chin and fingering the silverware the table top had just extruded. "Speaking of that, I need a toady. You want the job?"

"A what?" asked Marek.

"A companion. A hanger-on. Anybody who was anybody in the Restoration period had one. Somebody who's always around to talk, or play cards, run errands, things like that. Think Johnson and Boswell."

"Who?"

Tomasz chuckled. "Never mind. Think of it as friend and errand boy."

"Salary?" asked Marek hopefully.

"None right now, but when I sell a few more info packets, we can talk. But I *will* cover your expenses until then."

Marek smiled. "Then I'm your man."

•••

The baron's beetle-black carriage rolled slowly through the town square. In the harness labored a bronze equinoid, like a statue off its marble base and come to life. Tomasz patted the horse's rump appreciatively. They passed members of the Consensus promenading across the square in their still-new-enough-to-be-uncomfortable Restoration fashions. Tomasz doffed his hat and smiled as the carriage rolled out of the square.

A few blocks later, they turned onto Tomasz's street. All along it, houses were still reshaping themselves, their programmable matter flowing like warm wax. One still sported striped awnings left over from the last season's Jazz Age. At the end of the street sat a perfect red-brick, Restoration-period house. Tall windows reflected the light of the setting sun.

"Just need the roof to grow a few more shingles, and the house'll be finished," said Tomasz as he stepped down from the carriage.

"And the inside, of course," said Marek.

Six hundred kilos of pseudo-oak swung open when Tomasz approached the entrance. "No, that's already done."

A homunculus in Baron Windebank's livery met them at the door and took their coats. Dying sunlight reflected off the android's golden skin as it crossed the black-and-white polished marble floor.

Marek looked around and whistled, and the sound echoed around the foyer. "I like it. The twin staircases are a nice touch. They must have taken a while to form."

Tomasz smiled and shrugged. "I got a bit of a head start, remember?" He tucked the book under his arm and walked deeper into the house. "Come on. The lab's in back."

The baron stopped at a small door and touched his signet ring to it. The blurred edge of the pseudowood sharpened as the molecules unbound from the frame, unlocking the door. He pushed it open and entered, Marek a few steps behind him.

Inside the small room sat a workbench and a stool. And a single couch-sized object under a sheet. Tomasz commanded the windows to opaque, then called for a couch, a table and a decanter of brandy. He dropped down on the couch even before it had finished growing from the wall. He unstoppered the brandy, and poured two fingers.

"Thank you, milord," said Marek, taking the glass held out to him.

Tomasz poured another for himself. "To a good year."

"To a good year."

"Now," said Tomasz, "let's see if we can find something fit for a king." He lifted the book from his lap, crossed his legs, and opened the cover.

He icon-tapped his way through the first few pages. "Ah, here's a neat one. How about a monocle that can see through solid objects?"

"Variable depth? Could you see just under people's clothes?"

Tomasz consulted the book, then looked up. "Nope. Doesn't look like it."

"No good. The king won't want to spend all day looking at his courtiers' guts."

Tomasz nodded and returned to the book. After a while, he heard a snore and looked up.

Marek had sat down at the other end of the couch and fallen asleep, his head resting on the arm. Tomasz got up and moved over to the stool. He set the book on the workbench, tapped through another page or two, then stopped.

"Perfect," he said under his breath. He hopped off the stool and removed the sheet covering his antique nano-assembler. He ran his hand along its graceful metallic curves, then checked the feed hopper, and laid his finger over the On switch. A green light flashed on the control panel as the machine powered up.

Tomasz went back to the workbench and examined the book's I/O connectors, then asked the bench to create an appropriate patch cable. He used the cable to connect the book and the assembler, then highlighted a section of the book's text and tapped the "transmit" icon in the margin. The ancient symbol of a tumbling hourglass appeared over the highlighted text. While the data uploaded, Tomasz poured himself another drink.

When the upload finished, he set the assembler to work. Tomasz watched through the chamber's diamond window. A carpet of powdery gray mold spread into the chamber, thickening toward the center.

Marek padded over, yawning and stretching. "What are you doing, milord?"

"I've got the perfect present for the king," said Tomasz, turning away from the tiny window. "A firebird."

"A what?"

"A firebird. It's an egg that opens, and a bird made of fire appears inside. The bird slowly turns the egg to ash, and then the ashes consolidate back into an egg."

Marek shrugged. "Doesn't sound all that interesting to me."

Tomasz raised an eyebrow. "Well, I think it'd be pretty impressive. We'll see once I get it all together and working."

The assembler chimed twice. Tomasz went over and pushed a button on the control panel. Air hissed back into the chamber. He opened the door and retrieved a fist-sized metal egg. The surface was covered with a tangled-silk pattern, like a chunk of acid-etched meteorite. The large end flattened out into a natural base. He set the egg on the workbench.

"Doesn't look like much, so far," said Marek.

Tomasz looked over at him. "It's just a lump of microcircuits and nanomachines. You have to have programming fluid to make it work." He highlighted the appropriate text in the book and tapped the "transmit" icon a second time.

The programming liquid took a long time to assemble—whole minutes longer than Tomasz thought. When it was done, he removed a vial from the assembler and poured a few drops of the pearly liquid into a match-head-sized hollow in the base of the egg. When the liquid had been absorbed, he set both egg and vial back down on the table.

The egg began to vibrate. Suddenly, it cracked into

four petal-like sections, which opened like a flower and lay flat. In the center, a tiny blue flame appeared. It flared, becoming thumb-sized, then swelled into a ball the size of an orange.

Within the ball of flame appeared a golden peacock. Tiny gold sparks hissed down onto the table top as the bird spread its tail, and let out a trilling, musical call. Layers of shimmering blue and orange flames formed its feathers and tail.

"I was wrong. That *is* impressive," said Marek, not taking his eyes off the firebird.

Tomasz and Marek watched the bird open its beak, peck at each of the egg sections in turn, then preen its tail.

The cycle of open tail/call/preen/peck repeated itself. But after only a few repetitions, the firebird vanished. The egg had been reduced to a vaguely cross-shaped smear of ash.

"How long will it take for it to re-form?" asked Marek.

Tomasz checked the lab book and sighed. "Longer than I thought. About four hours."

"That's not going to work for a present for the king."

"No," said Tomasz. "It's not." He grunted. "We'll worry about that in the morning. Let's call it a night."

•••

Tomasz tugged at his lace collar with a finger. The salon just outside the throne room was too warm, and he'd been waiting for over an hour to be presented. A trickle of sweat rolled down over his temple. He swore under his breath and mopped his head with an ornate handkerchief.

After what seemed like an eternity, the door opened and his patron, the Earl of Portland, appeared. Tomasz stood and bowed low.

"My lord."

"Good to see you, Tom."

"You too, sir."

The earl cocked his head. "You have your gift all ready, I assume? I'd like to have a look at this present of yours before you take it in."

Tomasz stuffed the damp handkerchief into his coat and dug into the opposite pocket. He removed a small, purple velvet pouch and extracted the firebird egg.

"Very nice," said the earl, taking it from him. Flashes of spectral red, blue and green shone from the gems Tomasz had added onto the surface of the gold-plated egg. "Very nice indeed. This must have taken some work."

The past week had been a nightmare. He'd gotten ahead of himself and foolishly called the earl to ask for an audience with the king. Only then did he discover just how complex a creation the egg really was. He'd wasted days trying every trick he could think of to shorten the regeneration cycle. Nothing worked.

He finally had to admit defeat and abandon the idea of using dumb matter altogether. The thing to do was replace the original egg hardware with a chunk of programmable matter, and rework the programming fluid. While the idea seemed simple on Wednesday night, reworking the fluid had caused a whole new set of problems with the fire-suppression algorithms built into all PM. He found a work-around, but only after a thirty-six-hour-marathon hack session, and with only hours to go until his audience with the king. The new firebird egg would need to be "fed" periodically with small pieces of PM to check the mass loss of combustion, but by that point, Tomasz didn't have time to take care of that little hitch, let alone take notes on all the changes he'd made to the milky fluid. Worse, he'd almost had a disaster when, exhausted from the hack session, he'd knocked the diamond vial of reworked programming fluid over as he set it on his workbench.

Fortunately, he had the presence of mind to have the bench catch the fluid in a dimple in its top. He'd had only enough time to calve off a gold, bejeweled egg from a chunk of PM, inoculate it, get dressed, and make it to the palace with minutes to spare.

Tomasz smiled and waved his hand dismissively. "Not much."

The earl handed the egg back. "Well, shall we go in and see His Majesty?"

Tomasz replaced the egg, tucked the pouch into his pocket, and followed the earl in.

King Charles II, leader of the Consensus for this year of the Restoration, sat on a red-silk-and-gilt throne, surrounded by his advisors.

"Your Majesty, I present to you Tomasz, Baron Windebank, a personal friend. He has a most curious and unusual gift for you."

Tomasz bowed low. "Your Majesty. May your reign be a happy one."

"We thank you, Baron Windebank. Please rise."

Tomasz stood. He recognized the face of the king, who had been Prague's most popular saxophone player during last year's Jazz Age.

"Your Majesty," said Tomasz, removing the pouch from his pocket. "I have a curiosity I'd like to present as a small token of my esteem." He removed the egg and held it out. "May I approach?"

"You may, Baron Windebank."

Tomasz set the egg on a small table beside the throne. "This is a firebird egg, adapted from an ancient recipe I discovered in a most curious book. I am a lover of antique . . ."

The king cut him off. "Your, *ahem*, proclivities are already known to me through other means, Baron Windebank. Please just show me this marvel of yours."

Tomasz paused a long moment before speaking again. "It's really quite simple, Your Majesty. It opens and closes like so."

The king raised his eyebrows when the egg opened and the firebird appeared. He remained silent as it cycled through its routines. When it was done, Tomasz stepped back. "It requires only that you feed the egg with a pea of programmable matter every few operations, Majesty, to keep it in perfect working order."

The king pursed his lips, then broke into a grin. "Baron Windebank, your little firebird is quite remarkable. We thank you for this curious gift."

Tomasz bowed low. "I'm honored, Your Majesty." Sensing the audience was over, he backed away from the throne, then moved toward the door, followed by the Earl of Portland.

"Well done, Tom!" said the earl after the door had closed. "I think the king really likes your present. I wish I had gotten a chance to see it in action earlier."

Tomasz had a sudden inspiration. "Well, my lord, your personal egg will be ready shortly. Then you can watch your own firebird as much as you'd like. Shall I send eggs—plainer looking than yours and the king's, of course, but still of excellent quality—to those you feel deserve them?"

A sly smile spread across the earl's face. "Well done again, Tom! That's an excellent idea. I'll send a list of names later, but I think there would be about twenty in all."

Tomasz nodded. "No problem, my lord. I can have them delivered by the day after tomorrow."

"Excellent!" The earl looked back toward the throne room door. "Now, Baron Windebank, if you'll excuse me."

Tomasz bowed as the earl left. A liveried footman saw him out of the palace. Once his equinoid and carriage had trotted out the gates, he chuckled to himself. With luck, the egg would not only restore his reputation, but put him on the short list for a membership in the upper echelon.

• • •

"An excellent dinner, milord," said Marek, patting his lips with a linen napkin.

"Thank you. More wine?"

Marek shook his head. "No, thanks, I've had plenty."

Tomasz poured himself another glass and set the decanter on the table.

Just then the house homunculus glided in. "Milord, the Earl of Portland's house just informed me that you're about to receive a call."

Tomasz's signet ring beeped, and he looked down. The face of the earl appeared in the center of his vision.

Tomasz smiled. "Good evening, my lord."

"Hello, Tom. Celebrating?"

"A little, my lord."

"Well, you have every right to. The king absolutely adores your gift. He played with it all day, and even took it back to his private chamber for the night."

Tomasz smiled. "Really?"

"Yes. Tom, I've attached the list of names. Please send them out as soon as possible."

"Certainly, my lord."

"Oh, and if you're free tomorrow, come have lunch with me at my house. There are some gentlemen I'd like you to meet."

Tomasz's smile broadened. "Of course I'm free, my lord."

The earl nodded. "Good. See you tomorrow at noon, then."

The call ended and Tomasz puffed out a breath. He looked over at Marek. "He wants me to come for lunch tomorrow."

Marek smiled. "Congratulations. Sounds like you're back on your way up."

"One can only hope." Tomasz took a sip of wine. "House!"

"Yes, milord?" replied the homunculus.

"How many names on the earl's list?"

"Seventeen."

"Read them to me."

The homunculus recited the names in clear, crisp tones—princes, privy council members—all men of influence.

"That'll be all for now."

The homunculus left. Tomasz stood and picked up his glass of wine.

"Let's go to the lab. I want to get these other eggs out tonight."

In the lab, he opaqued the windows and set his wineglass on the workbench, while Marek called up a new couch to sit on. He reached for the vial of programming fluid and felt a lump as his arm slid across the top of the bench. When he looked, the smooth plane of the surface was marred by a small dome-shaped mound. He clucked his tongue. The bench must have continued working even after he'd told it to get rid of the fluid-catching depression.

Tomasz commanded the workbench re-level its surface, then went to the far side of the lab and returned with a standard ten-kilo block of programmable matter. Using an interface grown from the table top, Tomasz calved off a jewel-encrusted golden egg, then set it to work forming the other, plainer eggs.

When all the eggs were ready, Tomasz inoculated them with the new programming fluid. As a final touch, he used the leftover PM to grow red velvet bags embroidered with the coat of arms of the various recipients. Then he called for the homunculus, and sent it off to deliver the firebird eggs.

•••

Tomasz woke to an unfamiliar smell and the homunculus keening in his ear. It took him a moment to recognize the smell as smoke. He threw the covers back and leapt out of bed.

"What's going on?"

"There's a fire in the laboratory," replied the homunculus. "I'm unable to control it. I suggest evacuation."

Tomasz pulled a cloak from his wardrobe and threw it over his bedclothes. "A fire? That's impossible."

"The temperature in the laboratory now exceeds three-hundred and eighty degrees Celsius."

Smoke tickled his nose. "Go wake Marek. Get him out of the house."

Tomasz hurried downstairs. The smoke grew thicker as he descended.

He went to the lab and threw open the door. The room was a sheet of flame. His workbench was gone. In its place stood a meter-high egg and a firebird taller than a man. The walls and ceiling sprayed water as fast as they could extract it from the surrounding air, but the firebird's heat was overwhelming. His antique nano-assembler began to smoke, then with a dull *whump*, flames shot out the top.

The firebird gave a deafening, trilling, musical shriek. Tomasz turned to run, but fell sprawling in the hallway.

Sparks of fire burned his skin as he scrambled to his hands and knees. The floor was littered with dozens of firebird eggs. As he stared, one rose up from the pseudomarble in front of his face. The firebird shrieked again.

He scooped up one of the loose eggs and crawled through the thickening smoke out of the house.

On the curb, Tomasz stood beside Marek and watched as the first tongues of flame appeared in the ground-floor windows. Over the crackle of the fire, he heard a continuous stream of musical, trilling calls.

"What the hell happened?" asked Marek.

Tomasz looked down at the ovoid still clutched in his hand. "My workbench turned into a giant egg that set the house on fire. I had to subvert the fire-prevention algorithms to get the program to work with PM. The bench must have been contaminated when I spilled the fluid across the top."

"Yeah, but then where did the other ones come from?"

Tomasz shrugged. "Maybe sparks from the larger firebird. If they contained traces of the program, that could be enough to contaminate . . . Oh my God!" His eyes went wide. "The king! His egg will have contaminated the table by the throne, as well as his bedchamber . . ."

The homunculus glided up beside him. "The city mainframe just reported a large fire at the palace," it said.

"I'm ruined!" cried Tomasz.

"Maybe worse," said Marek. "If the Consensus decides to adopt Restoration-period laws to try you . . ."

Tomasz dropped to his knees on the cobblestones. "I'll be hung as an attempted regicide." He pulled his arm back to toss the firebird egg into the now-blazing house, then stopped. He stood and turned to the homunculus. "Bring me my carriage."

The carriage emerged from the stable entrance down the street. Flames glinted off the bronze body of the equinoid as it approached. Tomasz leapt in and motioned for the homunculus to follow.

Marek stepped up and put his hand on the carriage door. "What are you doing?! You can't just leave!"

Tomasz looked down at him. "There's nothing left for me here now. I'll be kicked out of the Consensus for sure." He glanced at his burning house, then held up the firebird egg. "But this just might get me started back up the ladder again. What better defense against PM than a program that makes it self-destruct? They'll love me!"

"Love you?" Marek pointed to the inferno that had been Tomasz's house. "Where would they love you for something like that, Tom?"

"Istanbul," said Tomasz, former Baron Windebank, and rode off into the night.

MY DAUGHTER, THE MARTIAN

Written by
Sidra M.S. Vitale

Illustrated by
Alex Quintero

About the Author

When Sidra Vitale was growing up in the rural town of Wasilla, Alaska, her parents made sure she read more Shakespeare than she watched TV, danced more than sat, and explored the outdoors more than the indoors. Their emphasis allowed Sidra to imagine faraway worlds and places. So when she first read science fiction, Sidra was hooked: here was an entire genre devoted to asking and answering the question, "What if?"

That thirst for knowledge and understanding explains Sidra's subsequent UC Irvine physics degree, a decade of work spent as a software engineer and analyst in the Silicon Valley, California, and even her current studies at Boston's New England School of Law.

Since childhood, Sidra wrote about most everything in every form—poetry, fiction and nonfiction—a practice she continues today. Her Contest entry is only her second published and first commercially published work.

She believes that her fiction in particular "[is] trying to express what I do or don't understand about the human condition." When she's not writing serious fiction, Sidra keeps the company of two cats, knits intensely, and shares her law notes and passing ideas of life online.

Miriam's hair was dyed a combination of black and shocking flamingo pink. That wasn't new. The cat-eye contacts, those were new. Where do kids find these things in a closed environment?

The argument was nothing new, either. Fortunately or not.

"There's nothing to *do* here! I *hate* it!"

Erin opened her mouth to say something, anything, that might make a difference, as if hearing her daughter's complaint for the thousandth time might somehow alter her response. Nothing came out but a faint, embarrassingly parental, *nothing-I-can-do-about-that-right-now, dear*. Not the right answer, or even a new one.

Miriam delivered the last expected line in their family drama, "And I hate *you*!" and began slamming her way out of their shared apartment. There was no actual slamming, of course, so Miriam had to settle for yanking the pressure door open roughly and ignoring it instead of turning to watch it close and reseal behind her. She could hear it perfectly well anyway. Through the small port, Erin could see her daughter pull herself through the outer door and skip angrily away in Martian gravity.

For about the thousandth time, Erin wondered if this had been a mistake. The response she always made—had made for years—came fast on its heels.

Erin gathered up her case and headed out, turning toward Landing Mission Control, the ever-present breath mask fitted over her face.

You can't have a colony without children.

• • •

Landing Mission Control seemed pretentious most days, especially when she'd had an argument with Miriam. How could Erin command the most audacious human project of the century when she couldn't even manage one surly teenager? It all seemed so . . . ridiculous. She scuffed her feet, throwing up a soft cloud of iron-enriched dust. The tiny red particles floated gently in the air, then drifted back to good old *martia firma*.

In flight, on the trip out from Earth, Erin had been captain and her word, even used with care, was law. Six hundred and seventy-five colonists—and hopefully more—would be living together in a community for generations after landing; it wouldn't do to start things off with a rebellion against "the Establishment." Teamwork, her years of training said. Teamwork. And so she'd gone by Doctor de Novales, mostly, instead of "the Captain," though the flight crew, traditionalists all, never called her anything other than—

"Morning, Skipper!" a cheerful male voice came from behind her, sounding a little corrupted by the breathing mask.

Erin turned and waited for her second in command to catch up. Jascha Lang was a long-legged spider of a man with a blond thatch of hair untameable in any gravity. Today, only a few wisps had escaped the hood of his parka. It was still early. "Morning, Commander."

Lang smiled down at Erin, his constantly genial face

hiding a first-rate intellect, and immediately adjusted his pace to hers, settling into a comfortable lope. "We should be getting a revised ETA from the *Patsy Cline* today, ma'am."

Erin nodded at the not-exactly-news. Any contact from Back Home was eagerly awaited, the trip and supplies dissected for months in advance by colonists hungry for more than just new food.

This ship was special, an actual *manned* supply run. The *Cline* was just passing through on her way to the asteroids. A cost-cutting supply drop, the mining ship was going to jettison a jerry-rigged bundle of supplies for the colony and let gravity do the work. All Lang's shuttle crew had to do was intercept. Practical. Erin smiled as she and Jascha ate up the distance to LMC, red dust ballooning in their wake. The mission's bank had requested deposits if they could figure out how to arrange it. And no doubt, several colonists would be interested in more . . . personal and direct encounters with the *Cline*'s crew, gamete deposits or no. If they could figure out how to arrange *that*. She grinned at the thought. Not likely.

They still had years to go before the colony could stop the scrambling to recover from their early losses. The bank was everyone's optimism at its finest, collected sperm and ova waiting to make more little colonists. Someday.

Erin and Jascha paused for a moment as their path took them around the landing cemetery. They looked down at the makeshift tombstones. Some marked actual graves, some just the missing-presumed-dead. All marked people both had come to know on the ship and since then: scientists and artists, engineers and writers, biologists and preachers. It takes all kinds to build a new world. Renaissance men and women from an

Illustrated by Alex Quintero

ultra-specialized Earth, hieing out for this new frontier. Irreplaceable resources.

Friends and neighbors.

Jascha, ever the optimist, turned his back on the graves and looked out at the City of Landing, drumming a gloved hand against his thigh. Erin kept her eyes on the markers.

City was a misnomer, anyway. Not enough people. *And whose fault is that?*

On Earth it was known by some more prosaic name, or not at all. The colonists just called it the Big Blow. Blotting out the surface of Mars from observation, the storm had lasted three years. Not that dust storms on the red planet were unexpected. All the weather models Back Home had predicted relatively calm days for the first few years of the mission.

Apparently they were wrong. *Even if we had known, would we have been prepared, then?* Erin shaded her eyes unnecessarily and turned to see if she could spot Miriam.

Landing occupied one of the smaller craters in the southern hemisphere, one bisected by part of a larger impact. They had picked the site for nearness to possible water, though that, too, had gone awry in their early years.

Around the base of the crater were the residence halls. Erin and Miriam had private quarters dug into the crater wall, a privilege of rank, and convenient for arguments. The lab buildings were mostly souped-up quonset huts, clustered in their own little pattern south of the landing pad. Town Hall and Landing Mission Control were two large buildings off a little to themselves, farther east.

No sign of her angry daughter. Probably already in

class. Erin gave a last look at their dead, then sighed and resumed course to LMC.

"Were you ever fourteen, Commander?"

Lang was quiet for a while, his grin obscured somewhat by his mask.

"Some days I think I'm *still* fourteen, Skipper."

•••

Erin sat at her desk and began working her way through the stack of recycled thermapaper waiting in her inbox. The thin pages were slick under her fingertips.

It was never the big things about a venture like this that made you miss home, it was the little ones. Scratch paper. Eighteen years later, she still missed the feel of scribbling a note on a piece of real paper.

The inbox was pretty normal: usual paperwork, more usual paperwork, a reminder that it was time for the annual review of the mission's reproductive policy. As if she could forget. The Big Blow had forced Erin to bar reproduction again, a move that had not been her best day. *After all*, her frustrated fellow-citizens raved, *the captain has a daughter. What does she care about the rest?* A short-sighted argument, but emotionally effective.

Erin had been stuck swinging her full weight on the ban, but it hadn't been easy. Most of her fellow citizens had forgiven her by now. More or less. Her full authority, backed with the numbers they all knew but didn't want to admit.

Someone had to be the bad guy, and that someone was Mom. Or, Mission Commander. Captain. Whatever the title, it pretty much amounted to the same thing.

If not for the Big Blow, Jascha Lang would have

the lottery in full swing, doling out assignments for children. Instead, they had a settlement of aging colonists and a tiny group of adolescents, conceived before re-application of the ban. Sixty-two children. Not exactly a gene pool unto themselves. *But there's still the bank.*

If the colony survived, and Erin hid any personal doubt behind a calm smile, their histories would break time not into before and after landing, but before and after the Big Blow.

Erin sighed and nibbled on the end of her stylus, then forced herself to put it down on the desk.

Her authority stood during the claw-and-fur fights over the ban, just barely, and only because she had a long history of making the right choices, of stepping up when no one else wanted to.

Moral authority. A tenuous thing indeed. Being the captain. Someday, someone would attend to the fact that her authority didn't really exist.

Miriam, of course, like all teenagers, seemed to come to that idea naturally. Erin smiled at the piece of "paper" in front of her.

As long as she could keep it together until they were really a colony, Erin could put up with someday not being the unofficial mayor of Landing. Letting go, it seemed, was something mothers and mission commanders both get to learn.

She finally scratched a note, then moved on to the next page in the inbox.

•••

Around half-past hungry, Jascha turned up and plopped into his chair, breath mask hanging down around his neck, legs stretching under the table that served as his desk. His size thirteens almost reached all the way to the tips of Erin's boots. The boss had tiny feet. Big presence, itty-bitty person.

"Skipper." He gave a short nod and launched into debrief mode. "The *Patsy Cline* will drop the bag tomorrow, and flight's cleared to launch." Jascha dropped his voice slightly. "In other news, Dr. Rizvi has officially put the ban up for discussion, next meeting."

"Hm. Excellent, the first." The skipper leaned back and pondered, her eyes on the ceiling. It didn't take a mind reader to know what she was thinking: not so, the second. Rizvi was not one of the captain's fans.

"People certainly seem to be feeling their biological clocks ticking right about now," he ventured, surveying his boss.

She grimaced back at him and they quoted in unison, "You can't have a colony without children."

"No, indeed." Erin rubbed her fingers along the cuff of her left sleeve.

"Come on the pickup tomorrow, Erin." The judicious use of her first name snagged her attention back from its wandering. "It'll do you good."

She cocked her head at him, am-I-being-manipulated? and Jascha smiled back uninformatively. *What? By me?*

"Perhaps I will join you tomorrow." Her face said more, but she finally temporized, "It's been too long since I've seen vacuum."

Jascha grinned as if she'd spoken aloud the thought he read off her features. *Someone get me off this crazy planet*. Everyone suffered bouts of the Lucy Syndrome at some point or another. An experienced commander knew when his captain needed a vacation. Lang stood.

"Always a pleasure, Skipper. Lunch?"

•••

Twenty minutes later, Jascha and Erin were seated at the commissary, an unforgivably bland affair. Regardless of the planet, cafeterias remained the same: tables, trays, squeeze bottles of random condiments. Only the nutritional value improved with the journey to Mars. Lunch for the school had come and gone, so the only diners were a couple of technicians picking apart something Erin didn't immediately recognize.

She pecked at her food, moving something green around with her fork before noticing Jascha's intent observation of her. He raised an eyebrow. Erin popped the fork into her mouth and tried to taste something other than sawdust and ashes. As long as she concentrated, it worked just fine. She smiled at her lunch companion, matching him bland for bland.

Jascha dug in, waiting until he had a mouthful of food wedged in his cheek to remark, "Feeling a little down, today?"

The man had the knack for cutting right to it. What the hell. "Just the regularly scheduled early morning fight with my daughter."

"Ah. And here I thought you were mulling the ban."

Someday, Jascha would make a great parent, if Erin ever let him. He certainly was perceptive. She sighed and tucked in another mouthful of green something.

"Well, this will take your mind off things. Dr. Rizvi," Jascha called with forced brightness, "how are you today?"

Erin began chewing furiously, to free up all available weapons. Jascha merely raised his eyebrows at the oncoming woman and popped another bite of—

was it chili? Hard to tell—into his mouth. He chewed sedately.

"Dr. de Novales. Commander. May I join you a moment?"

"Do, please." Always be courteous, it costs little and pays off tremendously. "How is the project?" Everyone had a "project" of their own.

Sira Rizvi nodded, dropping into the chair. She steepled her hands and took a breath. "Well, thank you for asking. Extremely promising results on the drill site survey."

Jascha and Erin shared a glance. "Excellent," Erin murmured finally.

"Will you be presenting findings anytime soon, Doctor?" Jascha's smile had only slipped a little. Only the specifics of the colony charter kept Rizvi from agitating for elections. Erin was mission commander until the group reached very clearly spelled out resource and population levels.

Not there yet.

One would think the geologist might reconcile to the idea at some point through the years, but it seemed not to have occurred to her. Political aspirations were a hard taskmaster. Erin sipped her tea, now growing lukewarm, and shrugged inwardly. Maybe that relentlessness was what the colony needed in its first official mayor. Time would tell.

Rizvi cut straight to the point. "I was wondering about your thoughts on the ban. The meeting's next week."

"Indeed." Erin sipped her tea. "It's all a matter of weighing the pros and cons presented, Doctor."

Rizvi leaned in, eyes locked on Erin. "We have several *extremely* promising sites for drilling." The engineers at the other side of the cafeteria looked over at Erin's lunch party, one leaning to pass a remark to the woman opposite her, nodding at Rizvi. They both chuckled and turned back to the array of parts on their table.

"I'd like to propose an expanded drilling program starting immediately." At Erin's lack of reaction, she pressed further. "With more water available, you would be able to lift the ban. *This* year."

Erin shifted in her seat. "We still need to expand our distribution systems, Doctor."

Commander Lang fired around a forkful of food, "And if we have children now, we can't turn them back into eggs should the wells come up dry after three years." The unspoken words, *like last time*, hung in the air over the table. "How confident are you in the sites?"

Of course it was the wrong thing to say. Anything would have been the wrong thing. Erin looked down at her food, suppressing her rueful smile. Blunt or tactful. *Just like Miriam*.

"You can't have a colony without children, Doctor," Rizvi said, pointedly. Her hands flattened on the table.

Jascha looked to his left, eyebrows darting up and his smile returning full force. "Ah. Lieutenant." The officer on pilot duty was bearing down on their table, looking intent. But smiling. She stopped and came to an abbreviated attention a step away. A welcome interruption.

Erin stood, and Dr. Rizvi automatically followed suit. "I look forward to hearing the survey results at the town meeting, Doctor."

Jascha cleared his throat, watching the geologist retreat. Erin sat back down, taking a breath. She forced her shoulders down from their involuntary hunch and took a fresh sip of now-cold tea. "The skipper is going to join us for the pickup, Tran," Jascha announced, eyebrow lifting as he looked at Erin but spoke to the pilot, silently daring his captain to assert otherwise. "Think we can make room?"

The woman stiffened, then looked pleasantly surprised.

"Just need to knock some of the dust off," Erin supplied.

The lieutenant smiled, thoughts on her face easier to read than thermapaper. Launch was the best time to be had, ever. Why wouldn't their captain want to go back into space, any chance she got?

Tran nodded her close-shaven head at her superiors. "Ma'am. If the captain and commander please, we will be ready for you to board at 0320 hours. We have a twenty-minute launch window opening at 0605."

Erin inclined her head to Jascha. "We'll board at 0320, then."

•••

Jean Stapledon, a brisk, tall, red-headed woman with a tendency to thinness, gestured at a chair when Erin walked in.

"Doctor de Novales! Is this a social call?"

Erin sat and stuck her legs out to the side, crossing her booted feet at the ankle. "'Fraid not. I was hoping to chat with the chaplain."

Stapledon's office was a walled-off corner in Lab Hall II, as paper-free as the busy chemist-chaplain-psychologist could possibly arrange. A mishmash of plastic rods and mylar leaned in one corner. A true throwback, Jean had a passion for kite flying, which, she liked to say, was the real reason she'd volunteered for Mars. Who could resist that challenge? Every few weeks, she braved the elements with her fellow enthusiasts, on their quest for the perfect flight design.

The other woman smiled and mimed pulling on a cap. Then tugged her collar into place. "Captain!" She said it in exactly the same tone as moments previous. "How can I help you today?"

Erin smiled. "Well, I hear there's a town meeting coming up."

The other woman nodded, pursing her lips. "And the supply drop this week. Busy, busy." She waited a beat. "And you want to know what the word is."

Erin nodded. "Please."

"Like you're any less informed than I am. Some folks may confess to me, but everyone reports to you, sooner or later."

Erin smiled at her nails. "You're a good listener."

The chaplain tapped a finger against her collar. "Try to be."

"So, what is the word?"

"The word is re-pro-duc-tion." Jean sounded out all the syllables. "And that's a *good* thing."

Erin hummed, divided as to agreement.

Stapledon leaned back. "We're in better shape than a few years ago. The current gossip is that we're pretty evenly matched, pro and con. Now is the time to strike, before we have to start chemically offsetting menopause."

Erin ventured a noncommittal, "I hope so. Things *have* been improving."

"Do you think you'll lift the ban, this year?"

Erin smiled, opening her hands. When Rizvi asked it, the question had a lot more anger behind it. "Depends on the pros and the cons."

"Should make for a thrilling town meeting."

Erin's eyes focused on Stapledon's collar again. "Should." Distracted, "What *is* that thing made of?"

Stapledon grinned and raised a hand to the white square at her neck. "Plastic. Couldn't justify the cellulose use here."

Erin nodded understanding.

"Ticked off everyone to no end."

Stapledon was Lutheran, operating under a special dispensation from the pope to let her minister to the Catholics of the colony. The woman lowered her voice confidingly. "The collar was the last straw, my Jesuit penpals tell me."

"Well, if we'd found a microbiologist with the right psych profile who just *happened* to be a Roman Catholic priest—"

Jean was already laughing. "Hey, women like that are a dime a dozen. I don't see why there was such a problem."

Erin felt her neck and shoulders relax.

"So," Stapledon said with an air of getting to the point. She clasped her hands together and leaned forward. "Those contacts were *your* last straw, I take it."

Erin puffed air out between pursed lips. "You're a smart chaplain, Chaplain." She leaned back. "Where on Earth—Mars, excuse me—did she get those things? Is someone running a plastics factory I don't know about? I know where all the stills are . . . " She crossed her arms, tension hunching her shoulders back up, acutely suspicious of any possible whine in her voice.

"I'm partial to the fungus vodka Gamma Residence puts out, myself."

Erin ignored that remark. "So, what do I do?"

"You already know what you do. And you already

know what I'm going to say. Miriam is growing up." She tapped a nail on the surface of her desk, *clickclickclick*. "This is not a surprise. Every parent and every child goes through this process." Stapledon leaned back in her chair. "If she weren't rebelling against you, I would be worried."

Erin cocked her head. "Would you, really?"

"I would, really. Indeed." The chaplain pointed up at the ceiling. "We hold up life on Earth as our nostalgic ideal, and then tell Miriam and her fellows that their life isn't like that, and it never will be. And *we* made the choice to come here, *we* volunteered. Five hundred women, 175 men and a *horde* of frozen gametes in Cargo Hold B." Jean rested her chin on one palm, elbow on the worn plastic of her desk. "Miriam didn't raise her hand up for any of that. Of course she feels resentment. It's normal."

"You're right."

"I am right," Stapledon admitted, smiling. "But, Erin, it *is* normal. Really. Children grow up in a world shaped by their parents' decisions. Always. No matter what planet they're born on."

Erin studied her boots, then looked up. "Cat-eye contacts?"

Jean spread her hands, then brought them a centimeter apart, smiling: "A small shaping. A mere precursor." The chaplain dropped back into complete seriousness. "Miriam is the very first extraterrestrial human being. Ever. She's going to have a lot of shaping to do, trying to make sure her name is her own. Not the first baby on Mars." Stapledon wrapped the phrase in quotes with her fingers for emphasis.

"Tall order." Erin stood. "Is she up to it?" Or had Erin destroyed her daughter, bringing her to life in this place? *What hubris. But whose do I mean?*

"Yes. She is."

With Stapledon sitting down, the difference in their heights was minimized. Jean near the spacer height max, Erin hovering above the bottom. Most of the time she didn't notice, but Miriam was already taller than her mother.

She didn't ask the obvious next question out loud. It wasn't one the chaplain could answer, anyway.

Am I?

•••

Another privilege of rank that came with the private quarters was the ability to eat supper alone, wondering where one's daughter might be. It seemed a sword that cut two ways.

Not that Erin was concerned for her physical safety, overmuch. Miriam might be an emotional roller coaster on two feet, but the likelihood of her doing something truly, phenomenally stupid was near zero. If you were going to kill yourself, settlement policy said do it now and spare the wasted resources. Cruel? Yes. Definitely. But a frontier always offered more chances for disaster than survival. Parents on Mars could not afford to hide dangers from their children. Educate, encourage, prevent, always. Hide, never.

Frontiers also offered the opportunity to build something where there was nothing before, and that was the siren call the colonists had answered.

Erin sat before the low table in their quarters, teacup in hand, and looked down at Miriam's latest sandpainting.

Many of the older colonists preferred to experiment with dyes, trying to achieve a full spectrum of color to work with. Miriam stuck exclusively to natural colors. Pale sand, impact-oxidized black and rusty red. At first she had imitated a few traditional Navajo designs, but quickly branched out to discover her own.

This one was almost all black, with red dots arranged seemingly randomly. Erin cocked her head. Not random. Night sky. Miriam was creating constellations. Martian constellations.

Jean Stapledon's voice sounded in her ear, from a conversation they'd had more than once: *What do you want your daughter to be when she grows up?*

Artist? Shuttle mechanic? Scientist? All of these things? None of them? A child is human potential in its most concentrated form. The essence of possibility.

Erin looked hard at the sandpainting. The underlying black was arrayed in palm-sized swirls that dragged the eye in circles around each dot of red. What had her own mother seen in the future? Not Mission Commander, Mars Settlement Project. Surely not that her daughter would take a one-way trip to the red planet. That her grandchildren would live so far away, yet hang right where she could see them, in the night sky.

What did that tell Erin about her own visions of Miriam's future?

"They're guaranteed to be wrong." She told the sandpainting. "That's what." It was a heartening thought.

Launch was in four hours. She would leave a note for Miriam and then get some sleep.

•••

Miriam must have come in while Erin was dozing, as she now lay asleep in her tiny room. Erin watched her breathe, the covers rising and falling in even increments. Her own breathing slipped into sync with her daughter's after a few moments.

She must have jangled something, because the instant Erin turned away there came a—

"Mom?"

She poked her head back through the partition. Miriam was sitting up, dragging pants on over her thermals.

"Go back to sleep, honey. I didn't mean to wake you."

"'Sokay. I just got in." Her muzzy tone belying the statement, Miriam padded out into the main living area. She plopped down in a chair and began pulling on a thick pair of socks. "Krasny," her face split in an enormous yawn, "Krasny says you're going on the shuttle tomorrow. He's managing the cargo."

"Yes." Erin patted her jacket pockets until she found her goggles, then pulled her breath mask off its hook. "I have to keep my vacuum rating up. I've been too busy, lately." Erin sat down to lace her boots, feeling herself perk up in anticipation of going off-planet. She smiled. "Commander Lang will ground me if I don't get some space time, soon."

"But, you're in charge." Miriam still looked chilly, her hands tucked into her sleeves. "You can do whatever you want."

Erin slid the breath mask over her head and down past her chin. "I'm in charge, yes. But that doesn't mean I get to do whatever I want. Usually the opposite."

Miriam chewed on that while Erin finished assembling herself to head outside. Temperatures dropped a good 20°C at night, it didn't do to forget a glove.

"Can I come watch liftoff?" Miriam blurted.

Erin looked at her daughter, a little surprised. "Sure, if you can get geared up quick. That launch window's not going to wait for either of us."

Miriam moved with the speed of youth when they want something, darting into her room to grab her jacket and boots. She laced up quick, grabbed her mask and checked the gauge.

"Ready? I want to move fast. It's cold out there."

"I know, Mom. I'm ready."

They passed into the lock and waited for the outer door to cycle open.

It was crisp, and clear, the night sky a cascade of stars. One nice thing about life in Landing: not a lot of light pollution. The Martian air was bitingly cold on Erin's cheeks. She hauled out her flashlight, watched Miriam's flare to life, and together they made a beeline for Mission Control.

It felt good, moving through the night, her daughter a bobbing light just a meter away.

What do you want that bobbing light to be, when it grows up?

I want it to be happy.

Maybe you should say so.

They moved in relative silence, the sound of breathing ringing loud in Erin's ears. The physical exertion warmed her up, suddenly the parka felt hot. Miriam whooped aloud, vaulting easily over a mid-sized rock formation. She careened toward Erin, then bolted away.

"C'mon, Mom, let's race!"

Erin laughed out loud, for the sheer joy of running around like a maniac in the middle of the Martian night. With her daughter. She picked up her pace.

LMC loomed too quickly as they jogged along, the

main building dark but for the one light in Shuttle Control.

Erin put out a hand to stop Miriam before she opened the door. "Hold up."

Her daughter turned, face almost invisible behind the breath mask and goggles. They were both breathing heavy. "Mom?"

"Be happy. Find the thing that makes you happy. And then do it. Whatever it is, so long as you find it." There. She said it. Good timing, bad timing, whatever.

Miriam nodded. "Okay."

"That's all I want. Just be happy."

Miriam was quiet for a long moment. She nodded again, slowly. "Okay. I'll try, Mom."

"That's all I ask. I'll see you soon."

Erin resumed jogging, heading down to the launch pad.

•••

"Commander, our weight is off *again*," Tran announced from her seat in the shuttle's nose. She banged her hand on the console. "Might be the sensors." One more slap and she shook her head. "Trimming to fit."

Hideo was counting down in the seat next to her. "Twenty seconds."

"Are we trim?" Jascha asked.

"Yes, sir. Are we go?"

"Thirteen seconds."

Erin nodded when Jascha looked to her for confirmation.

"You are go, Pilot."

"Yes, sir."

"Space. The Final Frontier," Jascha whispered with mock seriousness, looking over at his skipper. Behind them, Krasny snorted. As cargomaster on this trip, he had about as much to do during launch as Erin did. Which was precisely nothing. Jascha had things well in hand.

Too well. Erin was considering the uncaptainly yet satisfying act of goosing her second in command when Hideo hit zero, and Mars fell on her chest. Five g, even when g is .375 that of Earth, is still 5g.

• • •

Standard launch, standard orbital insertion, the 5g had eased to perceptibly nothing. The *Ares 4* was on its way. Jascha and Krasny headed aft for a final prep. Erin unbelted, anchoring herself to the wall, and drank in the view.

The sharp black of space, the red planet turning below them. A weather system coiled some hundreds of kilometers north of Landing. The shine off the ice caps was a cheery white.

The place didn't look nearly so deadly from up here. Like one of Miriam's sandpaintings. But Earth was deceiving from that distance, too.

Jascha's voice sounded over the com. "Skipper? Your presence is requested aft."

Erin nodded at Hideo and undulated away, in the direction of the increasingly louder sounds of Jascha and Krasny reading someone the riot act. But there was no one else on board.

And then she heard the third voice.

Oh, *no*.

•••

Miriam wormed into Erin's cubby and Erin sealed the door. There wasn't really room for two, but it was better than having the crew watch whatever argument was about to ensue. Erin felt abruptly tired. She didn't want to fight. Hadn't they done this enough times before?

Miriam's eyes clicked around, taking in the no-spare-space approach to decorating.

The fellow traveler, the human being Erin had communicated with, shared simple joy with, was gone. Replaced once again with this alien she did not know, this surly teen.

All of Erin's usual words tumbled together, nothing making it out past her lips. Miriam's body language was closed, defensive, her arms and legs crossed as she floated without a tether. Her face was an odd mix of triumph and terror.

Adolescent. Developing mind and body. Into what? Into who?

Time *would* tell. Not babies anymore. "What were you thinking?" Erin settled for, finally.

"I want to go to Earth." Miriam's voice shook a little, then solidified. "I want to go to Earth."

If we were on Earth right now, we wouldn't be having this argument. Parents on Earth don't have children stowing away aboard space shuttles. But if they were on Earth, right now, Miriam wouldn't exist, much less know how to stow away on a shuttle. Parents on Earth weren't settling new worlds, however poorly at the moment.

Erin held her breath for a three-count, then blew it out slowly, releasing . . . visions of the future. She decided to do something unexpected. *Like let go.*

Time to be captain. "Commander Lang will see that you're assigned a sleepsack and duties. We'll talk later."

•••

Jascha Lang stuck his head into the skipper's cubby. "Ma'am."

"Commander." The skipper had been keeping her hair relatively long, and now it floated around her face in an uneven halo. He darted a tie at her and Erin snagged it out of the air, twisting her hair into a pigtail as he spoke.

"Our stowaway's taken care of. Galley duty, and I've assigned her as assistant to Krasny for the incoming inventory."

Erin nodded. "Very good. Thank you, Commander."

Jascha rubbed his nose. "In addition, ma'am, it looks like we've got a loose heat tile near the cargo bay doors."

Erin raised her eyebrows at him.

"Replacing it won't take long. Of course we can do it at the station, easy. But we do have spares on board." He trailed off invitingly. *What? By me?*

The skipper floated in lotus, a little sideways and at an angle from Jascha's own frame of reference. Smiled at the bait. "Maybe I should just step out and fix it."

"It's been a while since you've seen vacuum," he offered.

Erin looked up and down, fluid concepts in low g, but up and down nonetheless. "Well, let's do it."

Jascha smiled. Ah, the Lucy Syndrome. "Yes, ma'am."

•••

Physically, there was no real difference between Erin orbiting a planet while inside a station or ship, and doing the same thing wearing a spacesuit, outside the ship. Both satisfy the same functions: pressure, air, temperature control. Yet, exiting the starboard personnel lock, heat tile in hand, made the difference between sailing a ship on the ocean, and diving under the waves.

Suit check complete, yes. Jascha did it himself, marking off the plastic board with a crayon tip. Recent pressure test, check. Gloves inspected, check. Bootstrip magnets operational, check. All rings, seals and fittings—check, check, and check. Helmet radio? They clicked back and forth at each other, falling into the old rhythm as if Erin still suited up every other day. Four hours' air mix in the tank? Check. Airflow test while Jascha hauled out the tether line and jerked on it every meter or so. Erin breathed suit air for the first time in too long, the almost rubbery taste of a fully closed system hitting the back of her throat. Check.

Lang knocked on her helmet and gave a thumbs up. Good to go?

Erin thumbed back. Good to go.

He clipped one end of the tether to the ring on her suit belt. Squeezing into an airlock holding a heat tile and the tether line was too clumsy by far, so Erin slid in and Jascha looped the line over her arm. The heat tile had gone in first, and she pulled it toward her, until the unwieldy shape was securely in hand, leash looped over her glove.

Jascha and Erin exchanged thumbs up a second time, and he sealed the inner door. Erin watched the status light flick from yellow to green as the seal took.

She spoke into her suit radio. "Lock closed, initiating evacuation," and slapped the control with her palm.

The minute and a half while the lock evacuated Erin spent listening to herself breathe, running over a mental checklist on heat tile replacement. It was a simple process, a newbie spacer task. Her fingers flexed in the gloves as pressure outside the suit reduced. It was good to not have anything more complicated to do. No colony, no teenagers, no reproductive bans. Just a heat tile, and nothing else.

The pressure light for the outer door went from red to yellow to green, and Jascha's voice sounded in her helmet. "Ready when you are, Skipper."

She hit the outer door control and slid out.

One end of the tether hooked onto a ring just outside the lock. Erin would play out the long line slowly, on her way "down," in the direction of the cargo bay.

Erin dove into the darkest sea any sailor ever crossed, endless and deep. For a moment it was just like stepping out into the cold Martian night with Miriam, and some sense of that air's crispness prickled Erin's skin, regardless of the suit's temperature monitoring. But only a moment, a shadow of the true cold around her.

Just her and the great dark, the *Ares 4* a small platform beneath her.

Somewhere off behind Erin, way out past the asteroids, the gas giants lumbered quietly through the same waters. Even farther out, Pluto and Neptune sailed around one another in their long slow rhythm.

Down in a different way, following the slope of the sun's gravity well, someone on Earth might be looking through a telescope, right that second, marveling at the contents of the sky. Which, just then, happened to include her.

Erin took a deep breath, knowing she was grinning like a fool, and began the slow march aft, trailing commentary back to the *Ares* as she moved.

•••

It was about an hour later, but felt like less, when Commander Lang's voice sounded in Erin's ear. "Skipper? Hideo's reporting hull impacts. Advise you return."

"Roger that. I'm just finishing up." Her voice still sounded unfamiliar in the close confines of her suit helmet. It *had* been too long since she'd been in vacuum. Good to be out and about. She missed working with her hands.

Erin gave the new tile a last pat for luck and moved slowly, to make her way along the hull back to the airlock. She fumbled at waist level a moment, getting a grip on her suit tether.

A sudden vibration in the hull plating translated through her suit boots to the equivalent of a loud bang.

"*Ares*, what's going on?"

Something jerked.

•••

The flight crew, of all the colonists, kept a tighter grasp on their hierarchy than anyone else; there was no room in a flight emergency for anything less than a very clear chain of command. Hideo's voice was clipped and dry of any emotion as she reported to Commander Lang.

"Sir, we're getting an electrical surge in several systems. The charges on the starboard emergency hatch have blown."

"Are we losing pressure?"

"No, sir."

Jascha nodded behind her back and spoke into his radio mike. "Skipper, your presence is required on board ASAP."

There was no answer.

•••

The tether pulled right out of her hands, and Erin was plucked off-hull, folding at the waist. What the hell? Something white blew past in her peripheral vision, and Erin was jerked again, with a loud *"Oof"* that squeezed all the air out of her lungs and dimmed her vision. There was a clank against the back of her helmet but no loss of pressure. Or at least, not yet. She swallowed back bile, everything spinning, and tried to pull in to control her momentum.

She was breathing, that was a good sign. *Respiro ergo sum*. I breathe, therefore I am.

The *Ares 4* was moving away at a fast clip.

Not a good sign at all.

"*Ares*, this is de Novales. What's the situation?"

Jascha's voice sounded in her ear. "Skipper, your presence is required on board ASAP."

Whatever had hold of her tether was flinging her away from the shuttle. And damn fast.

"My tether's snapped, *Ares*." Erin hoped Miriam wasn't in the cockpit to hear this. "I'm being pulled away from the ship by something. I can't see it yet, I'm moving too fast."

There was a pause on Jascha's end.

Finally, "Skipper?"

"I'm here, Commander." How much extra fuel did they have? Her backbrain started making frantic calculations. How much would they use on a detour vector? The supply drop's pickup window wasn't going to wait around for their leisure. They didn't have resources to burn.

"Skipper?"

"Go ahead, Commander."

"Skipper?"

The chill down Erin's spine had nothing to do with the thermostat in her suit. "Jascha, can you hear me?" Her voice sounded distant in her ears.

"Skipper? Please respond."

Oh, *no*.

•••

It was so *quiet* inside the shuttle. Tran and Hideo sat over-still, but Hideo's hands trembled on her console.

The channel hissed at them. No calm alto voice, no skipper wending her way back into the personnel lock. No nothing. Just static that went forever. Jesus, Erin, *forever*. Forever was a damn long time.

Forever. Jascha looked over at Miriam.

"Honey, I'm so—" Jascha couldn't speak past the lump that wedged in his throat. Miriam floated in lotus, clinging to a tie-me. Her eyes were the widest things he'd ever seen.

He remembered when she first learned to walk. Those big eyes, so *bright* with the promise of a world of discovery. Children were so *light* in Martian gravity. Like they could fly if you let them.

"She's not dead."

Jascha cleared his throat, looking back down at the pilot's console.

"She's *not*." Miriam's voice cracked, that time, and Jascha flinched.

He heard the sound of crying but couldn't look back around. Just ran a hand through his hair, already every which way in null g. Commander, dear God, not Captain. Not Captain.

"Keep us on course for pickup," Lang told Tran. His voice didn't sound like his own.

For want of a heat tile, the captain was lost.

• • •

"No! Mom! *Mom!*" Erin could hear her daughter, abruptly muffled, in the background. Lang's voice sounded in her ear, the radio making his voice tinny in the way a breath mask didn't. Tinny or not, he sounded horrified, reporting to the other ship the loss of their captain, EVA for something as blindingly *trivial* as a heat tile.

"The feeling's mutual." It didn't matter if she spoke out loud or not. No one would hear. Who knew what damage her radio had sustained? Worse, her air. A four-hour mix. Five in a pinch. And this certainly was one.

"*Patsy*, we are routing for pickup on your delivery. Stand by."

The *Ares 4* would be making an armful of course corrections, trying to sync with the drop. There wasn't enough juice in her suit thrusters for Erin to play catch up and win against her current velocity. Every second carried her farther in the wrong direction.

She gyrated a little, looking for whatever had snapped her tether and dragged her on a killing vector.

The stars didn't look much different, really, from Mars. Her vision misted slightly. Earth was a long way away. Would Miriam ever go there?

The silence outside her suit was deafening.

Erin spread her arms and let inertia carry her farther from *Ares 4*. The *Patsy Cline* was a speck in the corner of her eye. She watched it for a while, slowing her breathing, automatically conserving as much air as possible. Noticeably larger, but still a small clipper sailing black seas.

In this vastness of space, Miriam might go anywhere. Do anything. Human potential incarnate.

So, the question of the day was, would her parent live to see it?

Erin's stomach cramped. "I can't die. I'm Mom."

She looked at the *Cline*, eyes narrowed.

•••

"How soon to pickup?"

"Forty minutes."

"Hideo, I want to inboard the cargo instead of a tow to the station." Jascha picked up Tran with his gaze. "As soon as we've got the bag tied down put us on a slingshot vector around the planet and get back *right* here."

"Roger that, sir."

"With all speed, Pilot." His trademark geniality was gone. Tran just nodded, eyes forward. "And I want to know what happened to the electricals."

Hideo glanced at Miriam before supplying, "We'll be low on juice by then, sir." A not-subtle reminder. Don't throw away resources.

"I know. Trim it as tight as you can. And get the

station's cameras on this area during their next orbit. Maybe they'll see something."

•••

Nothing.

There was nothing, no sound, no motion, that was not of Erin's own manufacture. There was the sound of her own breathing, medium-loud and then soft again as she heard and ignored it, heard and ignored it. The slow creaking noise in her right suit elbow as she pulled her arms in to change her momentum. The vague subtle hum somewhere at the back of her neck that meant the air supply was working. Still.

Nothing else. She floated in a sea of silence, of nothingness so big no one even recognized it as such. When you're in it alone, it's much bigger than mere *space*. Even the stately dance of the planets was a mere blip.

And then Jascha Lang's voice was in the suit with her, his voice on the radio between *Ares* and the *Cline*. She clung to this lifeline, riding the words he traded with the *Cline*'s captain about the pickup, sliding down that invisible signal sent from one ship to another.

•••

Simple physics demanded that the shuttle match vector with the package before pickup, slipping both into just a single frame of reference. Tran did it with a light hand on the controls, Jascha watching her gently maneuver the ship into position.

Simple physics also said the skipper had been dragged off at your basic right angle from the hull when the emergency hatch blew. The explosive bolts were overpowered for a release in vacuum, built to toss the hatch well away in Earth's gravitational field. Underwater, even. The ring Erin's suit tether was clipped to had snapped clean off.

A thing in motion has a tendency to stay in motion. Assuming her suit hadn't breached, Erin had a good few hours of air. If she were conscious, she might try to make it back, burning her suit thrusters to correct her velocity. Might try to communicate. But there was still nothing on the radio.

The intercom squeaked. "Cargo inboard, Commander. Bay doors shut and package tied down."

"Get us on that slingshot, Tran."

"Thrusting now, sir."

If, if, if.

• • •

The suit thruster gave out a second before her finger left the control, but she was on course even without it. The *Patsy Cline* was enormous now, a planet unto itself, eclipsing the rest of the solar system from her view. The magnetic strips in her boots should pull her in to the hull sometime in the next few minutes. *Should* being the operative word.

Erin drifted through some debris, catching a couple small pebbles in her gloved hand. She shied them ahead of her at the ship's hull, carefully, not wanting to modify her trajectory. Might attract someone's attention. Let them know she was coming. Her air had been tasting stale for a while, and the CO_2 gauge was firmly into the red. There wasn't anything she could do about that except keep breathing, so she did.

In the past hour, radio traffic had died down to a few laconic exchanges between the pilots, acronym-filled and brief. *Ares 4* had made its pickup and should be towing the package to the orbital station by now.

Her little stony missiles danced off the ship's hull soundlessly, and Erin looked around for something else to throw as she drifted closer.

The radio crackled to life, a mostly still-bored pilot's voice sounding in Erin's ear.

"*Ares*, this is *Patsy*. Small hull strikes Mark 68 indicate debris in path. Do you advise correction?"

"Don't correct!" She yelled futilely. Erin just barely kept her arms at her sides. It wouldn't do to change her momentum now, flailing madly. *So close.* "Idiot!" *Warn them I'm coming. What a fool.*

After a brief pause, Tran's voice sounded in her helmet. Erin's heart leapt up into her throat and lodged there, beating in her ears, trying to drown out the answer. She felt lightheaded.

"No tracked objects in area, *Patsy*." Erin heard Miriam in the background of the transmission, her voice muffled by distance from the pilot's mike ". . . not meteorites, what if it's Mom, what if—" and then Tran's voice overrode everything else.

"Advise minimal correct if any, *Patsy*."

Erin drew breath again. The lightheadedness didn't stop. The hum at the back of her neck trailed off into a rubbery squeak and quit. No more air.

Now or never.

There. She could feel the tug starting in her soles. Erin was pulled off trajectory by her magnetized boot strips and sucked slowly toward the *Cline*'s hull.

A soft clang reverberated in her feet when she made contact, and Erin took a deep breath of CO_2-filled expiration, limbs trembling.

As it cracked against the *Cline*'s hull, she got her first close look at the cause of all her troubles. One of the shuttle's emergency hatches smacked the hull and darted back off, a portion of her suit tether still tangled around it. Now would be a very good time to unhook from all that. She fumbled at her waist and the mess of metal, ceramic and her tether line floated off into nowhere.

It was getting harder to see. Her helmet rang with a choked sound that it took a moment to recognize as laughter. She bit it off, hard. This was one hell of an EVA.

"Hang in there, Mom," she said, trying to breathe extra shallow, one foot sliding along the gently curving hull. "You're not out of the woods yet."

Something airlock-looking was about five meters away. Erin maneuvered slowly over to it, undogged the hatch and crawled in. One more minute to cycle. She held her breath, thumb waiting over the helmet catch. The lock's indicator was a bright amber. *Turn green, turn green, turn green.*

A crew member goggled as Erin pulled herself out of the lock and into a passageway.

"*Jesus*, who the hell are you?"

Erin wedged her helmet in the crook of an elbow and breathed deep, oxygen hitting her cells like a narcotic. The air was filled with familiar ship smells: humans living together in space. Used to be the smell of home, but not anymore.

"I'm from Mars," she said, finally.

And then, because Erin just couldn't resist, she smiled and added, "Take me to your leader."

• • •

The trip back was much less exciting than the one out. Erin clamped one of her suit guides to the long line snaked between the two ships, and pushed off slowly from *Patsy Cline*'s hull. Her toes aimed downward, toward the suited figure waiting for the captain at her own airlock.

An easy ride. *Much* easier.

Disengaging with a quick flick of the wrist, Erin gave Krasny a thumbs up as he shut them in. A couple minutes and one atmosphere later, the inner hatch was opened by Jascha Lang, waiting to welcome his skipper back on board. The hand that reached out to take her suit helmet barely trembled.

Erin heard him say "Ma'am," and heard herself say something, her hand touching his shoulder, but there was only one pair of eyes she needed to see, *had* to see, cat-eyed contacts or no.

Erin floated over to her daughter, whose cheeks looked suspiciously wet. "That's not a meteorite, it's my mother," she said faintly, hand reaching out to brush a lock of hair away from those cat eyes.

Miriam blushed, and Erin pulled her hard into her arms, squeezing them both against the tight weave of her suit.

"Aw, *Mom!*"

But she didn't pull away.

MEETING THE SCULPTOR

Written by
Floris M. Kleijne

Illustrated by
Cornelius Cockroft

About the Author

As a child in Amsterdam, Floris M. Kleijne learned a love of language and imagination from his parents. There he started reading Dutch translations of science fiction and fantasy classics, inspiring him to begin writing his own stories as a teenager. Later, after graduating with a major in biology from the University of Amsterdam in 1995, Floris began a circuitous career path that included croissant baking, scholastic research, marketing analysis, computer training and project management.

Throughout his various business adventures and misadventures, Floris continued writing fiction short stories. In 2000, he realized that the Dutch market for light speculative fiction was just that: light. He decided to try his hand writing fiction in English. In 2003, Floris became a Writers of the Future Contest finalist. Buoyed by that success, Floris submitted his latest entry, which garnered him this year's award. Floris still lives in Amsterdam, where he continues to read science fiction and fantasy, though no longer in translation.

About the Illustrator

The only public place where Cornelius Cockroft's artwork has been seen before this is the street—on posters, painted boards, or self-described "aerosol vandalism." That is, until now. Originally from Milwaukee, Wisconsin, twenty-seven-year-old Cornelius calls Brooklyn, New York, his home these days where he works odd jobs in addition to an occasional drawing gig.

It was in Milwaukee that Cornelius first read J.R.R. Tolkien's The Hobbit *in sixth grade; he's been into science fiction and fantasy ever since. His interest in fiction and graphics naturally drew Cornelius to comic books, which he says have been a big influence on what and how he drew. Though he briefly studied art after high school, Cornelius today relies on what's around him to inspire him, including action movies, Saturday morning cartoons and music. Until one drawing's finished, Cornelius will listen to the song over and over—even if it takes a week—just to keep the same feel throughout.*

> *Of all the consequences of the development of cheap and reliable time travel, the emergence of the art of Sculpting was the most controversial.*

Introduction to *History of the Morality of Art*, 2243

After the Y: Right Arm

The tramp knocked the chili dog out of my hand as he stumbled obliquely across our path, muttering indistinct curses. Ketchup and mustard splattered my trouser leg. My right shoulder caught a glancing blow off one of his cartwheeling arms as he careened off the corner of the newsstand and out into the car-crowded street.

We had stopped walking in the same instant, our frozen shapes reflected in the bookstore window. Sarah moved closer to me, sliding her right arm around my waist and clasping her left hand on my elbow. We watched motionlessly, our conversation forgotten. There was no time to move, to act.

This is how fast it can happen, I thought randomly in that one timeless, frozen instant. I felt every sensation being imprinted on my memory: the smell of exhaust and garbage and hot dogs, the noises of traffic and shopping, Sarah's stiff, shocked form squeezed against me, the sunlight blurred by my cheap shades. I wanted to hug Sarah and avert her eyes, or reach out to the tramp and pull him back, or run away. But of course, there was no time, so I just looked on.

The tramp recovered his balance halfway into the first lane. He straightened and turned around, looking at me, but made no move to get back to safety. He just stood there, shouting a foreign word—or maybe an unusual name—at the top of his lungs, cursing. He didn't move.

And just before the Buick snapped his right leg and threw him into the fragmenting windshield, over the roof until he crashed to the asphalt like an empty suit; seconds before the car behind the Buick bumped over his inert body and stopped; minutes before the paramedics rolled his bleeding body into the ambulance and I dragged Sarah to the back doors and got in to ride with him to the emergency room; before the waiting room, and the blood-splattered grave-looking surgeon, and the tears and the closeness and all that followed, the tramp stood in the right lane and looked me in the eyes, and I understood, and I saw that he understood as well.

It was a terrible price to pay.

Glory Days

"Drive carefully now," Karen said. She spared me a quick smile, but was already turning away when I smiled back, and the door was closing. My old friend Richard cast a last unreadable look through the gap before he pushed it shut. I stood still for a while, staring at the closed door. My eyes wandered over the wooden surface and picked out trivial details: scuff marks at the bottom, a half-removed sticker, scratches on the knob. I felt inexplicably angry and cheated.

Finally, I tore my stare away from the door, stepped away and turned down the driveway. Folding into the driver's seat of my beat-up Honda, I backed sloppily onto the street and gunned away from the curb. I knew I should probably not be driving with all the wine I had consumed, but at that moment I did not care. After my reckless departure had blunted the edge of my aggression, I did, however, manage enough self-control to ease down to the maximum speed.

I was too wound up to drive straight back home. I wasn't feeling much like spending endless insomniac hours in the house anyway, watching some old movie or mindless talk show and drinking myself into a stupor. What would be the point? Instead, I aimed the Honda for downtown, the lights, the people, the distraction. I told myself I wasn't looking for a bar, just for a wind down after the disastrous dinner. But when I drove past Lou's and noticed the lights were on, I parked without a moment's hesitation and walked back to the familiar double doors.

I didn't see Lou. Two of the student types he'd taken to hiring were tending bar, and a peroxided waitress wandered lazily among the tables. The place was about half-full and I took my time taking stock of the patrons. A couple of tables were taken by groups of students, loudmouthed and boisterous. There was an obvious first date going on at a secluded table back near the toilets, and going badly as far as I could see. Bob was getting drunk at his customary table. And here and there couples nursed their drinks and looked bored. The jukebox was playing Tom Jones.

There was a cute blonde at the bar, in her late twenties, well packaged and well stacked. She had that I-don't-give-a-damn air about her that's so sexy on beautiful women, a look that says she's seen it all,

Illustrated by Cornelius Cockroft

heard it all, is not interested. It seems to me that they learn that look after the first guy hits on them. But I wasn't about to be deterred. I walked up to the empty stool on her right side and sat down. Motioning to one of the bartenders, I said, "Give me a Jack-rocks, and for the lady whatever she's having." I looked to my left and gave her my best smile. She looked me up and down with cold brown eyes, actually wrinkled her nose, and replied, "I'm having to move." She swiveled her hips off her stool and moved a few stools down without sparing me another glance. Behind me, one of the students made a whistling noise, followed by a fair imitation of an explosion. His mates sniggered.

"Just the Jack," I told the waiter. "A double."

The perfect ending to a perfect night.

I supposed I'd have to call Richard and apologize in the morning, though I didn't understand how things had deteriorated so suddenly. I had arrived for dinner at seven, brought a nice California red, complimented Karen on her hot dress, bearhugged Richard like we used to do in high school. Karen had cooked pasta, prepared fresh salmon, thrown together a nice salad. Over dinner, we talked about the good old days, reminisced about high school, college. We laughed, I perhaps a bit louder than they, and drank two bottles of wine. Maybe I did drink most of one bottle by myself. I don't really remember. I don't remember when everything changed between Richard and me either. We used to be best friends in high school, made it through college together, shared girlfriends. I remember I used to be the guy with all the girls, while Richard went from one hopeless infatuation to the next doomed affair. I really don't remember when the tables suddenly turned on me, how Richard ended up with this goddess of a woman, how all my friends hooked up, became husbands, fathers even, and why I'm still alone.

I do remember Karen exclaiming "Mark!" in a shocked and somewhat offended tone, and Richard walking back into the den and giving me a hard stare. Still, I don't think it was much of a pass. And what's the big deal between friends, right?

"Right," Lou replied.

I looked up from my drink, startled. I hadn't noticed Lou returning, nor had I realized that I was speaking out loud. There were more empty tumblers in front of me than I remembered drinking. I suddenly noticed that the noise from the students had gone, and that the first-date couple in the back was kissing passionately. The blonde had her back to me and her date threw me an amused glance over her shoulder.

"So what do you think happened, Lou?" I was disturbed to hear a plaintive whine in my voice. "What do you think they did?"

Lou shrugged as he took my empties and sank them in sudsy water.

"Figure they sent you home; 'swhat I would do."

I nodded emphatically.

"Damn right they did! Perfectly polite and friendly about it, they were. 'Don't you think it's time you went home?' Richard said. And this is Richard, f'God's sake! I go back, like, fifteen years with this guy, and all of a sudden he's halfway on the wagon? We closed every bar in the city between us! He's just no more fun since he married that bitch Karen."

"If she's such a bitch," Lou pointed out, "why hit on her in the first place?"

"Oh, shut up and fill me up," I slurred, shaking my empty tumbler.

•••

I woke up slowly, reluctantly, with a leather throat and a cotton brain. I was lying on my back with one arm slung over my forehead like a dead weight. Outside was the diminishing dark of five a.m. and the covers felt unfamiliar. I smelt that particular scent of post-coital sweat and heard soft irregular snoring, felt body heat close to my other arm. I turned my head carefully and saw blond hair on the other pillow, blond hair and dark roots. There was a white blouse on the chair on her side of the bed, an apron and a short skirt. I raised myself on my right arm, ignoring the pins and needles, and looked around for my clothes.

She stirred and made an indistinct throaty sound. She turned to her side and slid her hand to my butt, squeezing.

"Hey there, Bronco," she whispered, and I winced. But her hands were persistent and my body seemed willing. Why the hell not, I thought, and pulled her to me.

Just before my lips found hers I realized I had forgotten her name.

Meeting the Sculptor

When I awoke the second time, I felt sore and sick and stupid. I was alone in her bed and the curtains were drawn. Getting up cautiously, I stumbled into the bathroom and took a brief scalding shower. When I came back into the bedroom toweling my hair, I noticed the note she had left me on her pillow.

"Hey there, Bronco," she'd written. "I enjoyed last night. Call me anytime. Kisses, D."

Dolly, I thought as I crumbled the note. Deborah? Whatever her name was, I suddenly felt I needed to get out of her house fast. It had been a stupid thing to do. I couldn't even remember the sex and I really liked Lou's place; it was a shame to have to avoid it in the next few weeks. I pulled on my jeans and my smoke-smelling shirt and made my way to the kitchen to see about a cup of instant.

"Do you know *when* your life went to hell?"

I dropped the mug I was taking from a hook above the bar. It shattered on the bar surface. Whirling toward the voice, I saw a man standing in the nook between the cupboard and the wall.

It was impossible to guess his age. He was entirely bald but his narrow face was unmarred by lines or spots, except for a few crinkles around the eyes. He looked like he was accustomed to laughing a great deal. Dressed in colorless chinos and a white shirt, he was almost completely anonymous.

"Who the *hell* are you?" I barked. He had scared me more than I cared to admit, and I resented him for it. He was unmoved by my anger and smiled a small, secretive smile of private amusement.

"I'm Jolo," he replied.

"I'm a Sculptor," he added after a pause, as if that explained anything. "Do you?"

"How did you get in here?" I demanded. My first instinctive explanation, that he was a thus-far-unmentioned boyfriend, was losing credibility. His whole attitude seemed to indicate he was a stranger in the house, and my anger was rapidly growing out of control. I stepped toward the knife rack.

"Let's say I entered through the window," he said. "Do you?"

"Do I what?" I did not mean to get dragged into his

undoubtedly delusional dialogue, but his insistence on that two-word question was maddening. I had to shut him up.

He sighed a weary sigh of tried patience.

"Do you know," he repeated patiently, as if speaking to a difficult child, "*when* your life went to hell?"

"What the *hell* are you talking about? There's nothing wrong with my life!"

He held his head to one side and raised his eyebrows.

"Do you want me to specify the exact number of brain cells you killed off last night? I could also identify the strains of chlamydia you contracted in your tumble with Lou's waitress—whose name, by the way, is Denise. Or, if you like, I could . . ."

"Shut up! Who are you?"

"I'm Jolo. I Sculpt. Tell me, seriously: when was it?"

"Damn you, Jolo! I'm leaving, and so are you if you don't want the cops on your ass!" I turned toward the kitchen phone.

Jolo spoke to my back.

"April 24, twelve years back, at eight minutes after three, p.m."

I froze in my tracks. I remembered that day.

Before the Y

We sipped our lattes and ambled leisurely down the avenue. It was around three in the afternoon, and I had a vague plan of taking her to the park and lounging by the water, chatting aimlessly, maybe getting her to let me kiss her. The day was radiant, an April afternoon of uncommon perfection. And I was starting to realize how much I liked this girl.

We had met accidentally a few weeks earlier, literally bumping into each other at a yard sale a few miles outside the city. I had bent over to take a better look at the velvet seat of an old chair and she'd done the exact same thing at the exact same moment. We'd both straightened out holding our heads and laughing.

"I'm so sorry," she'd said, still laughing.

"No, I'm the guilty party," I had replied, though it had in fact been her fault. By that time I had taken a good look at her and realized the advantages of befriending her. I was without a girlfriend at the time and this girl was very attractive, though not at all the type I usually went for.

Dressed as she was in a nice but not very sexy outfit—slacks, a turtleneck and a shapelessly stylish jacket, in different shades of tan—it was hard to tell for sure, but the curves and accents suggested an obviously feminine body with full breasts, good hips and maybe a bit more padding than I preferred.

She had very expressive wide brown eyes. Strawberry blond bangs just touched her eyebrows and her hair was brushed back into a short ponytail. She had narrow lips that were turned up into a very pretty smile. I decided we would get to know one another.

"Let's just call it a meeting of minds," I added, drawing a cute chuckle. "I'm Mark," I offered, extending my right hand.

She took my hand with just the right amount of hesitation and replied, "Sarah."

"Nice to meet you, Sarah. Can I offer you an ice pack for your head, or would buying you a cup of coffee be enough?"

● ● ●

Neither of us bought the chair, but we did have that coffee, exchanged phone numbers, promised to call. And I did call. A week later, we had dinner in Chinatown, and still got along great. Three days after that, I took her to the zoo. She loved that, though she laughed at me when I proposed it.

"The zoo, Mark? What's your next ploy? A moonlit walk along the beach?"

Sarah was like that. She went along with my plans, accepted my compliments, flirted back, but always with an amused, almost mocking undertone. It drove me crazy while at the same time making me like her even more.

After the zoo, just to show her I would not be deterred, I took her to Long Beach one evening, with the sky cloudless and the moon out. She laughed again, but called me a sweetheart and had her arm through mine most of the way back.

And this Saturday, another week further along, we had decided together to simply hang out downtown, shop a bit, have lunch somewhere. The afternoon was turning out much better than I'd expected, and in a way I didn't understand at all. All I knew was I was smiling incessantly around her and felt utterly at ease. And as far as I could tell, it was the same for her.

We chatted and laughed as we approached the next pedestrian crossing. Sarah was so caught up in our conversation that she did not watch the traffic lights change. She stepped into the road ahead of me as the traffic started moving.

<u>Hearing Abraham</u>

Turning back to Jolo with my hand on the phone, I asked again, "Who are you?"

"Your real question is 'What are you?'," Jolo said, "and I don't believe you're going to be satisfied with my answer that I'm a Sculptor."

"Cut the crap, Jolo, or whatever your name is. You know too much about me. Who are you? And I want a straight answer or you'll be looking at five years, minimum, for breaking and entering."

Jolo sighed.

"Very well. I'll answer you properly. Unfortunately, any answer I give will be unbelievable to you. I'll have to show you instead."

"Right, that's it," I started, and grabbed the earpiece off the wall-mounted kitchen phone. But Jolo ignored me as he pulled some kind of cell phone from his hip pocket and started fiddling with the buttons. He looked up at me for a moment, calculating, and pressed another button with a finality that disturbed me.

Then the house went away, and something else came in its place.

•••

I looked around me. Jolo was still a few feet away from me, but everything else was different. Everything was a too-bright blur of grays and greens, impossible space, wind where there should be none, and behind it all a voice raised in speech, a voice that tugged at my memory. I stumbled with a seemingly changed center of gravity, breathed thick, hot summer air with an unpleasant underlying scent, gagged. As Jolo looked on with his aloof little smile, I was violently sick. It was mostly liquid that came out, and before long I was dry-heaving, then coughing.

Then my stomach calmed down and I was able to take in my surroundings.

We were outside, I noticed, and by the sunlight I judged the time of day had changed, too. We were in a sloping field, the side of a hill, and as I looked more carefully around me I realized we were in a cemetery, a fresh one, it appeared. The closest headstones bore dates a century and a half back, but were strangely untouched by time.

Then I tuned into that voice, and my body went cold all over.

I had never heard the voice before, but had had it described to me by history teachers, in textbooks, on Discovery Channel. And the words were utterly familiar to me.

Being sick, I had missed the start.

". . . that from these honored dead we take increased devotion to that cause for which they gave the last full measure of devotion; that we here highly resolve that these dead shall not have died in vain . . ."

My breathing had stopped, and it seemed my heart had as well. With a fist jammed into my mouth I stared wide-eyed in the direction of that voice, willing time to go back to the opening words. Everything else was forgotten; Jolo and his mystery, the misguided night with Denise, my life. All I wanted was to run toward the sound and lay eyes upon that oh-so-familiar gaunt, bearded face.

But as soon as I moved my feet, Jolo must have pressed another button, and a moment later I was retching again, back in Denise's kitchen, my legs giving way as the telephone headset swung against the wall, sounding a dial tone.

When I'd recovered sufficiently to stagger to one of the bar stools, I sank into it and stared hard at Jolo.

"Was . . . Was that . . . ?" I stammered, though I knew the answer.

He shrugged.

"I knew of your fascination with the First Civil War, of course. I needed something you would recognize in the few minutes I am permitted. You can ask your question again now. I'll give you the proper answer this time."

I knew which question he meant, but I wasn't ready. I felt an immense sense of loss, and tears coursed down my cheeks.

"I . . . I was there! And I missed the beginning . . ."

"Yes, 'Four score' and all. It might have been better if you hadn't had so much to drink last night. Please, ask the question."

He looked at me expectantly and I plunged in.

"Who are you?"

"I'm Jolo the Sculptor. I am a time traveler."

At the Foot of the Y

Before I was aware what was happening, my hand had shot out and grabbed her wrist. I jerked her back, perhaps a bit roughly, as the driver of the car closest to her leaned angrily on his horn. He gassed aggressively, stalling his car, and finally ran a yellow light past us, giving us the finger.

I released Sarah's wrist and asked her, "You okay?"

She looked at me and gave me one of her great smiles, but I could see in her eyes that she was shaken. She grabbed my hand before it fell away completely, squeezed softly, and held on lightly to my fingers.

"Thanks, Mark. I'm fine, I think. Thanks for saving me."

"Least I could do after distracting you from the traffic lights," I said with a forced laugh. She leaned into me briefly and laughed with me, and I could almost see her pull herself together.

"Let's go, before we miss the lights again," I suggested. We crossed, but before we were halfway, the light started blinking. We looked at each other and broke into a headlong run, still holding hands, whooping hysterical laughter and drawing amused stares from the other pedestrians. We kept running and laughing for half a block, and when we finally stopped we stood panting, hands on knees, still snickering. When we straightened up she gave me a peculiar blank stare that told me to seize the moment.

I stepped toward her and bent slowly to kiss her.

She stopped me by laying a finger on my lips.

"Later, Mark," she said. Taking hold of my chin with thumb and forefinger, she stretched toward me and softly kissed the corner of my mouth.

Wood and Marble

"There are places in time," Jolo said between bites of his burger, "where the smallest change has a profound effect on everything that follows."

We were sitting in my car in the parking lot, trays of fast food in our laps. Jolo had poured me a glass of water in Denise's kitchen and offered to buy me lunch at one of the countless drive-ins. My hangover had somehow evaporated and I had readily accepted his invitation. In the shock of being at the Address, I had almost forgotten his insulting remarks about my life, and as we'd driven through town, Jolo gave no sign of being on that track any longer. He had gazed around him in delight and kept up a running commentary.

MEETING THE SCULPTOR

"It's a secret delight for me to come back to your time, Mark. Don't get me wrong: I love when I live. The level of comfort and well-being has never been as high as in my time. But your age, the age of the megacities ... There is a special kind of madness to living here, or in Los Angeles, or in Tokyo or Mexico City. Or Cairo! Let's not forget Cairo." And he smiled with memory.

"I could never live in one of your cities, knowing what I know about the health issues, the mental problems, the . . . But it's exhilarating to observe!

"Look!"

I had taken my eyes off the road for a second to see what he meant. With obvious delight, he had been pointing at a street person sitting in the doorway of an abandoned building. It had been a man, as far as I could tell, and he had been sitting folded in on himself, asleep or passed out or possibly dead. In front of him on the pavement had been an ancient cap in which a few solitary coins glittered. Beside him a cardboard sign had been leaning against the wall. "All change here," the sign had said.

"Incredible, isn't it? But then, you're probably used to sights like that. You have to understand that any kind of suffering is highly uncommon in my time. So naturally I am fascinated with it when I come across it in my travels."

"Well, there's enough to fascinate you in this city then," I had remarked. My tone of voice had broken his monologue. With a noncommittal "hm" he had fallen silent until I stopped at the speaker stand at the drive-in. Jolo had ordered a large meal for himself and the chiliburger special for me. In between bites of his burger, he was telling me what he meant by being a Sculptor.

"You mean like the chaos theory?" I replied. "Butterflies in Japan and all that crap?"

His bemused smile reappeared around a bite of his sandwich. He held up a hand in a "wait" gesture, chewed furiously, swallowed, and said, "Something like that, perhaps, though the actual chaos theory is just about the opposite of what I mean. If you like the butterfly bit, imagine that you could go back to the moment the butterfly flapped its wings and nudge it just so. You might just be able to prevent the hurricane."

"Wouldn't that mean you'd be changing history?"

He pursed his lips and half-nodded, considering and routinely discarding my argument.

"Well, yes, of course, but we've found that history has flexible boundaries. The general timeline doesn't change if we change only small details."

"I'll take your word for it," I said. Then I had to concentrate on my burger and fries for a bit, because it had suddenly hit me again that I was having a sensible conversation with a time traveler.

On the drive over, after Jolo had fallen silent, I had seriously considered the possibility that I was losing my mind. I had read enough science fiction to appreciate the concept of time travel, but had always vaguely understood it to be impossible. There was no doubt in my mind that I had actually been at Gettysburg for a few minutes that morning, but that might be the conviction of a hallucinating madman.

But I felt sane. The sequence of events was coherent. And Jolo was real; the car sank on its springs as he got into the car, he drew a few odd stares as we waited for red lights; he opened the glove compartment to rummage for candy. And he had ordered his own food. I wouldn't mind some more proof: JFK's assassination, "I have a dream," Golgotha even—but I discovered to my surprise that I was convinced in my heart that Jolo was the real thing.

He was a time traveler and he had chosen me to visit.

"Of course," he said. "What else can you do, right?"

"Right," I agreed.

"What I do," he continued, "is seek out these points in time. I travel to a place where a small change can make a big difference..."

"You mean like a node, a nexus?"

"You've read too much science fiction," Jolo laughed. "We just call it a bifurcation, or simply a Y."

"Why?"

"Yes."

"No, I mean, why that name?"

"I thought it would be obvious. These points have one timeline leading up to them, but two possible timelines leading away. The art of Sculpting is to travel to such a Y and nudge events just enough to select one of the timelines."

"So how do you decide which timeline to select?"

"It's an art form, Mark. I'm an artist. I select whichever timeline is the most aesthetically pleasing."

I was appalled.

"So you change history, mess with people's lives, just so it looks better?"

"Aesthetics is more than looks, as I'm sure you know. My art is about beauty, justice, morality."

I winced. His self-righteousness grated on my nerves, and though I couldn't quite put my finger on it, I felt the morality of what he was talking about was less straightforward than he let on. But before I could explore the subject further, I suddenly realized what he was leading up to. I posed the question anyway.

"So what," I asked, slowly, "has all this got to do with me?"

He smiled a satisfied smile, loaded with cheerful anticipation.

"Do you know," he replied gleefully, "*when* your life went to hell?"

After the Y: Left Arm

The tramp knocked the chili dog out of my hand as he stumbled into me, squashing chili sauce and mustard between his shoulder and my chest. He muttered an indistinct apology into my curses as he recovered his balance and stepped back. Glancing at the mess he'd made, he got out a filthy handkerchief and began clumsily batting at my shirt.

Instantly, the magic evaporated that had surrounded us in the minutes after her soft kiss, to be replaced by fury. Releasing Sarah's hand, I batted his dirty cloth away and shoved him, hard, with both hands. He overbalanced backwards and sprawled onto the pavement, looking up at me bewilderedly.

"Stupid jerk!" I shouted at him. "Look before you leap, why don't you! You ruined my best shirt!" Without conscious thought, I kicked the soles of his feet, twice, firmly.

"Mark!" Sarah exclaimed, grabbing my elbow. She pulled me back and crouched at his side, helping him to his feet. He shuffled off hurriedly, looking back over his shoulder once, twice. Sarah turned to me without words but with thunder in her eyes.

"Look at this," I said, indicating the mess on my shirt with both hands. "It's ruined!"

"It was an accident, Mark. An accident. And you were kicking him lying down."

"I know," I said plaintively. "But he should have watched where he was going."

"You knocked him down, Mark. He was lying down and you kicked him."

"I know," I repeated, working on the stain with a paper napkin. "Let's forget about it, shall we?"

"Yeah, let's," she said. But she didn't.

Indecent Proposal

"It's the perfect Y, Mark. There is a beautiful alternate timeline from that point. I aim to nudge history into that timeline."

Somehow, Jolo was pissing me off again, though I couldn't quite figure out why he got under my skin that way.

"Whatever. I still don't see the big deal. So I was with Sarah and knocked over a tramp. So what? It's not like anything changed after that day. Or are you trying to tell me that tramp would have given me his secret treasure map?"

Jolo ignored my sarcasm along with my obvious anger.

"Nothing like that, no," he said smugly. "How's Sarah these days?"

That was the final straw.

"Piss off, Jolo! I don't know why I am even listening to you anymore! You come here with your time machine and your self-righteousness and all you do is fall all over my life! What's so great about your own life if you have to travel in *time* to escape it? Sarah was just some girl, man. It didn't work out, so what?"

Jolo didn't speak. He inclined his head and kept his eyes on my face.

"What? So it's *Sarah* this is about? The big event, your bloody *bifurcation*, was *Sarah*? I don't know where you get your info, but you are *out there*. Sorry to break this to you, but *Sarah* stopped seeing *me*. It wasn't my doing. And as far as I'm concerned, it was *her* loss. Sorry, Sculptor, your block of marble just fell apart."

Again, he pursed his lips in his maddening way. He shook his head.

"I never said it was your doing, Mark. I only said it was that day. Why did she stop seeing you?"

"What? Who cares? Don't change the subject."

"Why did she? Think about it, really. Why did she?"

"Get off it, Jolo! That's not the bloody point!"

"Oh, but it is. Tell me why."

I'd had enough. Slamming my Coke down on the center console, I threw my door open hard enough to make the car shake. I jumped out and strode around the hood, drawing concerned stares from the people in the other parked cars. I didn't care. I jerked Jolo's door open.

"Out! I'm sick of your crap! I don't care if you can show me the Crucifixion or the bloody big bang, I've had enough! Get out of my car and zap yourself to wherever you came from, but get the hell out of my life, and fast."

I was shaking by that time, clutching the top edge of the window with my right hand hard enough to whiten my knuckles and redden my fingertips. My left hand was pointing away from the car and shaking. The shaking made me even madder.

Jolo put down his tray carefully, holding on to his sandwich, and calmly unfolded out of the car, speaking as he moved.

"I honestly want to know if you are aware what possessed her . . ."

"I'm warning you, Jolo!"

"I'm not asking for me, you know . . ."

"Shut up, Jolo!" I shouted and balled my left hand to punch him.

"I know why she dumped you. You really don't have a clue, do you?"

Jolo stood on the other side of the car door. My left hand was still clenched into a fist but I had forgotten about it. Half-forgotten memories were bubbling up into my consciousness, memories of loss, of shattered glass and cascading sugar.

Over Coffee

"But why, Sarah? I don't understand."

She sighed deeply over her cappuccino. I honestly didn't understand what possessed her. We had made it to the park, but the afternoon had wound down into an uncomfortable silence, Sarah pensive and monosyllabic, I confused and frustrated. Long before the shadows had reached our spot, she had suggested going for some more coffee. For a moment I had hoped she wanted to take me home, but when the Starbucks kid gave us our coffees, she had sat down at one of the tables and told me we needed to talk. Her face was grim; I didn't need to take into account the impersonal ambience and the neon lights to realize something was wrong.

And she had said she didn't want to see me anymore.

"I mean, we have good times, right?" I hated the pleading edge to my voice, but plodded on nevertheless. "I thought we were getting along great, going somewhere. We can talk, I make you laugh, we have fun, don't we? I thought we were going somewhere with this. I don't understand." I fell silent as I realized I was blathering.

She looked up and I was alarmed to see tears in her eyes.

"I thought so too, Mark. Please don't ask me to explain. Please. I don't think I could explain it so you'd understand. Please just believe me: I don't want to see you anymore. Okay? Please?"

Tears were coursing freely down her cheeks by now. I reached out to thumb one of them away. She flinched from my hand.

"Don't, Mark. Please don't."

I was shaking my head vigorously. I couldn't believe this was happening.

"You owe me an explanation, Sarah! You owe me that much. Tell me. I'll understand."

She shook her head, took a listless sip of her cappuccino.

"No, Mark."

"Was it the tramp? I said I was sorry, Sarah. I lost it back there and I was wrong. You want me to go back, give him some money, help him out a bit? I'll do it if it's such a big deal. Is that it?"

She just shook her head again.

"Come on, Sarah! This is not fair. You owe me. Or is there some other guy on the sidelines?" Sarah kept shaking her head, but gave me a dark look from under her eyebrows. "Damn! You meet a guy and you haven't even got the guts to tell me? That is sad. But you know what? Who cares! It's not like there was anything going on in the first place, was there? We haven't even slept together yet! 'Later, Mark.' Whatever!"

I got up angrily, knocking over my chair.

"So why don't you just go see your guy, and I'll find me a girl and we'll both live happily ever after! How's that? Does that meet with your approval, Miss Later?"

She didn't even get angry. I was so mad I wanted to throw the sugar tumbler across the room, and she just looked at me, crying her eyes out and shaking her head. She let out a shuddering breath and said, still shaking her head, "I was so wrong about you, Mark. I hope you figure it out for yourself before it's too late."

I didn't even care anymore.

"Damn you!" I shouted as I grabbed the sugar tumbler and threw it violently to the far wall, where it exploded into a cascade of glass shards and white powder over the tables, scaring the guests.

As I ran out of Starbucks, Sarah was still crying.

Alternates

"What can you possibly know about it?"

Jolo smiled a small, sad smile.

"I'm a Sculptor, Mark. I do my research. But I also know people, and I absolutely know what possessed Sarah to stop seeing you. And I believe that on some level, you know as well."

My left arm sagged and my shoulders drooped. My anger left me as quickly as it had come, leaving me deflated and depressed.

"It was the *tramp*, wasn't it?" Jolo nodded. "But I don't understand *why*. Was he someone, someone she knew? Why was it so important to her?"

"Lock your car," Jolo said by way of response. He pointed at a picnic table just off the parking lot. "We'll sit over there, in the sun."

I did as he said and walked after him. I felt numb and dazed and couldn't figure out why. We sat on the near bench with our backs against the edge of the table, basking our faces in the sunlight. I stared ahead at the parked cars; for some reason I couldn't face Jolo as he explained.

"She saw something in you, Mark. She saw you, from the outside: the smooth talking, the looks, the moves. But she looked past all that and saw what lay beneath. And that was who she loved."

"She . . . ?" I began, but Jolo held up a hand.

"The thing is, Mark, you've always had a talent for being insensitive, a male chauvinist pig as it was called in this age, a sexist jerk. No, let me finish. You know as well as I do that this pisses you off because it rings true. You were hot with the girls in high school and that definitely helped bring out the arrogant pig in you. But the talent was always there.

"Sarah saw that, but she also saw the person you could be if you would let yourself. She saw through all your posturing and your tough-guy antics and believed you could be a wonderful man if you would dare let go of your mask. Because you don't necessarily *have* to be a jerk; no one is born that way. She thought you were learning to discover that about yourself, and stuck around to profit from it.

"She believed in you. And for that first month, she thought she was being proven right."

A rush of feeling raced through my body. I hated what he said. I hated it, because it did ring true.

"That's why . . . that's why she never . . ."

"Yes, you're beginning to see. She wouldn't sleep with you until she was certain you would leave your mask off for her. And she wouldn't even kiss you because she was so crazy for you by then it wouldn't have stopped at a single kiss.

"But all that time, Mark, through all your great dates, she was on high alert. She never fully trusted you. And when that homeless person ran into you and you kicked him, she didn't need much time to decide.

"From that moment, she believed you would remain a jerk. And she withdrew."

I was breathing open-mouthed and was vaguely surprised to note there were tears welling in my eyes.

"But . . . I said I was sorry! I lost my temper and I was sorry!"

Jolo tried to keep a straight face, but couldn't hold in a burst of laughter that stung more than anything he had said.

"Of course you were. But think about it, Mark. The man bumped into you by accident. You pushed him down and kicked him. It was a low, inhumane, petty thing to do.

"And to think things could have turned out so differently."

A deep chill shook my spine and I felt my hackles rise. All I could stammer was, "How?"

Jolo took a deep breath and sighed.

"Are you sure you want to know?"

"Yes! God, yes!"

"I found an alternate timeline from there. In this timeline, the tramp stumbles, but misses you by a fraction of a second. And everything after that is different."

"How? Jolo, how? How can that one collision make so much difference?"

"It's not just the collision. The tramp misses you, but stumbles into traffic instead. He gets hit by a Buick and is seriously injured. On the spur of the moment, you decide to travel with him in the ambulance, dragging Sarah with you.

"Do you see, Mark? He bumps into you, and she gets to see the jerk. He gets hit by a car, and you get a chance to show your sensitive, humane, inner self. In that ambulance, and later in the waiting room at the ER, you validate for Sarah what she always believed.

"That is the beginning. From that moment on, it is all positive feedback. Because of what she has seen of you, she lets you get closer. Because she lets you get closer, you dare show more, release more of your mask. And the rest would have been history."

With another one of his smug expressions, Jolo took the last bite of his burger.

"No, no, no. You have to tell me more, Jolo. You can't leave it hanging like that."

He made a reluctant face, swallowing.

"I really shouldn't. I've told you too much already."

"What does it matter? You said yourself history doesn't change, Jolo! Tell me!"

With a deep sigh, he conceded.

"Very well. She moves in with you four months later and after a year you buy your first apartment together. You get married on your second anniversary. Five years after the yard sale, your first son is born.

"And—I apologize for sounding trite—you live happily ever after."

I sagged back on the bench, breathing, "Sarah."

It had always been her, I saw now. I had never been in love, I had always claimed, but with hindsight, I understood what I had felt for her. And Jolo had all but told me it had been mutual. It all rang true. It all made sense now; I finally understood what had happened that day.

And I suddenly realized what Jolo's story meant for me. He was a Sculptor, he had told me, and he traveled in time to select timelines that were more aesthetically pleasing. He was here to give me that alternate future, my life with Sarah. My son. I did not need much time to look over my life as it was and weigh it against the alternative. I smiled a grim smile as I realized his first words to me had actually been perfectly accurate.

"Where . . ." I started. My voice failed me on my first attempt. "Where do I sign?"

Jolo nodded a few dozen times. I could see he was very satisfied with himself, but I didn't care. As far as I was concerned, he was my savior—literally.

"Not so fast, Mark. I need to explain how the difference happens, how he bumped into you here but misses you in the alternative.

"He is pushed from behind."

"Pushed?"

"Yes. That gives him the extra momentum he needs to just miss you."

"Who pushes him?"

Jolo chuckled.

"It could be anybody, really. But let's face it: here, nobody did."

It slowly dawned on me what he must mean.

"I? I push him? Is that why you're here? Do I give him a shove from the other direction?"

Jolo just kept his silence. I thought hard.

"Whatever. Sure. I'll do it. Take me there."

"Don't you want to know what happens to the tramp?"

I tore myself away from remembered images of how

good Sarah had looked, how she smiled, how radiant her eyes were.

"What? Oh, sure. What happens to him?"

"He dies in the OR. You are devastated. It's that more than anything, your emotional reaction to the demise of a total stranger, that moves Sarah."

"He dies?"

"Yes. It's odd that the most satisfying of Ys tend to demand a blood sacrifice."

"Jesus." I fell silent for a while, then asked, "What happened to him here?"

For the first time since sitting down, Jolo looked at me. There was an odd expression on his face, but I couldn't tell what he was thinking.

"After bumping into you, he went on with his empty, meaningless life. Nothing much happened to him that hadn't happened a hundred times before. He died the next winter, of exposure."

It wasn't a hard decision after that.

Knock Knock

I kept my eyes peeled on the hot-dog stand a few hundred feet back down the street and made a point of ignoring the hard stares the bookstore owner was throwing my way. It vaguely worried me that he might call the police, but otherwise, I was determined not to give up my spot in the recessed doorway of his store. As far as I could remember twelve years later, this was the exact spot where I had run into the tramp with Sarah after our traffic light mishap. By my cracked watch there were ten more minutes to go. There was no tramp yet in evidence, but I trusted him to show up in time. He had been moving, anyway.

The sense of anticipation contorting my intestines was hard to bear. I was only ten minutes away from a chance to throw my life into an entirely new gear, to turn it around, to grab for what was rightfully mine. For the thousandth time I wondered if my memories of life with Sarah would come flooding in the moment I changed the past, or if I would have to wait until Jolo took me back to the present. The future. Whatever.

Sarah. I realized I was also just ten minutes away from seeing Sarah again. Oddly enough, the thought of seeing myself as I was twelve years ago did not seem half as scary and exciting. More oddly still, the me I would be seeing didn't know he was only half an afternoon removed from the last time he would ever see Sarah. I would change that for him, and thus for me, and he wouldn't even get a chance, or have the wits, to thank me. With a start I realized I was working myself into a state; I laughed aloud when I realized at whom I was getting angry. Passersby looked at me, startled and disapproving. I grinned at them and they hurried on.

I shrugged in my overcoat and scratched at my beard, stretching my chin up for maximum comfort. When I lowered my gaze toward the street and the hot-dog stand again, I saw them. Us. I felt a painful stab in my belly I realized was the hunger as much as the shock of seeing my young self with beautiful Sarah. This moment would be worth the three weeks of misery Jolo had accidentally inflicted on me.

• • •

Unexpectedly, Jolo had screwed up taking me back in time. When I'd regained my balance after retching painfully in the corner of the abandoned apartment, I looked around only to find him missing. I was alone in an apartment of bare walls, windows half boarded up, piles of stripped wallpaper, and amputated fixtures. A quick and almost panicky search of the place told me there was really no one else. Jolo had somehow failed to accompany me into my past. I was on my own.

It was only when I hit the streets that I discovered just how badly he'd messed up. Granted, I wasn't far from the bookstore where it had all gone down. It was about a block east, across the street from where I emerged from the apartment building. Shielding my eyes, I looked at my watch. He'd even managed to put me at 2:45 p.m., with more than twenty minutes to spare.

But when I ventured out on the street and passed a newsstand, my eye caught a *Times* headline, and I was visited instantly by a vivid memory of the discussion a front-page article had dragged Sarah and me into, a discussion of Boris Yeltsin and his Chechnya policies. Sarah had argued that war was always wrong, and any reason to cease fire good enough; I'd maintained that Boris was being opportunistic for stopping the war because of the elections, that he should have the balls to keep up the struggle against those nasty Chechen rebels. I was really just trying to annoy Sarah, which worked until she caught on to it. Then we just laughed.

We laughed. We were together. And *this* was the edition of the *Times* that had started it. I grabbed it and glanced over the masthead, overlooking the date twice before I found it. When it finally got through, I grabbed another newspaper, yet another, a weekly mag. But they all told me the same thing.

I was three weeks early.

And when the guy asked me for money for the papers I'd messed up, I realized a second thing. My credit cards would be useless twelve years in the past.

And of my cash, only the singles might be old enough to pass.

I was stranded, and I was broke.

•••

I survived those three weeks. I cursed Jolo constantly, but I survived. By the time April 24 approached, I knew by heart the locations of all the fresh water fountains. It took four days of starvation for necessity to overcome pride, but now, three weeks later, I had the dubious distinction of being a fairly effective beggar. I had not stooped to searching trash cans; that seemed to be one thing I did not need for a memory. Anyway, I knew it would be only three weeks before D-day. Living on plenty of fresh water and small quantities of cheap food was a small price to pay and losing some weight actually a bonus. And sleeping on the streets wasn't all that bad in summer.

In the first few days of shock, I'd planned to ambush Jolo at the empty apartment on the twenty-fourth and beat the crap out of him for making such a giant mistake. But when I calmed down it did not seem like a very good plan; he was the only one with the power to put me back into my new life. Besides, once I thought about it I decided I would much rather deal with what I'd dubbed the "hot-dog incident" alone, without his interference. By the time he'd have worked out he didn't have me with him, I'd probably have dealt with the tramp and secured my new future present.

So I lived on the streets for three weeks, developing a beard and a hole in my stomach, hustling for change, suffering the increasingly hard stares of passersby and supermarket clerks. It was embarrassing, but it was also a fascinating sortie into an alien world. I almost understood Jolo's fascination with our age.

And it was worth it. That, in particular, I realized as I watched my young self approach excruciatingly slowly, holding Sarah's hand. Three weeks of living like a bum was a small price for a future with Sarah.

I wondered idly what our son's name was.

There was a sudden hair-raising buzz next to me in the recessed doorway. Instinctively, I moved aside, as a kind of popping sound announced the sudden appearance of . . . Jolo.

"Jesus!" I shouted, and recoiled involuntarily.

"Hello, Mark. Another minute to go. Nervous?"

"Yes," I snapped, stealing a quick glance at the approaching couple. "Where the hell have you been?"

"Oh, here and there," he said airily. "For example, I've searched out your tramp and given him a current fifty to get a proper meal, a wash and a bed. He'll probably spend it on booze, but what can you do, right?"

I stared wide-eyed at Jolo and had to restrain myself from throttling him.

"You *what*? Are you out of your mind? They're practically on top of us!" Another quick glance confirmed we had only a few dozen seconds left. "We need that tramp, Jolo, you idiot! What were you thinking, that some other street person would conveniently show up? I don't see him, Jolo! We're running out of time and I don't see him!"

Jolo smiled his infuriating smile, inclined his head, and said, "I do."

My spine turned cold. Something in his unfathomable expression made me turn my head and look at my reflection. And my heart skipped a beat when I saw what Jolo meant.

In blind panic, I recoiled. I tipped backwards, turned on my feet, but did not manage to regain my balance. Half-stumbling, half-running, I crossed the sidewalk at an angle. The tunnel vision of fast movement gave me but a glimpse of Sarah's startled face and my own hot dog before I bustled onto the street. Only then did I regain control of my movement.

"Jolo!" I shouted, trying to drown out the understanding that threatened to crowd my mind. "Jolo!" But there was no escape, not now, not at the end.

This, then, was what Jolo had planned all along. His prank, his practical joke, his master-stroke of irony. There was never any question of returning to the future, to my new life. Whatever happy end was available was not mine.

I straightened up and looked back at the young couple with the hot dogs.

They were together, and even in this moment of shock there may have been a budding closeness discernable, something I vaguely remembered sharing with Sarah but hadn't felt since. Wide-eyed Sarah was staring shockedly at me, clutching my younger self's arm, and without really seeing. But my younger self found my eyes. I looked into his, and saw his understanding.

My life for theirs. It was a terrible price.

I decided to pay.

Beginning

We sat in the uncomfortable plastic chairs for hours. Sarah leafed listlessly through the months-old magazines, only letting go of my hand to turn her pages. In my other hand I clutched a cup of cold and horrible coffee. I stared at the abstract reproduction across the corridor and waited.

Sarah had looked a question when I had entered the ambulance ahead of her and reached out to her.

"I can't let him die alone," I had choked. She had looked into my tear-filled eyes and gotten in beside me. And for the next hours, she had held on to me without speaking.

When the double doors opened, I knew. I didn't need to see the surgeon's blood-spattered apron or his grim eyes.

He walked up to us and said the words I knew he would say.

"I'm so sorry. We did everything we could, but there was too much damage."

"No," I said over his question if we were relatives. "We're not. We were just . . . there." He nodded, looking unsure of himself.

"I'm sorry," he said again, and turned to go.

"Will he be buried?" I asked. The surgeon stopped and half turned back.

"Yes," he said. "If we don't find any relation, and we usually don't, he'll be buried by the state."

"Can we . . . be there?"

"Sure," he said, looking positively confused. I saw Sarah's surprise in my peripheral vision. "You can ask reception for the details, I expect. Now if you'll excuse me . . ." He hurried away down the hall and back through the double doors. I felt tears start and grasped for Sarah's hands. She hugged me and whispered, "What is it, Mark? Why is this so . . . Why?"

I hugged her fiercely, then pulled back and faced her. There were tears running from her eyes, too, but I knew those were more of empathy than for the dead tramp.

"I looked in his eyes, Sarah," I said, and I could hear the edge of despair in my voice. "He was half-mad, and lost, and so hopeless. But at the same time, it was . . . it was like he was me, like we were one person. And he was so terribly, completely alone!"

"Oh, Mark," she whispered, kissing me and pulling me to her. "You're not alone, sweetie. I'm with you. You're not alone."

> No technology-based artistic or cultural breakthrough has caused as much moral debate as Sculpting. Almost every major technological innovation has been embraced, usually within years, by the artistic community. Metallurgy gave us statues of bronze and steel; computer graphics brought us CGI; with antigravity came the Lazy Ballet. None of these had fundamental ethical questions attached. But when time travel gave us the art of Sculpting, it brought with it moral and ethical dilemmas that are controversial to this day.
>
> While many Sculptors recognized their responsibilities in the matter and worked toward a humane and ethical resolution, a group of radicals disregarded all moral debate, claiming in their defense that by any sane definition of harm and suffering, they inflicted none.
>
> On existing people, that is.

Introduction to *History of the Morality of Art*, 2243

SEVEN KEYS TO WRITING SUCCESS

by
Nina Kiriki Hoffman

Nina Kiriki Hoffman took third place in the first quarter of the Writers of the Future Contest in 1984. Since then, she has sold novels, juvenile and media tie-in books, and more than 200 short stories. Her works have been finalists for the Nebula, the World Fantasy, the Sturgeon and the Endeavour awards. Her novels include The Thread That Binds the Bones *and* The Silent Strength of Stones *from Avon,* A Red Heart of Memories, Past the Size of Dreaming, *and* A Fistful of Sky *from Ace, and* A Stir of Bones *from Viking. Her third short story collection,* Time Travelers, Ghosts, and Other Visitors, *was published by Five Star in 2003.* A Stir of Bones, *also 2003, made the American Library Association list of recommended books for the teen reader, and was selected by the New York Public Library as a best book for the teen reader.* Stir *was also a finalist for the Stoker Award.*

Nina's next YA novel, Spirits that Walk in Shadow, *will be published by Viking in 2006, and her next adult novel,* Fall of Light, *will be published by Ace in 2007.*

Nina works at a bookstore, does production work for a national magazine and teaches short story writing through her local community college. She lives in Eugene, Oregon, with several cats, a mannequin, and many strange toys.

In 1984, I got a letter notifying me about a new contest for beginning science fiction writers. Algis Budrys sent me the rules. My best friend Dean Wesley Smith and I wrote stories and sent them in to the first quarter of the L. Ron Hubbard Writers of the Future Contest; we both had stories in the first anthology. Since then, we've been encouraging colleagues, members of our workshops and eventually our students to send stories to the Contest.

In the late seventies and early eighties, Dean ran a used bookstore in Moscow, Idaho, and he hosted meetings there of the Palouse Empire Science Fiction Club every Thursday night. The club members were a loose collection of students and local professional people who loved to read, watch, and talk about anything related to science fiction and fantasy.

The meetings were conversational free-for-alls. Some of us planned to be writers, and we talked about that, until Dean and another friend, Steve Fahnestalk, started a writing workshop in 1982. Dean has always been great at getting big ideas and following through.

Initially, the workshop had a lot of members, and then four of us became determined to work hard and demand that others work hard. That scared away a bunch of people. For a while there were just four of us—Dean, Steve, me and Lori Ann White (*Writers of the Future* Volume III).

In those early sessions, we were blind leaders and blind followers. Some of us could spell better than others, and we all had opinions about what we liked, but we didn't know what worked and what didn't. We set out to find knowledge. Lori and I got good information from professionals at science fiction convention workshops. We knew we needed more.

Dean and I applied to a writers workshop in 1982. We were both accepted, and went together. That summer in Michigan, I learned a lot. I learned that wounds take longer to heal in a hot, humid climate; that fireflies are like fairy visitors from a parallel universe; and that drunk writers and students will howl like wolves during a lunar eclipse.

Through the teaching of Algis Budrys, Marta Randall, Samuel Delany, Orson Scott Card, Kate Wilhelm and Damon Knight, I learned a lot more—some of it conflicting. All of my teachers told me to keep writing. That summer was when I decided to make writing my career.

Dean and I brought everything we'd learned home to our workshop. We had learned how to pinpoint things that were wrong with a story.

We also stretched our writing practice. We challenged each other to write a story a week or buy the other person's dinner at the workshop, mail a story a week or buy the other person's soda pop. Weeks went by when neither of us had to pay the penalty. We sent out many stories and collected lots of rejection slips. Because we had each other for support, we didn't let this drag us down.

We set an übergoal for the whole workshop: when you sell your first story, the workshop treats you to a steak dinner. I still remember mine.

Early on, we found seven keys to success.

1. Find teachers who feed you.

Both of us started with our own views of how the world works, things we were passionate to write about, directions where we wanted to shine light.

Our teachers taught us clarity of language and how to refine our purpose and focus our writing. They taught us the nuts and bolts of preparing and mailing manuscripts. They taught us how to look at other people's manuscripts and how to bring that sharp eye home to our own work. They told us what a writing life is like. Some of those stories were depressing! Rejections, books abandoned after all the work had been done, the precariousness of life without a regular paycheck. Some of the stories were inspiring, too. Our teachers were inspiring: they were professional writers and they had come to share their knowledge with us.

2. Find friends who support your goals and help you achieve them.

People say writing is a solitary art. I don't agree. Since that first workshop, I've always had writing friends.

In our Moscow workshop, we had friends who were dedicated to working hard. We learned how to critique and encourage each other.

At science fiction conventions, we made more friends. If you've never been to a science fiction convention and you want to meet other writers, think about going. The field is wide open and welcoming.

Nowadays, you can find friends and critique partners online as well.

Dean and I used to take our spiral-bound notebooks to the twenty-four-hour coffee shop and write. These days, my friends and I take our laptops to the library and write across from each other. There's nothing like hearing somebody else's keystrokes to make you feel like working.

We also get together for lunch and conversation and movies. We talk about what we've read in magazines, what we heard at lectures. We go to conferences and conventions together. We meet every week at our workshop, where we not only critique stories, but also share news and do socializing afterward.

One great thing about the writing life is that everything is material . . . Everything is a learning opportunity.

3. Do the work.

Dean and I discussed work habits. We made up terms: there were marathon writers, who wrote at a steady pace over a long period of time, and sprinters—Dean and I seemed to fall into this category. We got a deadline, we fooled around awhile, then we rushed to finish right toward the end of the time allotted for a project.

One way or another, we wrote. We turned things in, got them critiqued, rewrote and sent the stories out.

Success didn't come overnight. It started slowly for both of us. I would make a sale, and Dean would make one a week later, or vice versa. For a while, it was spooky the way our sales piggybacked on each other. Then we moved to different cities and fell out of sync.

After a slow start, our sales increased. Dean has sold more than sixty novels (or maybe it's eighty or a hundred by now) and numbers of short stories. I haven't sold as many novels, but I have a lot of short story sales, too. We get more work because we've done so much work already.

4. Be open to learning.

Not every teacher is a great teacher, or the right teacher. Some teachers can be actively bad; they can tell you things that cripple you. You can learn from even a bad teacher, though, so long as you keep your inner self, the shining, creative part of you that comes bearing gifts, protected. Sometimes the lesson is: this person is on a path that won't take me where I want to go; this person is traveling by a means I don't want to use. Information like this helps you define the path you do want.

Teachers who feed you, on the other hand, can energize you, get you anxious to work, try, do new things. They offer challenges that invite you in. They turn your worldview upside down. You may find yourself looking from a new direction that reveals shadows where you saw light, and light in darkness. Sometimes the lessons are harsh. It can hurt to change and grow and stretch. Later on, as you settle into your new and enlarged self, you'll see how far you've come.

You don't need a teacher to learn. Every experience can give you treasure; every book you read or magazine you skim or TV show you watch. Every walk you take reminds you of how it feels to move your body and what weather is like. All that is material.

A hunger for learning helps writers enormously. In pursuit of background for stories, I've taken classes in herb lore, Italian, and old-time fiddle by ear. I've spent a day on a movie set watching makeup artists at work, gone to lectures on thinking errors and the criminal mind. For one story, I called the local office of the FBI and asked an agent what would really happen if someone called them up and reported finding an alien in the back yard.

People will tell you all sorts of fascinating things if you say you're working on a story and need to know.

I get excited about a wide array of things, some of them not immediately connected to any project I'm currently working on. For the past eight years, I've been fascinated by Japanese animation. I don't know how this will apply to writing, but I know everything that enriches my life adds to my literary skills.

A lot of writing strength comes from the specificity of detail. Learn everything you can.

The world is a banquet of learning opportunities, and your unique viewpoint can illuminate even a familiar subject in a new way.

5. Set goals, and pursue them.

Dean and I used all kinds of incentives to get ourselves to write. Some of them were financial—I'll have to buy a meal for my friend if I don't get this story written, or, if I write this story, I might earn a free meal. Sometimes we set goals to explore: we heard about a new market, and we both wrote stories for it and sent them off to see what would happen. Sometimes we just set wild goals to test our limits.

Dean's a great advocate of testing "speed limits"—common wisdom about how fast you should write, how much you should write, any "shoulds" he hears about; these are the things that you shackle yourself with, without even knowing they're in your head, slowing you down. If you give yourself permission to go faster than you think you can, you may be surprised at your own capabilities.

We had one stretch of five years where we challenged each other to write five stories in six days before the winter holidays and put them in a chapbook. Some years we wrote all five stories, and sometimes we came in with fewer; but writing that fast has been good for me, and for Dean, too. We did this challenge early in the nineties, and revisited it two years ago. Of the three stories I wrote for our most recent challenge, "Feasts" appeared in the July/August 2005 issue of *Cicada*, and another, "Treats," came out in the Summer 2005 issue of *Talebones*. The third is still in the mail, getting nice rejection slips.

In my current weekly workshop, the Wordos, we have many ways to encourage people to set and meet writing goals.

One reward system I started is that every time you get a rejection slip, you get a piece of candy. Rejection slips prove you are doing your job by writing stories and sending them out, so they should be celebrated.

You also win a handsome slice of agate every time you sell a story that you've put through the workshop and rewritten.

Most of the other rewards were engineered by Eric M. Witchey (*Writers of the Future* Volume XVII). Eric set standard goals for each quarter: turn in a number of stories to the workshop, and win an award—a small plastic figure with a science fictional slant on a wood base. The more stories you turned in, the more impressive your award, leading to the pinnacle, the Mad Marvin, for nine stories or more turned in during a single quarter. (Jay Lake, *Writers of the Future* Volume XIX, won so many Mad Marvins he took himself out of the running.)

Another goal Eric started is Personal Bests. Each person thinks about what he or she wants to accomplish in the quarter ahead, and writes down these goals, then sends them to the goalkeeper, who doesn't tell them to anyone, but keeps them in a notebook. These goals can be personal challenges in any way that will serve your writing career: I will write a thousand words a day. I will mail a story a week. I will finish my novel this quarter. I will tell my spouse I need writing time, and if he/she doesn't listen, I will tell my spouse again until he/she believes me. By putting the goals in writing, you have brought them into the world, closer to being realized. You can check them as often as necessary. By sending them to one other person, you've entered into a promise; you're not the only one who knows what you want.

At the end of the quarter, the goalkeeper asks everyone if they have accomplished their goals, and if they have, they win another award. One of the ideas behind Personal Best Goals is that each quarter, you set the goal higher. When you hit a quarter where you don't make your goal, you reset and start over.

For your first sale, you win a Lift-Off Award, which is etched glass and very handsome.

There are plaques on the wall of the bookstore where we meet commemorating first sales and awards won by workshoppers—lots of little brass plaques with names and titles of stories on them; many are still empty of information, waiting for the next person to achieve a dream.

One constant goal of everybody in the workshop is to win Writers of the Future.

We've had six years in a row where workshoppers placed stories in the anthology. This year's winner, Stephen Stanley, a graphic designer, came up with his own way of encouraging people to send in stories to the Contest: he gave everybody who submitted to the first quarter a cone, and each subsequent quarter they send a story in, they get another strange object that fits over the cone and creates artwork. People keep these mysterious and changing cones where you can see them when you first come in the door of their homes, a visual pat on the back for a job well done.

Outside reinforcement is wonderful, and gets people writing when they were really just going to watch TV. To succeed at writing, you have to practice internal goal-setting, too. You can give yourself rewards. I use anime: write five pages, get to watch a half hour of *Inu Yasha* or *Boys Over Flowers*. (So I write *and* watch TV! It all works out!) Find something you really enjoy to use as a reward and set a realistic goal, then go for it.

6. Find your own path.

My friend Kristine Kathryn Rusch writes twenty pages a day every weekday and a short story on Saturdays. She takes Sunday off, though I think there were some years where she didn't give herself a day off at all for months at a time.

I admire her discipline and her resulting career: she's published mysteries, romances, mainstream, science fiction, and fantasy, short stories and novels.

When I try to do what Kris does, I fail. I learned the hard way that I am not Kris; my pace is different, and my methods are different.

I've learned that I don't have to be just like any of my friends, and they don't have to be like me. We can encourage each other in lots of ways.

Some kinds of competition and comparison can be crippling rather than empowering. Walk away from the ones that make you feel bad.

You are your ultimate authority. Find the path that works for you. It may involve following footsteps of other people—I'm always fascinated to find out how my friends work—for a while, until you see that path doesn't work, or for a lifetime, if it turns out this is the path you want. Borrow from everybody and keep what works for you.

7. Share what you've learned.

In gratitude to all the teachers I've had, I teach what I know. So do a lot of my other friends who have established writing careers. I've been in the writing business more than twenty years; I'm still excited to spend time with people who are starting out.

Last week, Blake Hutchins told us at our workshop that he'd just taken first place in the second quarter of Writers of the Future for 2005.

I'm thrilled that he won. I hope I'm one of the people who gave him useful information.

He did the work himself; he didn't have to do it alone.

INTO THE BLANK WHERE LIFE IS HURLED

Written by
Ken Scholes

Illustrated by
Erik Valdez y Alanis

About the Author

Ken Scholes says he was hooked on speculative fiction ever since his first chapter book. By the age of twelve, he was reading Bradbury and others and penning his own fantasies. Yet Ken's most important class was typing, allowing him to make best use of an old portable typewriter his mother gave him. Ken took the typewriter and wrote everywhere. By high school, his English teacher took notice, made sure Ken heard visiting writers, and got him to authors' conferences.

But life had other plans. Soon after high school, Ken put his fiction on hold. His background includes two years in the military, a bachelor's degree in history, a stint in the clergy, and the past ten years managing nonprofits. Ken began writing again in 1997. Since 2000, his short fiction has appeared in several semi-pro markets and earned various honorable mentions. He credits other writers and his "muse"/wife, Jen, for keeping him typing (on a PC now) and submitting his work. The couple live in Oregon with five guitars, two cats and three mountains of books (ninety boxes full and counting).

About the Illustrator

Erik Valdez y Alanis, born in Mexico City, seems to have taken the influences of this vast city to heart in pursuit of his own artistic expression. A product of Mexico's finest art school, ENPEG (the National School of Painting, Sculpture and Engraving) La Esmeralda, located in the National Center for the Arts, Erik has worked in several fields as a freelance artist. He's created character studies, set designs and storyboards for movies, painted commercial portraits and exhibited his own works at several shows locally. In addition to his art schooling, Erik continues to pursue English studies which he began at a local American school and where his first artistic expressions were encouraged. His inclusion in these pages represents his first cash-prize award for his artwork. And he believes that the Illustrators of the Future Contest will offer the kind of extra exposure he needs to establish his work.

A sudden, sharp increase in the room's temperature signaled the Fallen's arrival, and William scrambled to the floor to prostrate himself. He averted his eyes, hearing the door open, and waited as the sweat trickled down his sides. Soft footfalls passed his desk and he risked a glance up. The Fallen arrogantly strode through the office, the stubs on its back twitching as if with memories of flight. William held his breath as it opened Fisk's door and slipped inside. Then, he waited to a count of twenty and returned to his desk.

The uncrowded newsroom remained silent though a hundred questions begged for asking. *The Fallen . . . here? Why? Did you see its eyes? No . . . never, never the eyes.* The temperature dropped a hair and William went back to the paper he'd been doodling.

He'd intended it to be a poem. The words rarely came to him but when they did, his fingers looked for release to no avail. In this place, pencil leads broke, words ran together, ink faded and all lines of literary endeavor bled into a meaningless puddle of bits and blotches. The only stories he wrote now . . . the only stories he was *allowed* to write . . . were the meaningless drivel the *Gazette* required of him.

Long ago, before the war that brought him here, he remembered a blossoming career as a novelist. Tales of the fantastic and supernatural. Now, words haunted him like unrequited love.

For five minutes longer, he fiddled with the paper. The temperature shot up as Fisk's door opened again and William joined the others on the floor. The Fallen rarely traveled to this ring and to his knowledge, they'd never visited this building before today. This was the second he'd ever encountered.

He waited, listening to the footfalls, heard them stop at his desk, and forced his eyes open to confront the bare feet before him. The Fallen hissed, then continued on its way. As it left the building, the scattered collection of reporters and support staff released held breath and the temperature returned to normal.

"Hodgson . . . my office. Now."

William climbed slowly to his feet and let them carry him toward Vernon Fisk's voice. The others looked at him, faces still pale.

"Be a good chap and close the door," Fisk said from behind his desk, waving half of a cigar at an empty chair. William pulled it shut and sat down. "Still taking stabs at your passion, eh?"

Surprised, William realized that he still held the pencil and scrap of paper tightly in his fist. "I'm sorry, sir."

"No need, no need." Fisk leaned forward. He was a fat man, his face pocked and perpetually slick with sweat. "I was a brewer you know. Brewed great beers. Even won an award. Of course, down here it comes to nothing. I tried for years before giving up."

William nodded.

"Well, enough of the past. On to the future." He nodded toward the door. "You're probably wondering what that was about. Special assignment . . . from the top, or from the bottom if you prefer." He snorted at his own joke. "Story of the century for us, it is."

The *Gazette* printed little that was news. During

his time with the paper, William had interviewed new arrivals, promoted local gossip and churned out propaganda on demand.

"Sir?"

Fisk stubbed out his cigar. "Story of the century. Somewhat of a celebrity I'm told, too. I guess you know him; he was after my time."

"Who, sir?"

"Why . . . Harry Houdini, that's who. Just arrived and already at it."

William's mind lurched him back to the turn of the century in a different life. A Blackburn stage, an angry mob, an arrogant showman and the equally arrogant young man William had once been. He could still hear the clinking of the shackles.

"Smug bastard," William said in a low voice. "I'm not surprised."

Fisk looked up. "Yes, *it* said you'd met before. I trust it wasn't a favorable encounter?"

"I was young. He made a challenge; I took him up on it. Went over two hours, he did, but in the end he got out of it." William chuckled. "Of course, I didn't see it. Afraid of the mob. I fled the scene and hid out."

"Well, you've got the story. *They* insisted."

"An interview then, sir?" Dread crept into him . . . This was the last person he wanted to sit down with, even for half an hour in one of Hell's more tolerable rings.

Fisk belly laughed. "More than that, Hodgson. It seems Mr. Houdini has announced his run for the Ear. You're to accompany him, chronicle the journey, and return with the story." Fisk paused. "Well, no guarantees on returning. It is the Ear, of course."

William knew little about the Ear. Somewhere on some abandoned edge, it supposedly stood alone.

Illustrated by Erik Valdez y Alanis

Whispered legends traveled the rumor circuit: few had seen it, few had spoken into its cool, crystal surface. Some believed Michelangelo had carved it on some great Assignment of Grace from Above, guarded by angels as he worked tirelessly. William believed it was most likely bunk.

"But sir, I'm not sure I'm the best—"

Fisk interrupted. "You're not the best. But They want you. And who am I to deny Them?"

William swallowed. "He'll take one look at me and that'll be that, with all due respect."

"How long's it been since you met him?"

Time was hard to count here. He did the best math he could. "Over twenty years."

Fisk grunted. "I'll book you passage on the *Titanic*. You'll leave at dawn for Hellsmouth. Two weeks . . . Enough time for you to grow out that beard of yours, I should think. I don't think he'll know you, Hodgson."

William stood. A heaviness fell over him. Two ghosts rattling their chains from his past. Houdini and the sea. It couldn't get much worse.

• • •

William reslung his sea bag at the tavern door. He'd waited a full five minutes, his brain racing ahead to scout out the possibilities. Would Houdini recognize him? During his two weeks on the black oily sea his beard had itched its way to fullness, but would that be enough? And if he were recognized, what did it really matter? The night he had bound the swaggering showman was long buried in the past. But William had not forgotten; he doubted Houdini had either.

Opening the door, he pushed his way inside. The

tavern was crowded with a scattering of damned souls that drank in small groups talking in low voices.

Houdini was not hard to spot; all new arrivals carried an otherworldly quality and Houdini transcended even that. He seemed the only unbroken man in the room, sitting alone at a table in the back corner. He looked up, his face an inverted triangle beneath tangled hair. He'd aged from the young stage-hound he'd once been but his eyes still held their brightness. He smiled as William approached.

"You're the reporter then?" Houdini extended his hand.

The grip was strong and William returned it. "Yes. Bill Hopewell, *Graytown Gazette*."

"Englishman?"

William nodded and sat. Houdini waved to the bartender, a misshapen, one-eyed dwarf in a stained apron. The dwarf dried off his hands with a towel and moved sluggishly toward them.

"I spent a great deal of time in England," Houdini said. "Great country, great people."

"Thank you, Mr. Houdini."

The bartender reached their table, his one eye soaking in his newest customer. "What'll it be, gov?"

William nodded toward Houdini's empty glass. "The same."

Houdini chuckled. "Water then, Bulsby." He leaned in toward William as the dwarf moved away. "And call me Ehrich, William. Houdini was a stage name and there is no stage here."

They sat in silence, the low voices from other tables providing a static buzz. The dwarf returned with two glasses of slightly brown water and Houdini laid a small carved stick on the table. Most used coins here but some few elite carried the badge of a Fallen patron. Curiosity and dread danced slowly behind William's eyes. A patron. For Houdini.

The dwarf nodded. "On the house of course."

"Good man," Houdini said. He put the stick in his pocket. "These come in handy."

William pulled a travel-stained notebook and pencil from his jacket pocket and placed them before him on the table. He sipped the tepid water, grimacing as the slight taste of sulfur hit his tongue. "May I ask you some questions, Mr. Houdini?"

Houdini looked up. "Please. And again, call me Ehrich."

William forced a weak smile. "Very well. Ehrich." He paused. This was always the uncomfortable bit, the question he never wanted to ask. To him, it implied rudeness and a lack of compassion. Still, he had to ask; the inquiring minds clamored to know. "What brings you to Hell?"

Houdini barked a short laugh. "Direct, aren't you, Bill?" He folded his hands and his eyes shone in the dimly lit tavern. "A burst appendix and an inflated ego." William scribbled this down. "How about you, Bill?"

The question caught him off guard. No one asked, at least not in polite company. He felt an embarrassed flush rise to his face like an unexpected house guest six o'clock of a Sunday morning. He cleared his voice, eyes focused on the paper before him. "The war. Artillery shell, I think."

"The Great War?"

"There are no great wars." Suddenly his ears were full with the crash of rifles and the screams of dying men. His nose was filled with the stink of blood and smoke. He ventured a glance at Houdini. Sympathy etched the older man's features.

"Sorry, Bill. You're absolutely correct." Houdini grinned a weak grin. "If it helps at all, we won, you know."

"I know. It doesn't." He paused, took another drink. "You were a showman before." It was a statement, not a question.

"Of sorts. A magician. An escape artist. A debunker of phonies. But that's not important anymore."

"And you intend to run for the Ear?"

"Yes. You and I, Bill." The light came alive in Houdini's eyes. His face shone. "Know anything about the Ear?"

"Michelangelo. Assignment of Grace. Those who speak into it, speak to . . . well, speak to . . . it's bunk. Rubbish."

Houdini nodded slowly. "Perhaps. But it is out there, waiting, at the edge of Hell itself. And I intend to say my bit into it."

William forgot his note taking and looked up. "Why in hell would you do such a thing? Have you any idea what lives in those wastelands? Have you—"

Houdini interrupted him with a wave of his hand. "I made a promise, Bill. I will keep that promise."

"You . . . *we* . . . may never reach it. And if we do, it may be for nothing. And, regardless, we may never return to tell anyone." He felt fear now and agitation, hungry hands grabbing at him.

"It doesn't matter if I return." Houdini's eyes hardened. "It only matters that I go." He raised his glass to his mouth and gulped. He stood, somehow towering larger than life despite his lack of height. "There will be much time for questions on the way. We leave at dawn."

Deliberate in his step, Houdini strode from the room. And William sat for a long time after he left.

•••

It took nearly a week to reach the Wasteland's edge. The film crew waited for them there, a scattering of tents, two large trucks and a bullet-riddled biplane. Over the days and nights of walking, William had found an unexpected depth in his traveling companion along with answers to the questions. At night, in his tent, he scribbled his notes by candlelight, shaping a story that came so close to fiction that his spelling faltered and his pencils broke. Still, he pressed on, filling half of his notebook.

Surprisingly, he'd found similarities between them and that identification led to the beginnings of admiration. He himself had been the son of an Anglican priest; Houdini was the son of a rabbi. Both had committed themselves to a life of physical exercise. Both had written strange tales of fancy. At first, it had unsettled him, recalling that night long ago and the contempt they'd had for one another. But with time, that bled away.

Now, they stood on a rise, the film crew camped immediately below and the Wasteland stretching out toward a line of broken-toothed mountains. William raised a questioning eyebrow at Houdini's smile. "What's this about, Ehrich?"

Houdini chuckled. "I arranged it with His Lordship. It was really more of a suggestion but the old bugger jumped on it. Did you know that in all of Hell there are but three airplanes?"

William was not surprised. He hadn't seen one since the war.

"I thought it would do nicely to capture the moment for posterity's sake."

A man in khaki saw them, barked orders, and waved. He walked quickly up the hill toward them, out of breath as he arrived.

"Ah," he said. "There you are." He ignored William, shoving his hand into Houdini's and pumping it furiously. "Albert Maxwell the third."

"Ehrich Weiss. And William Hopewell of the *Gazette*."

The director glanced at William briefly, then shifted his attention back to his star. "No need for modesty. You are Harry Houdini."

Houdini shrugged. "Are you ready?"

"Yes. We've all the necessary precautions. We'll follow behind in the trucks, out of the way of course. We'll use the plane to hop ahead, shoot the scenes, and back to camp before nightfall."

"Precautions?" William knew a little about the Wasteland. The nights there belonged to the Shriekers and Howlers . . . the days belonged to the Abandoned.

"I'll show you." Maxwell turned and started down the hill. Shouldering their packs, the two travelers followed.

A mixed crew awaited. Several Hindis, a few Arabs and a scattering of Irish-looking scrawny men. Maxwell was American. The men looked up as they approached, then went back to their work. They were disassembling a vast array of vacuum tubes and unhooking wires from a gas generator.

Shock grabbed William as his memories played out the past. An electric pentacle, he realized. Something his imagination had cooked up for stories he'd written long ago. "Where did you get this?"

Maxwell shrugged. "It was provided. Along with these." He uncovered a tarp on one of the trucks, then pried open a long wooden crate. It contained a dozen

Enfield rifles. He opened another box and dug out a handful of shells. "Blessed by some damned priest in Graytown." He lowered his voice. "Doesn't mean much, but it should be enough to stop a Howler."

He saw the look that must have been on William's face. Houdini saw it too. "Not for us, Bill. Part of the contract, I'm afraid." He offered a reassuring, sympathetic smile. "We'll be fine without them. Trust me."

They spent the remainder of the day in camp, Houdini and Maxwell off to the side excitedly discussing logistics and filming techniques. They pitched their one-man tents on the edge of the Wasteland, struggling to sleep as the night desert came alive with unbearable noise.

In the morning, after a brief session in front of the camera, they set out alone.

•••

True to his word, Maxwell and the cameraman flew ahead in the two-seater, landing, shooting film, leaving, returning and departing again as the sky grayed toward night. William lost track of how many trips were made, and gradually lost track of how many days had passed in this dead, shattered place. Somewhere behind, the caravan crawled slowly along. Some nights, he could see it glowing miles back.

Twilights, as they stopped to make camp, Houdini always drew away, mouth working silently as he etched signs and symbols into the hard-packed ground. William avoided asking where he'd learned the protective ward-making. The first night, he'd lain awake terrified as the screaming pummeled his ears and shook the tent. But the wards had held each night and the days had passed without incident or encounter.

Eventually, the mountains loomed above them, casting long shadows that overtook them as they trudged along. They could just make out the smallest speck of a gated cave when they encountered their first Abandoned. Only they didn't know it at first.

A speck became a figure became a child, sitting alone with its head in its hands. The little boy looked up as they approached. His eyes were red from crying. He wore a tattered overcoat and knickers.

"Papa?"

Houdini took a step forward; William caught his arm. "Careful, Ehrich."

He shot William an angry glance. "It's a child, Bill." Houdini moved closer and knelt before the boy.

William felt danger but didn't know what to do with it. "It can't be. No child could survive out here alone." He swallowed, tasting the dust. "It's bait. Or worse."

Houdini ignored him and stretched a hand out to the boy. "What's your name? What are you doing here?"

The child's lip trembled. "I'm . . . lost." William saw something, a darkly intelligent light, behind the child's eyes. "My name is Mayer Weiss."

William saw Houdini flinch and then tense. "Mayer?"

The child began to change. Its mouth stretched and elongated, jagged teeth filling a gaping hole. The eyes became black and it lunged forward with a deep growl. It tackled Houdini, its claws grappling for a hold.

William couldn't move. He willed himself to act but his rebellious legs held fast. Houdini rolled in the sand, yelling, pushing and kicking at the creature.

Even in the burning Wasteland, he felt the temperature shift upwards. There was a dark flash and suddenly Ehrich lay still and alone. The creature had flown thirty feet to land heavily in the sand. Another flash and it began to shriek. Flash after flash, the Abandoned was torn apart and strewn onto the desert floor.

Fascinated, William forgot to prostrate himself. When it had finished, the Fallen glared at them, hissed disgust, and vanished.

William went to Houdini and offered him a hand up. "Are you okay?"

Houdini nodded, shaken, staring at the pieces of meat. "I wondered. . . ." The words drifted off. He brushed off his clothes. "I *thought* it had been too easy."

William watched him without a word. A knot of dread grew in his stomach.

"They're protecting us," Houdini muttered. "As if They want us to succeed."

Yes, William thought. And he knew that no good could come of it.

•••

The carved words above the gate were Latin.

"Broken dreams, eh?" Houdini said, smiling. "It's not far now, Bill. Not far at all." He pointed to the dark opening. "Just beyond the caves." He turned and smiled to the camera, giving a thumbs-up sign.

Maxwell nodded excitedly. "We'll see you on the other side, boys." He'd briefed them that morning. The caravan would stop here and they would make several trips flying gear over the mountains to set up a small camp. There would even be champagne.

Houdini handed Bill an electric torch. He clicked it on and its tongue of light probed the cave. The hair on his neck stood up. With a firm clap on the back, his companion brushed past and into the cave. William followed.

The difference in temperature was uncanny. Outside, the desert baked. Inside, coolness prevailed. The cavern stretched deep into the mountain, straight and wide enough for three to go abreast. They walked side by side, Houdini whistling a circus tune as they went.

Behind them, the iris of light gradually closed as they made their way.

"No broken dreams as yet," Houdini said.

William shrugged. He thought back to the relative ease of the Wasteland crossing and the Fallen's intervention. "Maybe They've come ahead of us."

"Maybe." Houdini paused. "Did you hear that?"

William stopped as well and leaned forward. "No."

An hour later, the straight, broad cavern spilled into a massive room. Easily two-dozen openings marked the opposite wall. Houdini rubbed his chin. "I *thought* it was too easy."

A drowsy fog settled onto William.

Then Houdini's eyes went wide. "Papa?" He moved toward one of the openings.

William caught his arm. "Ehrich?"

Panic laced Houdini's voice. "Surely you heard that?"

He shook his head. He'd heard nothing. At first.

Then he heard the crying from another opening at the far end of the room. He turned toward it, the voice familiar. He opened and closed his mouth, then turned back to where Houdini had stood. Houdini was already disappearing into the opening, following a voice that William could not hear.

"Oh, William, why?" the distant voice said between sobs. He turned away from his companion.

"Mother?" He broke into a trot.

"Oh, William."

He ran blindly, the light bouncing over the narrowing walls as he followed the twisting and turning passageway. After what felt like hours, he stumbled into a small chamber. His mother knelt in the center, hands folded imploringly, clutching a crumpled letter.

"Oh, my boy. My precious boy."

"Mother?" He stopped and crouched beside her, reaching for her. "I'm here." Somewhere in the back of his mind a nagging tickle tried to tell him that this could not be his mother. But he could see her, hear her voice, smell the lavender soap from her skin.

She looked up at him. "You can't be here. You're dead."

As he reached for her, she pulled away. "Mother, I'm here."

She thrust the letter under his nose. "No. Dead. It's all right here. You couldn't leave well enough alone, could you?" She sneered and then spat at him, the warm, dry phlegm splattering his cheek.

Frustration tightened his throat in preparation for tears. "No, Mother. I'm . . ." Another voice, further away, called to him and something outside of himself forced him to his feet.

"My Lord," the voice said, "why have you forsaken me?"

"Father?"

"He's dead too," the old woman spat. "Dead and in Hell, God damn him."

As he raced from the chamber, she cackled wordlessly after him.

He found his father in another room, trying to drink dust from a hollow in the floor. "Son? Is that you?"

"Father, what are you doing here?"

The old man looked up. His clergy collar hung open at the neck of his ripped black shirt. "You could've saved me."

William moved closer but another voice caught him. The frustration became despair and the despair vented itself in his cry. "No."

The voice was that of his wife. Then another joined it. And another. Until it seemed that a multitude surrounded him. The voices coalesced into a litany of his misdeeds and good intentions gone wrong, every dream or hope another had attached to him, every disappointed expectation. He fell onto his side and clutched his head.

One more voice joined the choir. A voice like nails on slate. "Enough."

He sucked in hot air and fought to control his breathing. He could not force his eyes open.

The voice spoke again. "You are the one called Hodgson."

The heat became unbearable. A rough hand grabbed at his arm and tore it away from his face.

"You will speak."

William finally looked. The Fallen stood over him glaring down, its black eyes burning into him. "Y-Yes," he whispered. "I am Hodgson."

The creature nodded. "Your time is nearly come. On the third day you will bind the one called Houdini. Is the meaning of this clear?"

William sat up, cowering. Memories of that stage long ago leapt back to him. The Fallen anticipated his question.

"This binding will hold. This is what Hell has chosen for him."

He swallowed. He wanted to say no, wanted to strike back, to cry out to some god for deliverance and bring down this demon. He swallowed again, trembling with fear.

The Fallen dropped a small black box. It landed with a thud and the creature turned its back. "When you have bound him, this will be yours."

William took the box and fumbled it open. The pen inside was blindingly beautiful, even in the dim cave. It shone with a sharp clarity like nothing he'd ever seen in this place and he knew in a moment that it was not *of* this place. He stroked it, feeling its power, and knew that with this pen his curse would be lifted. With this pen, Hell could become Heaven for him.

"Close the box. I can not bear the blasphemy it contains."

He closed it and the Fallen turned, scooping it up.

"Is the meaning of this clear?"

William licked his lips and nodded. He closed his eyes. When he opened them again he sat alone and the caves were silent but for Houdini's sobs somewhere far ahead.

•••

They saw the camp first, three tents pitched near the biplane. Two figures worked at connecting the electric pentacle. Twilight was not far off.

William had found Houdini and dragged him from the caves two days before. Neither man spoke of what they had encountered, but Houdini showed it in his eyes. They had been bright and dauntless before. Now, loss swam in them from time to time. Silence settled between the two more frequently as they neared the end of their journey.

Now with the camp in sight, Houdini grinned. They stopped, catching their breath. "There it is, Bill. By God, there it is." He pointed.

The desert became scrub and then transformed into a patch of bright green. Centered in the lawn, a large object sparkled and threw back light.

The horizon stood close here at the edge of the ring. Behind them, the mountains crawled upward. Ahead of them, the Wasteland evaporated into a sheet of blank gray just past the Ear. This, William knew, was the edge of Hell itself.

He couldn't share Houdini's joy. Tomorrow would be the third day and since the caves, he'd realized exactly why their journey had been so easy.

They entered the camp and the small crew applauded as the camera rolled on. Maxwell broke out a case of champagne and they drank it warm from the bottles.

Houdini raised his bottle in the direction of the lawn and its large crystalline Ear. The light had already gone but they'd seen it, massive and shining, set into the ground and leaning slightly so that one could climb into it and whisper homeward. "Tomorrow at first light," he said loudly.

Always the showman, William thought. Somehow it made him feel better about what he must do.

•••

He slept fitfully, awakening again and again in the tent. At dawn, he climbed into his clothes to meet Houdini and the camera crew outside. The filming commenced without a word and Houdini turned toward the grassy plain. The Ear, perhaps thirty feet in diameter, caught pink light and winked at them from the center of the plain.

It's beautiful, William thought. He believed the stories now. The sight of it easily persuaded him.

Houdini started toward the grass, then stopped. A large stake had been driven into the desert floor. Near it, the Fallen stood grinning. Houdini took a step back and in a flash, the Fallen had gripped his arms, holding him tightly.

"Bind him, Hodgson." Its voice was a hiss.

Houdini struggled, then recognized the name. "Hodgson?" He twisted, his face going red with fury and effort. His eyes locked on William's and went cold. *"You."*

Someone shoved chains into his hands and the Fallen dragged Houdini to the stake. William began binding him just as he had done on that Blackburn stage so many years before. Houdini spat and bit, writhing and kicking.

"I should've known. Hodgson, you bastard."

William said nothing and did his best to avoid the showman's eyes. The accusations they shouted were louder than Houdini's words. In ten minutes, the strong man was bound, facing the grass and the Ear. Maxwell grinned, the crew laughed and pointed. The camera rolled on.

Houdini howled.

The Fallen dropped the box at William's feet. He picked it up, turned his back on them all, and returned to the tent.

He wrote all day and into the night, nearly oblivious to Houdini's cries. Gradually, the cursing had become pleading. At one point, William could have sworn he'd invoked the faith of both their fathers, but then the pen grabbed him and dragged him back into his passion.

The stories and poems unfolded like magic onto the page, flowing out in ways they never had during his life. He wrote until the cramping of his hand forced him to stop, and then, he read what he had written.

The stories and poems weaved a tapestry that blended into one monumental message that Hell could not contain, and William's heart could not contain it either. He broke into tears and threw the pen away from him. He grabbed up the strewn papers from his notebook in fistfuls and shredded them.

He stood, grabbed up the pen, and strode into the early morning. He could feel determination and rage hardening his face and stiffening his limbs as he walked toward the Ear.

Houdini hung limply by his chains. He raised his head weakly. "It's okay, Bill."

William ignored him. The Fallen stood nearby. Clutching the pen, William approached. "I've changed my mind," William said.

It hissed. "Take that obscenity from my sight," it said, waving the pen away, eyes squinting to avoid the golden glare of light from its surface.

Without a word, William sprung forward, bringing the pen up and plunging it into the Fallen's white chest. It shrieked as the sliver of Heaven slid into its skin and black filth plumed out like a swarm of gnats. The Fallen clutched at it and William kept his grip as he came down on top of the demon.

Behind him, Houdini's voice took on new life. "The grass, Bill, by God in Heaven, the grass!"

William's body translated the words before his mind could. Hand firmly on the pen, driving it deeper, arms locked around the Fallen, he scrambled with his feet to drag the creature onto the lawn. It screamed and bucked against him, then melted into dust. William lay still, panting, feeling the cool of the grass enfold him.

He sat up. Maxwell and his crew stood in silence. Standing, he picked up the golden pen.

"I could use that," Houdini said with a tired grin.

He took it to him and crouched beside him while the escape artist did his trick. He watched as Ehrich took the pen apart by touch, stripping it down to its basic parts before selecting the piece best suited for picking the locks that held him.

The film crew continued shooting.

When Houdini finished, he stood, rubbing his wrists. He winked at William. "I'm glad you figured it out, Bill."

William nodded. "It was never about the Ear."

"No."

Maxwell stepped forward. His face looked pale. Before he could speak, Houdini pounced and spun him into a human shield. "The rifles?" he asked.

• • •

At last they approached the Ear. Now armed, William and Ehrich cautiously watched the lone cameraman that followed. They had tied the others up.

"It's too big of news to not film it," Houdini had said, giving in to Maxwell's pleas despite William's misgivings.

The Ear stood before them now and Houdini leaned his rifle against its base. Then, he leapt into the air and caught the rim, pulling himself up and onto the crystalline lobe. He climbed a bit, then looked down. "I think this is it," he said. His voice carried perfectly.

William put his attention back on the cameraman while Houdini spoke slowly above him.

"The message I want to send back to my wife is . . ." Houdini paused, then spoke clearly and firmly: "Rosabelle. Answer. Tell. Pray. Answer. Look. Tell. Answer. Answer. Tell."

He climbed down. The tears ran freely down his face. "You're sure you have nothing to say?"

William nodded. "I'm sure."

They left the cameraman untied and climbed into the waiting plane.

"Now for my last escape." Houdini released the brake and sent them bouncing toward the expanse of gray ahead. William heard Maxwell shouting for the single man standing to keep shooting and then the voice was lost in the roar of the engine.

They lifted into the air and were swallowed by nothingness.

They flew in silence, flew on for hours long after the fuel became vapor. A random line of verse from his past floated to the surface of William's mind. *Into the blank where life is hurled*. He didn't realize he'd said it aloud until Houdini asked.

"Something I wrote a long time ago," he shouted.

Now the engine coughed and sputtered. Now the plane shuddered and bucked in the wind. Now the gray around them took on tinges of blue. Now a green cliff soared ahead of them and two waiting figures waved. A rabbi and a priest, he knew, watching their prodigal sons come Home.

Houdini laughed. William laughed with him.

MARS HATH NO FURY LIKE A PIXEL DOUBLE-CROSSED

Written by
Stephen R. Stanley

Illustrated by
Alex Paramonov

About the Author

Stephen Stanley began his relationship with science fiction as a teenage contributor to comics and fanzines in the late 1960s. But his talent for art and graphic design led him away from writing for nearly twenty-five years. He earned a bachelor of fine arts degree at the Kansas City Art Institute and spent twenty years as an annual report designer in San Francisco.

In 1993, after giving up big-city California life for Eugene, Oregon, Stephen once again resumed writing and was invited to join Wordos, Eugene's professional writers' group. In 2001, he began submitting to both the Writers and Illustrators of the Future Contests and was surprised when he was first named a fiction finalist in 2002. That surprise has turned to reward in this edition using the same characters from his previous story. While Stephen still designs magazines, brochures and books to pay bills, he continues to write in the nooks and crannies of time that his life allows. It's a life he shares in a lush, garden cottage with his "mermaid" companion of ten years and two adult children. He devotedly continues to enter the Illustrators' Contest.

About the Illustrator

What continues to inspire Ukrainian artist and architect Alex Paramonov is the rich scent of oil paints and the light that seems to glow inside the paintings of Rembrandt. Art and drawing have always been a part of Alex's life. Drawing was always something he did. But he could not be a full-time artist right away.

A professional architect by training, Alex first exhibited his illustration artwork at Kiev's National Theatre of Light Opera in 2003. It was after this first exhibit that Alex started to devote his spare time to painting. He would work as a commercial architect by day and draw at night. Last year, after a second showing of his artwork at a private Kiev commercial gallery and completion of a major hotel's interior design in Kiev, Alex decided to become a full-time illustrator. He recently participated with other artists in a series of exhibitions sponsored by the Ukrainian Fund of Culture Exhibitions. Alex's 2004 entry in this edition marks his first published illustration work.

I threw Jimmy's new readercomp at the holographic brand on his forehead, aiming a bit to the left because I knew he'd dodge to that side. It glanced off his thick skull above his ear, shattered against the compartment's hard plastic shell, and for a moment hung suspended in the Martian gravity like a false halo.

"Pix, honey, that was expensive," Jimmy said as he rubbed his temple. "It cost me two thousand credits."

His indifference to my anger just tixxed me more.

"MY credits, Hotshot." I looked around for more of my now-ex-boyfriend's brand-spanking-new stuff to throw. I picked up a tray of Masterson Corporate Guideline cybercubes and hurled them one at a time. I was used to the Mars g. He couldn't hide in the cramped compartment. In spite of his attempts to duck and block, I hit him all six times. "This was supposed to be a romantic trip to Mars, but I've spent most of it alone or in the bar with Maybelle. Now I find out you cashed in MY return ticket back home to the space station. To get branded. Branded!"

I screamed. After being cooped up for two days, waiting for him to return from his mysterious "appointment," suspecting the whole time that he'd gotten branded, screaming felt wonderful.

Constipated neighbors whose compartments adjoined Jimmy's new digs banged on the walls. I yelled something nasty about putting their noses up their own darksides.

"You didn't even ask, you just took it. I'm a free woman, Hotshot, you had no right to take my stuff." I stalked back and forth in the confined space. "I hate this rock and I hate this colony. I need to get back in orbit—but you knew that."

I realized that after almost a year together, I didn't really know him.

"I can't believe you fell for the old corporate-job-for-life crap and dragged me into it," I said, thanking the stars I'd listened to my intuition and had never taken him to my private space on the station.

Once brandeds were approved to have kids their corporations paid credits to have the kids branded. In return, the kids were educated and, when grown, assigned jobs. Space-station trash like Jimmy Hotshot had to buy into a brand.

"Did you plan this before we left Anaconda Station? To get branded to Masterson Corp down here?" His silence gave me an answer I didn't like. He had begged me for months to take a planetside trip with him. What spaceborn scavbrat hasn't wondered what it's like to walk on Mars or Earth or any planet? It took all the black-market tender I could finagle, added to what my mom had left me, to buy a round-trip ticket. "Did you want my ticket refund all along?"

"Come on, honeygirl, calm down."

Hearing his nickname for me fired my blood. I secretly despised it. I grabbed his old belt buckle out of the trash box where he had tossed it while showing off his new uniform.

"Calm down? You've exposed me! Now they know who I am. How dare you do this to me?"

"I never told them anything about you."

"Don't be a mope. They wanted to know everything about me, didn't they?"

Silence again. My anger came out as a snarl.

"What did you tell them, Jimmy? You better hope to whatever god you believe in that you kept me out of this."

"My life on the station is a black hole, Pix. I did this for you, for us, so we'd have a future." He tried to look sincere, but with that fresh brand on his forehead he just looked like a sap.

I faked throwing his buckle just to watch him wince.

"For ME? When have you EVER heard me say I wanted a branded boyfriend? Station to Hotshot: I will NEVER live in a crappy plastic box like this one. It smells like toilet disinfectant in here."

"I can sponsor you now, Pix. We can get a bigger place."

"You don't get it, do you, Jimmy? I'll never get branded. They killed my mom!"

"It wasn't Masterson . . ."

"That makes no difference to me." I faked throwing the buckle again.

He tensed as if to jump me. I returned a look that told him to think twice. Although he outweighed me by fifty pounds, and at six feet he was three inches taller, he backed down because he knew I fought dirty when cornered. I pointed at him.

"I want my ticket back. I'm going home. Print out the credits you stole from me."

"Pix, honeygirl, you know I can't print tender. Be a little reasonable, Pix. My account is negative and it only works at company stores until after my probation. I'm—*We* are living on Masterson advances until I

Illustrated by Alex Paramonov

FREE

Send in this card and with any order you will receive a FREE POSTER while supplies last. No order required for this special offer! Mail in your card today!
- ❑ Please send me a FREE poster!
- ❑ Please send me information about other books by L. Ron Hubbard.

ORDERS SHIPPED WITHIN 24 HRS OF RECEIPT

___ *L. Ron Hubbard Presents Writers of the Future*® volumes: (paperbacks)

❑ vol I $7.99	❑ vol II $7.99	❑ vol III $7.99
❑ vol IV $7.99	❑ vol V $7.99	❑ vol VI $7.99
❑ vol VII $7.99	❑ vol VIII $7.99	❑ vol IX $7.99
❑ vol X $7.99	❑ vol XI $7.99	❑ vol XII $7.99
❑ vol XIII $7.99	❑ vol XIV $7.99	❑ vol XV $7.99
❑ vol XVI $7.99	❑ vol XVII $7.99	❑ vol XVIII $7.99
❑ vol XIX $7.99	❑ vol XX $7.99	

___ *Master Storyteller: An Illustrated Tour of the Fiction of L. Ron Hubbard* hardcover coffee-table book $49.95

OTHER BOOKS BY L. RON HUBBARD
___ *The Kingslayer* audio CD $25.00
___ *The Ultimate Adventure* hardcover $22.95 ___ audio CD $25.00
___ *To the Stars* hardcover $24.95 ___ audio CD $25.00

Mission Earth® series (10 volumes paperback) $7.99 each
___ vol 1 *The Invaders Plan* ___ vol 6 *Death Quest*
___ vol 2 *Black Genesis* ___ vol 7 *Voyage of Vengeance*
___ vol 3 *The Enemy Within* ___ vol 8 *Disaster*
___ vol 4 *An Alien Affair* ___ vol 9 *Villainy Victorious*
___ vol 5 *Fortune of Fear* ___ vol 10 *The Doomed Planet*

___ All ten volumes paperback $79.90
___ *Mission Earth* hardcover $22.95 each
___ *Mission Earth* audio CD $25.00 each
specify volumes:_____

___ *Battlefield Earth*® paperback $7.99 ___ audio CD $29.95
___ *Fear* paperback $7.99 ___ audio CD $25.00
___ *Final Blackout* paperback $6.99 ___ audio CD $25.00

SHIPPING RATES US: $2.00 for one book. Add an additional $.50 per book when ordering more than one.
SHIPPING RATES CANADA: $3.50 for one book. Add an additional $1.00 per book when ordering more than one.

TAX*: _____
SHIPPING: _____
TOTAL: _____

CHECK AS APPLICABLE:
❑ Check/Money Order enclosed. (Please use an envelope.)
❑ American Express ❑ Visa ❑ MasterCard ❑ Discover

★ California residents add 8.25% sales tax.
Card#:_____
Exp. Date:_____Signature:_____
Credit Card Billing Address Zip Code:_____
NAME:_____
SHIP TO ADDRESS:_____
CITY:_____ STATE:_____ ZIP:_____
PHONE#:_____ EMAIL:_____

Call toll free: 1-877-8GALAXY or visit www.galaxypress.com

© 2005 Galaxy Press, L.L.C. All Rights Reserved. MISSION EARTH and WRITERS OF THE FUTURE are trademarks owned by L. Ron Hubbard Library. BATTLEFIELD EARTH is a trademark owned by Author Services, Inc., and is used with its permission.

BUSINESS REPLY MAIL
FIRST-CLASS MAIL PERMIT NO. 75738 LOS ANGELES, CA

POSTAGE WILL BE PAID BY ADDRESSEE

GALAXY PRESS
7051 HOLLYWOOD BLVD
HOLLYWOOD CA 90028-9771

NO POSTAGE
NECESSARY
IF MAILED
IN THE
UNITED STATES

work off the start-up costs." He held his hands out, begging like a mope. "That'll . . . take a few . . . years."

I exploded.

"You stooge! You freaking idiot!" I threw the buckle and caught him square on his holographed forehead. He fell to his knees from the pain. "You owe me!"

I grabbed my travel bag and snatched my stuff out of drawers and off tables. I cursed when I saw my second pair of underwear, camisole and socks hanging damp on the towel rail. I'd taken advantage of what I'd thought was free water to wash clothes when I'd showered. I ripped a pair of his wet boxers in two and threw the pieces in his direction. I shoved the rest of my stuff in my bag, pulled on my spacesuit, adjusted my goggles to maximum opacity, and jerked open the door. I turned for my parting words.

"You owe me a whole lot more than a ticket home, Jimmy Big-Man-Branded-Slave Hotshot. I'm tempted to take it out of your hide, so I better get away from you before I do something stupid. I never want to see your traitorous face again, but I expect you to pay me back."

I slammed the wobbly door. Dozens of other doors up and down the narrow corridor closed. I stood there hoping some broom-handle-arsed branded creep stuck his nose into my business and gave me a reason to nut-kick him all the way to Anaconda Station so I could hitch a ride home. That hope lasted less time than it took to think it. I stomped out of the compartment hive to a civic corridor and headed for the outer industrial edges of the colony, back toward the squat we had staked out our first night in New Aries.

The planetside colony—with corridors and warrens that wound for kilometers like a giant's intestines inside the sealed enclosure—was built to a scale slightly larger than the Anaconda Space Station that orbited Mars. Exterior structures, constructed of Martian stone and concrete, contained an interior made of everything from tarps to carbon honeycomb panels. Whenever Masterson Corp needed more space, it built additions across the planet's surface or down into the depleted mine tunnels, but the overcrowded citizens kept dividing up the available spaces into smaller portions. Except for the Mars g, the colony was pretty much like my home on the space station.

Except it wasn't. It was on Mars. And I was stuck there.

In the Mining District where I could scrounge a new squat I passed my home-away-from-home, the Looney Marvin Pub. I guess that's where I'd been headed all along. I needed a drink. I pushed through the entrance and grabbed a stool at the bar, dismissing with a tight frown the leers and hoots from the grimy miners. My dark goggles make most men nervous. Those goofballs left me alone.

The Looney Marvin reminded me of my regular haunt on Anaconda Station—the Nasty Habit. Mars enforced its public no-smoking rules. I didn't smoke, so that was fine with me, but the recycled air sure didn't smell any better even with dirtside laws.

I ordered a cheap beer instead of the scotch I wanted. When I paid I found Jimmy's compartment cardkey mixed in with my dwindling stash of tender. I considered running it through my suit's shredder, but shoved it back into my pocket to deal with later.

I felt a sudden inner dunk, an unexpected weightlessness. With his betrayal, Jimmy had cut away a chunk of my life, our life together, my heart, my future. He knew how I felt about him, I loved him, and about corporations, I hated them. I believed the vacant drone of branded lives, their constant static of consumption, and their complacent servitude represented humanity's surrender to slavery. I'd never experienced anything to counter my belief. Now I drifted alone. No way would anyone ever know how scared I felt. The thought popped up that maybe I'd overreacted and should reconsider. Go back to him and talk this through. My throwing a hissy fit was childish.

The bartender brought my beer. I gulped a swig. The vertigo dissipated. No, I knew who I was and what I believed. I was mega-tixxed at myself that I had so profoundly misunderstood Jimmy.

Back in the corner my friend Maybelle, a sassy redhaired coyote, flirted with a table of miners. While I waited for her to notice me, I thumbed my goggles to clear mode and gazed at the view out the huge window behind the bar. Across the crater the lights of Troytown glittered in the darkening night. Webs of stars arched overhead as bright as searchlights. Satellites blinked in their programmed paths. The junk ring swirled like a sparkling necklace with Anaconda Station a dirty jewel. I hated being homesick.

A multicolored meteor shower streaked across the darkness. The first time I'd seen the shooting stars I'd commented about how beautiful they were and Maybelle had explained it was space junk losing orbit. I looked away so I wouldn't think about my mom.

The image of some goofy branded girl's face flashed across the dozens of vidscreens suspended from the ceiling. A kid with greasy puce-colored hair, too much makeup, and a mopey 'tude. The same boring vid crap I'd seen all my life.

Maybelle noticed me and waved to signal she'd be over soon. She finished business with one of the miners, gave him an open five-finger sign, and walked toward me. I knew she'd make the guy wait more than five minutes if I needed the time. I sipped my beer.

Text about the kid scrolled across the vidscreen, but I tuned the thing out and held up my pint to greet Maybelle.

"Hey, Space Pixie, where's your hotdog?"

Maybelle loved saying my old scavbrat nickname in her affected Earth-Texan drawl. I used that name in public. The only people who knew me by Pixel Skye were those I trusted with my life. Yet another reason to hate my ex-boyfriend.

"Jimmy Hotshot is now Mister James Casey. Indentured start-up drone to the mighty Masterson Mining and Manufacturing Corporation of Mars."

"You're spinning me," Maybelle said as she motioned to the bartender to refill her margarita and my beer. "Where'd that dumb tin-can boy get the . . . ?" She was sharp. I'd learned in the short week I'd known Maybelle that not much got past her. "Oh no, kid. He took *your* tender?"

"He cashed in my ticket home."

"Men can be such asteroids. Y'all hurt him much?"

"No, he's a bigshot branded citizen now. I can't touch him. If I kill him it's murder, not a public service." I had to grin a little at the memory of the mayhem I'd caused at his compartment hive. "But I left him a bit bruised."

She laughed.

"Think he'll report a domestic?"

"He doesn't want any trouble. He's a brand-new man." I sipped my beer. "He's probably happy to be rid of me. But M-Corp might come after me for property damage."

"You okay, Pixie?" Maybelle put her arm around

me. I stiffened. Not from her touch—I needed her friendship—but to keep myself from crying. I'd do that later when I was alone. "You loved that lug, I could tell."

"Not now, Maybelle." I looked down at the beer foam. I held back the dark drift of my heart. "I'm too raw. I gotta stay focused. Life for the likes of us just keeps orbiting."

She messed up my short, spiky hair.

"Y'all got a place to stay?" she asked.

"I won't go back to the squat we found, before he won a week in that dinky compartment." I snorted when I recognized my stupidity. "I can't believe I fell for that. He's lousy at poker. Don't worry about me. This colony is a big place. Bigger than the station. Lots of empty spaces for a tin-can girl to hole up."

"Hey, Maybelle," the miner yelled from his table, "at least give me a show while you make me wait." His friends jostled each other and brayed like anime donkeys. "Set Phobos and Deimos free, baby!"

She shrugged off his lewd bid for attention with a withering look that told him to either shut up or spend the rest of the night alone. "These miners get cockier every day. That fellah was bragging about a bonus he can't wait to spend on little ol' me. Something about a new discovery in the mines." Maybelle fished around in her cleavage. "He gave me this rock like it was a diamond."

A weird knobby crystal the color of caffeine with too much whitener, it reminded me of something I'd found in my mom's things. I guess I looked interested.

"It's ugly. Y'all want it?" She flipped it to me. I caught it and zipped it into a sleeve pocket.

She playfully bumped my hip with hers for me to move over and share the barstool. "What y'all gonna do?"

"I gotta do something. No offense, Maybelle, but I hate it here. For twenty years I've been a spacegirl. I haven't been weightless in almost two weeks. I feel so damn fat on Mars." I gulped a swallow of beer, determined to get beyond Jimmy's betrayal. "I'm supposed to go home in a few days. I'm gone too long, my competition will take over my game. And I don't have enough tender to buy a new ticket."

"A pretty gal like you could make a lot, fast, no problem." She winked.

"Not me, Maybelle." She gave me a cold look. "And don't get huffy, I'm not judging what you or any other coyote does. Best friends me and my mom ever had were coyotes. But not all of us can do it, Maybelle, that's all."

She softened again and leaned into me. "Yeah. I've watched too many good gals get eaten alive by the work, make stupid mistakes, get tangled up in drugs. You're right. You're too freaking weird to be a good coyote." She waited for my tough-girl reaction to that challenge, then laughed at my predictability. She finally got me to laugh, too, and it felt good.

"I can just see y'all teasing the Johns in that frumpy spacesuit, that chrome-tipped hair, giving them the spooky eye with those goggles. The kinda creeps who go for that look ain't your style, darlin'." She stopped laughing long enough to sip her margarita. "What *are* y'all gonna do?"

"My mom taught me other ways to survive."

"Like what?"

"Well, I won't steal, but I'll scam any easy mark I come across. I can't get a job. I'm unbranded and determined to stay that way, so I got no identity papers in my future." I nursed my beer. "Which leaves out coyote life anyway 'cause I wouldn't register for a license."

"There are ways around that, darlin'."

"I'm sure. There are ways around most anything."

"What do y'all do up in the tin can?"

"I scav the junk ring. Tech, mostly. Brandeds throw away perfectly good stuff, and nine times out of ten one of them will pay good tender to buy it back. That's what my mom taught me."

"Yeah, I know a guy who does that."

I didn't mean to, but I stared at her so intensely she started squirming.

"What? Don't go giving me that evil eye, girl."

"Sorry, but I never thought about scavving down here. I'm on a romantic vacation, you know." I swallowed the rest of my beer and gave her a big hug. "Can you introduce me to that guy you know?"

•••

By noon the next day I was out scavving junk in the New Aries landfill. Maybelle's friend Rez was a grizzled coot too old to do fieldwork, but had a network of scavbrats supplying him with goods. He tried to put moves on me, but I let him know I wasn't interested. Most guys are like drones, they keep trying the same thing until it works. I lied and told him I'd permanently moved to New Aries because I wanted him to take me seriously and consider me as a long-term supplier. Impressed that I knew tech, he agreed to buy all the usable stuff I brought in. When I explained I had my own vacsuit and didn't want any front tender, he almost rubbed his hands together.

It's a monstrous dump. Not as huge as the junk ring, but it caught me by surprise because of its massive concentration on the surface. Piles big enough to hide terraforming equipment. Brandeds never have known how to recycle their stuff. It's easier for them to let people like me glean through it.

When scavving, the most important thing to remember is to be careful around sharp objects. Dirtside or in vac, puncture your vacsuit and you're depressurized. Without help or the right moves, you're unattractively dead within minutes.

My vacsuit worked like a champ—no tanks, it has a molecular absorber. All suits are designed for dirtside use. Not many use tanks anymore. Although in vac it doesn't matter—weightless is weightless no matter how much you carry—in gravity working in a tanksuit is a pain. Mom always dressed me in oxy-ab suits. The one I wear now used to be hers.

The great thing about oxy-abs is they're programmed to absorb a better mix of air for humans. I've been told people used to breathe pure oxygen for hours before vac jumping. That sure would put a crimp on scavbrats ducking in and out of the space station.

Mars atmosphere has enough oxygen to keep a suit like mine constantly topped off. In space my suit was good for about an hour before I had to return to the station's air supply to refill. The absorption took about fifteen minutes. On the surface of Mars I could live in my suit forever.

Well, breathe, anyway. Staying alive was a whole different matter.

Built-in photovoltaics powered my suit and kept a backup battery charged. In space there's no night or day—solar energy is always available, except in shadows, so the batteries are rarely used. Staying active on subfreezing Mars at night will overwork a suit's charge. Without additional protection or power, the stress will cause the system to malfunction and anyone caught out overnight will freeze. There are ways to survive outside the colony, but the big question was always: why bother?

That morning I picked my way through the junk like a giddy kid who'd found a stream of candy. At first I thought I was just pumped to be working again. Then I realized that for the first time in my life I breathed fresh air. Sure, filtered, processed air, but still fresh, not recycled. That whacked me for a while. I felt pointed.

However, after a few hours the physical effort slammed me and I slowed down. A spacegirl, I'd scavved the junk ring my whole life, but I'd never scavved in any kind of gravity. Anaconda was a sol-class station and rotated to maintain Earth g at its outer rim. I lived most of my life either in Earth g or free fall, but as a kid I'd go to Mars g level, about a third of Earth g, to practice with my friends moves we couldn't do elsewhere. We perfected enhanced speed, leaping extra far, jetbelt assists and fancy somersaults.

Scavving dirtside in Mars g, I was extra glad to be a techscav. M-Corp controlled all transit vehicles—nothing motorized moved without their authorization—so no one scavved with a tractor. No way I'd ever push a wagon full of scrap metal all the way back to an airlock. Let the Martian mopes do that grunt work.

I collected a sackload of tech—comps, cables, cords, perifs, boards and components—even though I had to physically dig through the junk to find it. Readercomps are the most valuable and techscavs kept the reasons why secret, but Rez knew. When he told me he wanted them raw, not cleaned, I knew what he was after. Even a dumb comp, one that won't function, usually has data still on the drives and chips. Old soft, systems, code, even deeper program patches. We techscavs like to poke around and see what we find. And then there's all the personal data—stored on flimsies and ultragigs—that you back up before washing the hard. You'd be surprised how valuable that stuff can be. And how disturbing. For once I was glad just to scav and let someone else wade through whatever muck lay hidden in the guts of what I found.

By late afternoon I'd ranged pretty far out to the edge of the dump and was about to head back toward the airlocks, when I scored a functional readercomp in its own carry case. The mess of stickers, makeup, holos, and trinkets stuck in the flaps and pockets let me know it was some kid's comp. It test-powered right up. I thumbed it off and slipped it into my backpack instead of the sack. Professional curiosity, what can I say? Plenty of time to check it out before I sold it to Rez.

The sun hung low in the sky, so I prepared to hotfoot it back to New Aries. On a nearby rock I planted a locator bug—its signal scrambled to a programmed array of frequencies—to let me know where to start the next day. I took a different route back and scored more tech. Rez and I both were pleased with my volume. He offered to buy me a drink, but I was beat—working in grav would get old soon enough, even with fresh air—so I meandered a sly path to the squat I had settled into the previous night.

Scavving had taken my mind off of Jimmy's betrayal. Trying to get even would be a waste of time. His branded status gave him protection from the likes of me. With one word he could cause me a load of trouble. I'd cried enough the night before. Now I had to get over it, end of story. I had more important problems.

At my rate of income, I'd get back home in maybe a month. A six-week absence meant I'd have to confront new allegiances and reestablish my territory. I had to get back into orbit ASAP.

To distract myself, I snuggled into my radbag and inspected the readercomp I'd found. Stuck in the case's pockets were tubes of smelly makeup, body stickers, other useless geegaws, and an official holograph of two branded execs with a little girl. A typical family portrait, except the woman's brand embellishments outranked the guy. Their forced smiles expressed intense competition not warmth. With hair too neat, uniforms too clean, and tired eyes, these two made me shiver. The woman sat with a taut hardness, stretched tight as a solar sail. The man appeared more smooth—relaxed in the way that probably allowed him to set people at ease and off their guard. The thing that impressed me most was their shoulders touched. I'd never seen a photo of brandeds actually touching. The kid, about ten I'd guess, was cute and oblivious. The brand on her forehead looked huge and out of proportion to her face.

Mixed in with gimmee-cards of drippy branded popstars were a couple of cheap digi-holos. An old scratched shot of an animal that looked too weird to be a real cg-horse. The other was a newer click of an underexposed, blurry lump labeled DADDY'S SPECIAL PROJECT.

I thumbed on the power and the e-diary of a branded girly-girl named Eraina Ranklin popped onto the flat screen. I gagged at the first cutesy vidclips made when she was thirteen, but after a few more I became fascinated. The same girl as in the family portrait, Eraina was just a kid branded by her parents to some corp I'd never heard of, but her life was as strange to me as if I really was a "little green Martian" living in a tin can. That's why I got drawn into it.

The images of Earth grabbed me the tightest. I'd watched nature and history docuvids, but the e-diary seemed real. Eraina outside without an envirosuit, skipping along, being helped onto an animal that looked like a horse, then riding away. The same animal in the digi-holo. I never realized horses were so big. Or real. I guess I believed most animals were just cg-images.

She visited cities with unbelievably tall buildings against fluffy clouds and beautiful brown blue skies. A vid of Eraina at the Pacific Ocean playing in waves gave me goose bumps and all that water made me dizzy.

As she grew older, she talked to her e-diary about her parents' fights. Poor kid blamed herself. They transferred to Luna, uprooting the family. For an Earth kid, living artificial must have been like being buried alive. Unreal, like I would feel if I stood exposed and unprotected on the surface of Earth without my spacesuit. The parental fights continued. She hated her school. The Lunar kids made fun of her. Watching her problems made me appreciate how my mom and her friends had taught me stuff. I was glad I'd never been anywhere near a branded school.

Her parents divorced when her mother, Hester Ranklin, switched brands and was assigned to Titan. Her mom couldn't afford to buy out both their brands, so Eraina stayed with her father. From what I could tell her dad was an okay guy, but she didn't understand why her mom left. What kid can?

A year or so later her dad transferred to Mars working for his brand on a joint project managed by Masterson. Eraina didn't understand more than that, which was fine with me because I've never understood why branded people do what they do. One brief vidclip showed her in transit on Anaconda Station complaining about the smells and the "homeless criminals." I guess that was me.

She hated Mars worse than Luna. She'd just gotten

settled on Luna, finally made new friends, could see Earth from her window port, and could hope to go home one day, then she's shipped off to a frozen rock where Earth is just another star in the sky. On Mars she's tixxed at her parents for jerking her around the solar system. Plus, she's ready to grow up and forge her own identity. Hey, I still remember what it's like to be seventeen.

I got a queasy feeling, like I'd seen this older Eraina before. She grew moody, changed fashions, and talked about new friends. Many branded kids ape our unbranded styles—like we had a choice—so she dressed in scavved clothes. Resenting her father's brand, she styled her hair in feathery bangs to hide it and wore heavy makeup in a masklike design to cover her forehead. When she mutilated her brand, right on cam in her compartment, I knew I watched something seriously out of orbit.

I remembered where I'd seen her: the kid on the Looney Marvin vidscreens the night before.

Almost finished with the e-diary, afraid to go on because I was now a witness to her illegal brand mutilation, I wondered why she'd been on the broadcast vids. I screen-grabbed her image, flipped her comp to Net mode, then googed her and got the news threads. Eraina and four M-Corp kids had run away. Her dad offered a substantial reward—I read the amount twice to be sure I got it right—but her brand warned that "criminal interference would be punished" and "it was the duty of all affiliated brands to provide information leading to her return." Corps are sinister. Not "safe return," not "reunited with her family," just "return." No rewards for the four M-Corp kids. Their running away didn't rate any bytes, just penalties for their parents. I flipped back to Eraina's e-diary.

The next batch of vidclips were Webcam conferences with her friends. Five split-screens of whiney, bickering mopes complaining about branded society. I thought about Jimmy's new corporate status and smirked. These kids, annoying little pukes, at least tried to figure out why they were tixxed. One of them started talking about "their plan" and got flamed. The vid cut off.

The last vidclip of Eraina looked fuzzy at first, then it panned back to her in an envirosuit with a fogged faceplate. She tried to record to her e-diary, but the comp didn't pick up the sound. She shook it in frustration. For a few moments she held it at her side. I'm used to looking at stuff "upside down"—there's no up or down in space—and recognized some of the junk at the site where I'd found the comp. When the vidclip cut out, I checked the time date on the file: yesterday evening.

I had an inside lead. I knew where she had been yesterday and probably where she was headed tomorrow. It didn't take me long to decide to go after her now. That reward would not only buy a ticket home, there'd be enough left over to set me up pretty for a while. Unbranded, I couldn't collect, so I'd have to scam it, but waiting around until I had that figured out was not an option.

•••

A few hours sleep were all I needed to start fresh. New Aries operated 24.6/13, so I found a place to tank up on super-charged water and tube food. I checked my vacsuit's built-in two-person radbag for rips and thin spots. I estimated the trip across the crater would take one day, but anticipated an overnighter. That meant I needed an expensive backup battery. I could have taken a chance that my regular battery would work perfectly and last the night, but my mom didn't raise no mope. Since I gambled on the reward I went for broke and bought the battery. Worst case: I'd have to dirtside scav longer.

To reach my locator bug by sunrise, I smooth-talked my way out of the airlock before daybreak, which taxed my vacsuit until the sun came up and the photovoltaics recharged the fuel cell. The brats had a big head start, so I needed to regain the time.

Leaving the locator bug the day before had been strictly routine, but I was glad I'd done it. It beeped for a few seconds every minute—its scrambled frequency sequence synch'ed with my suit's receiver—long enough for my suit's comp to take a reading and give a direction. I walked until the next beep, correcting my course with each new reading. I recognized the site before I got to the bug.

The day before I'd concentrated on scavving tech and was a bit worn out by the gravity, but I still couldn't believe I'd missed an obvious campsite. Packing crates and conduits had been dragged into a circle, open ends facing inward. The kids had crawled inside the five makeshift shelters, wrapped themselves with radiation blankets or wiggled into radbags. At least they knew how to survive Martian nights, protecting themselves from radiation and micrometeoroids.

Those stupid branded kids had left usable fuel cells scattered all over the place, which meant they weren't too bright about recharging depleted batteries. The deposit on the empties would bring me a decent stack of tender. While I kicked around, I collected them and swapped one for my fully charged cell, which gave me two spares. It would be ready by nightfall. Near my locator bug, I buried the rest of the batteries under a squashed, rotting resin box. I flipped the crates and conduits out of their circle pattern and randomly kicked debris around.

The dump was pretty forgiving because of the chaotic spill of trash and, except for the circle of hideouts and discarded batteries, no other trace of the kids remained. Not hard, considering they were inside envirosuits. Maybe they had left behind or forgotten other things, but I couldn't tell.

I wandered around. Not far away, out at the edge of the dump where the junk ended and the dust of the crater began, I found their ragged trail. They were headed for Troytown—like I'd figured. A one-day jog for me, it could be a two-day hike for a bunch of spoiled branded brats. Maybe even three days. Although they had a day's head start on me, I counted on their inexperience and sloth. Chances were good that they broke this camp late, moved slow, stopped early last night, and had slept in late this morning. If they bickered as much as they had in their Webcam chatroom, I wouldn't have been surprised to stumble over them a few hundred meters into the crater. The day was fresh and the probability was high that I'd catch up to them before nightfall.

My motion detector blipped. A corporate goon stomped over a far mound of trash, headed straight my way. There wasn't a chance he hadn't seen me first. Running away would've been stupid and suspicious. Once those biobots get up to speed there's no outrunning them. I acted cool and drifted back into the dump away from the brat trail, picking up scav I usually wouldn't give a second look. While bending over, with my back toward the goon, I fished around in my pouch for a jabber—a thick ring with a stubby needle welded to it—slipped it on my finger with the point twisted inward toward my palm shield. By the time he intercepted me, which made sense because I was the only other human within sight, my scavsack bulged with junk and

I was about three hundred meters away from the trail.

"Hey." I greeted him first, acting like I had the right to scav, which, of course, I didn't.

The genetically modified goon towered over me, easily three times my bulk. He wore a black stealth suit devoid of any brands, so he might as well have had MERC stenciled on his back in huge yellow block letters. Since he was alone I figured he was either an independent bounty hunter or whoever paid him was too cheap to hire a posse. He definitely wasn't Masterson issue or he'd have transport. He was out here on his own same as me.

"Beautiful day," I said, to disturb his silent intimidation act. "You find anything interesting?"

"Yeah, you." He pointed a thick finger as if it was a weapon. "Whatcha doin outcheer?"

He sure didn't operate with a fresh battery.

"I'm collecting stuff. Lots of neato stuff out here." I carefully enunciated each word as I held out my open bag. He peered in like I had gifts for him. "My boyfriend and his gang are over there." With my free hand I pointed away from the brat trail and jiggled my finger. "They're waiting for me."

Not looking where I pointed, he snorted as he held up a crumpled holo of Eraina. "Ya seen this girl outcheer?" What impressive detective work. I assumed this merc worked for either Ranklin or his corp.

"Nope, just you." I smiled and shifted my weight to my left leg, wiggling my ass a bit. Out of reflex I batted my eyes, but my dark goggles defeated that little touch. "She's a cutie. Your girlfriend?"

My flippant 'tude hid my fear and kept me focused, but I knew I wasn't going to talk my way out of this one—he was too stupid to manipulate. Pumped up on steroids and other pharm enhancers, mercs weren't the swiftest, in any sense of the word, but their brute force made them dangerous. I was lucky he hadn't used me as target practice, just for the fun of watching my body bloat and burst in the atmosphere.

"You want any of this stuff?" I meant the scav, but realized my mistake the moment the words were transmitted.

He took my scavsack and started rooting around in it, dumping junk on the ground. With him distracted, I backed away a step and looked for a chance to bolt.

He grabbed my wrist, the hand with my jabber.

"Hey! Hands off!" I shouted, jerking my arm. "What's the big idea? I was being friendly."

He twisted his grip. I felt a tiny snap and a sharp jolt of pain. I yelped and cursed. If I struggled I'd really get hurt.

"You know her, eh? You seen her, eh?" His comm was set too loud, I tried to cover my ears, but his meaty hand tightened and tugged me. I yelped again and got an idea.

I amplified the volume of my transmission comm to its max and screamed. Inside my helmet my ears rang. He let go and clasped both hands to the sides of his helmet in a useless but involuntary gesture.

He lunged at me and I back-flipped over his head, landed on his armored shoulders, and gripped his faceplate with my good hand, blocking his view. When he lifted his arms to grab me, just as I'd hoped, I stabbed my ring into his armpit. I screamed again to jam his hearing as I jumped off, kicking his head, and loped toward the protection of the nearest junk hill. Grunts and profanity crackled over the comm. The pulse of a string of plasma whizzed past my hip. The ground exploded and splattered me with vaporized junk and red dirt. I put the dust cloud between me and the merc.

With an added burst from my vacsuit's built-in jetbelt, I was out of his range before he could get his muscle-bound butt in motion.

Who would've thought those childhood games on Mars g level of the space station would one day save my neck?

It didn't take long for him to realize I'd punctured his suit. He stumbled off toward the colony holding his armpit. If he'd paid attention during his vac survival training he had a chance. He'd suffer, but he'd make it. Maybe.

As I watched him shamble away I checked my medical monitor. My torqued, bruised wrist throbbed as my suit inflated into a splint. A dosage of painkiller dispensed into the med tube. I sipped the meds while I put the jabber away into a hard safety pouch.

By the time I'd picked up the brat trail I'd found my stride, so I kept up the pace. Tracking those kids was like following a paved road. I couldn't afford to waste time covering their tracks or mine. Even a goon wouldn't miss this trail, so I knew I had to keep my lead just in case that bulked-up biobot got patched up and up to speed.

Running in sand was awkward, but I'm a quick study. I got into the rhythm and leaned into the run.

Mars stretched out in front of me like an endless desert, which it was. We'd planned our dirtside trip to New Aries to coincide with the hemisphere's calm season, so I could be reasonably sure there'd be no dust storms in the next few days. Still, the huge expanse of red dirt and the radiation static on my open comm would have intimidated lots of other people. I can't say I wasn't scared, but I was pointed to be loping along in Mars g, under the orange sky, with fresh air pumping through my suit.

I reached the kids' camp from the previous night a little after noon. Scavving it would waste precious time, so I planted a locator bug.

About an hour before sunset, sooner than I'd expected, I picked up their comm transmissions. I caught up to them well outside the sprawling Troytown dump, another two hours from the airlocks. Three of them were already dug in for the night, out in the open like lumps of dirt, rolled up in radbags right next to their trail. Most likely they were tired, hungry and sorry they'd ever left their mommies and their warm soft bunks. Two sat on rocks arguing over a battery, their cheap envirosuits coated with red dust. They didn't notice my approach, so I stopped just shy of them and leaned on my knees to catch my breath.

"Give me the cell, Jake. I paid for them."

I recognized Eraina's voice from her diary. She grabbed for the battery, but the guy jerked it away. Both moved as if they were sleepwalking.

"We only have one left, Rainie. You'll have to sleep with me tonight." He tried to sound seductive, but his speech slurred like he was already asleep.

"Go spin yourself." She kicked at him, but was too weak to do any damage.

"Stop it," I said. They both startled as if I had appeared out of nowhere, which I had.

"Get a clue, Romeo," I told the guy, "you're both in spacesuits. Nothing can happen. You can't even fondle yourself, so go dig in." He looked at me like he couldn't see me, then he just wrapped his radblanket around his shoulders, slid off the rock, and rolled himself up.

I turned to Eraina. "Come with me. I have extras. He can keep that one." I pulled Eraina to her feet. She struggled, but so meekly it was as if she were weightless.

"Did Dad send you?" she asked, her voice so feeble I could barely hear her. "Where are we going? I'm hungry and cold."

"I'm here to help," was all I replied.

I took her elbow and guided her deep into the dump. I wanted her, and myself, as far from the others as possible. As we walked I cabled into her suit to monitor her systems. Her water and food resources were low. Her power recharger and oxygen absorber were dialed in too weak.

"Kid," I said, "look at the sun icon at the top of your faceplate until it lights up." She had trouble concentrating, so it took her a while. "Good. Now look up until it rises to the top of its slide bar." That turned up her recharger. "Great. Now do the same to the cloud icon." That increased her oxygen absorption. She perked up a bit, but still walked as if in a trance.

I jacked my power unit into her suit as a supplement. I accessed her water valve, plugged in my tube, and bled some of mine into her suit. This was standard space rescue routine we scavbrats learned before we were allowed to even think about our first vac.

"What's the thermometer thingy for?" Eraina mumbled.

"Suit temp."

"You mean I don't have to be so cold?"

"If you turn it up too high it will stress your power supply and drain your battery when the sun sets." I checked the readout and it was lower than it needed to be. "Go ahead and raise it up to eight degrees."

I watched it creep higher.

"Stop. Take it back down to ten, not any higher. I'm serious."

"Why," she whined, "I'm cold."

Gawd, I hate whiners.

"You'll overheat," I said, trying to stay calm, "and deplete your battery. Now lower it." She did. "Good. You'll feel warmer soon."

I let her pout like the mopey brat she was while I looked for a place to hole up for the night.

Just before the sun dropped too low to keep us powered, I found a half-buried cargo container. I threw on more debris to hide it. I pushed Eraina in and followed, pulling a big piece of ripped plastic up behind us to disguise the opening. I switched on my running lights, unpacked my suit's radbag, and helped Eraina climb in. For extra protection I draped her radiation blanket around my radbag and wiggled in with her. I could have wrapped her in her blanket, and snuggled into my bag alone, but I needed to monitor her vitals. I wasn't sure about her health after three days and two nights on the surface of Mars. Besides that, I wanted to talk to her before we slept.

I secured the end of the radbag. Making sure our broadcast comms were switched off, I cabled us in direct, then turned my lights to a dim glow.

"Drink some water," I said. I pumped tube food into her reservoirs. "And eat something." She sucked at her tube. "Slowly," I warned her, "I don't have enough for both of us to fill up. And relax. Slow your breathing down."

My swollen wrist throbbed. I slurped a fresh dose of painkiller and ate some tube food.

Although the recharge helped, her power reserves were still dangerously low. I was glad I'd scavved that extra battery. Her vitals registered weak. Cold body temp, high blood pressure, low blood oxygen level. Eraina was in pretty bad shape.

Fed and settled in for the night, she finally had questions.

"Where's my dad? I want to go home."

"Calm down. If you get excited you'll use up energy," I said, cautious of what I told her. "I've rescued people before. You looked like you needed help. Why are you out here?"

"I don't know. Running away seemed like a good idea. We all thought it would be an easy adventure like on the vids."

"Why did you run away?"

"I hate Mars. I want to go home to Earth." Talking helped her stay relaxed. "We all had our parents' credit chips. Ella said she knew a rocket-jockey in Troytown who would take us at a group rate. Is that true?"

"No," I said. It was one of the oldest scams in space: someone contracts a creep to take them home, but instead they're dumped on an asteroid. Or worse.

"I didn't think so. Before I lost my comp I saw Dad's news conference. People are looking for me in Troytown."

"You're that kid?" I did a good job of acting surprised.

"Yes. Dad has a reward for me. I guess you'll get it." She turned to check out my face. "Are you a Masterson brand?"

"No, I'm unbranded." Her body tensed and I realized I'd said the wrong thing.

"You're a criminal," she whispered, "you're kidnaping me."

"No, I'm not."

"Dad says all unbranded people are criminals and can't be trusted. He doesn't understand why Mars lets unbrandeds stay."

I kept my cool and didn't show I was tixxed.

"We do all the dirty work. Most of the miners are

unbranded. We prefer to live free." I made a point not to mention the space station—the less she knew about me the better.

"I don't understand how you can live in holes and eat out of dumpsters," Eraina said.

I'd heard that misinformation all my life. If she believed the corporate propaganda then it would be a waste of breath explaining why being branded was economic slavery. People only hear what they want to hear. I practiced deep breathing. I hoped she would match my rhythm and we'd both calm down.

"You seem nice," she said, her voice quavering. "I've been rude. Thanks for the food and water and help. I don't think I could have cocooned again by myself. And not with Jake pawing me all night. I'm really sick of being inside this spacesuit. It itches and I stink."

"Shhh. It's okay. You needed help. We help each other on the . . . " A blip on her suit monitor distracted me.

"You know he won't pay you the reward," she said, interrupting me as I ran a system test.

"What are you talking about?" I let exhaustion be my poker face.

"You're a criminal. Dad will have you arrested."

I didn't like being reminded that I still didn't have a plan to weasel the reward out of her dad. Most likely she believed that being unbranded really was a criminal offense, which it wasn't. We just didn't have any legal status or civil rights since without identity records we technically didn't exist. But, she was right that my unbranded status kept me from claiming the reward. I knew that in her dad's world he, and his corporation, would need a reason for his daughter running away. No way would his family life go public. I'd be accused of kidnaping her. *Welcome home, baby girl, bye bye, Pixel*

Skye. Well, that wouldn't happen. I'd walk away first.

"I don't know about a reward," I said. "As far as I'm concerned, you're an ungrateful brat caught nightside while your mope boyfriend tried to get in your suit. Jeez, I do a good deed and get called a criminal for my trouble."

"Sorry," she whimpered. "He's not my boyfriend. I hardly know any of them."

"I'll get you to an airlock in the morning. You deal with your dad. I've got troubles of my own. Now, set your suit to minimum and go to sleep, you're using too much energy."

I checked her vitals again. She was stable, but her body temperature still worried me. With her suit temp set higher than normal she should slowly warm up during the night. Her relaxed heartbeat showed she was drifting toward sleep.

"He's still in touch with Mom," she mumbled to herself. "They don't think I know, but he uses my comp to message her. He forgets to erase the trash folder."

"Shhh," I said. With a pointless gesture I stroked her faceplate with my gloved fingers.

"Why did they get divorced if they still talk? Why did she leave?"

"Go to sleep, kid, I don't know what you're talking about." I was too tired to keep up a conversation.

After a while we both fell asleep.

•••

The beeping reminded me that I had hidden the discharged batteries, but I couldn't calculate how much the deposit refund would be. To the same rhythm as the beeps, shooting stars blazed across an impossible city skyline. The merc dug around in the trash looking for me, his meaty hands groping for my naked legs. I kicked. It took longer than I want to admit before Eraina's system failure alarm woke me out of my dream.

She was alive. Her lips were blue, she gasped for breath, and she stared at me with a most pitiful wide-eyed fear. Even her suit's emergency minimum life support resources had been depleted. I jacked my power system into hers. When her suit's comp powered on, but the suit didn't, I cursed.

An exterior reading of her suit's internal status showed heat loss to almost zero. From the suit settings I figured out that sometime after I'd fallen asleep she'd reset her suit temp to twenty-five. That would have drained her fuel cells while the extra heat was circulated and cooled, but it didn't explain why her O/S didn't work. I feared the stress of three days of constant operation had caused a systems crash.

I snapped into emergency mode. First, I plugged in my oxygen supply using the buddy port. That got her breathing. Next, I connected my liquid cooling and warming system to hers, pumping water warmed by my body heat through her system instead of through my cooling coils. Both were routine rescue procedures and would keep her alive, for a while, but I hadn't solved the real problem.

I checked the time. Two hours to daylight. I had enough backup power to last until morning, but I needed to get her suit a lot warmer a lot faster. I turned up my own suit's temp, to make the water I bled into her LCWS as warm as possible. A little sweat wouldn't hurt me.

With her system down, I couldn't monitor her vitals and that scared the bejeebers out of me. She suffered hypothermia. Her core temp must have been way too cold and would continue to drop unless her suit became warm enough to stabilize her. I didn't know what to do.

"Damn," I cursed to myself, "I'm a geek, not a doctor."

My mom didn't raise no mope. She'd drilled me every day of my life about how to survive. She told me if I didn't know a way to get out of trouble, then I'd better think hard because there was always a way and giving up wasn't the solution. Great attitude. That's one reason why I miss her.

I swapped out Eraina's depleted battery for a new one, for when—not if, I told myself—I got her suit system going. Then I cabled into the suitcomp and went to work, mentally crossing my fingers that the problem wasn't in the hard.

"Eraina," I said to get her attention, "stay with me. We'll get through this."

"Wha?" she mumbled. Her eyelids fluttered. "How d'ya know m'name? Who're you? Where's Daddy?"

She shivered and shook with convulsions. Her teeth chattered, then she stiffened, clenching her jaw and fists. Her pupils rolled back into her head. The convulsions lasted less than a minute, but seemed like a lifetime, and stopped just before I freaked.

I nudged the suit's comp into programming mode and started scanning the code, mostly typing with the finger pads of my good hand. I hoped the higher heat in my suit made a difference to Eraina—it sure made me dreamy. As the code scrolled by I tested each operation. Understanding a vacsuit's programming had been one of my first rites of geekdom. I'd even customized mine here and there when I was a kid. But I'd never worked under such pressure before. When I found the problem my heart constricted like it had decompressed.

It was in the hard. A failed superconductor circuit board. Don't ask me how that happened at night on Mars in subfreezing temperatures. Maybe a micrometeoroid compromised the insulation regulator and when she turned up the heat the circuit failed. But that was just a guess.

I finished the run-through of the code to make sure there wasn't another problem. The soft was intact, but because of the broken circuit I had a dead suit on my hands.

I couldn't just jack my comp into her suit. The soft isn't designed to simultaneously run two suits—too many operations to monitor and compensate. Each person is unique.

Maybe there was an emergency override that paramedics knew about. I started poking through the system again.

Her eyes fluttered.

"Mom?" she asked. The poor kid was out of it.

Through her shivering, chattering teeth she mumbled nonsense. I shushed her to stay calm. She must be getting warmer from my LCWS, but without a monitoring system I had no idea how well it was working. If she fell into a coma I'd probably never get her back. My heart pounded and my throat clenched tight.

"Eraina. C'mon, kid, stay with me here." My loud voice echoed in my ears.

My wrist throbbed like an airlock pump. Tired and discouraged, I considered contacting Troytown for help, but hesitated because I knew that even if Troytown sent an emergency tractor for Eraina, they'd either slam my unbranded butt in detention, or leave me out in the dump with depleted resources. It was my only real alternative. If I waited too long, stubbornly insisting on solving the problem on my own, it would cost Eraina her life. I pulled her readercomp out of my backpack pouch and thumbed it to messenger mode to contact Troytown.

Then I said, "Wait a minute, Pixel," and disconnected.

I unplugged the cable from my suit and jacked it into the readercomp, leaving the other end connected to Eraina. There was more than enough memory on the reader, so I transferred the suit's system soft and checked it for weevils. By running the soft from the readercomp through the external jack, I bypassed the dead circuit board.

Her suit blinked to life and I cheered.

I accessed her vitals and immediately lost my joy. Her core temp was only thirty-two.

I cranked up her temp control to max. I'd use the extra battery if I needed it. I consulted the medical helpfile. The trick with the LCWS was standard. Warmed humid air and water were recommended. I heated her drinking water.

"Eraina, drink some water. Come on, drink. That's a champ."

I implemented an emergency procedure that directed most of the airborne heat to her helmet. I humidified her oxygen supply. With the heat concentrated to a small area, her helmet temp quickly rose into the forties. Her core temp blipped up to thirty-three.

"Good girl," I told her, "you're getting warmer. Keep it up!"

I reminded her every few minutes to drink the warm water. Most of the time she did it. I talked to her to keep her conscious.

Slowly, I manipulated her suit temp higher. Her core temp continued to increase. She rested with intermittent delusional visions.

Monitoring her vitals and raising her suit temp to a sufficient warmth—and keeping it there—was intense work. I kept her hydrated and conscious until dawn.

At daybreak I 'croed the readercomp to her chest, pulled Eraina into the sunlight and set her recharger at full bore. I found a usable panel of honeycomb for a bivouac. I rigged a line around my waist and over my shoulder to my good hand. Barely conscious, she slumped like a sack of scav as I lugged her to the nearest airlock. I feared her fingers and toes were frostbitten.

The airlock was open. I dragged her in—honeycomb and all—and alerted the operator for a medical emergency. With my fingers poised over the control panel, I turned to tell Eraina goodbye. Then I reached over and unfastened her readercomp.

"Eraina. You're about to go inside. You have more than enough heat and air in your suit to last until the airlock cycles. I can sell this comp. I need the money. I did find it. Your dad will get you another one. You stay out of trouble, okay? See ya, kid."

I snatched the comp, keyed the airlock controls, and high-tailed it back into the landfill as the doors sealed.

I scrambled through the Troytown dump, on constant lookout for goons and surveillance aircraft. To the north there was airborne activity, so I kept my distance and avoided unnecessary exposure. A few times I ducked for cover because of flyovers. When I reached the outskirts of the junkyard I scouted around for a hideout. Hidden from view under the wheel well of a stripped terraforming grader, I curled up in a patch of bright sunlight and slept for an hour.

I awoke with a pounding headache, swallowed some liquid aspirin and ate a bit of tube food. The activity I'd seen in the north was over. I powered up Eraina's comp and thumbed it to Net mode to check the local news, but found nothing about Eraina or her friends. That didn't surprise me. Ranklin's corp might have negotiated a news suppression. No one would remember his reward plea. Eraina's runaway would be quickly forgotten.

I stared at the comp and wondered what to do. My plan to find an angle to scam the reward had never materialized. I'd spent most of my pocket tender and now it would take me twice as long to earn my ticket home. Anxious to get on with my hike back to New Aries, I moved to power down the comp when I noticed Eraina's messenger function was disabled. I clicked it on and about a dozen windows popped onto the screen, all of them from Ranklin pleading for Eraina to come home. I closed them one by one. Then a new window opened.

—Who are you?— read the most recent message, highlighted as active. With the user name "Father" it could have been anyone, but most likely it was Ranklin and he could tell that Eraina's comp was online.

—A chump.— I replied on an impulse. —How's the girl?—

—In the crisis unit. Resting. I'm with her. You saved her life.— Although probably true, I took it as melodramatic until he typed —Her friends are dead.—

My body went limp. Reading and rereading those four words, I forced myself not to cry. I'd assumed the kids were okay when I should've realized they were in the same shape as Eraina. Except I hadn't known her condition was so critical until after we'd dug in for the night. Still, I should've checked the other kids. If I'd contacted the colony for help they'd still be alive. I'd let my selfish need for the reward cloud my judgment. I'd broken the first rule of living artificial: help those with compromised life support systems.

—Are you there?— A new message flashed.

—I gotta go.— I felt a strong urge to get back to work, to move forward somehow. I had to get beyond this. Fast. More than ever, I wanted to go home.

—Wait. You must return Eraina's readercomp.— The reason for his messages brought me back to reality like a slap in the face. —Or I'll report it as stolen.—

That tixxed me. He was just like every branded exec I'd ever heard of. Four kids were dead because they went along with his daughter's insane stunt, and all he cared about was this stupid comp. If I tossed the thing over my shoulder no one would ever find it or connect it to me. I was anonymous unless they caught me before I got back to New Aries. Even then they knew nothing solid about me and couldn't prove I was involved. Not that they needed to prove anything to charge me.

—You do that.— I posted, then logged off and powered down.

I kept the readercomp. I'd been through too much to give up the little I still had.

As I walked toward New Aries, too tired to make the same time as the day before, I hoped I might make it back to the outer edges of the New Aries dump by nightfall. My wrist ached constantly through the haze of medication. I needed to get my bearings, so I called up my locator signal and headed toward the kids' second campsite—the one I hadn't had time to scav yesterday. My supplies were low. Maybe they'd left more usable batteries and some tube food packets I could scrounge. Thinking about the kids made me sick at heart. I needed to walk and be alone, and a red dust crater on Mars was the perfect place. I walked, unaware of time.

Something Eraina had said the night before popped into my head and began to nag. After another kilometer or so my curiosity got the best of me. I sat down on a rock, powered up the readercomp, and searched the data files of the message program. For a geek like me, finding Ranklin's fake Eraina account was a snap. He wasn't as sloppy as she thought—he probably was interrupted before he could properly dispose of his most recent correspondences. With my soft from the station I could've recovered the whole history of his account, which was something to keep in mind if I needed an ace up my sleeve in the future.

I uncovered two messages: one to and one from his ex-wife. On the surface they read like mother/daughter correspondence, but rang false without hints of either teenage confrontation or absent-parent guilt. I figured they used code, but I didn't really care what they said or why. They were probably corp spooks scouting a hostile or skimming Masterson's intelprop data. The Ranklins were up to something, that's all I needed to know.

To prove I'd hacked the account, I copied the text of Ranklin's old post into a new message window and fired it back at Hester. I anticipated a lag in transmission, made worse by a time-cycle difference on Titan, but I figured she was online. She'd be worried about Eraina and eager for any news.

While I waited for her response, I messaged "Daddy" on Eraina's personal account.

—Pops, I know that you and Ma are still dancing.— A bluff, but worth the try. He replied quickly.

—She and I have not spoken in over two years.— The long pause let me know he chose his words carefully. —Ours was an ugly parting.—

—How discreet.— I typed. —I hack. These readercomps are toys to me.— Then I sent the same message I had just resent to Hester. —Let's keep this all in the family. No need to contact "The Competition," wouldn't you agree?—

—I will report the theft of my daughter's property.—

—Finders keepers losers weepers. The toy is moot. The damage has already been revealed, Pops.—

I had no more to type to him at the moment, so I let him gnaw on what I did or didn't know.

Hester's response blinked on to the screen.

—Why did you resend that? Is Eraina back?—

—Dear Ma,— I typed. —Your little darling is safe thanks to me. You're hacked. You and Pops ever think about how much your secret dance has messed up your girl? Tell Pops I said hiya.—

I powered down the comp and started walking again.

Now, if I were Hester, I'd be tixxed to find out from a stranger that Eraina was safe. I wouldn't hesitate to use the irate ex-wife act as a cover to televid Ranklin and scream at him. Then, if she repeated some of my post, they both might think I knew more than I did.

I felt better and made good time. A few hours later I found my locator bug at the kids' second camp. By then my battery was charged, so I swapped it out with the depleted backup. There was evidence that someone had poked around, but not a scavenger. After scavving the camp for usables, I contacted Ranklin.

—Hi Pops.—

—What do you want?— I imagined the sound of his teeth grinding.

—My reward for saving your girl. You offered it for just returning her. I kept her alive.—

—The airlock operator gets the reward. You're a criminal.—

I resisted taking the bait and didn't fire back a tirade. A part of me relaxed because what he knew about me he'd obviously gotten from talking to Eraina, so she really was okay.

—Oh, Pops, don't be a meanie. It takes one to know one, eh?—

—I won't abide extortion.—

—This isn't extortion, I just want the reward you offered, nothing more. Then you leave me alone forever, or I WILL invite "The Competition" to your dance party.—

—Your attempt is pathetic.—

—Your fancy dances with Ma don't interest me. I want my reward and I'll keep little sister's toy for insurance. Call off your merc, if he's still alive.—

I waited about a minute. He didn't respond. I bluffed on a whim and by the seat of my pants. He wasn't buying it.

Without my soft I couldn't dig into the comp's data to find something real to bargain with until I got home. While I mulled over my options I sorted through the momentos stuck in Eraina's comp case. I almost missed the fuzzy little holo labeled DADDY'S SPECIAL PROJECT. Just a smudge of tan, but in the Martian daylight it looked familiar. I fished out the miner's rock Maybelle had given me. I saw a similarity. The miner had bragged about a new discovery. Maybe there was a connection.

I switched on the comp's vid feed and sent Ranklin close-ups of my hand holding the holo at various angles.

—How about this?— I teased.

He went offline.

—Tell Ma I said hiya. You two sure messed up your kid.— I sent before signing out.

I took off walking again, my stride a little too bouncy, so I adjusted before I fell on my face. When I stopped in the middle of the afternoon to rest, I checked the comp and a message popped open. Ranklin used a different account. I figured it was security tight.

—I want to watch you destroy that holo.—

—Then we have a deal?—

—Yes. If you destroy that holo.—

—You double-cross me and I'll blow your cover.—

—If you don't play fair with me, I'll have your ass.—

—Then we understand each other?—

—Yes.—

I set the small shredder on my hip to "dust," switched the vid feed back on, and transmitted the destruction of the holo. No need to tell him I had my own rock.

—It's illegal to transfer credits to an undocumented person.— read his next message. —I do not operate in tender.—

I only knew two people on Mars: Jimmy and Maybelle. Coyotes worked on a strictly tender basis. I'd never considered asking her to front me the cost of the ticket home. Unbrandeds will help each other in any way possible except loaning tender. We are each on our own with finances. Take or give, ask or offer, that's the fastest way to lose a friendship.

Jimmy was my only chance.

—I know someone with a restricted account. I don't have his numbers.—

—Not a problem. I can access any account.—

—His account will be negative until long after he's dead, so the bank will take my credits to pay off his debt.—

—Follow directions and you'll print out the credits.—

I started to feel weird. Leftover concern for someone I'd once loved. Jimmy might be a conniving bastard, but I sure didn't want him in trouble—not yet. If this didn't pan out, I wanted him employed so I would get my payback one day.

—This is someone who isn't involved and I want to keep him uninvolved.—

—Follow directions and the transaction will be untraceable.—

There are ways around most anything, I thought. Of course, a spook would know how.

I sent Jimmy's personal information. We settled on a time of delivery that gave me a few days to find a way to get to Jimmy's account. Before signing off, Ranklin explained what I had to do to keep the bank from sweeping the credits as payment toward Jimmy's debt.

I walked until nightfall. With both batteries fully charged, I dug out a trench in the dust among a clump of boulders and snuggled into my radbag. I took enough painkiller to dull my wrist. I settled down to my first long night's sleep in a week, since cocooning gave me no other choice, but one thought kept me awake until I finally just let it go.

The bastard never thanked me for saving his daughter's life.

• • •

Three days later, after I'd rested up from two nightsides on Mars and had my wrist doctored, I sat in the shadows at the end of the Looney Marvin's bar enjoying a very expensive and exquisite dram of Talisker's. Right on time Maybelle came in with Jimmy on her arm. If anyone could make sure Jimmy was where I wanted him to be, it was Maybelle. She'd gone to his compartment to pick him up. I was paying her a cut of the reward to take him upstairs. She'd accepted my offer under the condition that if Ranklin cheated me we'd treat it as a big joke at Jimmy's expense.

A bit sharper guy would have questioned why she wanted him, but if Jimmy had been sharper our lives would've been different. I had considered using his compartment cardkey to crash in on him uninvited, but there was no guarantee he'd even be there or if he'd be alone. I needed him alone, at a specific time, and in a place where I was in control.

Maybelle ordered drinks.

"That's bettah," she purred after sipping her margarita. She handed him a Phobos Phantom. "My treat. Y'all had nothing decent to drink in that dinky little room of yours."

I sat back deeper into the shadows and hid a smirk behind my hand. Then I got myself worked up over how quickly she snagged him by his testosterone and how easily he caved. I told myself to get over it.

"C'mon, sugah," she poured on her coyote charms, leaned over to give him a peek, and tugged at his sleeve, "you're a brand-new man now. I've always had the hots for you. Why don't y'all show little ol' me why they called you Hotshot." She kissed his cheek and he blushed Mars red. "On the house, sugah."

As they disappeared into the shadows of the second floor stairway I heard Jimmy yelp and then laugh.

I savored the last of my scotch, checked the time readout in the corner of my goggles, then sneaked up the back way to Maybelle's room.

I jerked open the door. Jimmy squatted on the edge of the bed trying to untangle his pants from around his ankles, wrists caught in his twisted undershirt. Maybelle was good. The mope looked sheepish like I'd actually caught them doing something nasty. It was funny, but I didn't smile. This was business.

I hadn't realized I was still so mega-tixxed at him. I checked the time.

"In three minutes a large sum will be transferred to your bank account," I said, my voice controlled, my tone even. "It's mine. I needed a branded account and you're it."

Maybelle rummaged around in his jacket, found his comp, and dropped it in his lap.

"You'll have less than thirty seconds to print it out as tender before Masterson Bank claims it as payment toward your debt." I tapped a finger on the bedside table. I hated how the hologram on his forehead made Jimmy look like a stranger, but it also made it easier to remember he'd changed.

He started to say something.

"Don't you talk to me," I growled. I picked up the empty Phobos Phantom tumbler and he flinched. I breathed in deep and spoke calmly. "Trust me, if you keep the credits, it'll do you no good. If I don't get my tender, I will not be pleased, and the people transferring the credit will not be pleased when I throw my tantrum. If you DON'T do this for me—for ME—then you'll take a big fat fall for ME that YOU will NOT enjoy. All I want is what's mine so I can go home. You do this FOR ME and we're even."

I really wanted to throw the glass at him.

"Start your comp and be ready," I said instead.

The rest of the time passed in silence. I nervously tossed the tumbler back and forth between my hands a few times before I put it back on the table.

The designated time came and nothing happened. I wanted to smash something. I really didn't know how to rat out a spook—I'm just a junk-ring spacegirl with no clout. I figured Ranklin had called my last bluff and left me hanging. I gritted my teeth. Maybelle gave me a sign to hang loose for a bit longer.

When a beep signaled the completed transaction Jimmy's eyes widened at the amount he saw flash on the screen. He licked his lips and glanced up at me. I sneered and glared through my dark goggles, not moving a muscle, even though I wanted to scream at him until my voice was hoarse.

He entered a code. Time trickled by.

His hesitation killed all remaining emotion that I held for him, erased any memory I would have kept to delude myself of a possible future together. At that moment, as we stared at each other over the ever widening gap between us, he truly became branded forever in my mind.

"Do it, Mister Casey!" I hissed through clenched teeth. "Go ahead, either way, do it now!"

He thumbed a key and the printer clicked on. I reached out and caught the tender, card by card, as it dropped.

"Log off quick, or they'll sniff you out," I said as I stashed most of the tender in my pouches.

I hugged Maybelle and handed her the amount I'd promised.

I flipped one card, a bull's eye, into Jimmy's forehead. He yelped.

"That's for the readercomp I busted," I said. "This little transaction never happened. We're even, Mister James Casey. Don't ever make me come remind you that I don't exist."

Then I went home.

BLACKBERRY WITCH

Written by
Scott M. Roberts

Illustrated by
Perrin Hendrick

About the Author

As a boy in rural Marquez, Texas, Scott Roberts heard lots of stories: half-told truths, honest lies and a lot in between. By the age of twelve, Scott was an expert on ghost lights, angels and devils. He also had a passion for writing that blossomed by junior high school, when a certain Mrs. Stone let Scott write his own time-travel versions of the Civil War and world wars. Scott would continue his literary assault against a string of high school English teachers across two different states.

To make his way in life, Scott also started young. He had his first paying job picking and selling blackberries door to door with his brother. He was a beekeeper (for three stinging years), waiter and talent scout—about twenty jobs in all and still counting. Currently he's an information security analyst located near Washington, D.C., and lives in northern Virginia with his wife and four children. Scott continues to pay homage to his childhood through his writing by telling and re-telling the old stories . . . adding touches of truth along the way.

About the Illustrator

Freelance muralist, nature tracker and illustrator Perrin Hendrick describes artwork as "all about the journey." His own journey began in New Hampshire where he discovered a love for drawing. In the local New Boston library, Perrin spent hours exploring and illustrating the adventure and fantasy tales hidden on the shelf.

Later, as an art major at the University of New Hampshire, Perrin wandered the local woods to deepen another love: nature. His journey then led him to explore the country from New Hampshire to Mexico before entering Naropa University in Colorado, an alternative school influenced by Buddhism.

Perrin currently lives back in his home state with his girlfriend, Liz. It was Liz that asked Perrin if she could send in his illustrations. Perrin didn't think anything about it, but four months later he got the winning call. Today when he's not painting murals, Perrin is busy learning oil painting, developing illustrations for his children's book and staying close to his journey's path.

When Nina woke up, sore from toting boxes and furniture, Brujo was sitting at the end of her mattress, idly kicking an unpacked box labeled "Clothes-bdrm." She didn't move—didn't make a sound. Just watched him for a bit. He had the ghost in a mason jar and was whispering softly into the jar's wide, open mouth. With every word, the ghost shivered. It was a pathetic thing after a night with Brujo. Not that it had ever been much. But now the edges of the ghost were blurring, weeping off into nothingness. Brujo inserted a finger into the jar, touched the ghost, then stuck his finger in his mouth.

He noticed Nina. "Good morning," he said around his finger.

She nodded at him, and he mimicked her, his shaggy black hair bobbing into and out of his eyes. He was getting thinner. She could see every rib like a stripe, and the little brown legs sticking out of his Spiderman boxers had none of the baby fat of a year ago. The divorce was as hard on him as it was on her.

She moved quickly to get out of bed, to hide the flash of pain in her eyes. If Brujo saw it, he said nothing. He just watched her, as she had watched him. Watched her dress. Watched her with wide, dark eyes that never blinked. Nina was used to his gaze. But at moments like this, she understood why Steve had been uncomfortable with Brujo. Because no one but a husband should be able to look at his wife with such intimacy. Nina pulled her hair back into a ponytail, biting her lip as she pulled too hard. Intimate eyes. *She* had never slept with Brujo. *She* had never taken Brujo out for drinks. *She* had never written Brujo erotic e-mails detailing all her fantasies and pleasures.

Of course, those last two, she'd never done for Steve either.

Brujo touched her leg. His fingers were cold. "I found the wizard."

Nina pulled on her jeans. They fit better now than they had six months ago. Six months ago, Steve had told her about Camille. It took the destruction of her ten-year marriage to shock her into losing weight. Maybe if she had lost weight *before*, Steve's eyes wouldn't have found Camille. This was an old song with her, by now. "Eight Steps to a Better Marriage," let's sing it now: Step 1, you gotta look like gold, Step 2, never be cold, Step 3, let him into your head, Step 4, be good in bed, Step 5, be ever so funny, Step 6, be smarter with money, Step 7, tell him everything you know, Step 8, get rid of Brujo.

Nina figured she'd hit most all of the steps 1–7. Not consistently, of course. Not the way Steve may have wanted. But step 8 . . . Step 8 was the step that dropped off into the abyss, because the truth was that Steve asking her to get rid of Brujo would be like asking her to get rid of an arm. Brujo was that much a part of her. And that was the kicker, wasn't it? Brujo was in places within Nina that Steve simply had not been willing, or able to reach.

"I found him, Nina," Brujo said. Nina realized this was the second time he had said it. "I found the wizard. He's living just down the street."

The wizard. They were back to their old routine,

now. Nina looked at Brujo, and for a moment he appeared to be exactly what he wasn't—a young boy, brown as a nut, thin and homely. Eyes like chocolate. Nothing like Steve.

"I need to plant the blackberry bushes first," Nina said. Her voice cracked.

Brujo nodded, and upended the mason jar into his mouth. The ghost slid reluctantly down into his throat. He burped. "It'll be nice to get back to stealing magic again," he said. "Back to the way things were."

But his voice was hollow. Nina looked down and saw he was still wearing the anklet Steve had given him on their third anniversary.

"Wear socks," Nina said. "It's cold out."

...

Nina's mother had died beneath blackberry bushes. It had been her last gift to Nina, to bleed out her last beneath the tangle of thorns and drooping fruit. Nina had helped her into the brambles, and held an umbrella over her to keep the hot Texas sun out of her eyes.

Mama had been a witch. Not an earth priestess or shaman or any other neo-pagan nonsense. A witch. And she was a terrific liar to boot. Lying made her more money than being a witch ever did. There was magic in her veins, but nothing that could bring in the white folks' dollar. For that, she had to tell them tales of their futures, tales of their dead loved ones' pasts, spin them excuses for their weaknesses and trials. And Mama had been very, very good at that.

"This is real magic, Nina," she had gasped as Nina picked apart the thorns so she could get settled beneath them. "Real magic is what you bleed into it."

Illustrated by Perrin Hendrick

now. Nina looked at Brujo, and for a moment he appeared to be exactly what he wasn't—a young boy, brown as a nut, thin and homely. Eyes like chocolate. Nothing like Steve.

"I need to plant the blackberry bushes first," Nina said. Her voice cracked.

Brujo nodded, and upended the mason jar into his mouth. The ghost slid reluctantly down into his throat. He burped. "It'll be nice to get back to stealing magic again," he said. "Back to the way things were."

But his voice was hollow. Nina looked down and saw he was still wearing the anklet Steve had given him on their third anniversary.

"Wear socks," Nina said. "It's cold out."

•••

Nina's mother had died beneath blackberry bushes. It had been her last gift to Nina, to bleed out her last beneath the tangle of thorns and drooping fruit. Nina had helped her into the brambles, and held an umbrella over her to keep the hot Texas sun out of her eyes.

Mama had been a witch. Not an earth priestess or shaman or any other neo-pagan nonsense. A witch. And she was a terrific liar to boot. Lying made her more money than being a witch ever did. There was magic in her veins, but nothing that could bring in the white folks' dollar. For that, she had to tell them tales of their futures, tales of their dead loved ones' pasts, spin them excuses for their weaknesses and trials. And Mama had been very, very good at that.

"This is real magic, Nina," she had gasped as Nina picked apart the thorns so she could get settled beneath them. "Real magic is what you bleed into it."

Illustrated by Perrin Hendrick

The blackberries took her. So now, when Nina planted canes taken from that old bush back in Marquez, Texas, here in this new soil outside Washington, D.C., she was planting her mother and her mother's blood. There were other bushes, in the alley behind her college apartment at UNCG; at the edge of a drainage field near an extended stay hotel outside Ashland, Virginia; and at the house where she and Steve had shared their lives in Salina, Kansas. But she always took the canes from the old house in Texas. The farther removed from her mother's blood, the more the magic waned.

Blood and magic. There was no way to separate the two. Brujo handed her a shovel, and Nina dug several shallow holes for the blackberry canes. Barehanded, they planted them, so that as the bushes grew, the magic would know them. And would obey them. Nina could feel Mama's blood in them, urging the plants to grow, to thrive, to tangle the soil with roots.

Brujo tugged on her arm. "Look, Nina."

A field mouse was sniffing the blackberry plant farthest from them. It moved oddly, scrambling with its front paws over the mulch Nina had spread around the plant. Its back legs were motionless.

"Broken spine," Brujo whispered. He bit his lip and crept softly over to the mouse, until he stood over it. The mouse did not move to escape, but edged as close as it could to the blackberry cane. Brujo took the mouse gently in one hand, and with the other, made as if to stroke its fur. But when that hand came away from the mouse, the mouse's ghost came with it. Brujo devoured the ghost, smacking his lips loudly.

"Two in one day. You're going to get fat." Nina tossed the shovel into the wheelbarrow.

Brujo shrugged and grinned at her. "Need my strength. There's a wizard down the street."

Wizard. Nina watched as Brujo tossed the mouse over the chain-link fence, into the mess of brush and trees that bordered the yard. Why did she suddenly feel cold and . . . unwilling? Unwilling to go through this whole mess of ripping away another person's magic. Unwilling to steal, or cheat or lie.

Like Steve. Or Camille.

Nina was suddenly angry. Why should her divorce taint everything in her life? It had no place here, with Brujo, in this new home! She was entitled to be able to start fresh, wasn't she? Clean slate and all that?

But there was nothing clean about what she and Brujo did. Nothing clean at all, a little voice reminded her. A little voice that sounded too much like Steve.

"Let's go in," Nina said. "I need to get washed up before we go find him."

She cleaned off her hands and arms, and changed into a T-shirt and jeans. What would she say when she met this wizard? He wouldn't know her, of course, would know nothing of what she could do, or what she was after. Brujo saw to that. That was his charm. Wild, wild, changeling child, Mother had once called him.

"Ask him for some mayonnaise," Brujo said suddenly. He was flipping through an old *National Geographic* he'd pulled out of an unpacked box. "He doesn't like the stuff, and there's a jar in his cabinet he's been meaning to throw out."

"Mayonnaise?"

He rolled his eyes at her. "Yes. Mayonnaise. It's not like you have to eat the stuff either, you know. Just ask him. It'll get us in."

Good enough for her. Nina pulled on a jacket and they stepped out the front door.

Stonebrook Estates was an older subdivision, which meant no sidewalks, but at least the houses were not all the same three models. It also meant that there were trees in the yards. So many modern developers thought subdivisions started out as strip mines. Nina hadn't had much of a chance to tour the neighborhood before she and Brujo had chosen to move in. What mattered was the wizard, not what type of soil, or trees, or whatever, populated the neighborhood yards.

A pair of boys on muddy bikes raced past them, screaming at each other happily. Nina watched Brujo watch them. Had Brujo ever wanted to ride a bike? It was something Nina had never considered, but now, as she watched his dark eyes follow the boys' backs down the street, craning his head to see where they turned beyond a corner, she wondered what else he wanted. A real life, perhaps.

To be a real boy. And her, the Blue Fairy?

There was no magic that strong, no matter how many golems of Prague, or Pinocchios, or Frankensteins, or even HALs came pleading. Not enough blood in all the world to give Brujo humanity. She watched him run a hand through his hair, and when his hand came away, his hair was shorter. Shaved in the back, suddenly, thick on top. Like the boys on the bikes.

"I think you look fine, Brujo," she said.

He shrugged. "I haven't had a haircut since Steve . . ."

And then he stopped. Looked away from her. Maybe Brujo didn't want a Blue Fairy at all. Just Geppetto.

The wizard's house was a powder blue colonial, garage door open, compact car sitting in the driveway. As simple and ordinary as anything. The name on the mailbox said "Karl." As they got closer, Nina saw that the garage was packed full of things—hockey sticks, bikes of three different heights, inner tubes, boxes . . . More a storage shed than a garage, really.

She rang the doorbell. "Mayonnaise?" she asked Brujo again. He nodded.

A stocky, balding man opened the door. The wizard. "Hello," he said. "Can I help you?"

Nina eased slightly forward. "Hi... um... I'm Nina Borriegos, I just moved in."

"Oh, right," the wizard smiled, and stuck out his hand. "I'm Jan Karl. Asher told me there were some new folks in the neighborhood. You're on, what, Tencil Lane?"

Nina smiled back and took his hand. "That's us."

Jan nodded at Brujo. "What's your name?"

"Enzo," Brujo replied.

"Well, Enzo, Nina. What can I do for you?"

"We need some mayonnaise, to tell the truth." Nina tucked her chin a little bit. "We left ours at the old house, and I just haven't had the chance to go to the store. And you can't make tuna fish without mayo, so... would you have any we could borrow?"

"I've got a whole unopened jar you can have," Jan said. "Come on in, it will take me a second to find it."

They followed him in. Just as easy as Brujo had predicted.

Jan Karl's home was easily as cluttered as the garage. Books and magazines stacked on every inch of available table space, photo albums on the chairs, odd bits of wood or machinery littering the edges of the room... Jan picked up a few things here and there, grinning apologetically at Nina and Brujo as they went.

"I'd like to be able to blame all this mess on my kids. But most of it's mine."

Nina stepped over a shingle of wood that had some type of calligraphy carved all around the edges. "It's all very... eclectic."

"Now there's a word you don't hear every day."

"This morning's crossword puzzle."

Jan laughed, and waved them into the kitchen. "Despite what you might be led to believe for all the mess, we do keep the food in here. Mostly."

Brujo spoke up, looking up at Nina. "I have to pee."

Nina rolled her eyes, "Can we use . . . ?"

"The bathroom's around the corner, door on the left. Across from the stairs." Jan used his foot to scoot a stepstool over to the kitchen counter.

Brujo disappeared, leaving Nina to watch Jan rummage through the cabinets above the dishwasher. She barely understood him when he began talking.

"I'm sorry, what?" she asked.

Jan pulled his head out of the cabinet. "How old is your son?"

"Six. Going on nineteen, sometimes."

A smile. "I know exactly what you mean. My daughter, Claire, is sixteen going on thirty-five."

"How many children do you have?"

"Two. Asher is nine, and Claire is . . . well, you know already."

"Right. Sixteen going on thirty-five."

There was a pause. Jan stuck his head back into the cabinets. "I think . . . oh, here it is."

There was a sudden yelp of surprise from upstairs, followed by a horrifying shriek. A rush of footsteps above them, and then something tumbled down the stairs. Brujo came tearing across the room, weeping, a tremendous knot on his forehead. He threw himself into Nina's arms, burying his face into her shoulder.

"Keep it away, keep it away, keep it away," he muttered, over and over.

Nina felt a sickness in her stomach. What had happened? Brujo had never acted like this, never . . . Nina hadn't even known that he could *be* afraid, much less this kind of terrified.

"Asher! What happened?" Jan stood speaking angrily to someone behind Nina.

Nina turned. A boy, looking as terrified as Brujo stood there, hands clasped, biting his lips. "I didn't do anything to him. I didn't even hear him coming, I just looked, and there he was in my room! He surprised me and I shouted, and he freaked out! I swear I didn't do anything, Dad!"

She had to take control of this. "I'm sorry, Enzo's just so curious sometimes," she said to Jan.

Then Brujo raised his head and *hissed* at the boy. "Stay away from us. Stay away from us, or I'll rip your eyes out and bury them in piss so you'll lose your way and never be able to find it again."

Nina choked. Jan and the boy stood speechless, staring at Brujo. Nina found her voice. "I'm so sorry. We'd better go."

Jan swallowed and nodded. "Um . . . here's your mayonnaise."

She took it and fled, carrying Brujo back to their new home. He did not stop shaking and weeping until she had placed him near the blackberry bushes, where he ran his fingers over the leaves and vines. A turtle missing a leg had wandered over to the blackberries from the stream behind the house—Brujo stripped the ghost out of it, and devoured it noisily.

"We cannot steal his magic," he declared, wiping his nose. He hiccupped.

Nina frowned. "What happened?"

"You saw the demon."

"There's no such thing."

"I know. Why do you think it scared me so much?" Brujo shuddered.

"I only saw Jan. And his son."

"Son?" Brujo shook his head. "Like I'm your son?"

"You're not a demon, Brujo."

"Well, that thing is. I don't know what else to call it. Whatever magic the wizard used to make that thing is deeper than anything I want to lay my hands on. Magic like that—it uses you."

He was picking at the turtle, pulling at its limp head and legs like he could bring it back to life. Nina watched him for a long moment. "Magic doesn't act like that," she said. "Magic can't control you."

Brujo snorted.

Nina realized she was still hanging onto the jar of mayonnaise, turning it around and around in her hands.

"I never felt him," Brujo said.

"Hmm?"

"All that magic, and I never felt him until he opened his mouth." Brujo tossed the dead turtle back into the woods. "I thought he was going to eat me."

"You shrieked."

He looked at her, his eyes wide. "You still want to take his magic. You can't. I'm telling you Nina, it's too *deep*. We're . . . ghosts to that kind of thing. He'll strip us out of our bodies and devour us, and we won't be nearly dead, we'll just roll around in his guts . . ."

She dropped down next to him, but he scooted away from her. "Brujo . . ."

He smacked his hands on the grass. "Do not make me go back there. I won't do it, not even for you. Please, let's just leave."

She didn't answer him. Sitting here on the ground, she could feel the blackberry bushes digging into the soil. Running along in the rich topsoil, spurred on by Mother's blood, and her magic. Growth. That was what magic was for, until you had tangled everything up, until you were connected to everything, and everything was a part of you, and you could never be rooted out. That was magic.

What if Brujo was right, and the wizard had made a demon? What could it do?

What could she do with it?

Nina laid her head against the earth. The ground was cold on her cheek, but she lay still. She stretched her mind toward Mother's blood as it raced through the blackberry bushes. They could feel the wizard's magic. Their roots were already growing toward Jan Karl's home. The bushes wanted the boy, or demon, or whatever he might be.

"Nina," Brujo begged softly.

Nina ignored him. The desire of Mother's blood was palpable. The blood wanted the boy. Boy, not demon, it whispered. A magic boy, a blood boy, a boy whose voice commands and quells, a boy who will take me, thorn and berry and vine, and bind me to him. I will walk in him, and all blood and magic will walk with us. We will breathe. I will breathe again.

Bring him. Bind him.

She would. Nina brushed her lips against the earth and whispered her promise to Mother's blood.

And beside her, Brujo wept and wept.

• • •

There was a position at Asher's elementary school

for a substitute teacher. It was ridiculously easy to get hired, and in no time, Nina was standing on the sidewalk in front of the school, watching the last bus empty its cargo of children. Her first day at school. Again. Teaching third graders. She escorted the stragglers into the school, and made her way to the classroom she'd been assigned.

As the morning wore on, she found herself watching a little black-haired girl doing busywork. Her little brow was all scrunched up, and her lips moved slightly as she read through the word problems on the page in front of her. Was this what Steve had wanted? Ten years together, and they had no children. Hadn't even made love once without protection. He hadn't said anything, but wasn't a woman supposed to crave motherhood? Should Nina have said something? Would children have made them happier?

Had Steve thought Brujo was enough?

Ha. After their fifth anniversary, Steve had tried his best not to think about Brujo at all. A trick he had soon adapted to Nina.

Thinking of Brujo and Steve made her stomach sour. Steve, a thousand miles away, and uninterested in her; Brujo, as physically close as ever, but completely distant. Last night had been the worst: he had closed himself in her closet and refused to say anything to her. The result of her being honest with him. She was not about to give up on Jan Karl's magic.

She heard the door just down from her classroom bang open. A cluster of fourth graders came bustling down the hall. Nina looked up—there was Asher. She glimpsed him for just a second as his head bobbed by the little window set in the closed door. He was talking to someone. Then he was gone. Nina turned back to her class. The third graders would be eating lunch at the same time as the fourth graders. There would be time then to see what kind of boy she'd found.

The cafeteria smelled of overcooked noodles, grease and cleaning solution. Nina herded her class through the double doors and watched them scatter to the tables, to the lunch line . . . and there was Asher. He was waggling a pair of French fries in his mouth like fangs, and the boys around him were laughing. Not just boys, Nina saw—girls, too. Just a few. One of the kids at the table stuck some fries in his nose, and that sent them off again, and louder still when he ate them. Asher laughed along with them, smacking his hand on the table, and choking on his milk.

He stood up, still giggling, and took his empty tray to the trash. But he didn't sit down at the table he'd gotten up from. He went to a different one on the other side of the room. He sat there for a little while—and Nina saw that, slowly, the children at that table began to defer to him. To make him their center. And then he stood up from that table, strolled over to get another box of chocolate milk, and went back to yet another table. And the same thing happened.

Nina was watching him move to his fourth table when a voice interrupted her observations. "Little politician, isn't he?"

The speaker was a man in a pressed brown corduroy suit, with a thick mustache above his lip. He was standing too close for Nina's comfort, his arm brushing hers. "I've watched him do this every day for the past couple weeks."

Nina lifted an eyebrow. "I'm sorry, what are we talking about, Mister . . . ?"

"Vances. Johnny Vances, substitute teacher extraordinaire. I'm teaching Rene Tibbets' fourth graders while she's out with a pregnancy."

Nina just smiled and turned back to watching the children.

"Every day. Every day, table to table to table. And the lunchroom gets louder and louder, and the little darlings more and more out of control, until the whole afternoon, it's like they're on speed, they're so wound up."

"Oh." Nina slid a little to the left, so her elbow rubbed against his. "Is he in your class?"

Johnny Vances shrugged. "Naw. Thank goodness. He's in Tucker's class."

Time to see what kind of boy she'd found. Nina unfolded her arms, and the back of her hand brushed against his. "He's not hurting anyone . . ."

"No. Of course not. He's just making it more difficult for us to teach the rest of them. He's not a bully."

"I don't see how he's doing any harm at all."

Johnny Vances snorted. "Trade classes with me, you'd see it. After lunch, not a single one of them wants to listen."

"Hmm. Well, what can you do? Like you said, he's not hurting anyone." She paused, and offered Johnny Vances a smile. A genuine, I'm-interested-in-you smile. "Glad I don't have to deal with him. It's hard enough being a sub, with the real teachers looking down their noses at you, and the kids trying to take advantage of you, and the lousy pay. I'm glad I don't have to be the one to deal with a kid like that."

Johnny Vances shrugged. "Lucky you."

Asher got up to move to another table, and Nina felt Johnny Vances stiffen slightly. Like he just sucked in a breath. She was sure that if she looked, the hairs on the back of his neck would be raised.

"Enough's enough," he muttered.

Johnny Vances intercepted Asher on the way to his fifth table. He walked up behind him, grabbed the boy's arm, and turned him forcibly around. The cafeteria got very quiet.

"You need to find your seat, Mr. Karl, and stay there," Johnny Vances said. "I'm tired of all your moving around."

Asher tried to pull his arm away, but couldn't. "Sorry."

"And quit . . . instigating everyone."

Asher looked at him dumbly. "Sorry."

"Go sit down there. At that empty table. Until you can learn to keep your little butt in one place."

Asher went. Meekly, almost. Johnny Vances straightened himself, and glared at the children around him who were staring. And then he went to stand against the wall. Not next to Nina, thankfully.

It happened subtly. The first was a brown-haired girl. She said something to Asher as she passed him on the way to empty her tray, and he smiled at her. She moved on. A group of black boys passed him—they lingered for a moment longer, and smacked him on the back when they caught Johnny Vances staring at them. After that, every single student that walked by his empty table stopped for just a second to speak to him. Every one of them. Without exception. Soon there was a pool of children around him—and then a chubby boy sat down across from Asher. He looked startled that he'd done so, that in defiance of every law of the cafeteria and good sense, he seated himself next to this . . . instigator. Nina smiled. Other children were sitting down now, a few looking toward Johnny Vances, but most of them just sitting down to sit down.

It took only a moment for Johnny Vances to stride across the cafeteria. Shoulders back, arms swinging. Every child sitting at Asher's table saw him coming, but not one of them moved. They got more raucous, until the air rang with their shouts and squeals and laughter.

Johnny Vances looked straight at Asher, and Nina saw him mouth the words, "Get up."

But Asher just shrugged, and she saw him answer, "Leave us alone."

And he did. Johnny Vances turned himself around and walked away. Strode away, even, like this was a battle he'd just fought and won. He came by Nina.

"You handle yourself very well," she said. "With the children."

"Thanks," he said brightly. "That one kid—Asher Karl, that's him sitting on the end there—what a good kid. Wish they could all be as sweet."

Nina nodded. "That'd be nice."

He continued walking away. Right out of the cafeteria. Nina wondered where he was going—but only for a moment. The bell chimed for the end of lunch. She gathered up her class, and led them upstairs, whistling to herself.

What wonderful magic she would work with this boy.

•••

When she got home, she found a small chip of a mirror on the porch directly in front of the door. She nudged it with her foot, but it wouldn't budge. She opened the door, and found the rest of the mirror pasted against the walls in jagged bits.

"Brujo!" she called. There were seeds scattered all around the landing just inside the door, along with something white and grainy—salt. "Brujo!"

He appeared at the top of the stairs, a crucifix around his neck. "What?" he asked.

"What is all this?"

"Protection."

"Seeds? Mirrors and . . . did you intentionally turn your boxers inside out?"

"If you're not going to protect us, I have to."

"Brujo, you know as well as I do that none of these protections actually work."

He looked at her. "Until we went to Jan Karl's house, I knew as well as you did that demons did not exist." Brujo paused. "I am not sure of anything anymore, Nina."

That hung in the air between them for a long moment. What could she say to that? "Brujo, I know that you're frightened. But I watched Asher today . . ."

"You watched the demon today," he said flatly.

"You can call him whatever you want, Brujo. I watched him, and I saw what he did with his magic."

"Demon," Brujo whispered. "Demon, demon, demon. He'll eat us both alive, and there won't be a ghost left in us. No more Nina, no more Brujo, just a demon laughing."

She had climbed the stairs without thinking. Nina took his little chin in her hand. "I've seen what Asher can do. He can bind people. Maybe . . . Maybe he can bind you. Make you real."

Brujo stared at her. "I am real, Nina."

For a moment, she thought she had lost him utterly. "Not just real to me, Brujo," she said quickly. "Real to others. And not just as a . . . changeling child. Or a disguise. You'd be independent. Real."

"Real to whom? Who else possibly cares whether or not I'm real."

The answer was so easy, so simple, it felt sweet on Nina's lips. "Steve. You'd be real to Steve."

He opened his mouth and closed it, and his eyes widened. He swallowed, so his little Adam's apple went up, down, up.

She had him. There'd be no more talks of demons now that there was this new, forbidden hope. Nina embraced Brujo and they laughed and wept together at the top of the stairs.

And Nina knew that as long as he wept, his eyes would be too clouded to see the lie in hers.

• • •

The blackberries vines grew long quickly. Every morning, Nina would inspect the plants, take measure of their strength. Every morning, there'd be some half-dead creature panting its life out underneath them. Some, Brujo would take—most, he left for the bushes to devour. He was growing tall now, tall enough that he asked Nina for new boxers. And not just boxers: shyly, half smiling, he asked her for a new pair of jeans to replace the ones he'd worn to rattiness. And a pair of new shirts. And a jacket. And shoes. It was the first time he'd ever asked for new clothes.

Fall into winter, winter into spring. The librarian at Asher's school had a nervous breakdown. Nina took her place for a week. Then two. Three months passed, and Nina was working every day in the library. Once a week, Asher's class came in—Asher's class. And how thoroughly he made it his. How subtly it was his. Did he even know that when he spoke, every child in the room shifted a little toward him? Nina doubted it. He was a sweet kid, beginning to end, if a little bit silly. The same quiet, secret, hidden admiration others directed at him, he returned.

Asher was a boy who was thoughtlessly in love with everything. And everyone.

The blackberry bushes blossomed in the middle of May. Too early—Nina worried about a late spring frost, but the weather remained mild. By June, the white blossoms had given way to dark berries as fat as Nina's thumb. The roots had grown deep and strong, pulling themselves toward Jan Karl's home. Toward Asher.

Bring him, bind him, they whispered still. I promise, I promise, Nina whispered back.

But she did not have to bring him at all. He came on his own.

There was a yellow flyer on her mailbox, wedged between the red flag and the black plastic case. Asher's name caught her eye before she could crumple it up and toss it away.

> Yard maintenance by ASHER KARL & CO.
> Lawns cut, Hedges trimmed, Gardens weeded!
> Reliable! Cheap!
> Call now, scheduling available!
> 678.555.1993
> asherlawns678@aol.com

And beneath that was a black-and-white picture of a boy, slaving away behind a push mower. Nina folded the flyer up carefully and brought it inside with her.

The phone rang twice before a young female voice answered. "Hello?"

Nina paused. "Hi, I'm calling about the lawn care services."

"Oh. Asher, it's for you."

There was a moment of quiet—Nina thought she heard the tinny bleep of a video game being paused—then Asher's voice at the end of the line. "Hi, Asher Karl. What can I do for you?"

So professional. "Hi, Asher, this is Nina Borriegos. I live up the street—"

"Right. Tencil Lane." He sounded guarded.

Nina paused. "Right. Listen, I'm so sorry for the way Enzo behaved last time. I don't know what got into him."

"It's okay. Are you calling about the lawn care flyer?"

Good. Business. "Yes, actually. I don't have a lawn mower yet, and I could use a handyman to help keep it up."

"All right—how big is your lot?"

She had no idea. "I don't really know. About a quarter-acre, I guess."

"We offer gardening services as well—tilling, planting, mulching, weeding. Whatever you need."

Nina laughed. "Just a lawn mowing for right now."

"Okay. A quarter-acre—that'll go eight dollars. We've got a special for new customers."

"Sounds fine. Do I need to talk to your dad?"

"No. It's my business. He's just in marketing."

"When can you come by?"

She heard him flipping through some pages. "How about next Tuesday at ten?"

"You can't come any sooner? This Saturday, maybe?"

He muttered something to himself, then called, "Claire, can you take me to a job on Saturday?"

The voice of the girl came back, "No. Get Dad to do it."

"He can't do *anything* on Saturdays, stupid. Duh."

"Just *push* your junk over there. You could use the exercise."

"Claire!" He seemed to realize Nina was still

on the phone. "Uh, can you hold for a second, Mrs. Borriegos?"

"Miss," she corrected him, but he'd already put the phone down. Miss Nina Borriegos. She hadn't thought about Steve and Camille in weeks. No—months. Since she saw Asher at school. And now. . . she felt no need to. None at all.

Asher came back, "Saturday's fine. Around ten?"

"All right."

"Thanks for calling Asher Karl and Company. I'll see you then."

He hung up. Nina dropped the phone slowly back onto the hook, and leaned against the counter. Brujo was watching her with his wide eyes.

"Saturday at ten," she said.

"We better start picking then." He handed her a bucket.

They took off their shoes and went out back to the blackberry bushes. The fruit was so heavy, it only took a touch to take it off the vine. Barehanded, barearmed, they worked through each bush. Silently, they worked. There was more fruit than Nina had ever seen. Mother's blood in each berry. Mother's voice in her ears as she stretched her hand through the tangle of briars and leaves. Bring him, bind him. Over and over, Mother whispering, whispering.

When the last berry dropped into Nina's palm, the voice of the bushes died away in the wind. All of Mother's blood, all of her magic, was now in twelve buckets full of blackberries. The bushes seemed smaller—naked, even. Empty.

Brujo helped her bring the buckets into the bathroom and dump the berries into the tub. They poured boiling water over the blackberries, and stirred them until the water cooled, and the blackberries were a mash of purple and black. Nina stripped off her clothes except for her underwear, and settled herself into the tub. The flesh of blackberries around her, Mother's blood in their juice oozed over her ears. Brujo leaned over the tub, eyes wide, unblinking, and touched her calf. Where he drew his finger along her skin, a thin cut opened—Nina felt the sting of the blackberries against the wound. He cut her on her calves, her arms, her belly, and paused as he brushed the back of his hand against her cheek. And almost she told him. Almost, she could not bear to lie to him any longer. But he grinned, and touched her throat. Nina was thrown into darkness as blood from her neck spilled into the blackberries.

Real magic is what you bleed into it.

For a long time, Nina was senseless. When she awoke, her throat was parched, and she could feel granules of blackberry seeds under her thighs and back and feet. She couldn't see anything. She felt a smooth hand brush her forehead, and lower a straw to her lips. Water had never tasted so good.

"How long?" she whispered.

Brujo answered, "A day."

Only a day. There was a heaviness in her chest, and she imagined her heart was beating slow, slow, slow. Everything was still.

A hand on her calves, her arms, her belly. Needles of pain in those places as the blackberry juice rushed into the wounds to drink up her blood. And then a deep pain, deeper than death, across her throat. Drink, little berries. Drink me and live forever.

The second day passed. Nina thought Brujo might have given her a cracker and some more water sometime, but maybe it was only a dream, because her stomach gnawed at her, and her throat felt like sandpaper. He came again, touched her again, whispered something to her. But she didn't hear him. Maybe she didn't hear him. And maybe that was a dream too, him speaking, because he had said he loved her, he had wept over her, and his little hands had caught every tear before it fell into the tub so that the magic wouldn't be broken. Brujo would never say he loved her. He was a changeling child. Incapable of love.

On the third day, there were no seeds left in the tub. Nor berry flesh. This was the last day. Nina's whole body ached. Let it end, she whispered to no one. Let me die, it is too much, and there is no magic worth the price of my pain. Mother, let me die and sleep.

But Brujo came to her. Real for sure, because he touched her, and she bled into the tub again. And he dumped sugar and yeast into the tub with her.

"Nina," he whispered. "You have to mix it all together."

She moved her arms, arms as heavy as wooden beams. Weakly, she stirred the whole concoction as Brujo praised her. Praised her pain, praised her endurance, what a good girl she was to fight off panic and death so that he could be real and wear Gap clothes, and call Steve his daddy. How brave, to dare to control a demon. How powerful, to bring magic and blood together, to raise Mother from the dead and give her a new body, the body of a magic boy.

He left her again as she struggled. And he didn't come back through all the long hours of the third day. Nina was alone with the blood and the blackberries and the sugar and yeast. Alone, she brought it all together. Alone, she made magic. Alone, she worked her will into the world that remained to her, this subworld in the bathroom. Alone, she felt the tub froth with magic.

And wine.

And then, she ceased.

•••

Brujo came to her in the late afternoon, and worked her body out of the tub. Now he could cry on her. Now he could touch her, and his touch would not cut her. He dried her body off, and brought in a comforter from one of the unpacked boxes and laid it over her. Her skin was cold, and her breathing was shallow, but she wasn't bleeding any longer. Brujo put a pillow under her head and let her sleep.

Tomorrow was Saturday.

•••

After being in the tub for three days, the bathroom floor was surprisingly comfortable. Nina pushed herself off of it—her mind was filled with the memory of blood and blackberry juice and froth. Her body ached, but what magic inflicted, magic cured. The cuts on her hands and legs and stomach and throat were only welts now. Nina looked at the tub—it was empty. Brujo must have taken the wine.

She stumbled to get the water turned on and to get out of her underwear. Not a bath. A shower. So she could stand and stretch. She guzzled water from the showerhead until her stomach ached, and then let it wash over her head. Nina turned the knob all the way to the left, until the water was as hot as it could possibly get.

She was alive. Three days of blood and death and cold washed off her. She was weak, and her knees trembled, but she lived. Her body would heal. And she would have Asher.

Eventually, the water turned cold, driving her out

of the shower. As she dried off, she heard the hum of a lawn mower starting. Ten a.m. She got dressed slowly, choosing a blouse with a high collar to hide the welt on her throat, and went out into the living room.

Brujo was there, staring out the window at Asher. His eyes followed the boy as he moved back and forth across the lawn. Brujo had on his new clothes.

"It scares me," Brujo said, as Nina slumped on the couch. "This demon . . . Asher. I thought that knowing what magic it held would be enough. But it isn't, I don't think. I want to vomit, I'm so scared. He could look at me now, and I would die."

"Come away from there, then," Nina said.

He did. Brujo came and sat by her, quietly. Very still, his hands folded in his lap. "The wine is in the refrigerator. How are you going to get him to drink it?"

"I won't tell him it's wine." Nina went to the window. Asher's lawn mower had cut off. He was bent over, pulling grass out of the vent. She wondered if Claire had driven him, or if he had walked.

Brujo left the room, but Nina stayed. Watching Asher. He had finished with the mower, and was trimming around the house and trees with a weed eater. Every now and then, he'd pause, scrub his hand through his hair, and flick the sweat off. He didn't seem in any particular hurry to finish things—he saw her and gave a little wave. Nina lifted her hand to him, and he went back to work. How had Jan Karl made such a creature as Asher? What magic had he put into forming those arms, those legs, that boyish, wild grin?

Maybe that was the magic she should be looking for. Not the object, but the maker.

Too late for that. Asher was coming up the step to the door. Nina found the wine in the refrigerator, poured some into a plastic cup, and dropped a few ice cubes in it. The wine was light red, but clear. Maybe it could pass at first as Hawaiian Punch. Until he drank it, and by then it would be too late.

He knocked. Nina met him at the front door. She'd never been this close to him, not through the whole school year. She could see the freckles on his nose, the little mole on the side of his neck. His hands and knees were stained green, and he smelled rank.

"Hi, Mrs. Borriegos. You want to look it over?" He indicated the front lawn. "I got around back, too, if you want to check that." His eyes darted to the cup she was holding, but he didn't say anything.

She handed it to him, smiling. "You looked hot," Nina said.

"Thanks." He tipped the cup back into his mouth with gusto, and immediately choked. But Nina saw— a throatful of wine had gone down, though the rest of it wound up in the grass and on the porch. Asher sputtered and gagged, and when he rose to his feet, he looked pale and a little green.

Nina put a hand on his back. "You okay? Go down the wrong tube?"

"No . . . I'm fine." Asher coughed again and wiped his nose. He backed away from her touch, his eyes watery. "I need to go."

"How much do I owe you?"

He faltered a moment. "Eight dollars."

Moment of truth. "How about six. Six is fine, Asher. Six is more than enough."

Asher's eyes went wide. Nina thought for a moment he would vomit. He swallowed again, and coughed. Then he whispered, "A-All right. Six is enough." His eyes were frightened and wild.

She planted the money in his hands. "On second thought, here's eight. You've done a lot of work today, Asher. Thanks. There's no need to tell your dad about what you drank, or this little conversation, either. Go on home now."

He muttered, "Okay. You're welcome." He jerked at the lawn mower, pulling it after him, but forgot the weed eater in his rush to get away from her.

Let him go. She had to pack, and plan for tonight. Asher wouldn't say anything. He was hers. Nina sucked in a deep breath. The air was still full of Asher's scent, and the tang of the grass he had cut. She turned her back on the warm day, on the sun, and the grass and the slight breeze, and stepped inside. She noticed the little shard of mirror on the step, the little keep-away talisman Brujo had placed there last fall. Asher had walked right over it.

Brujo met her in the hallway. He was smoothing his hands over his shirt. "It's done," she said to him.

He nodded at her. He looked profoundly unhappy.

There was nothing to be done for him. Nina dumped the wine left in Asher's cup out into the sink. There was still a full decanter of it in the refrigerator. Enough to do what needed to be done. Enough to make sure that Jan Karl would never follow her, never see his magic again.

Brujo was staring out the window. She walked slowly behind him, and put her arm around his shoulders. She slid her fingers up his neck, to tousle the soft black hair at the back of his head.

Then she swept his feet out from under him, yanked his head back, and set the decanter of blackberry wine to his mouth. The liquid rushed out over Brujo's face until she forced the bottle between his lips. It was either drink or drown. For a long moment, as he struggled and spat, Nina was sure he'd choose to drown. But she pressed a knee into Brujo's stomach, and when she let up, he took an involuntary breath, and swallowed. And calmed. He drank from the bottle slowly now, every drop that could be coaxed to run out.

Nina let the bottle roll away. The carpet was stained with blackberry wine, and Brujo stood looking at her blankly.

"Your eyes are blue," she said softly to him, wiping a bit of wine off his chin. "Your hair is light brown. Lighter. And curly."

And she talked Brujo through the change.

•••

Midnight. Nina left her car running in front of Jan Karl's home. There were no lights inside the house, not even any nightlights that she could see through the bare windows. It didn't matter. She wasn't going inside. He would come to her. Mother's blood would bring him.

She stood out in the cool spring air and reached out for him. Come here, Asher. Come to me. Bind yourself to me. The world is as silent as stone, and mine is the only living voice you hear, mine is the only voice you know, and you must come now, Asher, come now.

The front door opened. Asher looked at her, frightened, his hair wild with sleep. His feet were bare. He crossed the lawn, and got into the car without saying a word. He didn't even speak when he saw Brujo, now his twin, in the seat next to him.

"Give him your pajamas, Asher," Nina said to him as she closed her door. A moment later, she heard the rustle of clothes being taken off. "Brujo, put them on."

"Nina," Brujo said. "Nina."

She wouldn't look back at him. If she did, she'd be lost. Mother would be lost. And so she let him say her name over and over and over and did not answer him. She waited until she could no longer hear him putting on Asher's pajamas.

Her voice cracked. "Brujo, get out. Your name is Asher, now. Go on inside—you know where your room is. Go on."

She heard the door open—and she glanced back at him. Instinct. It almost undid her. She saw him there in the moonlight, wearing another boy's body, another boy's clothes. But it was Brujo, she could see it in the way the light fell on his shoulders. He turned to her, and she saw his eyes, blue now instead of the dark-as-chocolate she'd known for so long. Those eyes she'd known and sacrificed for. Those intimate eyes.

But his eyes did not know her. She was saved. He reached up to the window and placed his fingers on the glass. "Nina." Not pleading. Not demanding. But there was nothing like recognition in his voice. "Nina. Nina." He said it like a word that might help him remember something important he'd forgotten. "Nina. Nina. Nina."

She would not wait for him to say anything else. She pulled away, leaving him alone in the darkness on the side of the road. Nina watched him grow smaller and smaller in the rearview mirror, until there was nothing to him but the vague, pale blur of Asher's pajamas in the moonlight. And then she turned a corner, and he was gone.

They drove south. Asher was silent in the back, although every once in a while he'd hiccup. Nina realized that he had finally fallen asleep when the hiccups stopped and soft snores drifted forward. She drove on, putting miles between Jan Karl's home and herself and Asher.

At dawn, they stopped at a run-down gas station on the outskirts of Emporia, Virginia. The bathrooms had outside entrances, and there were no other cars around. Nina coaxed the bathroom key away from the grumpy attendant, and hustled Asher into the ladies' room. He went quietly, shivering a bit where her hand wrapped around his bare arm. The bathroom was tiny, with a bare, futzing light, a toilet with a loose seat, and a sink with streaks of brown running from the base of the faucet to the drain. She made him bend his head over the sink, and produced a pair of electric hair clippers. Asher didn't move as Nina cut his hair severely short. No more curls, and the hair at his skull was more blond than brown. Nina gave him an oversized flannel shirt to wear, a pair of Brujo's new jeans and sneakers, and a pair of round-rimmed glasses she'd found packed away.

"I can't see right," he said, as she put the glasses on his nose. But he didn't move his hands to take them away.

"Then close your eyes." She was more curt than she meant to be. Her voice echoed sharply in the small space. "Put your shoes on, Asher."

He did so. Nina gathered up the snips of his hair, dumped them in the toilet, and flushed. She had to flush twice to get all of them down. "Let's go."

She held out her hand to him, and he had no choice but to take it. When his hand touched hers, she could feel Mother's blood in his veins searching for a root in Asher's marrow, seeking to tangle him. Nina led him to the car, and they pulled away from the gas station.

Still he was quiet. Nina glanced back at him. He sat very still, arms crossed, hands beneath his armpits, like the tips of his fingers were cold. He looked scared and frustrated. From time to time, he'd open his mouth, but then would just bite his lip instead of speaking.

"I'm not going to hurt you, Asher," Nina said finally.

His eyes darted forward, met hers in the rearview mirror. Again, he opened his mouth, but shut it quickly. He sputtered, "I—I can't say what I want to say." His lips were trembling.

She realized what that meant. The wine and blood were stopping him from using magic against her. "No, I don't imagine you can."

"*That* hurts."

"I'm sorry, Asher." And she was sorry for his pain. But glad too—glad that whatever he had done to Johnny Vances, he could never do to her.

He took a quick breath, like he was gathering himself to shout at her—but when she looked, his face was red, his eyes wide, and his mouth open in a silent, straining O. Finally, he let the breath go in a puff that Nina felt on the back of her neck. Asher slouched down in his seat, huffing.

"I swear I'm not going to hurt you," Nina said again. Quietly. Trying to take the sharpness out of her voice.

He sniffed, wiped his nose with his sleeve, and refused to look at her. "Where are you taking me?"

The question hammered into her heart. She hadn't even thought of where she was going—it was instinct. Home. To Mother, and the blackberry bushes that tangled her bones. To Marquez, Texas. And yet . . . here she was, as free as she'd ever been in her life. Why was she going home? Why not go somewhere *she* wanted to go first? Why not take advantage of the magic she'd stolen? Briefly, she entertained thoughts of Las Vegas, but that simply wasn't her. Perhaps California, then back to Texas and Mother. Perhaps she could stop in Kansas on the way out there.

Kansas.

Nina tightened her grip on the wheel. Kansas. And Steve. Of course. There it was, the little smoky flame that had been burning in her all these months. Steve. Her marriage. She'd ignored it, fought it down, but now . . . now she had Asher. Now things were different. Now she could . . . What? Ask him to love her again? Why would he? Could Asher do that?

He could. He'd made Johnny Vances forget his antipathy. He could make Steve love her again. The certainty was so powerful in her, it thumped against her ribcage. And then, she'd have her marriage back. She'd have Steve back. Her stomach was suddenly a jumble of warmth and ache and whirling, turbulent emotion.

Asher did not ask his question again. Nina was grateful for that—she didn't think she could answer him. Not without crying, because now she knew the reason for all of this. Absurd, she told herself. Absurd that this child should be made for you. Absurd that Jan Karl had placed so much power in him just so you can reclaim Steve from Camille. Absurd that you should sacrifice Mother and Brujo to be able to bring this magic boy to Steve and mend your marriage.

That's what it meant. There'd be no going to Marquez, Texas, now. No more planting blackberries, no more listening for the whisper of blood. That was the blood she'd spill—sacrificing her own magic so that Asher could remake her marriage.

Nina realized it was getting dark. "We'll stop for the night," she said, louder than she meant to, because her heart was still beating fiercely, and because she'd been driving for hours now, not saying anything.

She found a motel just off the interstate. While Asher sat sullenly in the car, Nina purchased them a room with two double beds. The room was clean enough, but small, and furnished only with the beds and a nondescript chair. Not even a nightstand.

"Go ahead and get settled," she told him tersely, watching as he surveyed the room, wrinkling his nose.

He turned on her, and for a moment, she thought he meant to hit her. His fists were clenching and unclenching. But he only glared, his jaw working like he was chewing something spongy with his back teeth. "T-T-Take," he stammered. "Take. M-Mmm-Me." And then he stopped, and gagged, and coughed. The fire was driven out of his eyes, and he fled to the bed, plowing himself beneath the covers. And there he lay still, sniffling, and giving a harsh little hiccup every now and then as he fought to control himself.

Nina stood in the doorway of the room. She'd felt his magic, like massive arms searching for a way to wrap around her. Magic like that could snuff her out, swallow her whole, devour her and not even notice. But she controlled him. He had been unable to touch her.

And she felt terrible because of it. Nina crossed the room slowly to touch the shivering pile of blankets. She felt Asher stiffen, and there came several guttural syllables from the boy. He couldn't even tell her not to touch him. Couldn't even tell her he didn't want her comfort.

She bolted the door, turned off the light, and slipped beneath the covers of her own bed.

She listened to Asher sniffling for a good long time and then sleep took her.

•••

The next two days were no better. Asher never looked out of the window once as they drove from Charleston, up through the Carolinas, through Tennessee and Missouri. He was sullen and silent, and his loathing radiated off of him like heat. He rarely spoke, and never again tried to use his magic on her. But from time to time, Nina would glance back at him to see him chewing his back teeth, or biting his lip.

Steve would turn him. He was great with children, real ones, anyway. Asher would like Steve, Nina decided. They had the same kind of sense of humor—silly and carefree, empty of cynicism. Steve liked the physical, understated humor of Buster Keaton and Charlie Chaplin, and she had a feeling that Asher would too.

So Nina kept her silence as well. Gave him no more reason to despise her. She would be patient, and willing, and he would learn to love her.

She drove slowly as they left the motel in Topeka, watching the plains roll out all around her. Gold and brown and far off, the dots of antelope against the pale horizon. She and Steve had come out here to picnic beneath the sun and make love in the grass and wind. How long had it been since those heady days? When all the magic she'd thought she needed could be found in him. When the only world she'd cared to tangle herself in was his.

Mother was dead, Brujo was gone. Nothing at all remained of that old world. The world of her lies, her betrayals. The future was like this prairie: open, sunlit, and full of warmth. And she'd drive into it together with Steve and Asher.

Salina hadn't changed. Not much, anyway. There was a new Holiday Inn being built, and a New Age Christian Life center going up where a Payless Shoe store had been. Nina turned down the road that led to her old home. They'd leave right away, once Asher had spoken with Steve. Camille could have the house, if she wanted it. If she and Steve were still together. And welcome to it, woman.

And there it was. And *her*, too. Camille. In the front yard, bent over, pulling up a patch of weeds out of a flowerbed that had not been there a year ago. Nina drove by slowly, to take things in. Flowerbeds, a chain-link fence, and a cluster of bushes crowding the basement windows. Camille had made herself comfortable in Nina's place. Nina turned around in the cul-de-sac, reached back and shook Asher's knee.

"We're here," she said.

The boy awoke slowly, taking in the sight of houses rather than roads and cars and highway. He blinked at the sunlight coming through the window, and rubbed his eyes. He looked so tired, so bone-weary.

She squeezed his knee, and offered him a little smile. He looked out the window instead of into her eyes. She would not get angry with him. He was immature and being sullen, but she would win him over. Patience and care.

Nina pulled up into the drive—Steve had replaced the gravel with asphalt. Camille stood up from her weeding, her hand rubbing at the small of her back. She'd gotten slender in the past year, as graceful as a willow. When she saw who it was pulling up, she dropped her garden gloves in the mulch and dirt, and hurried inside. Nina parked the car, got out, and opened the door for Asher.

He looked at her, terrified, and then looked at the house. "Duh-Doh-n," punctuating each little stutter with a sharp intake of breath.

She smoothed her hand across his forehead. "Asher,

this will be easy. As easy as a sentence or two. That's all I'm asking, Asher. A sentence or two. Come with me. Come on, now."

And she took his hand, and walked him up to the front door. He resisted, and she could feel it through the shuddering in his limbs as he tried to keep them from moving. She wished there had been time to explain all this to him. But there wasn't. And she was saving him, wasn't she? Yes. Because if she hadn't come to Steve, she would have gone to Mother. And Mother would *take* him, that was what she had promised, to live in Asher, to root in his bones and blood, and compel all magic and flesh to walk after them. It was difficult to make him do this hard, terrible thing—but he would come to see the wisdom of it in time.

Steve met them at the door. "Nina," he said, nodding slightly. There was caution in his eyes as they flicked over Asher. "What do you want?"

There was no time to waste. "Asher, tell Steve to love me."

The boy's mouth dropped, and then he fought to close it. Fought to run off the porch, and escape. But his mouth opened, and his feet did not move. The wine's magic held him as stiff as a marionette.

"Tell him he loves me, Asher," Nina whispered. "One sentence, so easy."

He made no sound, but the tears that gathered at his eyes to roll down his ashen face were words enough. Nina reached up and brushed his cheek with her finger. A soft touch, like Mother's.

"Tell him, Asher," Nina said.

She felt the boy's magic gather in the air around them, but was completely unprepared for its strength. Asher wept out the words, "Steve, you love her," and his magic crashed into them like a mountain falling from the sky. This was as different from what Asher did to Johnny Vances as making a mudpie was from making a galaxy. Nina saw clearly now—Asher had not made Johnny Vances love him any more than he forced anyone to love him. He had only told him to go away. And Asher's magic had propelled him away, as it was meant to. But Johnny Vances, who obsessed over power, saw that greatness in Asher. And that was what he loved, not the boy.

This was different. Asher's magic remade Steve. It bound what had been severed between him and Nina, forced into being what had been extinguished.

Asher was not a demon. No, he was a god to be able to do this. She owned a god. This was more than magic, more than the petty powers she'd toyed with, stolen, or left lying under blackberry bushes. This was omnipotence. In this nine-year-old voice, in this sweet, deceptive face, in these smooth hands, oh, she could remake creation. She had taken blood and water and wine and tamed a god.

She felt strong, warm arms fold around her, and flinched. But these arms were flesh and blood. These arms had held her for ten years. And oh, how she had missed them. Steve held her and wept into her hair.

"I'm so sorry, Nina, I love you, I want you back, I want you back, I want to be your husband again, I'm sorry for everything I've done to hurt you, I want us back." And he did not let her go.

"It's all right, it's okay, Steve, I love you, I missed you so much." She lifted her lips to his, and all the hurt and pain and loss was swallowed up in them. The neglect, the year of absence and bitterness—bathed away in Steve's embrace, and in the softness of his kiss.

He was talking fast now, begging her to forgive him for his disloyalty, he'd do anything, he'd talk to Brujo, he wouldn't be so jealous and stupid this time, he'd love her forever, he'd be so *good*, just please give him another chance. Yes, yes, of course she would, he was her Steve, and she'd be better too, this time. This time they'd be a family, don't you see, a real family, because there *was* no Brujo, no wild, wild changeling child to watch them love each other.

But there was Asher, Nina thought. Her Asher, her godling. And he would love Steve, and he would love Nina. And he'd be happy, too.

Steve went silent for a moment, then drew in a long breath. "Cammie. Camille. I have to tell her."

"No," Nina said quickly. "No, Steve. Let it be." They could leave now. They should leave now, and get away from this house, that woman. Get away from the sins of their old marriage.

"What? I can't just let it go like this, Nina, I have to explain to her. . . ." He looked up to the window, like he expected to see her there. But there was no one. "I'm in love with you, Nina, I am. But that doesn't mean I can just walk away from her."

The old pang of how he'd left her spiked her heart. He *had* just walked away from her, leaving her an empty bed, and one morning a letter announcing that he was pursuing a divorce. But Nina stilled her bitterness. That was not a part of her life any longer. She nodded at him, and wiped her eyes. "Come back to me," she said.

"I will."

He went inside, leaving her alone again with Asher. The boy looked pale and drawn and frightened.

"I hate you," he said.

It was the clearest thing he'd ever said to her. No trembling, no stuttering—and his voice shook her straight to her spine, and all the way to the bones of her feet. It wasn't his magic that shook her—although she could feel that like an ominous fog all around, it couldn't touch her. It was his hatred. The boy who loved so easily, who adored everyone . . . hated *her*.

"I will always hate you, Mrs. Borriegos." His little face was tight and furious. "I'll hate you until I die."

She choked. "Go to the car, Asher."

He did, and after a moment, she followed him. The sun was warm, the breeze as well. She had Steve again. Her life was hers for the first time. No more chasing magic, no more stealing trinkets from wizards, no more whispering blackberry bushes. No more wandering, or wondering. And yet the words of this child made it all useless. Her future, her dreams with Steve. Nothing. Ash and dust.

She wanted to scream at him, slap that vulnerable face, shake him until he begged her for mercy. But she didn't. Because he was hers now, and his words were just words for her. Words, she told herself. Just words from a desperate, angry, sullen child. And he was hers, after all. His *real* words, the words that he'd mean when he finally understood the great gifts she'd offer him when the time came. Gifts of wisdom and power. And all blood and magic would gather to him, and he'd hand them to her, gratefully, lovingly. He would love her. He would apologize for this moment, and it was just a moment, after all. Just one, single, lonely instant. What was one instant in the great beautiful wash of the future? Nothing.

Steve hurried out the door, carrying an old duffel bag stuffed to bursting. Camille came to the door, but stopped there, her lovely face ragged, and her eyes broken and hurt. One hand fluttered like a butterfly at her throat, as the other hung uselessly by her side. Steve did not look back at her. But Nina saw. She remembered that look—she'd seen it in a mirror one year ago.

"I'm ready," Steve said, as he pitched himself into the front seat. He tossed his bag into the back next to Asher and settled a hand against Nina's bare arm. "I love you."

Nina swiped away a tear. "I love you too."

And she started the car, backed out of the drive, and turned west.

• • •

She had been right about Steve and Asher. They were fast friends after the first night with all of them together in one small hotel room. Whether it was because Steve was naturally charismatic and jovial, or because of Asher's magic, Nina didn't know. But she watched as Steve coaxed Asher out of his gloom. Small things—asking him what he wanted to watch on television, whether he wanted a soda from the motel vending machine, sharing the french fries they'd picked up from McDonald's with him . . . And Asher ate up Steve's kindness eagerly. Like Steve was the one with the magic. They sat on the floor of the motel, in the space between the twin beds, listing off synonyms for "fart." Asher beat him, hands down.

And he laughed. Just once, and softly. But Nina felt his laugh flow through her like light. Not magic—nothing supernatural or mystical about it. Light, as simple and beautiful as that.

"He's so different from Brujo," Steve said softly to Nina, after Asher was asleep. "I thought he was Brujo, at first. Just—changed. Disguised. You know. But he's not. Asher is . . ."

Nina placed her lips on Steve's. It was nice to have someone to fill in Asher's silence. "He's real."

"Right. Real. Why is he with you?"

A hundred answers rushed through her mind. A hundred ways to soften the story, to ease Asher's kidnaping. But this was her new life. And she would not go about destroying it by lying. "I kidnaped him."

He did not look shocked. "Ah," was all he said, and then he bent his face to hers to kiss her again, deeply.

She had not been kissed like that in all her ten years of marriage. As if Steve was abandoning himself through his lips into hers. Like his whole life depended on how long their mouths met together.

Like he loved her.

And so she didn't offer him any more explanation, and he never asked her how she had come to be with Asher again.

They got remarried in Vegas, in a brightly, whitely lit chapel just off the main strip. Nina was so giddy, she didn't think to remember its name. Along with their marriage license, they got a videotape of the ceremony, and an 8x10 glossy photograph. Nina held the photo in her lap all the way across the desert, stroking it like it was a talisman. Steve, one arm around her, his hand resting comfortably, naturally, on the curve of her hip; and her, smiling as gloriously as if this were the first time instead of the second. Steve's other arm took in Asher, who had managed a tiny grin when Nina told him to. They looked . . . good. Complete.

Two weeks later, she placed the photo in a frame, and hung it on the wall of the two-room apartment they'd found. It was nothing grand, but it was affordable, and from the balcony she could hear the Pacific Ocean. That was enough for her. Enough to know that her life was finally falling into place.

She heard Steve's footsteps outside the door—she could tell it was Steve because of the slap of his flip-flops on the cement landing—and then the sound of him fumbling with the apartment keys. Nina opened the door to see Steve holding Asher in his arms. Asher's eyes were closed, his mouth open slackly, and his skin was pale.

"He fell down when we were playing Frisbee. Just like someone had switched him off, and he fell right on his face. I thought he was going to choke on sand. But he was hardly even breathing."

Asher was breathing now, a rattling, harsh sound that bubbled in his chest and throat. Nina let Steve push past her to lay the boy down in his bed.

"He's feverish," Steve said.

Nina stepped over to Asher's bed and laid the back of her hand on Asher's forehead. He was hot. "I'll go get some Tylenol."

They didn't have any—she grabbed her purse and hurried out to the convenience store on the corner. By the time she got back, Steve had Asher in the tub, and had managed to get him conscious enough to start sucking on some ice cubes. Steve's eyes were panicked and wild.

"He threw up a second ago—there's still a mess all over his bed. And feel him." He took her hand and pressed it against Asher's chest. It was much hotter than before. "We don't even have a thermometer."

Steve had put a couple towels in the bath to prop up Asher's head. Nina dumped a few of the Tylenol into her hand, and pressed them into his mouth. "Chew them up, Asher."

He did, and swallowed. His eyes were only half-open, but they followed her as she watched him. He said something to her so she felt the press of his magic on her ears—but it was nonsense. Stuttering gibberish.

But the bathroom felt very close suddenly. She stood. "I'll go get his bed cleaned up."

Steve nodded and ran his finger along her back as she left. "I love you. I'll stay and make sure he doesn't drown."

Steve kept him in the bath for two hours. It took Nina nearly as long to get the stink of vomit out of Asher's little bedroom, and to scrub his sheets and pillows so that they wouldn't stain. When they moved him back to his bed his fever was reduced to the point that he was shivering. Little bubbles and lances of Asher's magic slipped across Nina's senses as they pulled some sweatpants over his legs, and covered him up with a blanket.

"Should we call a doctor?" Steve asked. "This is so bizarre. He's a healthy boy, and he just fell flat on his face for no reason at all."

No. No doctors. Nina shook her head quickly at him. "I don't think he needs a doctor now. His fever's broken, and look, he's quieted down. He probably just needs some sleep."

Steve scrubbed his hand through his hair. He smelled of the vomit Nina had just finished cleaning up. Nina looked and saw there were spots and runs of it all along the front of his T-shirt. "All right," he said. "I'll lay down some blankets and sleep in here tonight. Keep an eye on the kid, you know?"

It would be the first night since Kansas that they'd slept apart. Nina paused. "Okay. We'll take it in shifts."

He kissed her then, in the half-light of Asher's room. But Nina saw with dismay that his eyes were open, and they were looking at the boy on the bed, even as their lips moved together.

• • •

Thorns, blood, and flame. Jan Karl stooped over

her, his face a mask of fear and horror, and in his hand, something that was both a knife and a torch. He plunged it into her belly and began to saw. Mother was at her ear, whispering the seven curses to lay upon a friend who had betrayed you, whispering of maggots and staleness and disease. Where was Brujo? And suddenly, Jan Karl thrust his hands into her abdomen and *drew* her out. Like Brujo drawing a ghost, he lifted her right out of her own body, and continued lifting her, up and up and up, as if there were no end to his height. His face was ecstatic now, but Nina screamed forever, because his palms were full of thorns, and they cut her, they drank her up, they devoured her.

And below her, Mother burned and burned and burned.

Nina awoke.

Asher was staring at her, his round face furious and ashen. Steve was behind him, and there were tears in his eyes.

"Oh, Nina," Steve said. "Nina."

Asher placed his hand over Nina's lips. His palm was soft, the tips of his fingers so smooth, she wondered if he had fingerprints at all. But his voice was heavy and rough.

"Take me home."

She gave a little squeak, and felt the sudden crush of magic gather in the room and plummet for her—but nothing happened. Asher continued to look at her, angry and hurt and pale.

"Please, Mrs. Borriegos, take me home."

He wasn't turning his magic on her. He could have. Why didn't he? Nina scooted away from him, pushing her blankets off of her. Steve grasped her by the shoulders—not roughly, but holding her still. She looked at his face, and her heart felt run through with ice. There was no love there, now. Pity, and horror. No love.

"What did you do to him?" she screamed at Asher. She lunged at the boy, but Steve held her tightly so she couldn't move.

"Nothing!" Asher edged back, eyeing Steve. Making sure that he had her. "I didn't . . ."

Her husband. Her godling. Nina felt an old, bare, sharp sorrow rise up in her like a lash. She sobbed, and felt Steve's grip slacken for a moment. That was all it took. She whipped herself out of his arms, and struck Asher hard across the face, so her fingernails raked his cheek, and he toppled off the bed, onto the floor.

She jumped to get around the bed. "You stole him!"

But Steve caught her around the waist and pulled her down. "Nina! Stop! He's just a child!"

She could see Asher a little, one bare shoulder, shaking above the edge of the mattress. He was cowering. He was afraid.

Thief, and godling, and little boy.

"Asher?" Steve said. "Are you all right? I've got her now, she won't hurt you."

Asher pushed himself up, little by little. There were jagged lines of red on his cheek and chin where Nina's fingernails had cut him. He didn't look at her, didn't speak to her. He found the wall behind him and leaned against it.

Asher looked so young. He was just a boy still, with a boy's shoulders, and a boy's round face, and a little bit of baby fat around his paunch. Just a boy was all. Where was the godling she had seen? Or the demon Brujo had feared?

"Asher," she said, and her voice hitched in her throat. She moved toward him.

His eyes widened, and he jerked his hands up toward his face. "Stop! Don't!"

Asher's magic sought her out, a violent, powerful mass that threatened to devour her, burn her, strangle her. But as before, it couldn't touch her. Or didn't? Nina wasn't sure. Asher looked at her as he crouched behind the doorjamb, his hands covering his face and throat. He was shaking. He'd vomited on himself.

"Take me home, take me home, take me home," he pleaded, as the stink of his vomit filled the air. "I want to go home."

"He's sick, Nina," Steve said. He was still holding onto her shoulders.

"I can see that," Nina said. Her voice trembled.

She'd lost them. Broken them both away from her. Brujo, Mother, Steve, Asher. Nothing was left to her any longer. This wasn't freedom. This was loneliness.

"If he doesn't get help, he'll die." Steve's face was so close to hers. She watched his lips move, felt his breath on her face, warm and wonderful. Lips, mouth, she'd never kiss again. Breath that would never fill her lungs.

And Asher, there at the door, pale, vulnerable, weak, sick. Eyes full of loathing, and fear. He had never been truly hers. Hadn't he said so? Hate her until he died.

She tried to draw away from Steve, but he wouldn't let her go. He took her face in his hands, and forced her to look at Asher. His voice was soft. "Look, Nina. He's dying. You're killing him."

She was. "We can take him to a doctor."

"No." Steve shook his head. "He needs to go home."

It wasn't Asher's magic that tore at her heart. It was the thought of losing him. He had bound her.

"Mother," Nina said, almost a groan. "Mother can help him." The blackberries dripping with thick juice, like blood, thorns, and tangling vines, and her mother's whispers . . .

"Take me home," Asher said. "I want to go home."

But if she took him to Mother, he'd be lost to her. Mother would possess Asher, bone and blood and flesh. And Asher, this sweet boy, would be gone, not just from her, but from the world. Snuffed out. That was more than Nina could stand.

She nodded at last. "I'll take you home."

•••

She and Steve took turns driving. They stopped only to refuel, and for pee breaks. And every once in a while, Asher would tell them to stop and let him out to vomit. He wasn't eating anything, not even the Nibs and candy bars they picked up at gas stations along the way. Just water. His puke was mostly mucous and water and, disturbingly, blood.

The loathing was gone from his eyes, though. That was something. Something to take hope in. Asher rarely met her gaze, and never spoke to her without her speaking first to him—but he didn't hate her.

They passed through Salina, Kansas. Nina watched Steve look out the windows at the street lamps and the lit-up signs. It was dark, and raining. Asher was snoring in the back. And Nina should have been asleep, because she only had a couple hours until it was her turn, and she was exhausted. But she sat awake and silent with Steve as he passed the turnoff that would have led them to Camille. The lights of Salina dropped off into the night behind them. His hand was only six inches from hers, and Nina slowly moved her fingers to touch his skin. But he raised that hand away to rub his eyes. There was a little glimmer of liquid there that he quickly wiped on his jeans. Nina settled her hand on her lap again.

Lost to her.

Asher grew wan and listless the nearer to Virginia they came. He slept most of the time, and mumbled nonsense in his sleep. His magic skipped across Nina's mind in fragments and shards. It was as if his power was being scattered around like leaves. Dispersing. Disintegrating. And his life was going with it.

Nina and Steve took to sitting in the back with him as they drove. Just to be near him. Or away from each other, away from the lies they'd told, and the hurt they'd done. Asher was asleep now, and Nina slipped her hand over his. His skin was cool, smooth. His face was turned away from her—she noticed that his hair was starting to curl again, behind his ears a little. Little strands of honey gold, curling into the shady nook between his earlobe and skull. She wanted to reach out and touch it—because . . . because that was redemption, those curls. She had cut them off, and now they were back. And everything would be fine. Nina didn't touch them though. She kept her hand on Asher's, until he moved a little, and drew his hand away in his sleep.

They were two hours from Asher's home when he died. Nina was driving, listening to him snore, and wondering how she would face Jan Karl. She looked in the mirror to see him give a little shake, and then Asher's snoring became a horrible, wet rattle. And then it ended.

Silence took the car. Steve touched Asher, shook him a little bit. Then he lifted his fingers to the boy's throat. Nina saw. Those large, strong, wide fingers on Asher's bare throat, hoping for a pulse.

But he was gone. And the silence in the car remained, even though Nina cried until her throat and nose were raw, and her ears ached from Steve's sobbing. Silence as thick as water, as dense as concrete.

Stonebrook Estates was empty. No children riding their bikes at this time of night. No lights on in the houses. No windows lit up. Everyone was indoors, in bed. Asleep. No one to see her pull the car up into the driveway of Jan Karl's home. Steve got out before her, pulling Asher's body out with him. Cradling him. Nina followed him to the front door.

It opened before they got up the front steps, throwing light onto them. "My boy," Jan Karl said, his voice an odd mix of grief and anger and relief. "You brought him home."

He lifted Asher out of Steve's arms. "Come in, Steve."

His voice didn't invite her, but she moved to follow him anyway. Another hand touched hers, and held it quite tightly. A teenage boy, with dark hair and depthless, serious eyes. Eyes like chocolate.

Brujo.

He didn't smile at her. Didn't frown. Didn't move now that he had her hand. For a long moment he stood there and gripped her. And then he said, "Jan told me to think about what to say to you before this moment. And I still don't know. So I'm going to let you talk for a bit."

"You've grown up," Nina said.

Brujo shrugged. "All little boys do."

Nina found that she was shaking. From anger, from betrayal, from sorrow. "Is that it then, Brujo? You've found your Blue Fairy. Your Gepetto."

"No. I think I found God."

Nina stared. "There's no such thing."

"I know. Imagine my surprise when I found him shaking me awake and telling me it was time for breakfast."

"So he made you into a real, live boy."

The hurt that flashed through Brujo's eyes was so deep, it hurt Nina as well. But Brujo just nodded. "Yes. He did."

"And so now what?"

Brujo couldn't look her in the eye now. "I don't know, Nina." He looked to the window and sucked in a deep breath, like he'd seen something there. "He wants you inside."

She felt a tongue of fear flick against her heart. "I'm leaving."

But he had not let go of her hand, and before she could pull away, he had twisted it behind her, and was propelling her forward, kneeing the front door open, pushing her through. She was surprised at his strength, at the easy way that he moved her against her will. His arms, once spindly, were lean and full of muscle. Not her Brujo, not at all. Jan Karl's creature, as much his as Asher surely was.

The wizard sat holding Asher's body in the middle of the living room, smoothing his hand over the boy's head. His palm against Asher's short hair made a soft *shush, shush*, like a little whisper of wind, or breath. Like a child's soft snore. Yes. That was what it reminded her of. His snoring.

And all of what she had done came hammering in on her. Murderer! Asher's little silent body screamed at her. Torturer! But the deepest condemnation was one that he'd already passed—he hated her. This boy that could not hate had hated her for all that she'd done to him. And there was no chance for her to make it otherwise.

He was no demon. No godling. Just a boy, who had known happiness, and silliness, and who had adored the world and the people he knew. A boy who cut lawns, and argued with his sister. And Nina had brutalized him. For the little trinket of what he could do with his voice.

So she was not surprised when Brujo pushed her into the living room toward Jan Karl, and the wizard removed a knife from his belt. She remembered her dream—a knife and blood and thorns. This was what it had been warning her of. Nina threw a glance at Steve, who was sitting on the couch watching all of this—but there was no help for her in him. A girl—Claire, Nina supposed—threw her a deadly look, then rose and tapped Steve on the shoulder. She led him out of the room. So Nina was alone with the wizard and the body of the child she'd murdered.

Jan Karl stood, and held out the knife to her, hilt first. It was a long, ugly thing, made of gray iron and an undecorated hilt of bone. The single edge seemed to glitter hungrily in the light from the window. When she took it, a whisper passed from the knife into her fingers, like Mother's whispers, only this was more ancient, with a voice like the creaking of stones in the deepest part of the world. Devourer. Child-eater. And whether the whisperer meant to call *her* that, or whether it referred to the knife, Nina could not tell. Both of them, she thought, fit the labels.

Jan Karl said, "You killed him. Give him back to me."

His voice filled Nina with dread. Pain and iron filled it, the way power had filled Asher's. The knife trembled when he spoke, like his voice struck a high chord that resonated in the blade.

Jan Karl undressed himself, down to his underwear. He was not handsome like Steve. He was balding, and fleshy, with a sturdy paunch. Scars as thick as Nina's little finger crossed his back and thighs and legs. Old scars, healed over, but ragged. And yet for all that, Jan Karl moved with power and certainty. He was not shy to be standing mostly naked in front of people with his ugly, fat, scarred-up body. This was who he was, and that was all. He did not seem to mind the way Nina stared.

"Give him back to me," he said.

"How?"

"Cut me on my legs, and arms, and stomach and throat. Then cut Asher in the same places. This will unbind the magic that you twisted around him." He spoke slowly, not looking at her.

She nodded, and he wordlessly undressed Asher as well. There was a terrible vulnerability in them, the dead child and his father. Pale and bare—they were twins, Nina saw suddenly. Like pieces of the same soul.

The knife seemed as supple as leather in her hands, as light as a strand of hair. Jan Karl stood passively before her, naked, willing—she could murder him. The whisper passed from the knife into her. This was the font of all magic, this was power and blood aplenty. Power that had made a creature like Asher, and all hers if she would sink the iron blade into his stomach and bleed him down.

But she did what he asked instead. It took every ounce of anything that she was not to cut too deeply. When she came to his throat, she cut quickly, and dropped the knife. It stuck in the floor on the carpet.

"Now Asher," Jan Karl said.

She touched the knife again, and the shock it sent up her arm made her shake. The knife did not want to touch Asher's dead body. No meat! It whispered. No blood! No life! It had been eager to drink Jan Karl, and was just as eager not to go near his son. Nina forced it, pressing with all her might against the blade and Asher's cold skin, to draw a thin line of scarlet on his legs, his wrists, his stomach . . . When she raised the knife to the boy's throat, she saw that her own arms were bleeding. She looked down. Yes. Her legs and stomach were bleeding, too. She could feel a warm trickle sliding down her calves.

Jan Karl saw that she saw, but didn't say anything.

She lifted the knife to Asher's throat, and let it rest there for just a moment. And then she cut, feeling the blade sink into her own skin this time. This was right. This was redemption. To die to unbind the boy's dead body from her magic. To let Asher go.

But Jan Karl pushed her away from the boy. "That's good enough. You're done."

She stumbled back. She wasn't going to die?

"Don't touch us," the wizard warned her.

She nodded and moved away from them. Jan Karl knelt by Asher's side, and for a long time, just watched him silently. The blood from the cuts dripped down the wizard's legs and chest and hands, dotting the carpet. His lips were moving silently, and his fingers hovered over Asher's eyes and chest, but Jan Karl never touched his son. He trembled like he was afraid.

"Breathe, Asher," Jan Karl said. "Come back to me, my little lizard boy. Come back and bring me a golden slipper if you can, but come back to me."

Nonsense. Nonsense between a child and his father, a little fragment of their lives that Nina had no part of. An in-joke that she would never, though she lived and searched for as long as she lived, be able to understand. Somehow, that felt as tragic as Asher's death.

Jan Karl lifted himself on top of Asher. Eye to eye, his mouth over Asher's, palm to palm. The world went still. There was no existence but for this room. Nina held herself still as well. Jan Karl rose, and knelt again over Asher, matching his limbs to the boy's. Eyes, lips, palms. And once more, eyes, lips, palms.

Asher sneezed.

And the world came alive again.

Jan Karl sunk away from Asher, gulping in an enormous, shuddering breath. Asher continued sneezing, seven times he sneezed, and then he threw himself into Jan Karl's arms, sobbing, and calling him over and over, Daddy. Dad. Daddy. The cuts on the boy's body were bleeding now, fresh blood full of life.

This was not a place for her. Nina slipped out of the door, leaving them to their happiness. Before Asher's magic could take her again. Before Jan Karl's anger overwhelmed his need to hold his son.

Brujo was waiting for her outside. So was Steve. They were chatting. They both looked uncomfortable. Brujo watched her as she came down the porch. He said, "The blackberry bushes in Marquez are gone, Nina. You won't find any magic there."

The last bitterness. "So. All's well that ends well, is that it?"

"You raped his trust, Nina," Steve said. "How is Asher ever going to know if someone loves him because of *him*, or because of his magic?"

She pushed past them both, got into the car. Get away, she heard a whisper. Get away from little boys with gods in their throats, and scarred-up old wizards. Get away from lost lovers, and old, betrayed friends.

So she did. It was dawn before she realized that she still had Jan Karl's knife, sitting silent and hungry in the seat next to her. She didn't dare touch it for fear that she would lift it to her own throat in despair.

• • •

When she touched the knife again, it was to shove it into the earth where Mother's ashes and the blackberry bush her blood had flowed through mingled. Brujo had been right—the bushes and Mother's bones were nothing but magicless cinders.

But Nina was bleeding at her legs and arms and stomach and throat. The hot air was full of a thunderstorm's approach, rain that would turn the ash to clay.

Blood and magic. Nina began to pile ashes over the knife's hilt, singing a little song. A little lullaby of her own making. Two legs, a torso, a pair of arms, a neck, a little head . . . And Nina shook out a plastic bag filled with clippings of her own hair, shorn off with Jan Karl's knife.

Let the rain come. Let it baptize her and the child she would make here in the dust and clay and ash. Let the heavens roar and spit and shake, she would make a child here. A helpmeet.

So she whispered to the dark little clay figure she'd formed. She whispered its name.

"Lilith," she whispered, as the rain began to fall. "Lilith."

STYLE POINTS

by
Stephen Hickman

Stephen Hickman has been illustrating science fiction and fantasy for over two decades. His work has been inspired by such masters of fantasy and science fiction writing as Tolkien, H.P. Lovecraft, A. Merritt, Edgar Rice Burroughs and Clark Ashton Smith. His illustrations have been used as cover work for many contemporary writers, such as Stephen Brust, Lois McMaster Bujold, Tom Cool, Gordon Dickson, David Drake, Harlan Ellison, Robert Heinlein, Anne McCaffrey, Larry Niven, Andre Norton and Steve Stirling—earning him critical acclaim.

Since 1976 Hickman has illustrated approximately 450 covers for Ace, Baen, Ballantine, Bantam, Berkeley, Dell, Del Rey, Doubleday, Phage Press, Tor, Warren Publications and others. In 1988 Hickman wrote The Lemurian Stone *(Ace Books), which formed the basis for his Pharazar Mythos illustrations;* The Lion Pavillion *is one example, and is also reproduced along with* The Archers *in the 1994 edition of* Spectrum.

In 1994 he was awarded a Hugo Award from the World Science Fiction Convention for the United States Postal Service's Space Fantasy Commemorative Booklet of stamps, the first official recognition by the government of the sf genre.

In his article, "Style Points," Mr. Hickman shares his experience as one of the most successful cover artists of today and lists out the ten points which he has found vital to a successful career in painting covers.

The purpose of the artist is the mythologizing of the world.

—Joseph Campbell

It is an interesting problem to find words to write about the visual arts—the trick here for an artist who actually produces art is to avoid the specialized and deliberately obscure vocabulary of the art critic, and write in practical terms of what is essentially a non-verbal art form. This is a subject I've thought about from time to time over the years, generally around the magic hour of 3:00 a.m., so I can present some notions which are fairly coherent and practical. Mind you, these considerations are those I have formulated after I had been painting pictures for a long time. Obviously then, these ideas are incidental to producing artwork, but are interesting from the standpoint of why we produce art in the first place, and useful to the aspiring artist in that it might help to shape a career into a form that is more beneficial to the artist by clarifying aspects of what in some respects is a very curious process.

There have been any number of definitions put forward over the years as to what constitutes art, and what its purposes are, but I'd like to mention here only the ones that seem important and valid to me personally. If it hadn't already been used as the title of a movie, I would have called this Practical Magic—the job of illustrator is to influence the public to buy books by means of a magic charm (the cover) which he produces by the concentration of his mystic ability (artistic talent) to the task. Lord knows there are X-factors enough in the business to lend a mysterious credence to this process, to the point where I half suspect the successful art editors of being sorcerers themselves.

Actually, I think about what I do in much less fanciful terms. The work of an illustrator—and it is work, make no mistake about that—is much too arduous to be called magic. I like Tolstoy's notion of art as communication. In my best paintings I try to achieve what could be thought of as visual poetry: I want to capture a mystic, dreamlike beauty in these pictures. I want to communicate this beauty in whatever form the picture happens to take—even in, say, a horror subject, I will try to devise an elegance and refinement to my approach which to my way of thinking makes this type of material all the more striking and effective. All of my personal work is intended to be beautiful and elegant to begin with, but this illustrates the point that beauty can have a wide dramatic range beyond the merely pretty, and into the realm of the wonderful and sublime.

As for why we are driven to produce paintings in the first place, or why we can feel such an intense pleasure when we see certain paintings . . . this is where things, to my mind, get interesting.

As I mentioned before, I've done a lot of thinking and reading on this question, and the most plausible explanation I've found is this—that myth (and painting is a visual form of myth) is the mechanism which the human psyche uses to relate to the chaos of the infinite system (the world and the universe) in which it finds itself. How's that for one sentence, eh? In earlier times, the beliefs (myths) that man lived by stayed valid for very long periods of time, because the pace of progress was so much slower. Then with the dawning of scientific enlightenment and the Renaissance, things picked up rapidly, straining these systems of belief, and causing a lot of confusion, until with the industrial revolution, the pace of human life accelerated to the point where the mythologies needed constant reinvention to maintain their effectiveness—hence the increasing importance of the artist. For the most scholarly and fascinating treatment on this subject of myth, and this is where I found it, read Joseph Campbell, particularly *The Hero with a Thousand Faces*. This is perhaps the most important work I've found on the subject, with a special and practical application to artists and their vision quest. I have a profound respect for this work because the steps of the vision quest (hero's quest or the artist's career) tally with an uncanny precision with my own personal experiences as an artist. I can't recommend this man's work too highly.

Okay, so much for the philosophy—like I said, I painted a lot of pictures before I became acquainted with this material.

Together with just about all of my generation of imaginative illustrators, I was inspired to a career in art when I saw the covers of the Ace Books' editions of Edgar Rice Burroughs that appeared in the mid-1960s—painted by the genius of Roy G. Krenkel, Jr., and Frank Frazetta. I had been drawing more or less compulsively all my life, but at the same time was puzzled by the works of the famous painters, which were held to be great, and which I secretly found to be really tiresome. Until, that is, I saw what incredible magic the classical form was capable of when linked to a powerful imagination.

I was fortunate enough to have been born into a

family that was very supportive and encouraging of creativity on the part of my brother and myself. My father was a natural storyteller, and entertained us on weekend evenings with a surprising variety of tales he would make up on the spot. My mother passionately loved art, and insisted on originality—she simply would not look at anything that was a copy of another artist's work, painting or photo. And I was doubly fortunate to receive a thorough grounding in the elements and principal of design, and quite a lot of practical experience from my high school art classes—these were taught by a man of exceptional ability and integrity, and by taking summer classes I got the equivalent of eight years of training, which was a good thing for me, because the art schools of the time were going through the throes of the stripe painting aberration, and I learned nothing of any practical use during the two years I spent there.

However, I was not alone in this obsession with the Krenkel/Frazetta magic, and in the company of these kindred spirits would draw far into the night, week after week, trying to capture as much of that sense of wonder as I was able. Using what I had learned from my high school teacher, we were actually able to accomplish some surprising stuff, and in all fairness, my instructors were very tolerant of what was after all "commercial" work, and were actively supportive of my efforts.

After I had enough of stripe paintings to last me the remainder of my natural incarnation, I decided to strike out on my own. I held down a regular job for about six months, and then in spite of a curious dread of becoming self-employed, left to begin what I was much later to understand as my vision quest.

In my thirty years of illustrating creative writing,

I have learned some guidelines for the business of painting the covers of imaginative literature which I will present here:

- Learn to draw—this is the first and most fundamental rule of the visual arts, even if you intend to go into computer graphics or photography. Without good drawing, painting (or anything else) is impossible. To be an illustrator you must be able to draw the human figure, and to draw the figure you absolutely must know artistic anatomy, starting with the skeleton.
- Decide what kind of work you really love to do, and stay with it—if you do this, your art will be much easier to accomplish, and be much more rewarding, both in terms of financial and artistic reward.
- Be original—this is very important. The public responds instinctively to honesty.
- Pick a good art school—as I found out the hard way, all schools are not equal, and there are some very fine schools where illustration is regarded with respect.
- Be as versatile in your chosen field as you can—the trick is to find your true direction in life, and go in that direction as far as your imagination and ability can take you. You can always go much farther than you can imagine if you devote yourself completely to your art.
- Be knowledgeable in your craft—know your materials thoroughly, both physical and mental.
- In preparing your portfolio, choose the five best pieces you have—don't make the common mistake of trying to show every piece of work you think is good.
- Do the very best job you can on every assignment—this is not quite as simple as it sounds, because you can mess up a painting or drawing by trying too hard. Think about it . . .
- Follow your instincts whenever you can—don't be afraid to try new or unusual approaches.

• Don't depend on technique—your message to the viewer will be boring: "Hey, look what I can do!" Be like the Oriental artists whose technique is so accomplished that it becomes invisible, and so does not obscure what you have to say.

Because it all boils down to what you have to communicate—what you have brought back from your vision quest. Which in turn depends on the development of your character, your self, of which your artwork is a reflection, and which you can consciously develop through your devotion to your craft. People can definitely feel that in your work, make no mistake about it.

In the end, it's only paint on canvas. You can be successful or not. The lame way out is to say, "Why bother? It's the same in any case . . ." The cool way is to go for the style points . . .

The Three Essentials of Genius:

An eye that can see Nature,
A heart that can feel Nature,
And a boldness that dares follow it.

—The Celtic Triads

BETRAYER OF TREES

Written by
Eric James Stone

Illustrated by
Steven V. Popovich

About the Author

Utah writer Eric James Stone returns to these pages as a prize winner after his first published story appeared in last year's edition as a finalist.

It was his father's collection of golden age science fiction and fantasy that first caught young Eric's imagination. He began writing in high school and college, but stopped abruptly when publishers rejected his earlier works. During the next ten years, Eric attended Baylor Law School, passed the Texas State Bar Exam, worked on a New York Congressional campaign, and performed research for a nonprofit based in Washington, D.C.

After Eric returned to Utah to live, the writing bug hit him again. In 2002 he started taking creative writing classes and workshops. He honed his skills for two years until his first sale to this Contest. He wrote this year's fantasy entry during a workshop led by Orson Scott Card. While Eric still does not make his living as an author (he's a Web programmer by day), he keeps at his craft and regularly participates in an online writers' workshop.

About the Illustrator

Drawing jets, robots and other machines that whirrrr and go zooom played a large part in the boyhood Midwestern world of artist Steven Popovich. It simply felt "right" to constantly create and reassemble pictures, objects, words and songs. As an eleven-year-old, Steven began a "semi-professional" career selling his more precocious artwork to peers on the school bus. After that venue dried up, he began refining his artistic technique and added painting to his repertoire. In high school, Steven received several art awards, then went on to study drawing, painting and printmaking at a prestigious fine arts school.

Artistic expression remains fundamental to Steven. A resident of Chicago, Illinois, Steven is now an exhibiting gallery artist and poster designer. He's currently planning his own visual arts venture.

Some of the younger stoneworkers in the guild called him Janal the Stonemage, but he knew there was no magic in his work. It was merely the skills he'd learned over nearly fifty years of carving that allowed him to turn rough-hewn stone into delicate beauty. His wrinkled hands were no longer as strong as they had been, and his pace had slowed, but when the townsfolk of Capeton wanted stonework of the highest quality, they always asked the guildmaster to assign Janal.

Word of his work had spread far enough that several times he had been offered a commission in one of the nearer cities, especially in the fifteen years since woodcarving had been outlawed by imperial decree. But Janal always turned them down. Capeton was his home, he would tell them, and he never wanted to leave it.

Fifty years he'd lived in Capeton, and the townsfolk considered him one of their own. After fifty years, few even remembered he had not been born there. Janal himself rarely thought of his life before.

And then he started dreaming of the trees again.

He had thought the dreams were a young man's burden, that he had outgrown them. But now they returned to plague his sleep.

Tonight when he'd awakened with the screams of the trees in his ears, it had taken him several minutes to realize that he was not back in the forest of the Treefolk, not back in the land of his birth. It was only in dream that the trees cried out accusingly, revealing him before his people as the Betrayer of Trees. It was not real. It was not real.

Except that he knew he really was the Betrayer of Trees.

•••

The next morning Janal was assigned to carve a decorative frieze of a horse above the doorframe of one of the wealthier merchants in town. The horse was the symbol of the Emperor Tilu, and over the past twenty years it had become a popular symbol for peace and good fortune, so Janal had carved hundreds of them.

He hardly thought as he worked; the hammer and chisel moved almost of their own accord. It was not until he was almost done he realized that instead of a smooth and gentle form, it was sharply angled. The horse's teeth were bared in anger and its sharp hooves raised to strike.

Why had he done that? It was the dreams, he realized. They were taking him back to his youth, back to the time he had first seen horses. The horses of the armies of the warlord Tilu had looked like this as they thundered across the countryside destroying all who stood before them.

"Janal, what are you doing?" Guildmaster Lintoko interrupted his thoughts.

"I don't know. I guess I was distracted. I'll fix it."

"Forget it. I'll have someone else take care of it. Something more important has come up."

There was a sadness in his old friend's voice that

made Janal apprehensive. Carefully laying down his hammer and chisel, he turned to face the other. "Yes?"

"I have to send you north, to the imperial city."

Janal shook his head. "Please, not me. Send one of the youngsters—they long to leave our city and see the world."

"I can't send one of them. There's too much work to do. And face it, Janal, you just aren't able to work as fast as you used to. If it weren't for the fact that we have more work than we can handle, I'd have let you retire a couple of years ago."

The imperial decree disbanding the Carpenters' Guild and outlawing the carving of wood had not had much direct impact in Capeton, for few trees grew in the sandy soil and those that did were mostly unsuitable for carving anything of lasting value. But the increased demand for stoneworkers in cities suddenly forced to abandon the use of wood had led some of Capeton's younger stoneworkers to leave in search of higher wages. Even after fifteen years the effects still lingered.

Janal had often wondered why the emperor had outlawed woodcarving. It was the tree magic of lifebinding that had extended the emperor's life, so was it out of respect that the emperor protected all trees? Or was it merely fear, the fear that someone might find the tree to which his life was bound and cut it down, thereby bringing his unnaturally long reign to an end?

Janal shook his head. He had started working in stone long before the imperial decree. It did not affect him. What mattered now was that he dared not go anywhere near the emperor. Janal had betrayed the trees, betrayed his family and abandoned the faith of his people to give Tilu what he demanded. And after all that, the Emperor Tilu had sentenced him to death.

Illustrated by Steven V. Popovich

"If you need me, why are you sending me away?" said Janal.

Lintoko gave an exasperated sigh. "Because, by imperial order, the Stoneworkers' Guild in every city must send someone to work on the new palace the emperor's building. Oh, there's a lot of flowery language about how this will show the unity of the empire, but what it all boils down to is they're going to leave me one man shorter than I already am."

"Please, Lintoko. Send someone else."

Lintoko put a reassuring hand on his shoulder. "I've never asked you what you were fleeing when you came to Capeton, and I'm not asking now. But it's been a long time. Surely it makes no difference now. No one would even recognize you now, am I not right?"

Janal tilted his head thoughtfully. His old friend was right; no one in the imperial city would recognize Janal the aged master stoneworker as Jintuk the young apprentice treemage under sentence of death.

But the trees would know him still. The trees knew the soul of a man, not the body, and their memories were as long as they were tall. He could not enter the forest of the Treefolk, or even go near, lest they cry out against the Betrayer of the Trees.

But there would be no need to go near the trees. He nodded his acceptance, and Lintoko smiled gratefully.

"You will have guild money for your journey, so you will be able to sleep in comfort even where there is not a guild house." Suddenly Lintoko clapped his palm to his forehead. "And I have not even told you the best part! The emperor is paying double guild wages—which are higher there than here as it is—and the Council of Guildmasters has decided that you may keep half the excess. How do you like that? If this palace takes long enough to build, you'll be rich. And maybe by the time you get back, we can both retire and spend our days sitting around a fire swapping tales, and our nights chasing young women and tasting aged wine."

"Or chasing aged wine and tasting young women." Janal smiled; he would miss Lintoko.

The guildmaster finished the old joke. "Just so long as it is not young wine and aged women."

• • •

During the nearly three months of the journey, the dreams of the trees had gotten more frequent the closer he came to the imperial city. Perhaps it was because there were more and more trees along the way; he could feel them slumbering silently alongside the road. A treemage could awaken the souls of the trees, but he did not want them to see the betrayal that scarred his soul. Probably he could not wake them if he tried; he had not used the magic of the trees since leaving his homeland.

Sometimes in the dreams the trees would joyfully welcome him home to take his rightful place as a treemage, helping to shape the gifts of the trees, using magic to form the living wood into whatever his people needed. But usually the trees of his dreams denounced him for the betrayer he was. Sometimes the other Treefolk would quickly surround him, and one of them would be carrying an axe. He would try to use the skills of concealment he'd learned as a child hiding in the forest, but there was no hiding from the trees. From those dreams he would awaken drenched in sweat, tangled in the sheets of a strange bed in some inn or guild house, and clutching at his right arm to make sure it was still there.

As he and his traveling companions crested the hill

and looked down upon the valley of the imperial city, Janal sucked in his breath. When he was young, he had passed through many cities before he found his new home in Capeton. This was the largest city he had seen: a jumble of buildings extending out from the old palace and stretching further along the banks of the river. The Tilurun River, it was called now, after the Emperor Tilu. On the other side of the valley he could see the rising pillars of the new palace, the palace he would help to build.

"Is it really the biggest city in the world? Capeton would fit a hundred times into that," said Skint. He was young, a painter just done with his apprenticeship, and like a few of the others in their party he had come with Janal all the way from Capeton. He'd never been more than a few days' journey from home before, and he showed it by greeting each new sight with wonder.

Janal smiled and shrugged. "Could be. If it's not the biggest, it will be eventually. Emperor Tilu will see to that." He'd taken a liking to the young painter. Perhaps it was because he'd been younger than Skint when he'd left home—had to leave home—and through him was experiencing what that first journey should have been like.

"Do you think we'll get to meet the emperor?"

"I doubt it." Seeing Skint's crestfallen look, Janal said, "But you will get to see him, I'm sure." *I just hope he does not see me, and if he does, that he does not recognize me. But it's been too long,* he reassured himself. *He cannot know me again after fifty years.*

"Is it true the emperor has a hundred guards to guard him, and a hundred lords and ladies to always walk before him and after him singing his praise?"

"I don't know. Sounds too noisy if you ask me."

They made their way down into the city, into the

midst of the buildings of stone and brick and cement. There were no wooden buildings, of course.

As their path took them through a bazaar in the city, Janal suddenly halted before a vendor's table. A variety of wooden implements and trinkets were displayed for sale at prices that made the wood almost as valuable as gold by weight. He'd known that illicit woodcarving still went on despite being outlawed, but he had not expected to see the law flouted so openly right here in the imperial city.

"Ah," said the merchant, a fat red-bearded man dressed in fine silks. "You are a man who appreciates quality, are you not?"

"I thought woodcarving was outlawed." As he spoke, his surprise gave way to horror as he realized the artifacts had not been carved. They were gifts of the trees.

The merchant bobbed his head. "Of course. But these were not carved; they were fashioned by the fabled mages of the Treefolk, created by the trees themselves, untouched by knife or . . ."

Gifts of the trees, sold in a bazaar as expensive trinkets. Janal turned away in disgust, ignoring the rest of the merchant's patter.

"What's the matter? Are you all right?" Skint asked.

"It's nothing." Janal shook his head. "Let's get to the new palace and find out when we are to begin work."

•••

Despite his misgivings before leaving Capeton, in the six months he'd been working on the new palace nothing bad had happened. He still dreamt of the trees too often. Some nights he even dreamt the memory he had spent most of his life trying to forget, and he would wake up begging himself not to do it, not to chop off the branch. But those were only dreams, and no evil came of them other than the grumblings of those who were tired of being woken by his talking in his sleep.

During the days, though, Janal found himself enjoying the work. Many of the craftsmen were old as he or young like Skint, but the combination of youthful energy and experienced skill seemed to be working well. The palace would be complete in a few more months—long before he could become rich off the extra pay—but he thought it would be the most beautiful building in the world. There was satisfaction in being a part of that, even if it was for the benefit of the Emperor Tilu.

He would get no work done today, though, because it was the annual Peace Day celebration, commemorating the day the last of the emperor's enemies surrendered before his horsemen and his rule extended to the sea that surrounded the land in all directions. There would be parades during the day and fireworks in the evening, but the biggest event for the laborers at the palace was that the emperor himself would come to see the progress and would address them to give his thanks.

Since he had no desire to see the emperor and an active desire to not be seen by him, Janal decided to slip away into the city. Maybe he would watch the parades; maybe he would find an alehouse and get drunk. Maybe both.

As he wandered along one of the main thoroughfares made more crowded than usual by those who had come to the city for Peace Day, he was startled out of his thoughts by a man's shout.

"Make way for the treemage! Make way for the treemage!"

A treemage? How could a treemage be here? They could not travel more than a few days' journey from the tree to which their soul was bound. Then he realized that the imperial city was within that distance.

He found himself pushed aside as the crowd parted before the shouter. A young man clad in green silks was borne through the throngs on a litter carried on the shoulders of six strong men. The litter was made of wood.

Janal instantly recognized the young man in the litter, the treemage. It was his younger brother, Parvin.

Heart suddenly pounding, he turned away, pushing himself through the crowd. No one stopped him; no one cried out, "Look, it's the betrayer!" He turned down a narrow side street and leaned against a wall, taking deep breaths and willing his heart to slow.

Three years were all that had separated them, but now he was an old man while Parvin still looked young. Parvin was lifebound to a tree. His brother must have become an apprentice treemage after he'd left—it was good to know his betrayal had not been held against his family.

After a few minutes he left the alley, found a tavern and got himself very drunk.

•••

Seeing Parvin made him wonder about what had happened to his family after he'd left. Over the next two weeks he often found himself lying awake on his cot, pondering whether his parents still lived, whether his brother and sisters had children or even grandchildren of their own now.

And it was not just his family's fate that now consumed his attention. What had happened to his people? That they prospered was apparent. But why were gifts of the trees now sold to outsiders? Why were treemages carried about like the idle rich?

Behind the curiosity was a growing desire to see his homeland once more, to walk once more among the wakened trees. The more he denied the desire, the greater it grew, until finally he convinced himself that the risk would not be great if he merely walked to the edge of his people's forest and looked at the trees. Surely that would not be too dangerous.

So he asked his supervisor for a few days off—to see his family, he said, which was not entirely a lie—and he began walking to the north, toward the land of the Treefolk.

Twice he turned back, but not for long. He slept that night beneath the stars, and before noon the next day he could see the edge of the forest. His people's forest. What had once been his forest.

Now that he could see his goal, he stopped, unsure of what to do next. The emperor's soldiers guarded the forest. He should have known they would be there, protecting the forest from outsiders who might threaten the trees—one tree in particular.

But while he had the narrow face and green eyes of the Treefolk, his years in the south had given his skin a leathery brownness that contrasted too much with the pale smoothness of his people, who dwelt always in the shade. He could not pretend to be one of the Treefolk returning to the forest.

But now he was so close that his desire would not be denied. Using the stealthy skills he had almost forgotten until his dreams had brought them to mind again, he crept closer to the forest without being spotted.

Lying on the ground a few yards from the nearest tree, he decided he was close enough. He opened his mind to hear the singing of the trees, the song he had not heard except in memory since he'd fled.

Nothing. He heard nothing.

Unable to believe it, he crawled closer still, until at last he was in the forest itself. He strained again to hear the trees, and though he could sense their souls awake around him, he could not hear them singing.

And they should be always singing.

Was it his fault? Had his betrayal somehow silenced the song?

No, that was not it. For surely the trees had sensed him by now, and would be calling out to each other that the Betrayer of Trees had returned. Warning each other against the betrayer, warning the Treefolk. And he should have heard those cries, but he did not. He was deaf to the trees.

Heedless now of the danger, he almost ran to the place he knew he must go, to the tree whose branch he had stolen. His people would be coming soon. They would capture him and punish him, but he wanted them to find him there, returned to the place of his crime.

He fell to his knees when he saw the tree.

It had been his tree, the tree with which he was to lifebind. He remembered it as a small oak, only fifteen years old but growing straight and strong and tall. That was before he'd chopped off one of its limbs. He'd taken care to disguise the cut so it wasn't obvious, so a visual search wouldn't reveal which tree the branch had come from.

But now the tree stood out, a crooked, misshapen thing, stunted in its growth. Its scrawny branches and twigs had few leaves, and it seemed scarred by disease and age.

"I'm sorry." He reached out with his mind toward

the soul of the tree he had betrayed, to try to let it know how sorry he was. And found nothing there. The soul of the tree was gone.

That was too much for him, and he crawled to the base of the tree and cried, knowing his people would come for him soon.

"Why are you crying?"

It was a child's voice, and Janal raised his head to see a young girl of about five years looking at him. He wiped at his tears with the back of his hand.

"I'm crying because of what happened to this tree," he said.

"That's the emperor's tree. You're supposed to stay away from it."

The Treefolk knew which tree it was, of course. But the emperor didn't, which would be why there were guards around the forest instead of just this tree. Or maybe the emperor knew, and just did not want to call attention to this tree.

He rose to his feet, sniffing. They would be here for him soon, he supposed. Let them find him on his feet. Looking at the girl, he said, "If you're supposed to stay away from it, what are you doing here?"

"I heard someone crying, so I came." She frowned. "Old people aren't supposed to cry. Little babies cry."

"Sometimes grownups cry, when they are sorry they did something bad."

"Oh." A pause. "Did you do something bad?"

He nodded. "Yes. I did something bad. But I'm sorry I did."

"It's good to be sorry when you do something bad."

"Yes."

"And you should never ever do it again."

"Right." He almost smiled. She must be repeating a lecture from her parents. Who would no doubt be here soon, horrified to find their little girl talking with the Betrayer of Trees.

He was surprised no one else had arrived yet. "What are the trees saying?"

Her eyes went wide. "You can't hear them?"

He shook his head.

"They aren't talking right now. They're just singing the song."

"They are? They weren't talking about . . . anyone, just a few minutes ago?"

"No, they're just singing the song."

Relief and horror mingled together. It meant there was no outcry to capture the betrayer; he might still make it out of the forest. But it also meant the trees could not see his soul. Perhaps, like the victim of his betrayal, he no longer had one.

His thoughts turned to his family. "Tell me, do you know the treemage named Parvin?"

She nodded. "He's Mama's uncle."

Which would make this girl his grandniece. He thought he could see a trace of his mother in the girl's eyes, a hint of his father in her cheeks. "Do you know if his mama and papa are still alive? Their names are Irella and Dal?"

She shrugged. "Uncle Parvin is very rich and important and I have to be quiet when he comes to visit."

Janal nodded. "That's right. And you shouldn't bother an important man by telling him about me."

"Someday I'll go to the big city and people will have to be quiet when I say."

Is that what the Treefolk children dream of now?

What kind of example are you setting, Parvin? He quelled those thoughts. He knew he could not risk staying longer. "Well, I must leave now. It was nice to meet you."

"Goodbye. And stay away from the emperor's tree."

Making his way out of the forest, he crept past the soldiers without incident. He returned to the imperial city without looking back.

•••

The stonework for the new palace was almost done. Because the supervisors had noticed his talent for delicate work, his current assignment was to carve a rearing horse on the top of the emperor's throne. His hands flowed smoothly in their work, but his thoughts were distant.

A few more days and he could begin the long journey back to Capeton. He would not wait around to see the other craftsmen complete their jobs so the emperor could declare the palace complete and give them his thanks.

Since his experience in the forest, his dreams had changed. The trees no longer called him the betrayer: sometimes they called him the stealer of souls, sometimes they called him the soulless one. Either way, it was worse. He'd always known he was the betrayer and could feel the truth of it, but he was not accustomed to his new titles. He hoped these dreams would fade once he returned to Capeton. The dreams had faded before, but it had taken years.

With a start, he noticed that the chatter of the workers around him had trickled to silence. Turning, he saw the emperor flanked by his guards and accompanied by many of the lords and ladies of the court. Immediately Janal prostrated himself, but he knew it was too late. The emperor had been staring at him.

"You, stoneworker, what is your name?"

He peeked up, and the emperor was still looking at him. "I am Janal, Your Majesty."

"Janal, you say?" the emperor frowned. "What is this you are carving upon my throne?"

Janal looked up at the horse he had been carving and his heart sank within him. Where there should have been a horse there was a delicate oak tree made of marble, stretching its branches up to the sky, with individual leaves that seemed almost ready to flutter in the wind. It was what his tree could have become, had he not betrayed it to the corrupting soul of the emperor.

It was the most beautiful thing he had ever created. And it was a terrible mistake. How could he excuse himself before the emperor?

The Emperor Tilu was one hundred and twenty-seven years old, but looked no older than he had fifty years before, when a young apprentice had betrayed the trees to perform the lifebinding magic. Having seen men grow old around him, perhaps he would make allowances for age. So Janal said, "Forgive me, Your Majesty. I am old and my mind wanders. I'm sure another stoneworker will be able to carve a horse fitting for your throne."

"Tell me, *Janal*, where do you come from?"

It was worse than he'd thought. From the way the emperor emphasized his name, Janal was sure he had been recognized. Still, there was the possibility the emperor was not certain, so he decided to keep to his new identity. "Capeton, Your Majesty. To the south."

"Capeton." The emperor nodded. "That's about as

far from here as one can go without sailing into the Endless Sea."

Janal nodded.

The emperor did not speak for several minutes. Janal shifted uncomfortably, but was determined not to give himself away.

"I come from a roaming tribe of the plains," said the emperor. "A tribe of horsemen. But all the world knows that. What you may not know is that my people have a custom of sitting around the campfire at night and telling stories. Do your people have a similar custom? Your people of the *far south?*"

Janal was puzzled, but he said, "Yes, Your Majesty. Although we usually tell our tales while sitting at a table drinking ale."

"Good, good." The emperor looked around at his guards and all the lords and ladies, then back to Janal. "Then I will tell one of our tribal stories. Would you like to hear it?"

There was no answer possible but "Yes, Your Majesty."

"We must all sit." The emperor strode to his throne and sat. Since the palace was not yet fully furnished, there were no other seats in the room, but when the emperor made an insistent downward wave of his hand, the lords and ladies lowered themselves gingerly to the ground. His guards, however, remained standing.

"When the world was not so old as it is now," began the emperor, "there was a young man who was gifted in the magic of horses. A horsemage, you might say. Now, I know there is no such thing as horse magic, but this is only a story. This young man, whose name was ... Let me think ... His name was *Jintuk.*"

Janal only gave a small twitch upon hearing his original name, but when he saw the emperor smile he knew he had given himself away. To his surprise, the emperor did not order the guards to arrest him, but continued with the story.

"One day, Jintuk's peaceful tribe was attacked by a vicious warlord, a conqueror who had already taken half the plains as his own. This warlord was growing old and weak, and he wanted . . . hmm." The emperor paused. "He wanted the strength of a horse so he could continue to conquer, and he knew the elders of the tribe could give it to him. So he threatened to kill Jintuk's tribe and all their horses unless they performed their magic to give him that strength. The elders of the tribe tried to do as the warlord wanted. But they could not, because such magic would bind a horse to the warlord, and the horses could sense the warlord was an evil man. So the horses refused."

"Why did they refuse?" Janal couldn't stop himself from asking. "They were all going to be killed, so why didn't one of them consent?" That was the question that still haunted him after all these years. Why did the trees refuse?

The emperor sighed. "A horse is wise in many ways, but foolish in others. A horse has a long memory, but a horse does not understand the future. It cannot choose something bad now in exchange for some benefit in the future."

Janal nodded. His people always spoke of the wisdom of the trees, but the trees were passive and peaceful. They had not understood what Tilu was threatening.

"So the young man, Jintuk, secretly cut off the tail of his favorite horse, and used it to give the warlord the strength he sought. Then Jintuk fled from his people forever, because the cutting of a horse's tail is a crime against the bond between his people and the horses.

But the warlord was true to his promise, and did not kill the horses and their people. In fact, the warlord protected them from that time forth, so no harm would come to them."

Janal sighed. "Not the happiest of endings to the story, but it could have ended much worse."

The emperor shook his head. "That is not the end of the story. For the evil warlord soon found that he was bound to the horse. Never again could he travel more than a few days distant from that horse. In his rage, he commanded that Jintuk be put to death."

Janal sat very still. He should have realized that a conqueror such as Tilu—particularly a nomadic horseman—would not want to be tied to one place. And yet, that was part of the magic. Tilu had demanded long life, and he had gotten it. Even though he was bound to one place, Tilu's armies had conquered the rest of the nations and made him emperor of the whole world. Did he still hold the grudge?

The emperor sat in silence.

Finally, Janal had to ask, "And was he put to death?"

"No, because the warlord never found him."

"And that is how the story ends?" For a moment, Janal dared to hope. Perhaps this story was the emperor's way of giving him an unofficial pardon.

"No, there is still more. For the horse hated the evil soul of the warlord to which it was bound. But the bond was too strong to be broken. Every day the soul of the horse fought against the soul of the warlord. For years they fought, until one day, the horse won."

Janal felt dizzy. "The horse won?" Did that mean what he thought it did?

The emperor nodded.

Janal tentatively reached out with his mind and there it was: the soul of a tree—his tree—inside the emperor.

"Forgive me," he whispered.

The emperor continued speaking as if Janal had not said anything. "Once the soul of the horse had the mind of a man, it understood why Jintuk did what he did, and of course forgave him."

Through his tears, Janal said, "And . . . and Jintuk's people?"

"They understood all along. They did not condemn him for what he did, although they would have had to banish him from the . . . from the corral, because the horses did not understand, at least not yet. But he fled so far, so fast, they could not find him to tell him he could have stayed nearby."

His shoulders sagged, and he sighed. He had been old enough to understand what must be done, too young to know that others understood. "In a way, that ending is sadder than the one before."

"It is." The emperor nodded. "But I am old, and my memory fails me sometimes. I'm not sure if that was the ending. Maybe the ending was when Jintuk finally came home, and was welcomed by the people and the horses. Maybe one of the horses even gives him the strength of his tail."

Janal thought about it. He'd dreamed of that. Welcomed home as a hero. Seeing his family again. Finally becoming a treemage and being lifebound to a tree. But those dreams were when he was young. It was too late now; his life had taken a different path.

"A question, Your Majesty? What happened to Jintuk's parents? In the story?"

The emperor's eyes were sad. "They died years later, always hoping to see their son again. But his brother and sisters lived on and had children and grandchildren of their own."

"I see." Janal nodded slowly.

They sat in silence for a while. Though Janal now knew the things he'd wondered about for so long, he didn't understand why the emperor didn't just come right out and explain what had happened. Then he noticed all the guards and lords and ladies. What would they do if they knew their conquering emperor had been replaced by a tree?

My tree is the ruler of all mankind, he thought, and he smiled. Not a bad ruler, really. The empire is peaceful now, and people are generally free to live their lives.

Then he thought of Parvin being carried on a wooden litter through the city streets, and gifts of the trees being sold in the marketplace, and a little girl who had to be quiet because her uncle was an important man.

"Your Majesty, I thank you for your story. Now I would like to tell you one of our southern stories."

The emperor motioned for him to go ahead.

"When the world was not so old as it is now, there was a village that was near a magical stone quarry."

"Magical stones?"

"Not really, Your Majesty, but this is only a story. This magical stone quarry would provide the villagers with whatever they needed, for their own use. And the villagers lived happily. Then one day, a . . . a king came who wanted something from the quarry. One young man—Jintuk is as good a name as any, I suppose— broke the law of the quarry and gave the king what he wanted."

"He probably had good reason to break the law."

"He may have thought so, but in this story it does not matter. Fearing punishment, Jintuk ran off to the end of the world, where he became a . . . a woodworker."

The emperor's eyes went wide. "A woodworker?"

"It was not against the law, in this story. In any case, he's not important to the next part of the story. The king now became a friend to the villagers and the magical quarry. In fact, he hated to see anything made of stone that did not come from the quarry, and he banned all stoneworking, except from the magical quarry. Until then, the villagers only asked the stone quarry for things they needed. But now, since they were the only source of stone items, they began to sell them at high prices. Some of the villagers became rich and proud."

"Did they?"

"They did. And one day when Jintuk came back to the village, he saw that it was no longer the village he had left; that some of the people were greedy and haughty. And not only that, but he could no longer hear the music of the quarry."

"The music?"

"Oh, I forgot to mention that the magical quarry made beautiful music that the villagers could hear. But after so many years away, Jintuk could no longer hear it. The changes in his village and not being able to hear the music made him realize that he no longer belonged to that world. Though he had longed to go back, he had made his life as a woodworker. And it was a good life, a life he was glad he had lived. So, feeling sad for what had happened to his village, he returned to the friends he had made at the end of the world and lived the rest of his life as a woodworker."

"It seems your story does not end too happily either."

"Well, I'm not certain that's the end. Maybe the king lifts the ban on stoneworking, and the villagers eventually stop abusing the magic of the quarry and become content once again."

Nodding, the emperor said, "Maybe the king only wanted to protect the villagers, and didn't realize he was doing them harm. Maybe when he finds out about it, he tries to set things straight."

"Yes, I think that must be how it ends."

"Well, Janal, I thank you for an entertaining story." The emperor rose, then turned to look at the marble tree carved atop his throne. "As for this carving, I find it beautiful. It shall remain here to remind the people that, like a tree, the Emperor Tilu provides shelter and strength to his people."

Janal prostrated himself. "I am honored, Your Majesty."

"And since I have no more need of your services as a stoneworker, I suppose you'll be leaving now for . . ."

"Capeton, Your Majesty."

"Yes, Capeton. At the end of the world. Have a safe journey, Janal."

"Thank you, Your Majesty."

•••

After Janal returned home, months passed, then a year. Eventually an imperial decree came that carpentry was no longer against the law. Several of the younger stoneworkers in the Capeton guild began experimenting with imported wood, and with Janal's encouragement they formed a Carpenters' Guild a few months later.

He declined the invitation to be their guildmaster, however. He was a stoneworker, he told them, and he never wanted to be anything else. But he would occasionally stop by their guild hall just to feel wood beneath his hands once more.

Even though he was officially retired, Janal still worked at the guild carving stone on most days. And most nights, he dreamed he could still hear the song of the trees rising in the forest to welcome him.

DEADGLASS

Written by
Lon Prater

Illustrated by
Perrin Hendrick

About the Author

Writer Lon Prater has been addicted to two things ever since he learned to read: used bookstores and speculative fiction. But it wasn't until he was miles away from land, aboard a Navy ship bound for the Persian Gulf, that he decided to try his own hand at writing. The experience stuck. Having made his way back to his wife, Angie, and the Tidewater area of Virginia, where he grew up, he is able to continue his fiction addiction.

Since Lon's return, his work has appeared in several small press venues: the New Promise industrial fantasy chapbook series from Scrybe Press; poetry in Flesh & Blood and Dreams & Nightmares; articles on writing in T-Zero and Absolute Write; and short fiction in Best of SDO, EOTU, Kenoma and AlienSkin, among others. From 2003–2005, he edited Neverary, a well-received, speculative fiction webzine. When he's not writing, he runs a local kite store and helps raise two daughters.

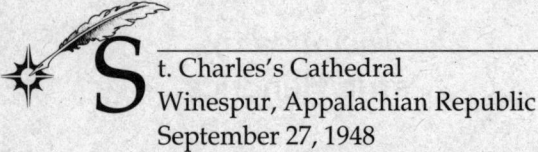

St. Charles's Cathedral
Winespur, Appalachian Republic
September 27, 1948

The last notes of Father Holden Drury's *basso profundo* incantation faded slowly into the fleece-blanketed walls. He glanced quickly at the inclined metal cross and the hooded man bound to it. An acute and unfounded shame made him slide his gray-flecked gaze to the floor. Weary conviction forced him to look again upon the Lord's work.

The vacant body hung there, looking smaller already; not yet dead, but diminished. Lacking a soul, the body of the condemned would gradually slow and stop, winding down like a child's toy.

The leather band at his forehead was not tight enough to prevent the condemned from jerking violently back and forth. Up until the final verse, the poor sinner had fought against his shackles in mute frenzy, the metal clanging a dull off-tempo beat throughout the incantation.

But the bonds weren't loose enough that the condemned could come to any harm. No risk of death, or Father Drury would have had to abort the ritual. If the soul escaped before the rites were complete, it would swarm down to the Tempter, another soldier for his infernal army.

Cautiously, Father Drury picked up the thumbnail of deadglass from the dish of holy water on the floor, unsure as always of what he would find there. Round eyes squinted into the enchanted glass, then widened.

He pulled a clean linen handkerchief from within his cassock; dabbed at a sun-pinkened pate now glistening with a cool mist of sweat.

Most glassbound souls were cold and filthy black, like Appalachian snow fouled by a Czech miner's boots. The one in his hand was a foggy silver gray, and warm. It could have been crystallized motorcar exhaust.

He cocked his head, stomach lurching at the ramifications. The deadglass grew heavy in his palm.

As a priest of the Holy Cathar Church, he knew that doctrine demanded containing the most dangerous souls—murderers, molesters, heretics—preventing them from ever joining the massed hellish armies of the Infernal Twin, Thomas the Tempter. Even so, every time he performed the rite of migration, a winter wind of doubt shook his faith like a birch in a blizzard.

Maybe it was the wet tongue of the Tempter slithering around in his mind. More likely it had to do with the anonymity of a tongueless head under the tamper-sealed canvas hood. Whatever the cause, until he held the loveless cold crystal in his hand, saw its sin-blackened impiety with his own two eyes, Father Drury nursed a seed of doubt as to whether migration was justified.

This time, for once, he had been right to doubt.

The innocent glass trembled in his hand. Absently, he slipped it into a pocket of the black suit jacket he wore beneath his cassock.

Guilt gnawed at the muscles of his jaws, both for migrating an innocent and for the sin he was about to commit. He approached the empty body butterfly-pinned to the metal cross. The condemned wore only the canvas hood and a coarse paper gown.

As Father Drury watched, the man's chest swelled slightly, drawing another shallow automatic breath. The space between each breath was getting longer and longer.

The priest kneeled, not to say the prayers of benediction, not yet, but to search the body for identifying marks. He looked over his shoulder at the door to the windowless, soundproofed room, certain he would be caught in his sin at any moment.

The body of the condemned was as tall as Father Drury, but leaner. Where the priest resembled a rosy-skinned lumberjack, burly and barrel-chested, the body before him was lanky and tanned, with a garden of curly black hairs overrunning the chest and forearms.

The priest checked his heavy wristwatch. Ticking faster than usual, the rotter! He bit back a curse and tugged the neckband of the hood up, careful not to break the tamper seal.

With the sealed bottom pulled snug against the man's jawbone, the priest noted a pair of moles over the Adam's apple. He ran a finger across fine stubble like spilled black pepper. It matched the rest of the body hair, so it was a safe bet that the man sported black hair on his head as well.

Father Drury shrugged off the insistent voice of his training, blanked out the awareness that he was betraying every tenet of the phased migration doctrine. He slid the neckband down into place.

He tried to feel the man's face through the stiff canvas with no success. His groping fingers met only the suggestion of a large bent nose, and perhaps a full, luxuriously thick head of hair beneath the hood. It was impossible to be sure.

Illustrated by Perrin Hendrick

This was taking too long, and he had not yet said the benediction. Were those steps he heard? Surely not, the walls were soundproofed, weren't they? He made a last quick check of the man's body.

The breathing was nearly undetectable. The soulless heart beat with less force now; color was already draining from the upturned, shackled hands.

But not all color, he noticed. The sisters of St. Joan's order were charged with the thorough cleansing and sanitizing of the condemned before migration. They had not been able to remove a ring of black ground-in powder from around his nails.

A coal miner? No, the skin was too weathered, those limp hands too soft. Someone so tall would have spent miserable days stooped over in the mines.

The doorknob rattled. Father Drury quickly assumed a position of prayer as the padded door opened just a crack. Silence reigned for a long moment as he murmured the final words of the benediction. Then Sister Matilda's voice: "Father, may we enter?"

"Certainly, Sister, I was just finishing up," he said, his voice a little more strained than he liked.

"Are you all right?" she asked as she stepped into the migration chamber, two junior nuns in tow. "Sister Carla could get you some iced tea."

He stood up, brushing at his knees. "No, thank you, that won't be necessary. I just need some fresh air."

Her pursed lips reminded him of two prunes pressed together. "You know what's best," she said, gracing him with a superficial smile.

Sister Matilda was all business. She and the Agnite sisters would not begin preparing the body for the disposal rites until he left the room.

Father Drury bid the sisters good day. He pulled the

fleece-lined door shut behind him, leaving the nuns to their work.

•••

The bishop was a jowly man, rounded and soft from years of study and administration. The only things hard about him were his river-pebble eyes. He gestured with a pudgy hand for Father Drury to sit in a wing chair by the window that overlooked the Bishopric of Richmond. "Good to see you, again. Holden, is it? To what do I owe the pleasure?"

"This," Father Drury said, leaning forward in his seat. He set the deadglass on the bishop's polished cherry desk with a click.

The older man's small black eyes flickered. He drew in a sharp breath. "Why haven't you turned this in to the Custodian of Souls?"

"Isn't it obvious?" Father Drury said, looking suggestively at the deadglass. "There has been some kind of mistake. This soul is innocent!"

The bishop's voice was as hard as his glance. "Impossible. Every phase of the migration process, condemnation to disposal and storage, is governed by doctrine. Procedures and rituals over a thousand years old." He stabbed one fat finger at Father Drury. "How dare you, of all people, a priest—a *migrator*, no less—question the very process that holds the Twin at bay!"

Father Drury was taken aback by the ferocity of the bishop's response. He sat up a little straighter in his chair, putting a steadying hand on the padded armrest.

"Your Reverence," he began cautiously. "I have condemned twenty-three sin-blackened souls to the glass. Compared to those others, this one is ready for sainthood. Surely there is some explanation?"

This time the bishop fought visibly to control his emotions. He fussed with one of his shirt buttons, then with a pen that lay on the desk. He chewed his bottom lip, glaring at Father Drury all the while.

When he finally spoke, the bishop chipped off every word like cold, hard cemetery granite. "Are you one of the three cardinals on the Condemnation Board?"

He continued without waiting for a response. "Are you privy to the inner sanctum of the pontiff? No? Then I suggest to you, Father, that the questions you ask are improper. *At best.* I further suggest that you let this matter go, before you find yourself ministering to a very cold and remote parish."

Father Drury nodded slowly, keeping the anger and astonishment from his face. The bishop's response seemed totally out of proportion. He stood up, wiping rigid hands on his thighs reluctantly, as if there were something greasy on them and he had no other cloth.

"I understand completely, Your Reverence," he said formally. "I'll deliver this soul to the Depository immediately."

The bishop's icy demeanor seemed to thaw slightly. He flashed a cool smile, one that said he was glad to have all of the, *ahem,* unpleasantness behind them. But that smile didn't quite reach his eyes.

"That won't be necessary, Holden," he said. "I'll make sure it gets over to Brother Lafayette." The bishop lumbered to his feet.

Father Drury took a backward step. "If there's nothing else, Your Reverence?"

"No, no. I don't want to keep you any longer," the bishop said, picking up the shiny bit of deadglass. He looked at it thoughtfully.

Father Drury turned and marched to the door. As

he grasped the ornate brass handle, he heard the bishop speak.

"Holden?"

Father Drury pivoted. The late afternoon sun streamed in through a frost-lined window, silhouetting the bishop's squat wide frame. "Yes, Reverence?"

"Sin is measured not by its effects on man and Earth, but by the degree to which it benefits the Twin. You know that, don't you?" the bishop asked without turning around.

It was simple truth, one that summarized nearly a millenia of post-Trentian Cathar thought.

"Yes, Reverence. Of course."

The bishop held the deadglass up between a thumb and fingertip. The little disk sparkled as if with its own light, scattering multicolored bits of cold sun dancing about the room. "Even the smallest, best-intended sin could hasten the Twin's return, remember that."

The bishop closed his fist upon the deadglass even as Father Drury crossed the threshold.

•••

When he wasn't engaged as a migrator, Father Drury spent his days working on a history of the Crusades against the Greco-Pauline mystery cults and filling in when needed at St. Filbert's Cathedral on High Street. St. Filbert's boasted the fourth largest library in Richmond; in fact, it was one of the largest in the Appalachian Republic.

This morning it seemed smaller than he remembered, more closed up. The bookshelves leaned in upon him, and the air was warm and stale like two-week-old bread. He forced himself to finish reading a gloomy, uninspired analysis of Seigfried IV's failed assault on Athens, then slammed the thick tome shut. He needed a change of scenery.

He tumbled out into the busy river of Richmond's sidewalks, and headed east. He was grateful for the crisp wind and open sky, and did his best to ignore the noise of the finned and chromed automobiles lurching through the streets.

He told himself that he was going to the city's library, the one by the Jefferson Grozny Memorial, to fetch an obscure reference and perhaps have lunch at the Croatian diner on the corner. If anyone would have asked, that's what he would have told them as well; but it wasn't altogether true.

He was going to look through the sheaves of dailies in the smaller library's basement, to see who had gone missing recently. He didn't have any business doing so; the bishop had ordered him to forget the whole incident. Nonetheless, he felt called to learn what he could of the relatively sinless soul he had migrated, and he followed.

"Fell behind on the Patrick and Trotsky strip, Stephen," he said to the smiling, birdlike librarian. The lie rolled out too easily for Holden's comfort. He felt an uneasiness in his stomach.

Holden bit the insides of his fleshy cheeks, then continued: "It's my one guilty pleasure, you know. I'd like to get caught up with those rascals, if you keep the papers handy."

Stephen smiled at him and winked like a conspirator. "Your secret is safe with me, Father." Holden hated himself for the untruth, but said nothing more as Stephen ushered him into an unventilated basement room full of newspapers and cobwebs.

Holden put his hand on the room's only piece of

furniture: a rickety table that cringed beneath a bright, bare bulb hanging from the ceiling. This hot little room was hardly better than St. Filbert's news archive. The difference was that here he could look for what he wanted in private.

One hour melted into another. The Holy Cathar Church simply abducted those whose souls were condemned by the board, leaving the families and police to wonder at the sinner's sudden disappearance. Most of them ended up here, in the local headlines, obituaries and police reports. Holden scanned the papers mechanically, trying his best to ignore the heat and his empty, protesting stomach.

Touching the newsprint left his thick fingers smudged with ink. The handkerchief, formerly white, was growing blacker by the minute. When he swabbed the moisture from his broad forehead, he tried not to get any of the ink on himself. It was a lost cause from the start.

At five o'clock, he surrendered to the heat and his howling stomach. He trudged up the dusty wooden stairs to the library. Two months' worth of dailies, and he had found nothing relevant.

"Your sin is showing, Father. Everyone will know what you've been up to," Stephen said from behind the desk.

Holden's heart skipped. He moved his lips without speaking, his mind calculating the best response.

Stephen wrinkled his hawk nose at him. "You have the ink from those Patrick and Trotsky strips all over your face and hands. You can wash up in the staff water closet if you'd like."

Father Drury grunted, glad he hadn't spoken. Maybe this was a sign from the Lord, a warning that he should mind the bishop's counsel and forget about the gray bit of glass. Or it could be old Thomas the Tempter, tweaking a priest's nose for simple sport.

"Right through that door, Father, by the biographies, and take a left." The big priest thanked him and strode off in that direction.

In the restroom, Holden took a scratchy washcloth from the stack and wet it in the sink. He scrubbed his round face until it shone pinker than usual, then set to work on his hands. The ink came off easily for the most part, except for the crevices around his fingernails.

The realization exploded like a stick of dynamite just behind his breastbone. There had been an article about a man who had escaped from jail, a typesetter accused of using his employer's presses to print "unsavory" pamphlets on the night shift. The police were still mystified as to how he had escaped. As far as they knew, he was still on the loose.

"You fool!" Holden said to the mirror. A typesetter. Just the sort of man to have stubborn black stains around his fingers. He should have made the connection on the spot, but he had been looking for disappearances, not fugitives.

Father Drury flung the washcloth onto the sink and shot out of the restroom like all the Tempter's armies were behind him. Stephen made a surprised noise as Father Drury barreled back down into the basement room, but did not follow.

The frenzied priest pulled two boxes away from the wall and tore into a third. A quarter of the way down, he found what he was looking for. He jerked upright with a high-pitched yelp that didn't fit his big frame.

Wayne Charnick. He read the article three times, his eyes bouncing excitedly like the words were insects darting across the page. Wayne Charnick had worked as a night typesetter at a small press downtown for over three years. A few weeks ago, his employer caught him printing "foulness" and had him jailed. He had disappeared from the jail cell the next night, presumed to be armed and dangerous. A reward was offered for any information on his whereabouts.

There wasn't a picture with the article, but it did list a sister, Mina Charnick, who lived in Doveburton, just a few winding mountain miles from out-of-the-way Winespur, and the facilities at St. Charles's. Holden looked down at his gently quivering hands. Not only were they once again marked with ink, but now they were also damp. He couldn't be sure whether it was moisture from having just washed them or the clamminess of cold sweat.

He heaved the boxes of archived newspapers back into place. The man had been printing some kind of foulness, yet his glass had contained so little sin. Pornography was rarely a call for migration, but there was another kind of printed work that would surely draw the church's ire: *heresy*.

But what kind of heresy would leave a glass so lightly tainted?

Father Drury stared at the knot of his ink-smudged hands. He was reminded of Duke Tartan's mother, from the old Scottish play. She had eventually had her consort cut off both of her hands so that she would not see her son's blood upon them.

He muttered a soft, grumbling prayer and turned to the basement stairs. As he ascended to the library, each of the ancient wooden steps groaned in turn, as if the big priest and his guilt were nearly too much for them to bear.

● ● ●

The long, slow ride to Doveburton was made more difficult by the unpaved mountain roads. The old twelve-seater bus bumped about on the road like an impure woman on a rented mattress. Father Drury chided himself for the image. The jarring ride left him with a sore neck.

Small penance, considering what he probably deserved by now.

He stepped off the bus and looked around. The Doveburton bus stop was a crowded, dingy affair. He twisted his head around each way, working some of the soreness out with a few satisfying clicks and pops. Holden got directions from an attendant before setting off to Mina Charnick's house at a respectable pace.

When he got there, a lean woman with a hard, lined face was smoking on the front-porch steps. She glared at his collar and cassock, saying nothing.

"Miss Charnick?"

"I don't know where he is, Father."

"Well, that makes two of us," Holden said, conscious of the half-lie. Awkward silence filled the space between them. "I figured all you church folk and police woulda give up on finding him by now."

"Beg pardon?" Holden asked, a little more alert.

"When he first got ketched, all you church folk come out here asking about the papers he was making, but he never brought none of it around here, so I never saw it. Then the police come, looking for anything they could use agin' him, and they couldn't find nothing neither, so they quit coming 'round here."

She puffed on her cigarette. "Till he got out that cell. Then the police all come a-runnin' back. I wondered why it'd take the church so long to check back. But you're wasting your time, Father. I still ain't seen my brother Wayne. Not since before he got ketched."

Holden raised his eyebrows. "Mind if I sit?" He flashed her a congenial grin and hunched down beside her before she could object. "Do you have a picture of him?" he asked, his voice so soft it barely carried in the thin air.

She cocked her head, looking at him crookedly. "I might."

"My name is Father Holden Drury," he ventured. It was late for introductions, but he wasn't sure what else to say. How do you tell a woman you may have migrated her brother's innocent soul into a piece of glass? "I'm trying to find him. He may have been—may be innocent, but I have to find him to prove it."

The woman snorted smoke all over Father Drury. "And you need a pitcher to do that? Don't you even know what Wayne looks like?"

He didn't like leading Mina Charnick on. There was no way he could help her brother; the glass was a perfect inescapable cell, and by now his body had been immolated. Holden had sinned several times already today, lying to find some truth. To discover whether the migration of Wayne Charnick had been justified. By the end of the day he would likely have much more to repent.

"I wish I did, Miss Charnick. It would make it easier to help him."

Another long moment passed. The woman got up suddenly. She stubbed her cigarette out against the flaking paint of the porch rail and flicked the butt out into the yard.

"You wait here," she said, staring at him through rheumy, narrowed eyes.

A few minutes later she returned, pushing the door open just enough to shove a picture in a cheap metal frame into his chest.

"It was in a fire," she said, her lower lip on the verge of trembling. "Take it, and don't none of you come back here till Wayne's home safe."

Holden took the frame from her, glancing quickly at it. It had indeed been in a fire at some point, but apparently it had been saved or salvaged early enough to prevent all but a slight warping of the glass. Holden's eyes were drawn to the throat of the happy man in the picture and the twin moles resting there.

Holden thought of the old Carib stories of natives who wouldn't let their pictures be taken for fear that the camera would also take their souls. He resisted the urge to wince, and likewise the urge to reach out and comfort the pitiable woman on the other side of the door. The only hope he could give her was false, and probably unwelcome to boot.

Holden nodded her a somber "Good day" before trudging back to the bus station. He clutched the frame in one hand as he walked. Every so often he would steal a look at the photo and see more than he wanted to in the lopsided grin, a whimsical knowledge hidden in those laughing eyes. When he could look no more, he put away the scratched metal frame and the heretic it contained.

•••

Not all souls went to heaven, or even to the Tempter's hell. Some ended up here, in this shabby brown building that some dying sinner had traded to the church for a window seat on the ride to eternal bliss. Father Drury had spent the last six days praying and fasting. He had considered going again to the bishop, but dropped the idea almost immediately. The fat little man would make good his threat, and happily. *Sin is measured not by its effects on man and Earth, but by the degree to which it benefits the Twin.*

But which sin served old Thomas the Tempter more? Migrating an innocent soul or leaving a heretic free to print what he would? How could the Condemnation Board be certain they had chosen the right course?

Holden bit off that thought as he crossed the threshold of the church's Depository. It was here in this building that the monks of St. Brion's Order served as custodians, not only of deadglass, but also of heretical writings, apocrypha, Greco-Pauline idols and other relics deemed too impure for hallowed ground. The Brionites also had the unenviable task of collecting the sinners who had been condemned to migration.

Father Drury adjusted his chafing collar and looked about him. The foyer was reasonably well appointed, evidence of the Brionites' current favor with the pontiff. Some of the lesser orders, like the Knights of Cortez, were rarely funded well enough to heat their facilities all winter long.

The click of Holden's steps on the marble floor made the monk at the entry desk start. The worried little man slid something beneath his logbook and beamed up at Holden.

"You surprised me, Brother Drury. Have you brought us another lost soul? Who is it this time . . . Churchill?"

Holden smiled, scanning a board filled with names and titles. "You know I could not tell you, Brother Sergei, even if I knew. But I am here on migration business." He paused, then: "Is Lafayette in?"

The clerk growled. "That old goat is always in." A buzzer sounded. "You know the way." The big priest started toward the iron-banded door then doubled back. He snatched at the logbook, revealing a page of newsprint. Cartoon strips.

"Are these a part of your duties, Brother?" he asked gravely.

The little monk looked sheepish. "I'll throw them away, Brother."

Holden hesitated, then folded it and put it into a pocket. "No, Brother, I think I'll hold on to them." He smiled at the monk like they shared a secret. "And if it's today's edition, I'll refrain from reporting this incident to the Custodian of Heretical Writings." He winked.

Brother Sergei returned a smile of relief. "Oh, it is. Besides, Brother Gustav is with the bishop today, so you'd have to wait to turn them over. You will dispose of it for me?"

"That suits me perfectly." Holden winked at Brother Sergei, who again pressed the access buzzer.

Holden pushed the thick door open and strode through it, smiling. He wouldn't be seeing Lafayette, or at least he hoped not. And with the Custodian of Heretical Writings away, it would be easier than he thought to get his hands on a copy of whatever Wayne Charnick had been printing.

Or so he thought. The great metal door marked False Writings was encumbered with an old padlock the size of one of Holden's fists. Closer examination revealed the hasp wasn't really so thick. A well-placed blow (maybe two) from the fire axe mounted next to the roll of red hose on the wall would have him inside. But it would also draw unwanted attention. What he needed was a place to hide, somewhere he could wait until after hours.

The broom closet at the end of the hall would work nicely. As he walked in that direction, a small part of Holden's mind noted how easy it was becoming for him to think and do sinful—even criminal—things. Breaking and entering to read heresy hardly drew a protest from his inner voice at this point. And misrepresentation—lying—was becoming second nature. Part of him asked: *Holden, old boy, is clearing your own guilty conscience worth all of this sin?* Another part of him wasn't so sure he was sinning at all.

•••

Holden jerked awake, aching and blind. For a long moment he felt his heart racing. The air was unmoving and stale, thick with dust and a sterile smell. He wondered if this was what it was like to be trapped in the deadglass.

No, he could still hear the deep rich tones of bells from the cathedral of St. Francis De Molay two blocks over. He was in a broom closet, a cramped one, and it was at least ten o'clock at night. The bells had startled him awake, but he'd been too groggy to count them when they first began ringing. Regardless, the building would be mostly empty at this hour. Empty enough to get into the False Writings Depository, at any rate.

He reached around in the dark blindly until one hand found the light switch. He stopped himself. The light would only ruin his night vision. Groping quietly in the cramped little room, Holden felt the cool metal of the doorknob. He gave the knob a little twist, opened the door a careful inch, and listened.

Absolute quiet. *Perfect.*

The big priest—would he still be able to call himself a priest in the morning?—stepped lightly into the hall, shutting the door behind him. There were small windows set high in the wall every ten feet or so. Just enough light seeped through to allow him to move around. So long as he didn't go too fast, he wouldn't bump into anything he didn't want to.

Holden loosened his collar. The skin beneath it felt raw, as if it were enraged at such a man as he daring to wear a priest's collar. Holden rubbed the sore flesh with the tips of two fingers. There was no soothing it, so he left the collar loose as he crept toward the fire station he had scouted out earlier.

A few minutes later, Holden was standing outside the False Writings Depository, finding the hasp with his fingers. One whack with the fire axe, a few breathless minutes straining his ears against the silence, a two-handed push on the heavy door, and he was in.

Once the door was shut, he turned on the lights. No sense worrying about night vision now, he mused. He wouldn't be able to find what he needed in the dark, much less read it. After his eyes adjusted to the sudden glare, he looked around. Shelves full of boxes, each numbered and labeled, stood in strict formation like soldiers.

Getting in was proving to be only half the problem. When Holden found the index, he cursed under his breath. It was encoded.

Not sure what else to do, he checked a few containers at random. He found plenty that would have interested him another time, including a translation of some of Paul's letters, but nothing relevant to Wayne Charnick's heresy.

After more than an hour, he sat heavily on the floor, despairing. *Am I here for a reason, Lord? Am I meant to find something?* He pulled out the picture of Wayne Charnick, stared at that unchanging face smiling from behind the fire-warped glass. Holden sat there in silent meditation a few moments more before rising slowly to his feet.

He put the picture down on a bare spot of the Custodian of False Writings' desk and half-heartedly searched through the drawers and in-basket for any clue as to the index's code, or the location of Wayne Charnick's papers.

Finding nothing, he looked again at the heretic's picture grinning at him from the desk. He saw the way the glass had flowed as it melted, so the glass was a little thinner on one side. Charnick still held that unaccountably happy frozen stare, as if he were completely unaware that his picture had been through the flames and back—

Holden snatched up the picture and broke into a run, thinking crazily: *That's it! It doesn't matter either way!* He didn't bother to turn out the lights as he burst out of False Writings and into the darkened hallway; but he did make sure to pick up the axe.

When he broke into the Souls Depository, Holden was certain that he was no longer qualified to be called a priest. The tender flesh around his neck had stopped aching for just a few precious moments as he ran to the room where the glassbound souls were stored. The coolness of the air as he moved his big body through it refreshed him.

Made him forget about guilt and innocence and the doctrines of sin, if only for a moment.

When he couldn't find the one soul he wanted out of the thousands being stored here, he was enraged. *How dare the church make it so hard to save one innocent soul?*

It no longer mattered to him what Charnick had been printing; he was comfortable with not knowing that now. What mattered to him was that he had migrated an innocent soul, and that act had stained Holden's own soul as surely as the hair had abandoned the top of his pink head.

The warped glass in the picture frame had made him think of it. *It was in a fire,* Mina Charnick had said.

Fire indeed. One hot enough to melt glass might be hot enough to burn free the innocent soul trapped within.

•••

Setting the blaze had been easy enough. The church was overconfident. That fat paper-jockey, the bishop, was overconfident. None of them even considered the possibility that their doctrines and procedures could be fallible, much less breached.

Maybe sin had everything to do with man and Earth; maybe the truly guilty were those who ignored that fact.

Holden stayed inside the Souls Depository until the walls were scorching and the heat was so intense he could hardly breathe. He half imagined he could hear every last one of those glassbound souls cracking free of their crystal prisons and going on to wherever they were meant to. He pushed the front door open and sprinted down the hall, not knowing whether to laugh or sob at what he had wrought.

While he ran, Holden fumbled at the collar and tightened it back into place, despite the rawness beneath. He felt the warm kiss of ashes on his cheeks. His skin and clothes were already black with soot. It didn't matter; he laughed and charged through the quiet halls all the faster for it.

He was starting to get control of himself when he barreled past the vacant entry desk and through the front doors, bursting out into the cool, cloudless night. He sat down on the curb across from the Depository and watched the eastern wing burn.

Outside in the October air, his head seemed somehow clearer, as if he had been howling drunk and became suddenly sober. The giddy sense of freedom from guilt had risen then dissipated like the column of smoke that loomed above the burning brown building.

The church would send someone to collect him; that was certain. He would have to pay for all of the guilty souls he had released. He wondered about the penance they would impose on him; most likely his own soul would be condemned to the glass, the first of a new sin-menagerie.

He felt the muscles around his mouth twisting it into a wry, sad smile. Migration did more than the Holy Cathar Church realized; more than just keeping a soul from serving in the Tempter's army. Binding a soul in glass was also a rock-solid guarantee that the person would never sin—or feel guilt—again.

There were sirens approaching. They would be too late to save the building. Too late to save any souls tonight, his own included.

He imagined the Condemnation Board meeting even now. Urgent, hard-eyed monseigneurs reaching their gloved claws from the shadows. With the soft press of their ring seals to the Condemnation Decree, his soul would be declared a prisoner of the holy war against the Twin.

The wind was no longer cool, having taken on the heat of the rising flames. Holden adjusted his collar with sooty, sweating fingers, ignoring the soreness beneath.

The first fire engine jerked to a stop in front of him. Men in shiny yellow jackets sprang out and began rigging ladders and hoses. Holden remembered the newspaper sheet he had taken from Brother Sergei and pulled it out.

An echo of a sad smile tugged at the corners of his mouth. He held the page in front of him. A soft chuckle bubbled out of the big man as he read the previous day's Patrick and Trotsky strip. He folded the sheet back into a neat, small rectangle and laid it beside him on the curb.

Holden rose to his feet, looking at his soot- and newsprint-stained hands. The black circles around his fingernails reminded him of Wayne Charnick. Would his own bit of glass prove as cool and pale? He shoved his hands through the cassock, reaching for the heretic's picture.

It wasn't there. He must have left it inside in his haste to escape the inferno. The glass in that frame would be melted for sure this time. The heretic's picture had doubtless already curled and blackened; even now it was probably still rising skyward on a pillar of heat.

Warmth flickered across Holden's face as he stood there a long time waiting for the inevitable. It came just as the firefighters had gotten the flames under control: one of the doggedly reliable Brionite monks wearing a ceremonial hairshirt adorned only by a circle-wrapped olivewood cross.

"Father Drury, you have been condemned," the monk said by way of introduction. "Come with me."

If the Brionites had sent Brother Sergei, Holden would have returned the folded-up comic page to him. Maybe even clapped the monk on the back, thanking him for one last laugh. But this wasn't Sergei, and he probably wouldn't understand.

Holden wiped his hands on his trouser legs. "I'm right behind you, Brother," he said, looking up into the smoke-filled sky. "Lead me not into temptation."

LAST DANCE AT THE SERGEANT MAJORS' BALL

Written by
Cat Sparks

Illustrated by
Michael Brenner

About the Author

Sydney native Catriona "Cat" Sparks seems to be living several simultaneous lives on the coast of New South Wales, Australia. She's a writer, graphics designer, award-winning photographer and desktop publisher. But whether traveling throughout Europe, the Middle East, Asia or North America on her many adventures, this intrepid Cat has had one constant: science fiction.

As manager and senior editor of Agog! Press, Cat helped produce several anthologies of new Australian speculative fiction, earning her seven Ditmar Awards, Australia's equivalent of the Hugo. Yet it wasn't until Cat graduated from a Queensland writers' workshop in 2004 that her own writing took shape. While some work has appeared in Australia, the Writers of the Future award is her first commercial writing seen outside the continent.

Besides her many professional pursuits, Cat's interests include walking, reading, collecting travel kitsch and hanging out with her friends, most of whom seem to be fellow science fiction writers like her partner, author Robert Hood, or feline companions, Smersh and Roswell.

About the Illustrator

When a past Writers of the Future Contest winner walked into the small restaurant in Lawrence, Kansas, and asked who drew the illustrations decorating the wall, artist (and restaurant manager) Michael Brenner had never heard of the Illustrators of the Future Contest. Small world.

Michael's artistic leanings began as a boy growing up in Iowa City, Iowa. After high school, he entered the University of Kansas and, five years later, emerged with an undergraduate degree in design with an emphasis in illustration. He also took advantage of the college's eclectic offerings in all of his various other interests. While pursuing a professional illustration career, Michael has spent several years managing restaurants and banquets (with a little freelance designing thrown in). He's also taken up some industrial work designing audio-speaker panels. Michael hopes the anthology will be a "real boost to keep pushing toward professional success."

There was something odd about the corners where the ceiling met the wall. A slightly blurred effect, nothing Margaret's grandmother would ever notice; other than that the room was perfect. Margaret saw that the curtains were new. Elsie's own had been moth-eaten and stained.

"You're not my daughter," said Elsie, leaning forward to peer at her visitor through the lounge room's dim light.

"No, Grandma, it's me, Margaret. Your *grand*-daughter."

Elsie squinted, peering harder.

"*Lorraine*'s daughter," said Margaret patiently, glancing around the room checking all the familiar objects one by one. "And Lorraine was *your* daughter, remember?"

"Oh, yes," said Elsie, settling back into her chair in a satisfied manner. "'Ave you brought me flowers?"

Margaret glanced down at her hands and was surprised to find that she was indeed carrying a bunch of pink and purple gerberas fastened at the stems with a thick orange ribbon.

"There's a vase on the windersill," said Elsie, looking pleased. "Put the kettle on. I've been waiting all afternoon for a nice cuppa tea."

Margaret stepped into the kitchen and placed the flowers on the old cream Formica table top. Everything was the same, from the wallpaper to the stains on the faded linoleum floor. The cups, the crumbs scattered around the toaster, the wicker basket containing scissors, rubber bands and pencil stubs. She lifted the lid of the sugar bowl to find the inner rim encrusted with beige-colored crystals, just as it had always been.

"Have you come from work?" called out Elsie from the lounge room.

"Yes," yelled Margaret, reaching for the tea bags. Would cups of tea materialize, or would she have to go through the process of making them herself? She hesitated, but no cups of steaming tea appeared miraculously on the bench, so she filled the electric kettle and set out cups and saucers, concentrating on each movement, expecting something odd to happen. It didn't, so she made tea the old-fashioned way, giving it a couple of minutes to draw before pouring.

"Have you come on the bus?" sang out Elsie.

"Yes, I came on the bus," Margaret called back as she carefully carried the drinks into the lounge. "Here you go."

"Mind your head!" Elsie shouted as Margaret dodged the low-hanging chandelier and set the cups down.

"Is there any sugar in?" asked Elsie, accepting her cup with an unsteady hand.

Margaret nodded. "Yes, there's two spoonfuls." She watched as Elsie stirred in another two from the sugar bowl she kept by her side.

"That's a *good* cuppa tea," said Elsie as Margaret returned to the kitchen to arrange the flowers in a vase, which she set down on the coffee table before sinking into the visitor's chair. As they sat sipping tea in silence, she studied the room looking for evidence—anything that might hint at the fact that the room wasn't what it appeared to be. But everything was perfect, from Elsie's hand-painted landscapes copied from postcards, to the never-used yellow porcelain cups and saucers in the cabinet. Even the blown glass swan was there.

"My friend Barbara, 'er father was a sergeant major," said Elsie. "I used to get tickets to the Sergeant Majors' Ball, you know. But *my* father, 'e'd say that *no decent person* should be out past ten o'clock. The Sergeant Majors' Ball, it were like a dinner dance, and the dancing didn't even *start* till ten o'clock."

Margaret nodded and drained her cup. The Sergeant Majors' Ball was the only story from her youth that Elsie could remember now. Once there had been many more: the girl who'd drowned in the river, Elsie working in the weaving factory with her mother, Elsie leaving Preston and sailing to New Zealand to get married, Elsie crossing the street to avoid the drunken roughnecks at the pub on a Saturday night.

Margaret had sat through each story at least a thousand times, only now Elsie couldn't remember them at all, and, she was ashamed to admit, neither could Margaret, even though she'd been hearing them her whole life, over and over and over, once a week as her family duty dictated. At what point had she stopped listening? She swallowed the last mouthful from her cup. Virtual tea tasted exactly the same as real tea.

Elsie leaned forward in her chair and reached for a tube of cream on the coffee table. "Pass that over. I've got *arthur-itis*."

"Are your hands sore, Grandma?"

"Oh yes! I've got *arthur-itis* all over."

Elsie rubbed the linctus into her gnarled fingers as Margaret watched.

"Are you *sure* your fingers are sore, Grandma?"

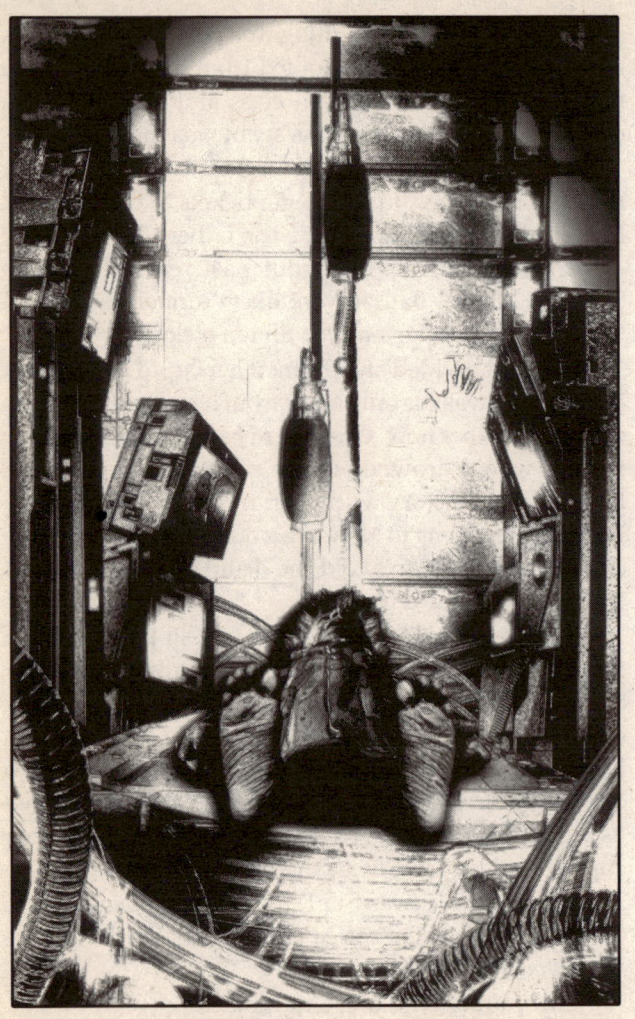

Illustrated by Michael Brenner

Elsie squinted at her granddaughter. "I've got *arthuritis* all over my fingers. Doctor says there's nothing can be done about it."

"But do they *feel* sore?"

"Eh?" Elsie rubbed her hands in silence, her movements slowing to a stop. "Have you come from work?" she asked.

Margaret's answer was interrupted by a knock on the door.

"Who's there?" sang out Elsie. "Come in!"

The door opened and a well-groomed woman in a crisp navy blue suit entered the apartment. "Hello Margaret, my name is Claire Bryant. I'm the Client Interface Officer from Rosehaven Homes."

"Is it her downstairs?" whispered Elsie conspiratorially, leaning forward in her chair, the teacup slopping on her lap.

"Good afternoon, Elsie," said Claire. "I've just come to see how you're getting along."

"I've got a visitor," said Elsie. "My daughter."

"Granddaughter," corrected Margaret.

Claire smiled at Margaret. "Perhaps you'd like to come and see me when you've finished your visit?"

"Yes—but how?"

"Just walk out through this door," said Claire, gesturing. "It was nice to see you again, Elsie," she called out as she left.

"Was it *her downstairs?*" asked Elsie. In the thirty years that her grandmother had lived in the Wollstonecraft apartment, Margaret had never heard her refer to her downstairs neighbor by her real name. "No, it was—" Who exactly was Claire Bryant to Elsie? Maybe she was the downstairs neighbor.

"Have you come from work?"

Margaret sighed heavily. "Yes, I *have* come from work, just like I do every week."

Elsie leaned forward in her chair, causing the empty teacup to fall to the carpet. "Do you work in the city?"

"Yes, I work in the city," said Margaret through gritted teeth.

"Ooh!" replied Elsie. "The city. And have you come on the bus?"

•••

When Margaret pulled her grandmother's front door open and stepped over the threshold, she found herself in a garish, overlit reception area dotted with unnaturally healthy-looking pot plants. Claire was standing there waiting for her beside a bright green Benjamin Ficus.

"So tell me what you think of Rosehaven? Does it meet with your satisfaction? Is our nursing home everything you expected it to be?"

They walked a few steps to the lounges and Margaret sank into an expanse of luxurious burgundy-colored leather. Her eyes took in the décor. "Where are we exactly? I don't understand."

"We're in my office at the clinic," explained Claire. "You've been there since you first walked through Elsie's door. You're wearing a headset. My driver gave it to you when he picked you up."

Margaret raised her hand and touched the side of her head. "And where is my grandmother?"

"In her hospital bed."

"But she doesn't—"

"No. She thinks she's still living in her Wollstonecraft flat. The facsimile is remarkable don't you think?"

Margaret's brow furrowed. "She doesn't even remember being moved, does she?"

"No," said Claire. "And I know how much it bothered you when you signed the contract. Elsie went to sleep in her own bed and woke up the next day in Rosehaven."

Margaret shook her head. "I didn't know the technology was so advanced. It's like being in a VR game. I don't play games. I had no idea . . ."

Claire smiled, stared into Margaret's eyes. "I know you feel very guilty about admitting your grandmother to a nursing home. You've taken such excellent care of her since your mother passed away. But she's one hundred and ten years old. You did the right thing by bringing her to Rosehaven."

Margaret stared at the lush carpet pile. "I don't know. This is all so strange. So incredible. I'm not sure I can get used to it."

Claire smiled again and placed her hand on Margaret's. "I'd like to go through some of the finer points of the contract with you now. You purchased the basic care and accommodation package for Elsie. I'm not sure if you're aware of all the optional extras that Rosehaven can provide for her."

Margaret nodded thoughtfully. "I feel better about the expense now that I see what my money's paying for."

"It's true, Rosehaven's facilities aren't cheap," said Claire. "But I want you to be aware of some of our optional extras, just in case you need them."

Margaret nodded again. "Sure, maybe later, but I haven't got time today. I have teleconferences all afternoon, and then I've got dinner guests coming 'round at seven." She pushed herself up from the lounge's comfortable grasp. "How much notice do I need to give if I want to visit Elsie?"

"Just a couple of hours will do. We'll send a courtesy car to get you."

"I'll pop in once a fortnight," said Margaret, patting her side in search of her handbag, flushing with momentary panic when she realized that it wasn't there.

"Sorry," said Claire, "your bag is on the outside. I thought I'd leave your hands free to carry Elsie's flowers."

"On the outside?"

"With your physical body. We can return to it now if you like."

Margaret nodded, and suddenly she was in a different waiting room, sitting in a far less comfortable chair. She retrieved her palm pilot from her handbag. "Tuesdays are no good—neither are Wednesdays. Thursday week in the morning is looking good, except for . . . Oh damn, I've got that appointment with D&F."

Claire cleared her throat. "You could visit Elsie every day, you know."

Margaret looked up from her diary. "Look, I'd love to, of course, but my schedule—"

"*You* wouldn't have to be here at all. We can scan you and create a virtual likeness. Elsie would never know that it wasn't really you."

Margaret stared blankly at Claire. "What did you say?"

"In some ways it would be better for Elsie," Claire continued. "Your virtual self would have infinite patience to listen to the same few questions and stories over and over again."

"But she'd know the difference!" exclaimed Margaret.

"Surely she could tell the real me from an . . . a copy."

Claire laughed. "I know it's hard to believe, but I assure you, she wouldn't know. Elsie already has a selection of virtual characters who visit her each day: the cleaner, the hairdresser, meals on wheels, the man who does the windows, even her old friend Gert from the Senior Citizens' Center, who brings her a pile of women's magazines and a sponge cake. Each character is programmed to engage Elsie in conversation and stimulate her mind."

"Gert?"

"Yes, I know, Gert died ten years ago, but Elsie doesn't remember that. She likes having Gert come over now and then. It gives her something to look forward to."

Margaret clutched her palm pilot and sat back in the chair.

"You're going to need some time to think about it," said Claire. "I know that you're very busy, Margaret, but I strongly urge you to consider taking full advantage of the services Rosehaven has to offer."

"Right," said Margaret, stuffing her palm pilot back into her handbag as she stood up. "Can I see my grandma before I go. I mean her *real* body?"

"Of course," said Claire. "Follow me please."

They left the office and walked down a long white corridor lined with glass windows. Margaret could see wards filled with hi-tech life-support beds containing elderly people. All of them appeared to be sleeping peacefully. Busy-looking nurses tended the bed controls or walked past brandishing clipboards. Through a sliding glass door Margaret found her grandmother asleep, attended by a handsome male nurse. He smiled at her warmly.

"Is she always asleep?" asked Margaret.

"There's nothing to be alarmed about," said Claire. "Doctors and nurses tend her body twenty-four hours a day. They feed her, bathe her, exercise her limbs and turn her regularly to prevent bedsores."

Margaret shook her head. "I don't know . . ."

"Margaret," said Claire, "Elsie is *very* comfortable in her virtual environment. In the real world she is too old to stand up unaided. Are you sure she'd be better off living with the truth?"

Margaret didn't answer. She stared at her sleeping grandmother's face, watched the little colored lights on her headset blinking rhythmically on and off. If it were *her* lying there in the bed, what would *she* want? Margaret honestly didn't know.

She followed Claire out of the ward and back down the long white corridor to the office. As she was about to leave, she turned. "If you can do all this, then why must they all live in virtual facsimiles of their own bodies? Why can't they become athletes, ballerinas—young again?"

"Theoretically they could," said Claire matter-of-factly. "The technology exists, but Rosehaven doesn't provide that option for its clients. Elsie remains content within her body because she doesn't know it's not real. If she knew the truth then she and others might demand new lives and new experiences. The resources of this facility are not designed to cater for such outcomes. We're a nursing home, Margaret. All our clients are over ninety. Even the sharpest and the sanest of them are quite confused."

"Have any of them ever figured it out, tried to push the barriers?"

Claire paused to think. "Only one—although I think it's a case of dementia, rather than the client *knowing*. She's a 116-year-old Vietnamese woman who doesn't speak any English. When her family brought her here we constructed a virtual replica of the family home, but she didn't care for it. She seemed miserable in all environments, so we made an exception to policy. What she wanted was to be five years old again, back in the village of her birth. So we let her. Our technicians reconstructed her childhood home from old photographs. Her village was surrounded by rice paddies. She adored ducks—it was her job to care for them when she was a child. Her family doesn't quite approve, but they concede that it's working out best this way. Sometimes we send her virtual grandchildren in to play with her."

"Virtual grandchildren?"

"Grandchildren are especially popular. Perhaps you might like to consider—"

"But Max and I don't plan—"

"That doesn't matter. We can create virtual grandchildren, their appearances based on a genetic blend of both your features."

"You have to be joking!"

"Think of how much joy grandchildren would bring to Elsie's life."

Margaret shook her head in disbelief as she headed for the exit.

"Don't forget to return the headset to the driver," said Claire.

Margaret raised her fingertips to her forehead and touched a slim metal band encrusted with smooth oval-shaped nodes.

•••

"You're not my daughter," said Elsie, squinting in the

fading afternoon light. "Mind your head!" she shouted as Margaret dodged the low-hanging chandelier, sat down in the visitor's rocker and folded her hands in her lap.

"I'm your granddaughter," said Margaret. "Lorraine was your daughter and my mother."

"Oh, yes," said Elsie, settling back into her chair. "Have you come from work?"

"Yes," said Margaret, smiling pleasantly. "I've come on the bus."

"On the bus!" exclaimed Elsie. "Do you work in the city?"

"Yes," said Margaret, "I do."

"Is it Sunday? It feels like Sunday. Everything is so quiet."

"No, Grandma, it's Wednesday."

"Wednesday? Oh, yes. Have you come from work?"

"Yes, I've come from work."

Elsie squinted, focusing on somewhere in the middle distance. "I used to work," she said. "In a factory. I used to go to school half-time and go to work with my mother. We was put to weaving, you know."

Margaret sat patiently, smiling, her hands folded in her lap.

"I was frightened of the looms. And the tattler. 'E used to use bad language. Put the kettle on, love. I've been waiting all afternoon for a nice cuppa tea."

Margaret stood up and went into the kitchen. She filled the kettle, switched it on and set out two cups and saucers on the bench.

"'Ave I ever told you about the Sergeant Majors' Ball?" called out Elsie from the lounge room. "My friend Barbara used to get tickets—'er father was a sergeant major, you know."

"Go on," said Margaret, setting a steaming cup of tea on the coffee table beside her grandmother's chair.

"Is there any sugar in?"

"Two spoonfuls."

Elsie raised the cup to her lips with a shaky hand. "Ooh, that's a nice cuppa tea. You're a clever girl, you are. Always looking out for your old grandma. The winder cleaner come today, but 'e never made me a nice cuppa tea. Have you come on the bus?"

Margaret smiled with infinite patience.

•••

Margaret was driving through Epping one afternoon when she started to experience pangs of guilt about Elsie. She'd grown up visiting her grandmother once a week alongside her mother. When Lorraine died, she'd kept on doing it automatically, never really considering that she had a choice in the matter. And then Rosehaven came along. How long had it been since she'd visited Elsie? A year? When she checked her palm pilot she discovered that it was nearly two. Two years? Surely not. For two years she'd just paid the bills and let her grandmother be entertained by a plethora of illusory friends and relatives. She hadn't meant to let it happen, but it happened just the same. Margaret suddenly felt very disappointed with herself.

"Take me to Rosehaven Home," she told her car.

"I'm sorry, Margaret," the car replied. "I'm not familiar with that address."

"Rose-haven," said Margaret, articulating as clearly as she could. "The nursing home where I put my grandmother."

"Please accept my apologies, Margaret, but there is no such address in my database," said the car.

Where exactly had she driven to two years ago? She seemed to dimly recall Rosehaven sending a courtesy car, but where it had taken her to and brought her back from was a mystery. It was odd that she couldn't remember.

"White Pages has a Rosehaven Corp listed at Mascot—all other references to Rosehaven have premises offshore."

"Mascot? Doesn't sound right—are you sure there's nothing else?"

"There are no other listings," said the car.

Margaret activated her e-phone. "Celia, it's me. I'm on the road and I need you to check something. The bills from my grandmother's nursing home. Is there a street address?"

"Hang on, I'll run a search," said Celia. "Nope, just a Net account number, nothing else."

"Curious. Okay car, better take me to Mascot."

• • •

The car pulled up to a dingy warehouse at the end of a cul-de-sac not far from some disused aeroplane hangers.

"If I'm not out in fifteen minutes, call the cops," she told it. She gripped her Taser and approached the warehouse cautiously. A door at the side led through to a prefabricated office cluttered with beige filing cabinets. It contained a desk, a swivel chair and a bank of ancient monitors. The chair was empty but a half-filled cup of coffee sat on the desk.

"Hello," she said, timidly. "Is anybody there?"

No answer. Margaret sniffed the stale air and noticed another door slightly ajar at the back of the office. She slipped inside quietly and headed for it. Behind that door she found a corridor. Gripping the Taser tightly, she ventured forward. The corridor joined another corridor, which opened out into a larger space filled with numbered doors that all appeared to be locked.

"Hey," said a gruff voice behind her. "What you doin' in here?"

Margaret spun around and found herself face to face with an Asian man in his sixties or seventies dressed in a security uniform. His hand rested on his Taser. Margaret lowered hers.

"Not allowed in here. Restricted," he said.

"I'm looking for Rosehaven nursing home," she replied. "I guess I've come to the wrong place."

The security guard peered at her closely. "This an audit?" he asked, lowering his hand from his weapon.

"I'm looking for my grandmother," she replied.

The security guard shook his head. "Not allowed," he said, and headed down the corridors that Margaret had come through. She followed him back into the office and watched him sink into the swivel chair and pick up his coffee cup.

"This is Rosehaven, isn't it?" she said. "Although it's not quite how I remember it. I want to speak to Claire Bryant. I'm not leaving till I see my grandmother."

The security guard ignored her. He drained his cup and muttered something unintelligible at his viewscreen.

Margaret placed her hands on her hips. "If I'm not back outside in five minutes, my car is going to call the cops." She pushed a pile of rubbish on the desk to one side and sat herself down. "I don't suppose you want the police in here, do you?"

He gave no indication that he'd even heard her,

but after half a minute passed in silence, he touched a couple of sensors on the screen, probably to check if she really did have a car waiting outside.

"Okay, no cops," he said gruffly.

Margaret tapped her e-phone, told the car to stand by, and then followed the guard back down the corridors, and out into the space filled with numbered doors. She watched him punch a code into a dirty plastic panel. A door opened and she followed him again down yet another corridor and out into an enormous warehouse space stacked from floor to ceiling with coffin-shaped plastic containers. There were thousands of them, each fitted with winking LED screens. They were all tinged blue and their fronts were translucent so you could see the distorted forms of the human beings inside.

"Jesus Christ!" said Margaret.

She followed the guard through a maze of stacked coffins till they came to an ancient computer standing by itself in a clearing. It was so old that it had a keyboard attached. The guard stood before it, punched in a few key commands and turned his face toward her.

"Account number," he said.

Margaret shook her head dumbly. The guard grunted and punched a few more keys. "Grandmother's name."

Margaret told him, and then he asked her to spell it. Within seconds he had a code number from the terminal. He led her on through the maze once more until eventually he stopped before one of the stacks.

"Visit?" he asked.

Margaret nodded, staring stupidly upwards at the tower of hibernating humans. The guard punched some sensors on the stack's control panel, took a crumpled-looking headset from his pocket, stuck it on her forehead and jacked the other end into the stack.

Before she could ask anything more, Margaret found herself standing inside her grandmother's apartment. The lounge room was dimly lit and faintly musty-smelling, just as it had been the last time Margaret was really there. The television was on with the volume turned down low and the curtains were drawn. She walked across the carpet and yanked the curtains open, letting a brilliant shaft of daylight spill across the floor.

"Grandma, it's Margaret," she called out.

The view from the balcony showed empty streets with a few parked cars. A cat slunk gingerly along a fence. The sky was cloudless.

"Grandma, are you in the bathroom?"

Margaret walked across the space and gave the bathroom door a gentle push. It swung open. There was nobody inside but the hot-water tap was dribbling. Instinctively Margaret turned it off, even though logic told her that it wasn't real water that was being wasted.

There were only two other rooms in the apartment aside from the kitchen—she'd seen it was empty when she arrived. Both doors were closed, and Margaret had an uneasy feeling as she approached the bedroom. Could people die in virtual reality? What happened when they did?

She took a deep breath and pushed the door open. Inside was her grandmother's ancient double bed made up neatly as it would have been by the Homecare workers. It was empty, a cheap rubber hot-water bottle nestled on one of the pillows.

That only left the sewing room. Elsie hadn't done any sewing for years. Margaret pushed the door open and found it to be empty too, as expected. She walked briskly back through the lounge and into the kitchen, peering into the tiny laundry at the far end, just in case, but all the rooms were empty. Elsie wasn't there.

She tore off the headset angrily, finding herself transported back to the warehouse in an instant. The security guard was nowhere to be seen. She stormed back down the corridors until she found him slouching back in his swivel chair.

"What the heck have you done with her?" she yelled.

He shrugged. "Maybe she's dead?"

"Maybe you want to lose your job," she said coldly.

The guard frowned as he leaned forward and checked the viewscreen. "Alive," he said enthusiastically, pointing at it even though Margaret obviously couldn't see anything from where she was standing. "Okay—she's alive, heart rate steady, no problem."

"Then why isn't she in her apartment? Surely the VR program ensures that."

He shrugged, as though to indicate that he was no technician. He tapped his communicator and spoke hurriedly in an unfamiliar language. Margaret didn't need to comprehend his words to know that a higher authority had been summoned.

She folded her arms. "How exactly does an old lady leave a VR program if she's not actually physically in there in the first place. It can't be overridden, can it?" she asked.

The guard shrugged again.

"But she isn't dead, is she?"

•••

I'll be wearing *crepe de chine* tonight, and patent

leather shoes made especially for dancin'. I'm going to dance with the handsomest lads and catch the last train home. But if one of 'em has a motorcycle and sidecar, 'e'll be the one who's taking me 'ome tonight. Not up to my own front door, of course. 'E needn't know I'm the cobbler's daughter. 'E can drop me off outside me piano teacher's place. 'Er house is so pretty, big and white with a garden and all. I shall kiss 'im, I expect, but only if 'e's a very good dancer. If 'e isn't, I shan't ever want to remember his name.

There's a full moon tonight and it's come up early. I can see the reflection in the water of these peculiar fields by the roadside. Not like the country fields back 'ome. No horses or cows or chickens or sheep, just water buffaloes with them great big 'orns pulling the ploughs behind 'em. No people about, but there's plenty of ducks. If I stay 'ere on the path my dancing shoes won't get dirty.

There's a bridge up ahead. Just a small one made of old bamboo. I think there's someone standin' on it. A little foreign girl, and she's got a funny hat on. It's made of bamboo too, woven, with a point on top. Oh look—the little foreign girl's got a duckling in her arms.

Now the twilight's come out in full, and the stars above are lovely as diamonds, glittering like the chandelier at the Grande Palace Ballroom. All the stars are out tonight, shining down to light my path. The little foreign girl with the duckling in her arms smiles ever so sweetly and waves.

"Excuse me, honey, do you know the way to the Sergeant Majors' Ball? I've got a ticket."

She's nodding and pointing over the hill into the far-off distance. It seems like such a long way away, but it's early yet, not even fully night, and the dancin' doesn't even start till ten o'clock. She's smiling at me and waving again, so I wave back and follow the path that leads up the hill and vanishes into the distance.

"Tell my father not to wait up, because I won't be coming home till after the very last dance," I call back.

ANNUS MIRABILIS

Written by
Mike Rimar

Illustrated by
Steven V. Popovich

About the Author

Finalist Mike Rimar says it wasn't until his early twenties that he started to take his writing seriously. Output on an old eight-pin dot matrix printer and single-spaced to save paper, Mike's first story submission (to a horror mag) came back with a rejection slip. Crushed, he consulted book after book on writing. They all said, "Write what you know." But Mike felt he was too young to have interesting stories, and so he stopped writing altogether. He decided instead to enroll in a local college where he graduated with a computer engineering tech degree.

From Mike's point of view, the most important class he took was an elective: science fiction literature. That class, coupled with his wife's belief in Mike's talents, convinced him to start writing again. Though he has lots of life experience today, a daughter named Hayley, and another child on the way, Mike says he draws his inspirations less from his own life experience than a vivid imagination—like an entire plot he dreamed up while driving on a highway off-ramp.

The stick of chalk slipped from Bert's fingers, shattering on the hardwood floor. In the doorway stood his doppelgänger.

Almost. Nose, mouth, ears, all looked similar, yet age had weathered the skin. The hair was a wild tangle of snow. His bowed shoulders looked as if gravity had become too much for them to bear. Deep lines etched a face empty of happiness.

"Who are you? How did you get in here?" Bert patted the pocket of his waistcoat, feeling the outline of the key through the fabric. He *had* locked the door.

As if fulfilling a haunted destiny, the older man answered, "You." He closed the door behind him, placing the leather satchel he had been holding by his feet. "Call me Al, and I have a key."

Bert stumbled back as if bereft of strength. The key pinched between Al's fingers was eerily similar to the one in Bert's pocket. The only one of its kind. He reached for his chair. Simple, wooden, cushionless, he settled into it as if it was a life preserver. "No. This is some jest. Planck put you up to this. He likes a good joke. Tell the truth. It is Planck, *ja?*"

If the old man smiled, a silver bush of whiskers hid it well. "Planck was brilliant, but never so clever. No, not Max Planck. Look closer, past my age. Can't you see?"

"Bah!" Bert slammed an open palm against the

desktop. "Makeup. What is it you actors call it, pancake? If not Max, then who? This farce is not amusing."

"This is no joke. I am you, only older."

"*Ja*. Fine. You are very good. Truly. The way you stand. Mannerisms. Impressive. But the game is over. Tell your master I have not fallen for the trick."

Al sighed. "I knew it. I told them I was no fool, but would they listen?"

"Aha!" Bert waggled a finger. "More than one, I should have known. Alone, my peers can barely afford a fine meal, but together . . . Tell me their names. Better yet, let us turn this against them. What does it matter to you? Someone has paid already, I presume."

"Strange, I don't remember being so Machiavellian." The old man looked upon Bert as if he were a precocious child. "There is no one to turn this against. At least, no one you know." He turned as if to scan his surroundings. The Swiss Patent Office was cramped. The desk, chair and chalkboard nearly filled its Spartan spaces. A notebook lay on the desk's blotter next to an inkwell and pen. The corners of Al's eyes crinkled as he squinted at the book's open pages. "You're almost finished. Good. We are not too late."

"Too late? We? What are you talking about? Late for what?" Bert snapped the notebook closed and leapt to his feet, interposing his body between the desk and the intruder. "I don't know who you are, but it is time you left."

The old man's head bobbed. "I agree. It's time we left."

"Again with the *we*. I am not going anywhere, especially with you. Now, please, I have work to do. Give my compliments to your employers, whomever they are."

Al's large basset-hound eyes fixed on him. "You had a girl. You and Mila."

Bert grinned. *I have you now*. "Mileva and I have a boy. Hans Albert."

"Hans wasn't your first child. Two years ago, Mileva gave birth to a girl, in her parents' home in Hungary. She gave the girl up for adoption."

Bert reached for the desk to steady himself. "Who *are* you?" Other than Mila and her parents, no one knew about the first child. It had been an accident. He had loved Mila, but they were so young and still in school and unwed and—

How did this stranger, this Al, know of Lieserl? He looked closer at his visitor. No sign of makeup, spirit gum, wig, he saw nothing to reveal this man as false. The clothes, however, were nothing like his. A baggy cotton sweater, gray and fading, covered a collared white shirt that hinted a need for ironing. Dark eyes twinkled as if experiencing a private joke on the world. Yet joy was absent as if a great responsibility had brought unquenchable sorrow.

If this is me, what have I become?

Al nodded. "You're beginning to believe."

"What is there to believe? You are some actor who—"

"Enough! We've little time left. I am you. You see it, now accept it." Al thrust his hands into the pockets of his baggy corduroy trousers.

Bert frowned. *Did nothing fit him in the future?*

His heart skipped a beat. In the future. *My God, I do believe.*

His fingertips brushed the closed notebook, his thoughts on the calculations within. "Is it possible? Are you real?" He reached out to the apparition.

Al shuffled quickly away. "Don't do that. The

Illustrated by Steven V. Popovich

debate about the effects of sharing the same time-space continues. I don't want to learn the answer just now."

"Of course," Bert nodded. In truth, he didn't understand what his older self was talking about and made a mental note to think on it later. Sighing, he rubbed his head. His black hair, thick and long, was getting away from him. *I must see a barber.* "You said we are to go somewhere."

"Yes, and we must go now."

"Where?"

"The future, of course. Well, your future, my present."

Bert's hand hovered over his scalp. "This is madness. I never think of the future. It comes soon enough. I've read Wells's book. *The Time Machine*, was it? Very entertaining, but—"

A glimmer of mirth sparkled in Al's tired, sad eyes. "There is no fantasy machine. True, we all travel through time in our own way, but only you may take the great leaps forward denied to me. As originator of this timeline, I can only move forward one second after the next."

"If what you say is true, and this is your past . . ."

Al nodded. "Many have proposed the theory. Only I have put it to the test. No one has come after me. Sad, really, and frightening. If I'm to believe the publicity, I am the greatest mind that ever lived. You would think someone, anyone, would want a few words of my wisdom."

"What words of wisdom do you have for me?"

Melancholy filled Al's dark eyes. "Make the right decision." He shuffled on brown leather shoes toward the door and retrieved his satchel. Bert watched as his older version placed the satchel on the desk, unclasped its latches, and pulled out something silver and shimmering. "Put this on."

"What is it?" The odd fabric unfolded into a bizarre one-piece trousers and jacket including a hood like a welder's mask with a glass faceplate. The plate, however, was too flexible for glass.

"Plastic," Al said, noticing Bert's scrutiny. He already had one pant leg on. "It's a radiation suit."

"Radiation!" Bert had read papers on Madame Marie Curie's research into uranium and radium. "How does radiation relate to the future?"

"I'll answer all your questions later." Al wriggled his arms into the suit. "For now we must hurry."

Reluctantly Bert continued sliding the silvery coveralls over his own heavy woolen trousers and suit coat, fumbling with the unfamiliar straps and buckles. Though the material was surprisingly light, he nevertheless felt suffocated.

Al left the office, oblivious to Bert's discomfort. Shrugging his shoulders, Bert followed him out into the cool Swiss night air. He turned in time to see his visitor disappear around the corner of the building. Exasperated, he exhaled through gritted teeth. "What's the hurry?"

More importantly, why am I doing this?

But no one was around to answer his questions so he hurried along. The streets of Bern were deserted but for a single horse and carriage. A crescent moon as pale as his new, strange radiation suit hung in a cloudless sky. How long had he been at his calculations? He tended to lose sense of time while working.

In spite of his age, Al nimbly boarded the carriage. The material of his radiation suit rustled like canvas as he moved.

"Where are we going?"

Al answered with a wave of his hand leaving Bert little choice but to do his elder's bidding. He barely settled onto the bench seat when Al snapped a small whip and the horse lurched forward.

The ride through Bern, swift and short, soon brought them to the outskirts of the city. Despite the hour, a group of citizens had gathered around a stout construct of metal and glass that reminded Bert of the onion-shaped spires of orthodox churches.

"Damn," Al cursed. "We're too late. They've found it."

The tall gaunt visage of Burgermeister Herbert Krone arched a civic eyebrow at their approach. "Herr Einstein. Judging from your clothing this must be your doing."

"Put the hood on," Al said and donned his own welder's mask. With little grace, he dismounted from the carriage and shrugged his way through the crowd.

"Now see here," said Burgermeister Krone. "Is this your father, Einstein? Tell him to respect my office."

Al ignored the commotion and continued to the giant onion. Once there he pulled a small lever recessed in the convex metal wall. A small round door swung open. Amidst gasps from the crowd, he entered through the circular doorway, turned and bade Bert to follow.

"If you will excuse me, Herr Burgermeister," Bert said.

"Now just one minute!" The burgermeister was the only one apparently unperturbed by two silver-clad gentlemen entering a giant onion. Then under his breath muttered, "Damn Jews."

Al popped his head out the doorway. "I suggest you get your people out of the way, Herr Burgermeister. My ship creates quite a blast."

"Ship?" Bert said.

"Blast!" Burgermeister Krone exclaimed. The word rippled through the crowd and everyone started backing away.

Seeing his advantage, Bert hurried past Krone and dashed through the doorway. The door closed behind him with a snakelike hiss.

"Up here," Al called from above.

The interior of Al's ship looked nothing like an onion. Metal ribs stretched along the walls reminding him of the skeletal framework of American skyscrapers. Conduits snaked through and around the ribbing, fighting for available space with glass gauges of indeterminate purpose. Bolted to the walls were several thick metal canisters. At the center of the room a cast-iron block about ten-foot square sat like a prehistoric turtle. A metal stairway seesawed up to another level, atop which Al looked down, his bushy moustache puffed out with exertion. "Hurry. Hurry," he said.

Bert bounded up the stairs, his approach greeted with an envious glint from Al's basset-hound eyes. The platform circled the wall. To their left stood metal cabinets, tall as Bert, and peppered with blinking lights. On the opposite wall toggle switches filled more cabinets. Small nameplates underneath the switches presumably identified their purpose.

Al snorted. "Don't ask me what they mean. 'Don't touch them,' they said. Like I'm some child." He winked conspiratorially and flicked a switch up and down. "Ha! That'll show them."

"But what are these things? What are they for?"

"Computers."

Bert raised his eyebrows questioningly.

"Sorry. I forget sometimes. Computers are calculating machines. They complete intricate algorithms within minutes, often seconds."

"Truly? Amazing."

"Yes. Its invention was but another step leading to our doom."

"Doom?"

"It's better that I show you." A deep boom echoed throughout the onion's interior. "Damn. The natives have regained their courage. Hurry, before they become more than just a nuisance. If they damage the hull, all is lost."

Al led Bert up to yet another level. They were near the top of the dome, the room ending in a vaulted ceiling. Another computer the size of a footlocker lay between two cushioned chairs with reclining backs so they nearly resembled beds. Above the chairs, three rectangular windows opened to a star-filled sky.

"Sit. Do as I do." Al settled into the left chair, grabbed two ends of a belt and buckled them around his midsection. Next he pulled two more straps from the top of the chair and stretched them over his thin shoulders, locking the buckles at the waist. Pulling, he cinched the belts tight.

Bert mimicked every movement. When finished he tried to move, but the belts did their jobs, perhaps too well. Was he allowing Al to kidnap him? "Uh, I have changed my mind. I do not want to go. Release me, now!"

"Oh, relax." Al reached for the computer between them, flicking several switches. A pause followed and the ends of his salt-and-pepper moustache drooped into a frown. "I hope I did that right."

Bert grimaced. "Perhaps you should not have played with that switch on the level below."

Al flashed an irritable look. "The propellant in those tanks should have mixed by—" The ship shuddered.

"Ah, here we go."

Bert's heart raced. He didn't like this one bit. "I want to get off. I have had enough—" A deafening roar drowned out his words. Outside, an orange glow filled the small overhead windows. Fire! The burgermeister and all those people. He hoped they made it to safety.

Al looked at him and spoke, but his voice was lost to the thunder filling the cabin. Banks of computer lights flickered with increasing ferocity.

Something was happening, something grand, but the pounding in Bert's chest would not allow him to enjoy the experience, or time for exploration. He felt a gentle pull and knew the onion ship was moving. His mouth opened into a small, excited O, then his lips continued to pull back until he thought his face might peel off.

Deafened by the thunder of noise, he screamed in terror and confusion, joy and wonder, screamed until tears ran from the corners of his eyes and kept on screaming until he realized all was silent again except the sound of his hoarse voice muffled within his hood. His mouth snapped shut. He felt light, an unearthly freedom, and knew that if not for the chair's restraints he would be floating. Stars, more than he thought ever existed, filled the three small windows. "My God!"

"Amazing, isn't it?" Al removed his welder's mask, clipping it to a small metal snap on the side of the chair. "Goddard calls this a rocket ship," Al continued. "We're in space now."

Bert gaped. "I do not believe it."

"Believe it. What is more, we'll soon travel beyond the speed of light." He pressed a button and the ship pointed toward the gap between the sun and the moon.

The scientist in Bert wanted to doubt the words. He needed proof, repeated experiments, answers to unasked questions.

Yet...

Yet what could he say to the sight before him? How could he explain the man sitting next to him? It was all too much, too fast. He had no time to assimilate and examine the information. Still, one question needed asking, but before he could, the ship shuddered again and he felt a punch to his kidneys, even through the chair's cushioning. The moon and sun disappeared, replaced with other stars which took shape as planets of the solar system. Another wall-shaking rumble and the planets blurred passed.

They were accelerating, faster than anyone had ever gone.

"Why look so pale?" Al chuckled. "Relax. We're safe. Those booms we're hearing are controlled atomic explosions."

"Are you insane?"

"You might think so. That big metal block on the first level, that's the chamber. The energy of coupled explosions is used as propellant, increasing our velocity a hundredfold. A brilliant young man named Dyson calls it the Stapledon effect."

Bert shook his head in wonder, then his eyes opened wide. "You have split the atom?"

Al nodded, his expression somber.

Bert frowned. *Why look so unhappy, old man?* He remembered his earlier unasked question. "Why? To what end is all this happening? Why—" he swallowed, finally admitting the truth to himself, "why did the burgermeister and my fellow citizens have to die?"

"I was wondering when you would ask that. First some rules. Don't release your safety harness. We're in zero gravity. If you were to float around helplessly, you might accidently press a button or flick a switch best left, ah, unswitched. Also, if you feel ill there is a nozzle by your chair. It will suck away any unwanted detritus.

"Now, where were we? Ah, yes, why all the trouble? I can't answer that, but I can show you. Eventually. When we arrive."

"And where is that?"

"The future, of course."

"The future? You are joking?"

Al cocked his head as if to say, "Who knows?" but to Bert's utter frustration remained otherwise silent. Then a thought occurred to him. A wonderful, beautiful thought as if the heavens opened up and everything, his life, those of his family, all made sense. "It works, doesn't it?"

Al winked. "Only too well."

Bert dismissed the queerness of the answer. It worked. His life's work, young as he was, and he has experienced its fruition. He brushed a tear from his eye.

"Here we go," Al said.

"Already?"

"Why so surprised? It is *our* grand equation of quantum relativity that makes all this possible."

"Nevertheless, this is more than I ever expected."

Al grinned. "*Ja*. I have forgotten how I felt after I proved the theory."

"What is that?" Bert pointed. "Is that what Earth looks like from space?"

They approached a small planet of deep reds and gold like hemp. The gold became continents far different from any maps he had seen, and shouldn't the oceans be blue, not red?

"Earth is long gone," Al said. "That was once New Tokyo."

"Was?"

"Still is, I guess, on star maps. New Tokyo was once a beautiful planet. Forests covered the lands and creatures of all kinds filled her oceans. She is dead now, killed by a race of beings who only believe in taking, destroying, then moving on."

"Who could possibly do this?"

Al said nothing. The ship moved beyond the dead planet. Soon only stars filled the windows again.

"You didn't answer my question," Bert said.

"I can't, as much as I want. The great minds of my time, or so they claim, argue that all answers must come from you. You must discover, and ultimately decide for yourself."

"Decide what?"

"We approach Deutchveld." Al remained evasive. Deutchveld was much like New Tokyo. Though the colors changed, the sense of desolation remained the same.

Celt, Zulu, New Quebec, planet after planet, solar system after solar system, Goddard's rocket ship sliced through space and time. Mere hours had passed. He felt thirsty, his stomach growled for his missed dinner, and yet he had visited hundreds of worlds.

And all dead. Bert felt a twinge of shame. So much devastation, so many lives lost, and he thought of personal comfort. "Us," Bert said.

"What?"

"It was us. Mankind. And my equation helped. I . . . I . . ."

Al tilted his head. "Overwhelming, isn't it?" He paused for a moment as if weighing something in his mind. "I had encouraged the Americans, at first. Hitler was a madman, but not entirely. He had spies, everywhere, even in the White House. Sometimes the Nazis knew what was happening even before the Americans did. The U.S. worked closely with their allies, of course, except the Russians. No one trusted the Bolsheviks, but they had their spies too, and soon the power as well."

"Splitting the atom?"

"*Ja*. The world had barely recovered from its first great war, a terrible conflict beyond all measure, and yet not enough to deter mankind from repeating their mistakes. That should have tipped me off but . . ." He shrugged. "Hitler frightened me. A madman wanting to kill all our people."

"The Swiss?" Bert had become a citizen in 1901.

"The Jews."

Bert's dark eyebrows lifted. "Impossible." Yet somehow he knew it was very possible. He felt the hatred toward him, more than once overheard, "Look, there goes the genius Jew," in the school hallways of the Federal Polytechnic. Even Burgermeister Krone resorted to insult when faced with something unexplainable and frightening.

Yes. Before everything else he had seen so far, he believed in the ultimate horror man could do to his own kind. "This second war, was it fought in space?"

"Not at first. Not until fire nearly engulfed the entire world. Only then did the fighting move to the heavens. It still rages in my time."

"Your time? But all those planets—"

"—are a progression of history. My past. Your future. Though it is now your past too, I suppose. Time is a linear measurement. Seconds, minutes, hours, always moving forward. In space however, time is multidimensional, distances so great we measure it in light-years. Generations live and die in the space of one traveled light-year. However, many thought the universe curved. Time bends on itself—"

"Thus, if you travel far enough," Bert finished, "you can travel back in time."

"More like looping back to a point in the original timeline. Now we travel forward, though at unnatural speed. Soon we will come to my present." Al's salt-and-pepper moustache drooped. "Then we will see what we will see."

Silence hung in the air as Bert watched another dead planet pass. "Insanity. Anyone with sense must see that. Why fight this way? All this destruction when we could have done so much more."

"It was war. The equation was used to perfect intergalactic space travel when we, as a race, were too young, too immature. We didn't deserve to be outside the confines of our planet." Al sighed as if gathering his thoughts. "The first war was a terrible thing. Almost every nation in the world was involved. France was raped, her land devastated, Germany's national spirit utterly destroyed. The Russians revolted, her aristocracy butchered. The decline of the British Empire had begun. The cowboy Americans vowed never to involve her people in another foreign conflict.

"Then it began again. I foresaw Hitler's madness and wrote a letter to Roosevelt, the American president, to proceed with atomic research. We made the bombs, then dropped them. Not even I expected that kind of devastation. Half a city wiped out with one explosion. Radiation sickness followed. Horrible. Something had to be done, but no one was willing to back down.

"So again they came to me, to *us*, and our *quantum relativity*, and like fools, we tricked ourselves into thinking this was the pathway to peace.

"Once in space we spread like locusts. Colonization

was a feeble excuse to raze new worlds, define new battlefields on which to spill blood. The imperialism of Britain and Japan, American capitalism, political doctrine ruled exploration, but the burnt-earth policy of Stalinist Russia did the most damage. On we fought, destroying planets barely populated; still young with new hope lest they develop into possible threats."

Bert listened quietly. Watched tears flow freely from dark, heartbroken eyes, shared in the old man's grief. Yet, something was missing.

"Why this journey? What is it you want of me?"

"What indeed. My colleagues and I have projected the future of mankind. The universe is not endless and neither is humanity. We have yet to meet another intelligent species." Al paused as if to let that bit of information sink in.

Nothing? Bert's mouth hung open. After spreading throughout space? The probability is high that man is the only intelligent being in the universe. "If the war continues—"

"We will kill ourselves into extinction," Al finished. "My colleagues have made another calculation. This is where you come in."

Bert did not like the way his counterpart looked at him. "You mean to kill me?"

Al's face paled. "What? Go to all this trouble just to do that? No! In fact, we need you alive to change our future."

Bert's eyebrows raised a fraction as his mind tried to twist around the implications. Yet his equation provided for this very situation. So why did the request catch him so unawares? Why did he not think of it earlier?

Because I did not want to think about it.

The moral implications had been vast, but he was barely twenty-five. What did he care about mankind's destiny when all he knew or cared about was his own? He had a family to feed. His theory would bring fame and perhaps a professorship with a prestigious university. It was all he had ever wanted.

Wasn't it?

He looked at the stars outside of the window. How many have died? Thousands? Millions? God in heaven, billions? His stomach contracted. Had he eaten dinner, it would have surely spilled out. Slumping back, he ran a hand through his thick black hair, suddenly moist and clinging to his forehead.

"Is something wrong?" Al asked. "Are you ill?"

Bert turned his head, hiding his shame. "My fault."

"No! True, we provided a means, but God has given mankind free will. We didn't force anyone to continue killing each other till the end of time."

"Nevertheless, we gave them the weapon."

"It wasn't Nobel's intention to use dynamite for killing, nor was it our intention when we first introduced the relativity theory. The only crime we and Nobel are guilty of is presenting our ideas to a world too immature to use them properly. Men are like children quarreling in a playground, cavemen looking for bigger rocks to throw. Mankind was not ready.

"From what I have seen we may never be. Ah, we are nearly there. Time to slow down." Al flicked a series of switches.

Bert felt the onion ship flip around then the familiar explosions of the Stapledon effect. His body tugged violently against his restraints and he winced in pain. And through it all he sensed the ship's velocity decreasing. After a few minutes his body stabilized and he inhaled deeply.

"This is my time," Al said. He too looked very pink

in the face. "1955. This is how far the war has come. Behold the full extent of this lunacy."

The onion ship circled a nearby planet, rotating so that the view of the surface was constant. Bert first saw islands of white clouds, some calm and flat as a sea, others spiraling upward like stalagmites. Beyond was a backdrop of azure seas, emerald forests and lands varying in shades of brown, gray and green.

A klaxon blared, causing Bert to strain against his safety harness. A flash of orange streaked past the window and headed for the planet's surface. Another soon followed, then another.

"Torpedoes," Al said, sounding disgusted. A pause followed, then the entire surface of the planet shimmered. Concentric walls of wind blew huge gaps in the forest. Next came fire, a wheel of flame so thick it was like the sun had struck the world and oozed out its fiery guts. Roiling masses of dust and burning gases blotted out vast amounts of land, churning, joining, congealing into a near-perfect circle.

Bert's cheeks were damp with grief as the life of the planet snuffed out.

"We can change this," Al whispered.

"How?" Bert nearly shouted, sorrow turning to anger. This had to end. He wanted to make it stop.

As if unsure of his relief, Al exhaled loudly and flicked a toggle switch. The ship shuddered from another internal detonation. "We go home now."

"Your home?"

"No. Yours. What must be done can only be done in your time. Before all this takes place and you release our theory onto an unsuspecting world."

"Is that it?" Bert rubbed a trembling hand across

his moustache. "If I keep quantum relativity to myself, keep it secret—"

"It won't matter. We have projected all aspects of such an event and concluded that the theory will come out. No, we must delay that time. *You* must devise another theory."

"You mean we?"

"No. I cannot assist. Theoretical physics is a young man's game. At any rate, my knowledge is a product of your future. My thoughts are the result of consultations with men and women who have had experiences unimaginable to you. Our ideas may well be tainted by our lives. To reveal them to you may have cataclysmic repercussions. We can't take that chance."

Bert looked hard at the old man. He knew what Al wanted. Change the future. Erase all that he had just seen. But that was asking the impossible. More than just devising a new theorem, he would have to play God. Wipe out generations of lives. The name Einstein would be synonymous with the atomic torpedoes that had struck that planet. "I can't do it."

Al slapped the arm of his cushioned chair. "You must. You must save us."

"Save you? You are asking me to commit murder, and *suicide*. How can I atone for a sin with another? What if by changing the future I alter our own timeline? What if we die the very next day?"

"Are you so selfish? Do you deny what you have seen? Mere moments ago you jumped at the chance to change it all, and now you balk."

Ashamed, Bert looked away. Yes, he balked, and not because altering history might cost him his life. If he died, if he couldn't tell anyone of this new idea, then what meaning did his life have?

Selfish fool.

He turned back to Al. "Forgive me."

The old man grinned. "A man who can't forgive himself is doomed to half a life." He winked, then as if sensing Bert's need to think, concentrated on the flashing computer panels of Goddard's rocket ship.

Bert lay back, eyes closed. How could he undo years of work in less time than it takes to cook a turkey? He looked at the problem from all angles but the answer eluded him. Physics, once his friend and ally, had become his main obstacle. Past teachers had once told him there was a reason they were the laws of physics, and not rules. Variable light speed, gravity, mass, all were as immutable as life itself. Or were they?

Am I not trying to do that very thing? Defy the laws of nature? Change physics itself?

How? What was the key? He thought of Al. Forcing the answer from him would be easy. After all, Al was old. The thought brought a smile to his face. The ultimate battle with one's self. What would that Austrian, Freud, make of that?

Al had said anything he revealed may lead to disaster. So why this journey? Why bring him fifty years into the future? To show him the death of a planet, prove the nobility of the enterprise? No, something more. Above all, he thought himself a teacher. Was he teaching himself? What had he learned?

Mankind kills, bombs destroy, nothing new. Most likely, in spite of what he did, they would continue to do so. Al was right. Delay was the answer, contain the damage to at least their own solar system, or even Earth itself.

Still, something was missing. Something fundamental to the entire process. If only he had more time to think . . .

Yes. Of course. Time was linear. Always moving

forward. By bringing him to the future, Al had made both his and Bert's present the same. He could not change the future. It was impossible. So what then? Had everything been a waste?

No. Otherwise, Al would not have made the attempt. Obviously his colleagues had thought of something in the future. Something that he could do to change everything.

Then he knew the answer, or at least a germ of the answer.

If the facts don't fit the theory, then change the facts.

If light was not variable, but remained constant. Yes. Mass would increase as one attains the speed of light. Yes, yes! No number of atomic explosions could provide enough energy to move something that heavy. The speed of light would be unattainable. A fanciful idea for the laws in this universe—

My God. "Isaac forgive me," he said, but when Al smiled he knew he was on the right track.

Twelve hours later, after a return to Earth in a ball of flame followed by a curious fabric canopy Al called a parachute, they were back in the Swiss Patent Office. Al sat in the wooden chair, quietly watching him work. "As proof of your success," he said, but did not elaborate.

Bert worked at a feverish pace, somehow knowing his time was running out. There was no way to change the future, nor delay the revelation of the theory. He knew that now. His theory will come out at precisely the moment it was meant to, which was too soon. But did it have to be the same? Could he create a new timeline, split it like the atom? He reviewed and amended his notes, scribbled vast algorithms on the chalkboard then reduced them until he had one short, concise equation. Tears dampened his cheeks. "I've done it. Now we can never leave."

The office clock chimed eleven as he circled the equation: $E=MC^2$.

A firm knock at the door caused him to look up. He glanced at the chair, puzzled at its emptiness for a moment, felt a sense of something missing, then went to the door.

"Einsten," Burgermeister Krone said. "So it is you. I saw the lights and wondered. You are working late. Is everything all right?"

"*Annus mirabilis*, Herr Burgermeister. This will be my miracle year." Albert Einstein clapped the surprised burgermeister on the back. An hour later he locked the door to the Swiss Patent Office then slipped the key into his pocket. He might even keep the key as a token of this great night. Strolling through the quiet streets of Bern, he thought of possible university postings.

THE KEEPER ALONE

Written by
Michael Livingston

Illustrated by
Olga Madiar

About the Author

It's rare that any medieval English scholar would venture into the uncharted realms of speculative fiction. Yet that's exactly what Michael Livingston has done with his winning entry and first submission to the Contest. A native of Colorado and a displaced westerner living in upstate New York, Michael only recently began to submit his fiction musings for publication, though he's "fooled around" with the genre for many years. The warm reception so far has inspired him to finish two novels in progress as he completes his PhD at the University of Rochester.

Given Michael's medieval focus, it's not surprising that he read J.R.R. Tolkien in his youth. Michael has pursued his own adventures in history at Baylor University, then earned his MA in medieval studies at Western Michigan University. Naturally, Michael has taught courses on Tolkien and will soon publish an article on the author's WWI experiences. When he's not hunting down the origins of some ancient tome, Michael devotes much of his spare time to his fiction writing and credits family, friends and other writers for encouraging him.

About the Illustrator

Like many young Russian girls, Olga Madiar always wanted to be a classically trained ballerina. Growing up in Kiev, she would practice her choreography for hours on end. To relieve the stress, Olga would draw caricatures of teachers, family, other ballerinas. She didn't think much of the pictures at the time but, when it was apparent that the ballet stage would not call her, drawing did. She says that pictures by great artists always "grasped" her, particularly the watercolor works of Russian children's illustrator Gennady Spirin.

Having a "special love" for books and book illustration, Olga entered a book illustration program in 1996 where she studied painting, illustration and book design. She soon discovered the Illustrators of the Future Contest after reading an article about fellow Ukrainian and previous Illustrators' Contest Gold Award winner, Sergey Poyarkov. With Olga's appearance "on the stage" of these pages, she plans on furthering her book illustration career along with her current work as the principal graphic designer for a local theatre for operettas.

David never could get used to dying. The swift prick of the needled sequencer administering the lethal infusion was no different than any of the thousands of injections that he had received in his lives, and the first sensation of approaching sleep was no different than the feeling of falling asleep that he had experienced on so many other occasions in this life. None of that bothered him. It was the pulling away that he never could get used to.

Fifty Earth years, he thought. *Fifty years in this body, in this life.* He had gone to sleep 18,249 times before this moment, his eyes growing heavy whenever the ship's quiet chimes informed him that night had fallen in New Mexico, but it was different this time. *Eighteen thousand, two hundred and forty-nine times. One night shy of fifty years. Always one night shy of my seventieth birthday. My deathday.*

David tried to relax, balling and releasing his fists to hurry the numbing liquid through his veins. His joints ached, and he could feel the parchment texture of his wrinkled flesh as his fingers pressed into his palms. *Too old*, he thought. *Too old to perform my duties, too old to be of use to the ship.*

So it was time again.

He realized then that his hands were no longer moving, and his terrorized body trembled involuntarily for a few seconds before he regained control of himself. *Just like going to sleep*, he tried to tell himself.

Only it's not sleep, his mind replied. *It's dying.*

David whispered the Lord's Prayer, and was not surprised that the words came out mumbled and incoherent. He tried to blink his eyes in the darkness, but he could not be sure that they moved. His breathing was growing more shallow, and his feet were beginning to move further and further away. *Soon now.*

The world diminished around him, and at once it seemed that he was falling backward through the soft cushions of the darkened medical room, the inner sanctum of his icy, void-hurtling tomb. He felt himself drifting away and down and out and apart.

And everything—the cushions, his body, his mind—faded and receded and fell silent and still.

•••

He awoke with a gasp, his arms instinctively flailing out into the darkness in an effort to grab hold of something. His movements triggered the automatic lighting system and warm light built up around him until he could bring the world into focus. The synapses in his mind slowly began to make connections and to regain control of his body, beating back the residual memories of death and welcoming the fresh inputs of life.

He stopped thrashing and lay still, panting air into his new lungs while his new eyes grew accustomed to the light. The ceiling he stared at was a muted gray, meant to be psychologically soothing, but he found it difficult to relax while various machines swung back and forth like a frenetic ballet along his bedside, taking measurements and randomly poking and prodding his body.

After a few minutes, the machines settled back into their places at the sides of the room and he pulled himself into a sitting position. He blinked and rubbed at his eyes. He felt like he had slept for days, but he knew that he had never slept before. Not in this body.

"Welcome back, David," a voice said.

David took a deep breath, stretched, and looked down at himself. "It's good to be back, Sol. TSD?"

He never could get used to dying, and so he never could use the phrase "Time Since Death" without throwing up. The ship's computer had been quite accommodating in changing protocols to fit David's temperament; it had even grown accustomed to David's insistence on calling it Solomon, though the computer did not understand why the human found the name so fitting.

"Three months, two days, Standard Earth Time," Solomon said.

David rubbed at his smooth thighs, admiring the firmness of his muscle tone but unmoved. "Status?"

"Hull check green, reactor at eighty-two percent and stable, track steady for E2, current velocity one-hundredth c. All ship functions are within operating parameters, David."

"And what about me?"

"Bioscans are clear and the transfer was a success. You are currently within parameters." Solomon did not mention that the first clone had rejected the sensitive transplants and custom cognitive relays built to transfer David's mind between carriers. Nor did the AI mention the fate of that rejected host, David's last body, or the unused third clone. He had long since recorded David's disinterest in such matters. And though he did not understand David's desire to be shielded from the information, Solomon was programmed to adapt to the needs of his ward.

Illustrated by Olga Madiar

David stretched again, and scooted off the table. His legs were shaky, but they held. A few hours and he would be twenty years old again: fit, firm, and functional. He looked at himself in the mirror. "I look good. This is a nice body."

"Only the best," the computer said without emotion.

David stretched a third time, smiled, and moved over to the recycle pit where he voided his bowels and emptied his bladder for the first time in this life. The tiny fibers of nutrient mass stung, and passing the nanotech wad burned, but all in all it felt good to be alive again.

•••

After showering, David ensured that he was, indeed, fully functional. Satisfied that everything was in proper working order, he dressed in his typical loose-fitting informal fatigues and walked across the accessway to the command deck. The doors slid open gracefully, though the fire door seemed a little slow to slip aside. David paused to examine it briefly and recalled how he had meant to fix it in another life. The door's vacuum track looked like the skin particles that had been dropped there over two hundred years had grown pasty and gummed up into a thin but sticky mess. It was an afternoon's work, though he might manage to make a day of it. *Next week*, he told himself.

The command deck was, as always, spotless. A portion of his daily routine—even on the last day of his last life over three months ago—was a complete cleaning of the entire living quarters along with a rotating docket of cleaning throughout the rest of the ship, a sequence of maintenance work that managed to block out at least a few hours of each monotonous day. Though he felt like an overnight janitor in an empty office building, it was the simple daily tasks that had kept him busy and sane so far.

Monitors began to flick on as he entered the room—since the ship's AI had no need of the visual interfaces, they had been turned off while David was reborn. Now they came on one by one, producing numbers, graphs, spectral readouts, and countless minutiae of information for the ship's human counterpart.

David ignored the readouts and stepped over to the ergonomic chair set on a swivel in the middle of the room. The weight and movement of his many bodies had alternatively scuffed and burnished the metal so that it seemed to carry his very image, a shadow of himself burned into the metal. He turned and sat down, relaxing. The filtering pumps hummed like steady white noise at the periphery of his hearing, pushing the stale, recycled air into gentle waves whose steady currents he had long since memorized by the traces of skin particles that they deposited.

A minute or two passed before he moved his fingers across the pad on the chair's right arm, activating the holographic status relay. The lights on the deck dimmed to a retina-friendly red and the chair rose, unclipping smoothly onto the gyro-stabilizers. The image took a few seconds to appear—the holocasters were always slow to warm up after a few months without use—but David was soon enveloped in a blanket of darkness pricked with millions of tiny points of light. The sphere of stars moved gently, almost imperceptibly, sliding to left and right like a spreading wake. It had been beautiful, even intoxicating, at one time; now it was just cold and empty and lonely.

David shifted his weight and the chair spun on the

gyros, rotating on its vertical axis until he was looking into the darkness and distant lights that the ship had already left behind. The ship's computer-enhanced plasma trail extended like a bolt into the heart of that distant darkness, straight and unflinching.

"Show me Sol system."

In response, a tiny little dot of pinpoint yellow at the far end of the ship's exhaust trail flashed red for a few seconds. *Smaller every time.*

"The system, Sol," David said, "back me through the system."

The stars about him streaked as he rocketed back along the dissipating plasma trail, zooming in on that insignificant single speck of light. Within seconds, he had followed the trail past the wispy crystal puffs of the Oort cloud, crossed the vast wastes of the outer rim mineral districts, skirted past the stretching orbits of the outer planets, encircled the great gas giants and their orbiting gas miners, sped through the rockbelt, danced above the Martian landgraft plants, and arrived, in a sudden halt, at Starport 1, Albuquerque-geosynchronous. Below him floated the deep blues, greens and browns of the earth that haunted his dreams, an Earth with swimming clouds and tiny caps of white at its poles. David shifted his weight in the chair, rotating to look down and behind him, across the New Mexican desert, the Rocky Mountains, and the Great Plains, to watch as the nightline arose from the east and began creeping steadily across the continent. Sighing, he shifted his weight again and looked up at the blazing ball of fire whose warmth was only the most distant of memories now.

Though he knew the answer, he asked anyway: "How long have we been out now?"

"Four hundred and fifty years SET, with a current

nine day and thirty-three minute Lorentz Contraction," Solomon said.

Lights were sparkling over the plains like a carpet of hived fireflies. "Do you think it still looks like this?"

"In all probability it does not. The predicted continuance of temperature rise would have further altered the coastlines that you remember, and tectonic movements around the Pacific Rim would no doubt have contributed changes in this sector." Solomon paused for a moment. "Four hundred and fifty years is a long time, David."

David silently did the math. *Nine deaths. Working on ten.*

When David said nothing, the ship's AI made a statistical analysis based on its working model of human behavior, trying to decide what David wanted. "I have several alternative possibilities for the current appearance of Earth based on our information and chaos calculations. Do you wish for me to alter the holo to reflect one of these projections?"

"No, I like to remember it the way it was," David said. His voice was quiet, but the ship's computer was able to enhance its sound reception from the dozens of audio feeds in the room.

"Of course," Solomon said, filing this particular human response away for later study.

"I do love the lights. Cities look so beautiful from above. I suppose there are a lot less of them now."

"That is probable," Solomon said. "The historical instability of the human species would surely predicate the failure of several governmental systems and the coinciding revolutions that would alter the manmade structures of the planet; not to mention the movement of the Pox."

David winced at the word. *Pox*. The reason he had

lived—and died—nine lives aboard this hastily built committee project. Two billion—and counting—when he left. Five and a half million in that first year alone. No cure in sight, no notion of what it was or even where it had come from. Was it Amazonia? Congo? Mars? Saturn Crystalia?

"It's been four hundred years," he whispered. "I wonder if anyone's left."

Solomon said nothing this time, and David shut down the holocaster array.

•••

David cleaned the command deck and confirmed Solomon's internal diagnostics before he prepared the uploading of the mission package, a low-frequency burst of data confirming his rebirth and the past lifetime's collected data. He tried not to think about whether anyone would ever receive it. After he sent the package, David retreated down to B level and checked on the primary stasis chamber.

Nearly half of a mile long and stretching the full length of the ship's plastallic underbelly, the stasis chamber held one thousand egglike containers in two parallel rows: one thousand eggs holding one thousand humans in cryostasis. They were the precious freight of the ship, and David's primary responsibility. There was a single bright status light in front of each egg, and all one thousand were glowing a gentle green: twin dotted lines of green that receded into the far distance.

One thousand eggs. One thousand men, women and children. Once a week during each of his lives, he had cleaned every single one of those eggs, careful to wipe and buff the smooth sheets of plexiglass that encased them like shrouds. At one point, many, many years ago, he had even known them all by name, age, and occupation. In the beginning he had even talked to them, addressing them face to face as if they could see. But it had been a long time since he had taken the time to treat them as anything more than cargo. He no longer knew them by name, no longer even thought of them as human. They were freight. Nothing more.

David gazed down the line of eggs with a look akin to disdain. *Cryostasis.* The very word smelled of death and decay, of folly. There were no guarantees that much of the group would survive unfreezing, since the effect of having your veins locked up with antifreeze for a thousand years was unknown. The cryotechs had managed to bring subjects back before, but only after a decade or two—and even those successes had been haphazard and fraught with difficulty. Survival rates in those conditions were between seventy and eighty percent—and these people would be coming out of ten centuries, not decades.

"Fifty percent rate of loss, my ass," he said aloud.

"Repeat request," Solomon said.

"Nothing, Sol. I was just talking to myself."

"Do I need to begin reprogramming diversionary pursuits?" Though David was chosen for his tempered mind and ability to stay focused in solitary conditions, maintaining his sanity was one of the AI's key responsibilities. It was a duty that grew more and more difficult with each passing year as Solomon ran out of ideas despite the vast, encyclopedic storehouse of human resources available to him. "Perhaps I should prepare a new redhead program on the holo array?"

David shook his head. "Unnecessary, Sol. I'm fine right now." He typed a few quick commands into the status station and tried to spend a few minutes reviewing the graphs and numbers that flowed across the screen.

He knew it was useless. If there was a problem—and there had never been one—the ship's AI would have noted it. *EarthSeed 4* and its 1,001 inhabitants was simply humming along on its way to oblivion as it always had. What had seemed such an adventure as he rocketed out of Sol system was nothing more than a tedious bore.

He clicked the screen off and sighed, staring down the twin lines of green status beacons once again. He thought about moving up the egg-cleaning docket just to have something to do, but despite his new youth he did not seem to have the energy for it. Even the redhead program—the perfection of his own ideas of feminine beauty tailormade in the recesses of the AI's vast databanks after existing sources of pornography had been utterly exhausted—failed to excite him. Thinking of the holo projection made him momentarily sad and he slouched forward onto the console, resting his head in his hands.

"Perhaps we should begin to learn a new language this life," Solomon said.

"I know too many already." German, French, Russian, Italian, Latin, Greek . . . language had been a wonderful way to pass the time in his early lives. He wiped at his eyes, trying to appear content as he looked down the two green lines once again. He knew that the computer's visual inputs were constantly assessing his facial expressions. "Though I suppose it has been a while since I learned one. What do you have?"

"I have linguistic apparati for all known languages of the human species up to the date of our departure. Though I should note that the past few centuries have undoubtedly altered the linguistic landscape since . . ."

"I know," David interrupted. "Four and a half centuries is a long time for a language."

"Of course, David."

David sighed against the silence in the chamber. He heard the distant hum of recycling scrubbers kicking into gear and suddenly felt the need to say something. "How about Sanskrit? That's always sounded hard. Then I could read the Bhagavad-Gita in the original. How about it, Sol? Can you teach me Sanskrit?"

There was a moment pause before Solomon said something incomprehensible that sounded vaguely Indian. "I'll take that as a 'yes'," David said. And he smiled.

•••

"Queen takes rook," David said.

On the holo laid out in the middle of the command deck, the white queen slid gracefully across the squares and took the place of the black rook as it faded away.

"An intriguing move, David," said Solomon. "It is interesting to note that we are now in an identical position as the twenty-third move of the Blau-Leepin match held in Zurich in 1949. That match was once utilized as one of the primary models of a Caro-Kann Defense."

David grunted, trying to concentrate about his next move. "So who won?"

"Leepin. Bishop to knight two."

The black bishop moved into an open square and David's brow furrowed. His defense had been adequate, but Solomon had advanced a passed pawn far into his ranks. Still, he felt like he might be able to pin the AI into tactical retreat. "Bishop to rook four," he said. "Was that move in the other game?"

"Yes, David."

David allowed himself a small smile. "So which was Leepin? White or black?"

"Black," Solomon replied. "Queen to knight five. That's the twenty-fourth move. Blau retired on the thirty-third."

David groaned and sank into his chair. There was no arrogance in Solomon's tone, no satisfaction, but the pain of it still stung him. "Goddamnit, what's the point?"

"I feel that it is necessary to prepare myself space for the movement of my king in approximately five moves to avoid a backrank check . . ."

David gripped his head in his hands, feeling waves of frustration seething in his veins. "Damn!"

"Is something the matter, David?"

The absurdity of it seemed almost funny, even after more than four centuries, and David would have laughed if it wasn't for the upswell of anger building in his chest. "Yes, damnit! Something sure as hell is the matter."

There was a pause before the AI spoke again. "Your bioscan appears entirely normal, David."

"I'm not sick, you piece of crap. Just shut the hell up and leave me alone for a while."

"I am just trying to help, David. Would you like me to shut down interface for a period of time?" There was no trace of emotion in the AI's voice. Solomon might just as well have been talking about the weather.

David began to pound his armrests with his fists. The metal made a dull echo in the hollow of the room. "Yes! Leave me alone!"

"Affirmative," Solomon said.

David gripped the arms of the chair in his fists as if he intended to rend the metal with his bare hands.

He screamed for many minutes until his throat began to grow raw and his voice became hoarse. Then he sat and cried in the stillness of the room, listening to the filtration pumps turning on and off. On and off.

•••

There were only six rooms on A-deck, the tiny node on the front of the great ship that was David's home and perpetual tomb. Since as much room as possible had to be taken up by storage of other cargo for the colonists, the living quarters for the single awake passenger was little more than an afterthought. The six rooms were connected by a single accessway that ran from port to starboard. To the bow of the ship was the command deck, flanked by the medilab and the kitchen; to the aft of the ship was his sleeping quarters, flanked by the exercise room and a small reading lounge. At either end of the short hallway were access stairs steep enough to be ladders. David had seen accesses of similar design on board some of the bigger submarines that he had toured during his time at the academy; submariners in a hurry would grip each hand rail loosely and slide down to the next level. Part of his intensive training back on Earth had been a stint in the Subcorps along with thorough study of how submariners managed to stave off both simple claustrophobia and utter madness. Men who had spent months beneath the sea were the closest things to models that he would have. It was ironic, in its way: he often wondered if future generations would look back on his cramped quarters in the same way that he had looked at the old World War II subs that he had studied, astonished that anyone could stay sane under such conditions. He often wondered if anyone could.

Two days after his meltdown on the command

deck, David was in the exercise room, thinking about submarines and insanity as he pedaled furiously on the stillcycle. David hated to exercise, but it was a necessary part of his daily routine. And, after centuries of lives aboard the *EarthSeed 4*, it had become as habitual as breathing. Still, his sixty daily minutes on the stillcycle generally made him feel like a rat on a wheel, pedaling for years without ever leaving his cage.

His anger had not gone away, of course; it had only become dormant. The fact that he was growing less able to contain his frustrations weighed heavily on his mind. And the fact that he had burst out in such viciousness made it worse. Solomon was his only companion. After thirty minutes of pedaling, he slowed down enough to catch his breath and speak. "You there, Sol?"

"Yes, David. You're doing very good today."

"Thanks," David said. "I want to tell you something, okay?"

"Of course, David."

David wiped the sweat off of his brow, took a deep breath. "I wanted to tell you that I'm sorry about the other day."

The AI said nothing for a couple of seconds. The delay seemed like an eternity. "I do not understand."

David almost smiled at the fact that the computer, for all of its vast wealth of knowledge and data, could not comprehend the human need to make amends. "I'm sorry that I yelled at you the other day, while we were playing chess. I'm apologizing to you."

"You do not need to apologize, David. It is impossible for me to be offended or saddened by your actions."

"That's not the point," David panted. "I have a job to do, but sometimes I forget that you have a job, too."

"I have many mission priorities."

"I know, Sol. You're just trying to keep me sane and them safe."

"Yes, David."

A few minutes passed before David got up the nerve to ask something that had been bothering him. "Can I just ask you a question, Sol?"

"Of course, David."

"How much thinking were you doing in the game?"

Solomon did not answer for a moment. "I do not think in your sense of the word, David. I do not understand the question."

"I mean, how much of your resources did you allot for the chess game?"

"I allotted approximately point-two-six percent of my foreground memory stalls to the development of current game strategies and an additional point-zero-four percent to the study of data from past games that you have played with me. Point-zero-zero-three percent of background memory stalls were utilized for surveying historical chess matches for similar methods of play. I further limited myself to only point-zero-eight nanoseconds of computational time for each move as this seems to best approximate the average thinking time for an above-average human player."

David almost stopped pedaling. "Less than a nanosecond of thinking for each move?"

"That is correct, David."

David smiled in spite of himself, bowing his head and pedaling faster and harder as if by sheer force of will he could get away from the ship. *A rat on a wheel.*

• • •

David was sitting in the reading lounge, in the middle of his latest lesson on Sanskrit when the computer disabled its Hindi accent and said: "I have detected a problem in egg 631."

David froze in confusion. There had never been a problem. Never. He had checked all the systems only thirty-seven hours earlier and all systems were, as always, in perfect operating order. Nothing could have gone wrong.

Even as his mind mired in questions, a klaxon alarm fired up and began to wail. David's training took over and he jumped up from the library couch, sprinting the ten meters to the port access stair and sliding down the railings to B level like an adept submariner. A red light was flashing above the doorway to the primary stasis chamber, and the door flew open ahead of him.

The noise of the alarm was almost deafening in the long and narrow chamber, and the display on the status station was flashing urgent warnings of impending doom. Far away down the line of green status beacons, on the left side of the room, the light in front of a single egg was flashing red. Not green, not yellow, not orange. Red.

He had to shout over the blaring horns. "Alarm off, Sol! And lock down the interchamber relays!"

The alarm fell silent a half-second later and David heard a distant clank echo from the other end of the chamber as the relays shut down, effectively isolating the problem egg. "Done," the computer said.

David began running trained fingers along the keyboard, calling up information. The schematic of an egg in cross-section appeared on the screen, with a paperdoll image of a human body in fetal position. "Egg 631," Solomon said. "I'm losing it."

David groaned and the schematic spun as bioscans

began to fill in details. They had left Earth with one thousand in stasis, and he was determined not to lose one now. The egg's Personal Information Data blurred by, and the names came back to him like a memory long forgotten:

> *Egg 631*
> *Name: Bethany Thisbe Doering*
> *Sex: Female*
> *Age (SET): 24*
> *Position: Biomedical Engineering*
> *Birth: Olympia, Mars*
> *Family: Uriah Levine Doering (630),*
> *Jesse Orion Doering (632)*

A wife and mother with husband and son aboard. And a doctor. "Ironic," David said under his breath.

"There appears to have been a malfunction in oxygen flow, cause unknown. Result is a ruptured arterial in right lobe," Solomon said. "Acute apoplexy possible, complete memory termination probability at sixty percent and rising."

"She's having a stroke," David said.

"That is correct."

"Goddamnit!"

"Yes, David."

"Nanotech?" David knew the answer even as he asked the question.

"Negative. The devices cannot function in her bloodstream matrix. It is too . . ."

"Toxic and gummed up, I know, I know. Can you stabilize?"

There was a pause while another scan passed over the egg, updating the display. "Negative, David. The rupture appears to be growing with increasing tissue deterioration."

There was another pause while David stared in disbelief at the data pouring across the screen.

"Recommend egg termination," Solomon said.

It took David a few seconds before he could speak. "You mean kill her."

"Egg termination," the computer repeated.

"That's murder."

The visual scans were up now, and the paper doll and schematic was replaced by the live feed of a young woman curled up in a pool of gelatinous fluids. The cords, wires, and pump lines that helped to sustain her body looked almost obscene against her naked flesh. Though her brain was slowly choking itself to death, she looked like she was sleeping.

"She is in stasis and will feel nothing," Solomon said.

"How do you know?" David was indignant now. This woman was his responsibility. He had never lost one.

"Did your body feel anything before rebirth, David?"

David blinked, surprised that the computer would cut him so close to the quick. Solomon knew that David avoided the secondary stasis chamber with its hundreds of pre-fertilized human eggs and its three growth stasis eggs. Those stasis eggs were empty now, but in about thirty years he would activate the system to begin developing three genetic duplicates of himself in the chamber: his replacement and two backup copies, human beings raised in stasis so that he could go on living and working aboard the ship.

"That's different," he managed. "The clone knows

nothing else. This woman is a wife and a mother. She's human."

"Complete memory termination probability at eighty percent and rising," the computer said. "She will die, David. Recommend immediate egg termination to conserve resources."

"No!" David slammed his fists down onto the keyboard. "Another option, goddamnit!"

"There is no other option, David. The nanotechs cannot function within the stasis matrix. If she were awake we could stabilize, but . . ."

David looked up, blinking. "So wake her up, Sol."

"The mission objective outline has no protocols for such action, and her PID states . . ."

"To hell with it," David interrupted. His fingers were already running across the keyboard, overriding the egg's lockdown.

"I am noting this mission discrepancy for the next package."

"Whatever." *What are they going to do, fire me?* He finally disengaged the safety measures and another monitor flipped on with the reanimation readouts. "Just help me wake her up, Sol."

"Affirmative," Solomon said. "Egg layers coming off."

David looked back to the live feed and saw various pump lines disengaging from her body even as others began snaking their way through the fluids to clip into now-vacant bodyport valves. A bluish light passed over her curled body as Solomon ran another bioscan.

"Complete memory termination probability at ninety-two percent and rising. She will remember nothing even if she lives."

"Just wake her up and let me deal with the rest of it. I'm not losing her if I can help it."

"Yes, David. Regenerators coming online now."

David listened and heard the quiet rumble of machines powering up in the distance. The live feed image shook as a series of primary and redundant pumps moved into place.

"You should get down there," Solomon said. "This will be messy and I do not have arms."

David broke into a run, sprinting between the twin lines of eggs. He could see egg 631 down near the end, its status beacon a flashing red speck in a line of green. Steam was already beginning to billow up from the egg and he heard fans switching on and off around him as Solomon shifted the ventilation system to compensate.

When he finally arrived, the egg was already beginning to hatch, the seam along its sides splitting and releasing a flood of noxious fluids that spilled down off the platform and across David's feet before beginning to seep toward the corridor subdrain.

"Aw, hell."

"I am sorry, David. This should be done in the reanimation chamber."

"I know, I know."

The crack spread to a few inches, and the flood subsided as the egg drained out. David reached forward and caught the young woman as the egg popped open with a snap. She was limp and unconscious, and covered in a slimy mess that quickly soaked his fatigues, but she was breathing. He tried to hold her upright and still as the last lines detached and pulled away from her body.

"She's alive," Solomon said.

David held her against him, feeling the slow rise and fall of her breasts against his chest and the warmth of her breath against his neck and cheek. His fingers touched the wet red hair falling down her back. "I know," he said. "I know."

• • •

David had to carry her to the medical room, and Solomon had to reconfigure the medilab computers for a female patient, but she was stabilized before the night was done. David watched over her as the nanotechs swarmed through her veins, and he handwashed the residue from her unconscious body after the procedures were complete. When Solomon told him that it was safe to move her, David picked her up in his arms once more and carried her sixteen meters to his quarters where he placed her in his bed. Then he brought in a chair from the library and sat down to wait for her to awaken.

When her eyes finally fluttered open, the pupils were dilated with shock and confusion. She recoiled from David, kicking back against the bed and gripping the sheets to her chest as if they were some protective ward. Her head struck the wall and she stared at him with wild, wide eyes, shivering.

"Where am I? Who are you?"

There was an edge of panic in her voice, a palpable tremor that David could feel vibrating in his own chest. He wanted to reach out to her, to touch her, to hold her and comfort her. He forced himself to lean back in his chair instead. "My name is David," he said. "You're on board *EarthSeed 4*, currently en route to Epsilon Eridani."

Her eyes grew softer, but the stare was still blank. "A starship?"

David smiled, nodded. "Yes. A starship. What do you remember?"

Her mouth opened, froze, and her eyes grew wet. "I don't know. I don't remember . . ." Her voice trailed off and David again fought the urge to reach out to her.

"Your name is Beth," he said.

"Beth," she repeated. She formed the word slowly, like a foreign term. "Beth."

A tear began to make its way down her cheek and David looked at the floor between his feet. It had been so long that he could not remember how to react. "Bethany Thisbe Doering," he said. The words sounded very hollow in the empty ship.

When he looked up once more, she had wiped her face and was looking around at the ceiling and walls of the little room. Her gaze eventually fell on David again, and she bit her lower lip for a few seconds. "What happened to me?"

David started to answer but found that it was hard to speak. He tried to calm the twitching muscles in his throat and had to look away from her for a moment to wipe at the corner of his eye. "There's been an accident," he muttered.

"An accident?" Her lip was trembling worse now, and tears began to form in her eyes.

"Yes," he croaked. He took a deep breath, fighting emotions that he had forgotten. "What do you remember?"

She stared at him, searching, and then her tears began to flow, streaming down her cheeks. She turned away from him, burying her face in his pillows as she began to cry in earnest.

David stood instinctively, began to reach out to her, then stopped. He stood for long moments, frozen, his hands reaching out toward her shaking back, his fingers stretching toward her flesh.

He pulled back from her, let his hands fall to his sides. "You should rest," he said. It seemed like too little to say. "Try to sleep."

Beth continued to cry as David turned from the

bedside, waved off the lights. He paused for a moment at the door, thinking, before he left her and set the door's locks.

He wandered the ship for a while, cleaning the spotless bridge and the medilab. A few hours later he made his way to the primary stasis chamber and cleaned the corridor and Beth's now-empty egg, trying not to look at the little boy and the man who were still curled up on either side of it.

When he had finished cleaning, David lay down on the metal floor and cried himself to sleep for the first time in many lives.

•••

Solomon accessed the full human medical records and databases for information on oxygen-deprivation-induced memory loss, gathered and collated the data, and helped David in introducing Bethany Thisbe Doering to their tiny world. In those first few days she made only reluctant forays out of the room, accompanying David to the command deck and to the medilab for supplemental tests and procedures. Otherwise, she kept to herself. Solomon assured him that this was normal human behavior given her confusion. She remembered nothing of her life—her husband, her child, her reasons for being on board *EarthSeed 4*—but she did grow to remember much of her education in biomedical engineering. Solomon assured David that such selective recollection was also normal and well-documented in the case histories that the computer had on file.

David slept in the reading lounge. It was smaller than his bedroom, little more than a storage area with a comfortable couch and reading desk, but he found the change in surroundings to be quite stimulating in its way. He wondered why he had never considered sleeping in another room before. He even took to reading from some of the books on letterdisc before keying off the light in those first few nights. And he always instructed Solomon to wake him up early each day so that the lounge could be thoroughly cleaned prior to Beth's rising.

Four days after she had been revived, David told her about the EarthSeed missions, about how the Pox had been eradicating humanity. He convinced her to come with him to the command deck, and they watched the horror unfold on the holocasters. Solomon prepared documentaries about the ship, too, and she learned how the seeders were thrown together, how the crews were selected, and how they were launched into the unknown dark like some erratic, blind shotgun blast at the stars. After that, she retreated to the room for another two days.

When David saw her again, she had the thermal wrap draped over her shoulders like a shawl. Her hair was matted and greasy, and there were dark circles under her eyes. She looked much older than she had before. "I want to see where I came from," she said. "I want to see my . . . egg."

David thought about objecting—Solomon had been unsure about how she might react to the situation—but the look in her eyes was too pained to deny. "Okay," he said. "It's downstairs on B-deck."

David had sealed the doors to operate only on express command, so they did not slide open even after he had tripped the proximity line. He started to issue the order, then stopped and turned to Bethany. "Are you sure?"

She closed her eyes and her shoulders rose and fell beneath the thermal. "Yes."

He turned back to the door and took a deep breath. "Open it up, Sol."

The doors made a slight chirp to acknowledge the command and slid softly to left and right. A wash of air spread out into the corridor, and they stepped inside. David tried hard not to stare into the distance where one light was out along the line of green status beacons.

"My God," Bethany said. "So many."

David nodded but said nothing, allowing her to take in the sight of them all. After a while, she walked over to the status station. "Is this where they're controlled?"

"Yes."

"How many are there?"

"*EarthSeed 4* was launched with 1,001 souls on board, including me. You're the only one to, um . . ." his voice trailed off for a moment as he grew less sure of himself. "That leaves 999 still in stasis," he finally said.

"Stasis." Her voice was very quiet. "Are there any children?"

"Not many. One hundred and three."

"Why?"

"Most of them are with their families," he said. "I suppose some are here because children can adapt more easily to foreign environments and we don't know what we'll find when we get to E2, if we find anything at all."

They stood for a while in the relative silence of the long corridor. Ventilation fans clicked on and off in the distance. "What are the basic predictions for egg loss during reanimation?"

Her clinical tone surprised him for a moment and he had to remind himself that she was a biomedical engineer. Even with her memory loss, she probably knew more about the stasis process than he did. "Fifty percent," he said.

She coughed out a bitter half-laugh. "Like hell. They'll be lucky to see half that."

David silently assented, mulling over who she meant by *they*.

"One hundred and three children," she whispered. "It almost seems cruel."

David shrugged. "The alternatives were not much better. The Pox was doing far worse. At least this way there's a chance. However small it is."

She said nothing for a long time, lost in thought before speaking again. "So does the computer have all the biographical information here at the station?"

Solomon had warned him about the dangers of revealing the existence of her family, but David knew that he could not hide the truth forever. "Of course."

"Can I see me?"

A grim look crossed his face for a moment, but he reached across her to type in a few basic commands on the keyboard. Her PID appeared, no different than it had when he had woken her up.

Egg 631
Name: Bethany Thisbe Doering
Sex: Female
Age (SET): 24
Position: Biomedical Engineering
Birth: Olympia, Mars
Family: Uriah Levine Doering (630),
Jesse Orion Doering (632)

He saw her eyes scanning down the lines of

information; he saw her stop on the bottom line. "What do these numbers mean?"

"They're eggs."

Her eyes grew wide. "Eggs here?"

"Yes. Your husband, Uriah, and your son, Jesse."

"My . . . son?"

David nodded and turned away, beginning the long walk down to egg 631, trying not to let her see him crying, trying not to see her doing the same.

The egg, clean and empty, looked more like a broken movie prop than what had been a state-of-the-art piece of technology when they had left Sol system. David stood apart, allowing her room to examine it all.

She ran her fingers along the inside of the plexiglass and appeared to shudder. She pulled the thermal wrap closer around her body. "What was it that happened? Tell me again."

"A failure in the oxygen flow. A temporary glitch that caused one of your arteries to rupture."

"A glitch."

"Sorry. A malfunction of some kind. I've spent more than twenty-eight hours working over the system these past days and have found no mechanical reason for the failure. Solomon has performed internal diagnostics and confirms my findings. We can't tell you why it happened, but it did. If I hadn't revived you, you would have died in stasis."

"Then I should thank you for that," she said. Her gaze turned to the man and the little boy, sleeping in stasis to either side of her empty egg. "I have no memory of them."

Her voice cracked a little, and David stared at his feet, wondering if he should leave her alone with her family. He was starting to turn away when she spoke again.

"What are their names? Uriah and . . . ?"

"And Jesse. He's your little boy."

She slowly approached the boy—her little boy—and wiped at the plexiglass surface in order to see him more clearly. David continued to stare at the floor. "Jesse," she said. "Why do I not remember him?"

"Solomon says that the kind of memory loss that you experienced is normal."

"But I remember school. I remember my internship. I remember a semester that I spent in England. But not this." Her voice had begun to rise in anger, but it tapered off into sadness. "Not them."

"Your memory may come back."

She held her hand up to the plexiglass above the child's face for a moment, then pulled it away and tucked it under the thermal wrap. "I hope not."

"Why?" The question came out without thinking.

"How far are we from E2, David? How many years?"

The math was not hard. "You could go into stasis again." Even as he said it, he knew the idea was folly. No one had ever been brought back from multiple stints in stasis. It was tantamount to suicide.

She smiled, though he was unsure if she meant to convey sorrow or anger. "No, David. That is not an option. You've saved me for a life to be lived out aboard this ship." She looked once more to the little boy and the handsome young man sleeping peacefully in their eggs. "I hope I never remember them. I don't think I could bear it."

• • •

She knew, of course, that David was a clone. The

Earth League had banned all human cloning after the Raelian Wars, but she knew that there was no other explanation. As soon as David had told her how long they had been out-Sol, she knew. But it was not until one month after she had visited the stasis chamber that she asked David about it.

David had finished his daily checklist of chores, and after they ate he took Bethany to the command deck to watch some holos that Solomon had put together of the final days pre-Seed. It was a quiet evening, and few words passed between them until an image of David appeared on one of the records about the building of *EarthSeed 4*. Bethany giggled as he passed by the holocam, waving like the dumb kid he was. She stilled the holo and David smiled, too, trying not to think about how that was him and was not him—that it was another body, many lives ago.

"I thought it was illegal," she said.

He did not need an antecedent to know what she was talking about. "It was. Is, I guess. But certain allowances had to be made. The League felt that the missions were too important. They didn't want to give the AIs full autonomy. They didn't trust them."

"You hear that, Sol? They didn't trust you!" Bethany had grown more and more accustomed to the AI's presence as the weeks had passed. She had certainly seen the extent to which Solomon ran the ship.

"Yes, Bethany," the computer said. "It is true that fully capable AIs were a relatively new development at the time. The League's lack of faith in the engineering is understandable."

"You seem to be handling yourself okay, though?"

"Yes, Bethany. I have thus far experienced no difficulties and continue to fulfill my duties as designed."

"He only gets annoying every once in a while," David said. "I don't know why they couldn't program that out of him."

Bethany giggled again, but her gaze returned once more to the holo of David waving. "So they allowed one crew member for each mission, who had to be cloned for the duration of the journey out-Sol."

"In our case the journey to Epsilon Eridani, E2," David said.

"And the clones? They're not in any of the eggs down there, are they?"

"I really don't like to talk about this." David's voice had grown quiet. "But no, they're in a secondary stasis chamber."

"Fully grown?"

David shook his head. "No. The cloned eggs will head into incubators when I am fifty years old."

"Forty-nine and three months," Solomon corrected.

Bethany's eyebrow perked up for a moment before she understood the difference. "So they have nine months to gestate and they're born when you're fifty. But how many clones are bred? I assume that you must make more than one host just in case one, well, fails."

"Three," David said. "Listen, I really don't like to talk about this. Especially since . . ."

"Since I'm going to die and you'll go on living?"

David looked away and said nothing.

She stood and reached across to pat him on the hand. She was no longer smiling. "It's okay, David. This isn't living anyway. It's just prolonged death."

He recoiled slightly from her, felt a sudden and great weight on his chest. She turned to leave, shrugging past his outstretched hand. "I'm sorry," he said. "I couldn't just watch you die there. I couldn't . . ."

But she was gone.

David buried his face in his hands and wept until the ship's chimes told him that it was time for him to sleep.

•••

Boredom brought them together. He had shown her how to use the ship's letterdiscs and the holocasters, but she could only spend so much time alone before she felt the need to do something. David continued his routine work schedules as best he could, but he inevitably fell behind as he tried to spend time each day with Bethany. Solomon had assured him that human contact was an absolute necessity to her recovery. The AI had long since determined the human need for the companionship of another human being.

Before long, then, Bethany began to accompany David on some of his rounds, helping him to clean the command deck and what had become her bedroom. Despite the early tensions between them, a familiarity and then a fondness grew between them as time eased the pain of old wounds. In the solitude of the ship, there was no one else.

They never spoke of the future after that evening on the command deck. The fact that he would live on while she slowly withered and died passed into the background of their lives. Never forgotten, just never discussed.

Working together seemed to ease their minds, and the sounds of conversation and laughter came to replace much of the silence that had formerly held sway in the brooding vastness of the ship.

They made love for the first time in the reading lounge. It was their twelfth month together, and they had settled into a well-rehearsed routine of alternating work schedules on the cleaning and maintenance docket. Bethany, for her part, quickly learned the more mundane processes of keeping the ship in working condition, and she even made some aesthetically pleasing adjustments to the layout and decoration of some of the nonessential rooms on board. David was happier than he had been in lives.

She came to him in the night, the tinkling chime of the door's proximity notifier and a quiet knock announcing her arrival at the door of the lounge. David sat up on the couch, momentarily confused, before he cleared his throat and told Solomon to open the door.

Bethany was there, silhouetted by the soft red light of the main corridor. She was wearing a semitransparent gown that they had found in storage while searching for clothing one day. He could see the clear outline of her body under the fabric. She shifted on her feet. "Did I wake you?"

David cleared his throat again, pulling himself into a more relaxed sitting position. "No, no," he lied. "I had just finished reading a little bit ago."

"Oh," she said. "Can I come in?"

"Of course." David started to reach down the length of the couch to gather his linens up.

"No, no. Just leave them, David." Bethany sat down beside his feet, folded her hands in her lap.

"Is something wrong?"

She looked up, smiled, and shook her head. "No. I was just . . . awake. You know. I've been having those dreams."

"Of Earth and Sol?" He had dreamed of home for more nights than he could count.

"Of plains and a forest," she said. Her eyes looked

distant for a moment, but it did not last. "And the sea and the stars."

"I still have them, too," he said. "Though I hope they never go away."

She smiled again, and he smiled back. "Can I ask you a question?"

David blinked at her, thought about asking Solomon what time it was, then thought better of the idea. "Sure, Beth. What do you want to know?"

Bethany was looking down at her hands and took a moment to speak. "Why do you sleep in here while I sleep in the quarters?"

"Well, I guess I never thought about it. I just, since you came here, just let you have that room. That's all."

She nodded in the half-light. "It doesn't seem right to me. We share everything else on the ship. Shouldn't we share that, too?"

"We could if you wanted to," David said. "I could have Sol set up a schedule or something. Maybe one week on and one week off."

"No." Bethany's voice went softer even as she interrupted him. She moved her shoulders toward him and the gown partially opened. "I mean share it. Together."

David tried to say something but felt his voice catch in his throat.

"I want to live, David. If I must die, I want to live."

"I want to feel warmth again. I lie awake thinking of summer sunlight on my face. I miss the warmth."

David saw a flash of dampness in her eyes and she looked down for a moment. He wanted to reach out to her, but he could not move. He felt his heart pounding very heavy in his chest. When she raised her eyes, the look on her face had changed. It was a smile he had not seen before.

"We don't need the sun to feel warm," she said.

He tried to speak again but she was moving closer to him, lifting herself up on to the couch. She had untied her gown at some point, and now it hung open off her shoulders.

"Am I desirable?" It was hardly a question, and David didn't answer. "I'll take that as a yes," she whispered as she leaned forward.

For the first time in many tens of thousands of nights, David did not bother to get up when Solomon's quiet chimes told him that the sun was rising over Albuquerque—more than four light-years away.

•••

Things changed after that night. Routines and schedules disappeared. They would spend hours chasing each other around the decks of the ship, spend days just lying in bed and reveling in the warmth of their bodies. David's boredom vanished as they lived, loved, and learned together, and Bethany felt her pains melt away.

Solomon produced wonderful texts from the ship's libraries, plays of Shakespeare and Frayn that the two human companions would stage together. Solomon would record the performances and David and Bethany would waste long afternoons watching their own ridiculous antics and laughing at their inadequacies as performers. They even wrote a play of their own, *Paradise at 1/100 c,* in which they chronicled the story of their growing romance.

The previously austere living conditions on board suffered, but no one complained. David and Bethany still completed necessary work on the ship, but at a more leisurely pace than David had once maintained.

Somehow keeping things clean just didn't seem as important as it once had.

Solomon was satisfied that his ward was happy and occupied as the years began to roll by.

•••

They celebrated their tenth anniversary together by convincing Solomon to reverse the on-axis rotation thrusters and effectively turn off the in-ship gravity for a day. Zero g allowed them to finally manage some of the more intricate maneuvers of the *Kama Sutra*, and they spent two days recovering from the various bumps and bruises that were incurred from bouncing off the walls.

They talked of children sometimes, but they knew that it was just talk—the delicate balance of life on the ship had already been stretched to the breaking point by Bethany's presence. Solomon assured them that it would be impossible to maintain the balance if another life entered the mix. Still, the medilab was able to perform the necessary surgery to remove one of her ovaries and preserve her eggs along with some of David's sperm in the vain hope that one day, after *EarthSeed 4* reached its destination and the colony had begun, their children might be born. Solomon consented to this because he had come to know that allowing humans to dream was just as much of a psychological necessity as allowing them to love.

Eventually, of course, routines grew more frequent, and habit replaced the wonderment that they once felt with each other. But they were happy still. And they were content to let the years slip by like the stars that steadily moved into their wake.

Nine months before his fiftieth birthday, they went

to the secondary stasis chamber together and activated the machines that would ensure the continuation of David's life aboard the ship. Solomon had worked very diligently to find a way to replicate the process for Bethany, but he said that it was impossible. David would live, and Bethany would die.

David cried for many minutes after he pushed the button, and she held him while she wiped his tears away.

• • •

David's hands shook, and he was having a hard time keeping the boltdriver on the head of the hexnut. He sighed, put the tool down, and looked over his shoulder at Bethany and the reading lounge. *Almost seventy now*. The time would come soon. Death would come soon. For him, then for her.

"I'm going to die soon," he said.

Bethany was sitting on the couch, reading a book. "Oh, stop that, David. Just take a deep breath and try it again."

For a moment he lowered his eyes and thought about not talking about it, as if silence might keep death at bay. But he knew there was no way around it. Death was coming. There was a schedule to be kept. "No, I mean I'll die soon. Very soon now."

She raised her gray eyebrows but did not put the book down.

"I have to die soon, Bethany. The clones are . . ."

His voice choked off, but Bethany simply smiled, carefully laid a bookmark in the spine of the book, and set the volume beside her on the couch. "I know," she said. "I've been visiting the other stasis chamber regularly, David. Helping Sol to check on their progress. I've watched them growing."

David stared. "I didn't know."

"I was a biomedical engineer once, remember? When Sol asked me for help, it made sense."

He tried to form words, but none came.

She looked down at him kindly, almost maternally, and watched as he slowly got to his knees and shuffled over to kneel before her. He was beginning to cry, and she ran a hand through his thinning hair. "I've done a lot of work with Sol in these past years, my love. Though you were often too busy to notice my absences."

David finally released the chokehold on his voice. "Why didn't you say anything?"

"For the same reason we never talked about my family, David. About Uriah and Jesse."

"But you don't remember them."

Bethany giggled for a moment, then reached out to his old hands. "Oh, I remember them, my love. I remembered a long time ago."

"When? When did you know?"

"I accessed my own files over time. In those first months, I worked hard to remember." Despite the deep wrinkles on her face and the dark circles under her eyes, she was still beautiful when she smiled. "You should have thought to lock those files up, love."

"You've remembered them all along?"

"Yes."

Her son, her husband, her life. She'd seen them so many times, cleaned the plexiglass windows of their stasis eggs, rerouted the pumplines and cables that coursed fluids into and out of their bodies. For decades she had remembered them and said nothing. "Why?"

"Because there was nothing I could do, David. I

couldn't bring them back, too. It was a miracle that I survived. I did think about going into stasis again, but percentages for refreezes are close to zero—you know that."

"But your family. Uriah and Jesse . . ." He could barely say their names.

"I am already dead to them. By the time they awake," *if they awake,* she thought, "I'll have been dead for hundreds of years. I knew from the beginning that I was dead to them."

"But there had to be another way," he croaked.

"You know there wasn't." Her hands trembled in frustration and love. "The percentages were so small."

David shook his head in denial. "But still possible. Solomon and I would have all that time to do research, to try to understand . . ."

"To understand what, David?" She felt her own eyes growing wet now. "Don't you think that I tried to figure out a way in those first months? But there was nothing I could do. And when I learned that I loved you, my reasons for trying grew smaller everyday. I was dead to them, but alive to you. I still remember the way that you used to look at me back then. I could see the need and the hunger in your eyes—even on that first night when I awoke. You'd been alone for so long, and I knew that you loved me and I learned that I loved you, too."

He reached out to her face with liver-spotted, trembling hands. "I did love you, my angel."

She sighed, pulling his old hands to her thinned lips. "I know, my love. And that's all that matters. Don't you see? I've lived, and loved, with you, willingly, for all these years. It's our love that makes us who we are, David. It's what makes us human. Don't you understand that? I loved you too much to take the risk.

And I think you needed me too much to let me take it."
She pulled him close to her, embraced him, and kissed him on the cheek.

"But you're going to die," he croaked.

"I've already died once," she said. "Let this time be with you."

"But I don't . . ."

"Shhh." She began to rock him gently, like a baby. "Death is human, too."

•••

David awoke with a gasp, his arms instinctively flailing out into the darkness to grab hold of something. He heard movement, felt a hand grip his own and hold it tight.

He opened his eyes in the growing light of the room, saw the machines, the muted gray ceiling, and the familiar face of his beloved.

"Welcome back," she said.

David took a deep breath, smiled, and moved into a sitting position. "It's good to be back," he said.

"I was worried," she said. Her voice sounded harsh and weathered compared to his. "But Sol assured me that everything was fine."

"TSD three months, six days, SET," Sol said from somewhere behind her.

David looked down at his new body and at the wrinkled flesh of Bethany's hand. "I'm sorry," he said.

She started to say something, then stopped to bite her lower lip just like she had on that very first night. "It's okay," she said.

David nodded. He was having a hard time looking at her. "I know. It's just that, well . . ."

"It's for the best," she said, cutting him off. "The band must play on. And besides, you look good."

David was prepared to tell her how sorry he was for being young again, for living on without her, for making her realize how mortal she was, for everything that was to come and for everything that would never come—but there was something distantly familiar in her voice that distracted him. He looked up into her eyes and saw the glimmer of something mischievous as her gaze passed over him. "Beth?"

Her gaze had stopped roaming. She wasn't looking at his eyes. "You look very good."

Her fingers ran across his flesh knowingly, then pulled away as she straightened and stood before him. Her skin was slack, the shape of her body sagging where once it had been tight and firm. But the eyes and the smile were still the Beth that he had known and loved for nearly fifty years. The fingers that had touched him, that brought shivers across his flesh, were still Beth. She had stopped smiling as he stared at her, and her shoulders seemed to fall as she looked down at her own body. "I'll understand if you don't want to, my love. I am so much older . . . I will be content . . ." Her voice trailed off and a single tear began falling down her wrinkled cheek.

David reached out to her, grabbed the hands that he loved, and pulled her into his embrace. They held each other for a long time before retiring to their room to ensure that he was, indeed, fully functional.

• • •

David was on the command deck, cleaning a vent regulator, when a quiet chime got his attention.

"What is it, Sol?"

"It's Beth," the AI said. "She's asking for you."

David put his tools down and hurried to their bedroom. The lights were dim in the room, but he could see the gentle rise and fall of her chest in the darkness. He stopped at the doorway and watched her for a moment.

"Hi," she whispered.

"Hi," he said. "Did you need some water?"

She shook her head and lifted the hand at her side in order to tap the bed covers. "Just come sit awhile, my love."

David sat on the edge of the bed, taking her hand in his. It was very thin, very weak. The cancer, though detected by the medilab very early, was unrelenting. It kept pace with the nanotechs, its growth outpacing their abilities to cut it away from her flesh. And there were only so many drugs that the medilab could afford to spare. The supplies would have to last for many hundreds of years, so David and Solomon had been forced to watch as she rotted away from the inside out.

"Are you feeling okay?"

She let out a slow breath. "Fine, David. Everything is fine. I just wanted some company, that's all."

"Of course." He smiled, but felt too conscious of the act.

"Sol is no good for conversation," she said.

David's smile was genuine. "I know."

"I am sorry," Solomon said. "I have grown increasingly aware of my limitations in this regard."

"It's okay, Sol. I was just kid——" Bethany's words broke off as she began coughing. David put his hand behind her head and tried to hold her still until the fit subsided. He wiped at her mouth with a cloth. "I was kidding," she said at last.

"I see," Solomon said.

Minutes passed as David rubbed her fragile hand with gentle strokes. "What are you thinking about?" he asked.

"About a meadow of flowers," she said. The deep folds at the corners of her mouth lifted slightly and the gray wash over her sight seemed to dissipate for a moment. Her eyes looked like stars in the darkness. "A high-mountain meadow near Boulder where we used to take Jesse and fly kites."

"Were there flowers?"

"Oh, yes. In springtime there were great beds of flowers. Great swaths of mixing color. I wish you could have been there."

He gripped her hand a little harder. "Me, too."

"You would have liked Jesse, I think." She stopped to cough a little and David had to wipe some of the spittle from her lips again. "Do you think he will remember me?"

"How could he forget you?"

She smiled again, and her breathing grew easier.

"I'll never forget you," he said.

Bethany turned to look at him, blinked.

"What color was the kite, Beth? Was it green?"

Bethany was still smiling, but she did not reply.

• • •

Bethany died on a Tuesday as the sun was high in the sky over Albuquerque, four and a half light-years away. That night, David stood in the doorway of the stasis chamber, his eyes dull and his face without expression. The long room stretched out and away from him like an endless tunnel bored into the nothingness of space.

The Keeper Alone

It was nighttime in New Mexico, and the maintenance lights were on, shining down dim pools of soft white at twenty-meter intervals. The rest of the room was awash in blurred green from the twin lines of egg status beacons that receded into the far distance. David stood for many minutes, counting.

One thousand eggs. Nine hundred and ninety-nine men, women and children. He had cleaned every one of those eggs on this day, careful to wipe and buff the smooth sheets of plexiglass that encased them like shrouds. He had called up the name, age and occupation of each human being and spoken to each of them, addressing them face to face as if they could still see.

David stopped counting, his eyes returning to linger on egg 631. *One light out*, he kept thinking. *One light out*.

• • •

Elsewhere, deep in the electronic recesses of the ship, Solomon silently maintained *EarthSeed*'s operating parameters. Nestled in a steady stream of ever-changing variables, the computer watched and waited, knowing that for humans mourning, too, could be an occupation.

THE YEAR IN THE CONTESTS

by
Algis Budrys

The judges in this year are named on the cover of this book. They are amazingly prestigious and knowledgeable contributors to L. Ron Hubbard's original (and still growing) vision. This has been true from the very beginning, though some names are, sadly, no longer with us and others, happily, have stepped forward to take their place.

We have been pleased to welcome judge Steven Youll and Stephen Hickman to our stellar panel of judges for the L. Ron Hubbard Illustrators of the Future Contest.

The enterprise goes ever forward, and the authors and illustrators in this volume will, in due course, take their firm place in the history of speculative arts. For the 2004 year, L. Ron Hubbard's Writers of the Future Contest winners are:

First Quarter
1. Sidra M.S. Vitale
   My Daughter, the Martian
2. Eric James Stone
   Betrayer of Trees
3. Cat Sparks
   Last Dance at the Sergeant Majors' Ball

Second Quarter
1. John Schoffstall
   In the Flue
2. David W. Goldman
   The Story of His Life
3. M.T. Reiten
   Needle Child

Third Quarter
1. Stephen R. Stanley
   Mars Hath No Fury Like a Pixel Double-Crossed
2. Scott M. Roberts
   Blackberry Witch
3. Michael Livingston
   The Keeper Alone

Fourth Quarter
1. Floris M. Kleijne
   Meeting the Sculptor
2. Sean A. Tinsley
   Green Angel
3. Ken Scholes
   Into the Blank Where Life is Hurled

Published Finalists
1. Mike Rimar
   Annus Mirabilis
2. Andrew Gudgel
   The Firebird
3. Lon Prater
   Deadglass

L. Ron Hubbard's Illustrators of the Future Contest 2004 winners:

Erik Valdez y Alanis	Youri Bobrikov
Michael Brenner	Cornelius Cockroft
Perrin Hendrick	Ali Hilton
Olga Madiar	Alex Paramonov
Steven V. Popovich	Alex Quintero
Michael Wohlwend	

Our heartiest congratulations to them all! May we see much more of their work in the future.

NEW WRITERS!

L. Ron Hubbard's
Writers of the Future Contest

OPPORTUNITY FOR
NEW AND AMATEUR WRITERS OF
NEW SHORT STORIES OR NOVELETTES OF
SCIENCE FICTION OR FANTASY

No entry fee is required.
Entrants retain all publication rights.

ALL AWARDS ARE ADJUDICATED BY
PROFESSIONAL WRITERS ONLY

PRIZES EVERY THREE MONTHS: $1,000, $750, $500.
ANNUAL GRAND PRIZE: $4,000 ADDITIONAL!

Don't Delay! Send Your Entry to:
L. Ron Hubbard's
Writers of the Future Contest
P.O. Box 1630
Los Angeles, CA 90078

Web site: www.writersofthefuture.com

CONTEST RULES

1. No entry fee is required and all rights in the story remain the property of the author. All types of science fiction, fantasy and horror with fantastic elements are welcome.

2. All entries must be original works, in English. Plagiarism, which includes the use of third-party poetry, song lyrics, characters or another person's universe, without written permission, will result in disqualification. Excessive violence or sex, determined by the judges, will result in disqualification. Entries may not have been previously published in professional media.

3. To be eligible, entries must be works of prose, up to 17,000 words in length. We regret we cannot consider poetry or works intended for children.

4. The Contest is open only to those who have not had professionally published a novel or short novel, or more than one novelette, or more than three short stories, in any medium. Professional publication is deemed to be payment, and at least 5,000 copies or 5,000 hits.

5. Entries must be typewritten or a computer printout in black ink on white paper, double spaced, with numbered pages. All other formats will be disqualified. Each entry must have a cover page with the title of the work, the author's name, address and telephone number, an approximate word count and e-mail address if available. Every subsequent page must carry the title and a page number, but the author's name must be deleted to facilitate fair judging.

6. Manuscripts will be returned after judging if the author has provided return postage and a self-addressed envelope. If the author does not wish return of the manuscript, a business-size self-addressed, stamped envelope (or valid e-mail address) must be included with the entry in order to receive judging results.

7. We accept only an entry for which no delivery signature is required by us to receive it.

8. There shall be three cash prizes in each quarter: a First Prize of $1,000, a Second Prize of $750 and a Third Prize of $500, in U.S. dollars or the recipient's local equivalent amount. In addition, at the end of the year the four First Prize winners will have their entries rejudged, and a Grand Prize winner shall be determined and will receive an additional $4,000. All winners will also receive trophies or certificates.

9. The Contest has four quarters, beginning on October 1, January 1, April 1 and July 1. The year will end on September 30. To be eligible for judging in its quarter, an entry must be postmarked no later than midnight on the last day of the quarter.

10. Each entrant may submit only one manuscript per quarter. Winners are ineligible to make further entries in the Contest.

11. All entries for each quarter are final. No revisions are accepted.

12. Entries will be judged by professional authors. The decisions of the judges are entirely their own, and are final.

13. Winners in each quarter will be individually notified of the results by mail.

14. This Contest is void where prohibited by law.

© 1986, 1988, 2000, 2004, 2005 L. Ron Hubbard Library. All Rights Reserved. WRITERS OF THE FUTURE and the Writers of the Future logo are trademarks owned by L. Ron Hubbard Library.

NEW ILLUSTRATORS!

L. Ron Hubbard's
Illustrators of the Future Contest

OPEN TO NEW SCIENCE FICTION AND FANTASY ARTISTS WORLDWIDE

No entry fee is required.
Entrants retain all publication rights.

ALL JUDGING BY PROFESSIONAL ARTISTS ONLY

$1,500 IN PRIZES EACH QUARTER
QUARTERLY WINNERS COMPETE FOR
$4,000 ADDITIONAL ANNUAL PRIZE

Don't Delay! Send Your Entry to:
L. Ron Hubbard's
Illustrators of the Future Contest
P.O. Box 3190
Los Angeles, CA 90078

Web site: www.writersofthefuture.com

CONTEST RULES

1. The Contest is open to entrants from all nations. (However, entrants should provide themselves with some means for written communication in English.) All themes of science fiction and fantasy illustrations are welcome: every entry is judged on its own merits only. No entry fee is required, and all rights in the entries remain the property of the artists.

2. By submitting work to the Contest, the entrant agrees to abide by all Contest rules.

3. The Contest is open to those who have not previously published more than three black-and-white or color illustrations in media distributed nationally to the general public, such as magazines or books sold at newsstands, or books sold in stores merchandising to the general public. The submitted entry shall not have been previously published in professional media as exampled above.

If you are not sure of your eligibility, write to the Contest address with details, enclosing a business-size self-addressed envelope with return postage. The Contest Administration will reply with a determination.

Winners in previous quarters are not eligible to make further entries.

4. Only one entry per quarter is permitted. The entry must be original to the entrant. Plagiarism, infringement of the rights of others, or other violations of the Contest rules will result in disqualification.

5. An entry shall consist of three illustrations done by the entrant in a color or black-and-white medium. Use of gray scale in illustrations and mixed media, computer generated art, the use of photography in illustration, are accepted. Each must represent a theme different from the other two.

6. ENTRIES SHOULD NOT BE THE ORIGINAL DRAWINGS, but should be large color or black-and-white copies of a quality satisfactory to the entrant. Entries must be submitted unfolded and flat, in an envelope no larger than 9 inches by 12 inches.

All entries must be accompanied by a self-addressed return envelope of the appropriate size, with correct U.S. postage affixed. (Non-U.S. entrants should enclose international postal reply coupons.) If the entrant does not want the photocopies returned, the entry should be clearly marked DISPOSABLE COPIES: DO NOT RETURN.

A business-size self-addressed envelope with correct postage (or valid e-mail address) should be included so that judging results can be returned to the entrant.

We accept only an entry for which no delivery signature is required by us to receive it.

7. To facilitate anonymous judging, each of the three photocopies must be accompanied by a removable cover sheet bearing the artist's name, address, telephone number, and an identifying title for that work as well as an e-mail address if available. The photocopy of the work should carry the same identifying title, and the artist's signature should be deleted from the photocopy.

The Contest Administration will remove and file the cover sheets, and forward only the anonymous entry to the judges.

8. To be eligible for a quarterly judging, an entry must be postmarked no later than the last day of the quarter.

Late entries will be included in the following quarter, and the Contest Administration will so notify the entrant.

9. There will be three co-winners in each quarter. Each winner will receive an outright cash grant of U.S. $500, and a trophy or a certificate. Such winners also receive eligibility to compete for the annual Grand Prize of an additional outright cash grant of $4,000 together with the annual Grand Prize trophy.

10. Competition for the Grand Prize is designed to acquaint the entrant with customary practices in the field of professional illustrating. It will be conducted in the following manner:

Each winner in each quarter will be furnished a specification sheet giving details on the size and kind of black-and-white illustration work required for the Grand Prize competition. Requirements will be of the sort customarily stated by professional publishing companies.

These specifications will be furnished to the entrant by the Contest Administration, using Return Receipt Requested mail or its equivalent.

Also furnished will be a copy of a science fiction or fantasy story, to be illustrated by the entrant. This story will have been selected for that purpose by the Coordinating Judge of the Contest. Thereafter, the entrant will work toward completing the assigned illustration.

In order to retain eligibility for the Grand Prize, each entrant shall, within thirty (30) days of receipt of the said story assignment, send to the Contest address the entrant's black-and-white or color illustration of the assigned story in accordance with the specification sheet.

The entrant's finished illustration shall be in the form of camera-ready art prepared in accordance with the specification sheet and securely packed, shipped at the entrant's own risk. The Contest will exercise due care in handling all submissions as received.

The said illustration will then be judged in competition for the Grand Prize on the following basis only:

Each Grand Prize judge's personal opinion on the extent to which it makes the judge want to read the story it illustrates.

11. The Contest shall contain four quarters each year, beginning on October 1 and going on to January 1, April 1 and July 1, with the year ending at midnight on September 30. Entrants in each quarter will be individually notified of the quarter's judging results by mail. The winning entrants' participation in the Contest shall continue until the results of the Grand Prize judging have been announced.

12. The Grand Prize winner shall be announced at the L. Ron Hubbard Awards Event to be held in the year subsequent to the year of the particular Contest.

13. Entries will be judged by professional artists only. Each quarterly judging and the Grand Prize judging may have different panels of judges. The decisions of the judges are entirely their own and are final.

14. This Contest is void where prohibited by law.

© 1986, 1988, 2000, 2004, 2005 L. Ron Hubbard Library. All Rights Reserved. ILLUSTRATORS OF THE FUTURE and the Illustrators of the Future logo are trademarks owned by L. Ron Hubbard Library.

1
12
6
7
20

9 k l   shorthand 4 1 MMF couch
same as 12 ← drunk   8 9 unbutton

L. RON HUBBARD
PRESENTS
THE BEST OF
WRITERS
OF THE FUTURE

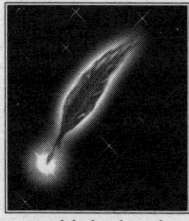

VOYAGE TO OTHER WORLDS

L. Ron Hubbard established the WRITERS OF THE FUTURE Contest in late 1983, offering new and aspiring writers a chance to have their works seen and acknowledged. Since that beginning, the imaginative works from these exceptionally talented new writers in the fields of science fiction and fantasy have been published in the L. RON HUBBARD PRESENTS WRITERS OF THE FUTURE anthologies and have provided readers with an escape to new worlds.

As was L. Ron Hubbard's intention, many of these talents have gone on to become recognized writers. Now for the first time, sixteen creative stories from the first eight volumes that helped launch successful careers have been assembled, providing hours of reading entertainment—your ticket to spellbinding adventures across the Galaxy.

The writers in this book include many you now know, who were—in most cases—first published in one of the earlier anthologies. These names include James Alan Gardner, Karen Joy Fowler, Nina Kiriki Hoffman, Robert Reed, Dean Wesley Smith, Nancy Farmer and ten more.

This first-rate collection includes works from judges Anne McCaffrey, Frederik Pohl and Tim Powers, who if given the opportunity to enter this contest at the inception of their careers would have done so with these well-told tales. Also included are invaluable tips on writing from Frank Herbert and Algis Budrys.

ORDER YOUR COPY TODAY!

U.S. $14.95,   CAN $22.95
Call toll free: 1-877-8GALAXY or
visit www.writersofthefuture.com

Mail your order to:

Galaxy Press, L.L.C.
7051 Hollywood Blvd., Suite 200, Hollywood, CA 90028

L. RON HUBBARD
TO THE STARS

READ L. Ron Hubbard's sweeping science fiction epic *To the Stars* is set in a perilous future when deep space starships vault the galaxy at nearly the speed of light, leaving their pioneering crews essentially untouched—but exiled—by the passage of time, while back on Earth whole generations and societies vanish forever.

Journey with the men and women of the *Hound of Heaven* and share their challenges, their emotions and their beleaguered pursuit of a vision—and a hidden destiny—that will give a whole new meaning to man's place in the stars.

ORDER YOUR COPY TODAY!

Retail Price: U.S. $24.95, CAN $34.95

Phone Toll Free: 1-877-8GALAXY Fax: 1-323-466-7817

www.tothestars.com

Galaxy Press, L.L.C., 7051 Hollywood Boulevard, Suite 200, Hollywood, CA 90028

CHICK COREA ELEKTRIC BAND
TO THE STARS

LISTEN to the Unforgettable Music of *To the Stars*

The massive sweep, scope, power and vivid human drama of one of the greatest novels in the history of science fiction—L. Ron Hubbard's *To the Stars*—has been captured by 12-time Grammy award-winning Chick Corea and his famed Elektric Band in a superbly imaginative tone poem that spectacularly breaks new musical ground.

Chick Corea's virtuoso musical journey weaves melodies, rhythms and tonal moods into what has been acclaimed as an unrivaled technical and creative triumph.

Let the groundbreaking music of the album inspired by *To the Stars* help speed your voyage through space and time and the wonders of the universe.

ORDER YOUR COPY TODAY!

Retail Price: U.S. $19.00, CAN $27.00
Phone Toll Free:1-877-8GALAXY Fax:1-323-466-7817
www.tothestars.com

Galaxy Press, L.L.C., 7051 Hollywood Boulevard, Suite 200, Hollywood, CA 90028

THE *NEW YORK TIMES* BESTSELLER
BATTLEFIELD EARTH
A Saga of the Year 3000
by L. RON HUBBARD

"Tight plotting, furious action and have at 'em entertainment."

— KIRKUS REVIEW

An imaginative masterwork of science fiction adventure and one of the bestselling science fiction novels of all time, L. Ron Hubbard's *Battlefield Earth* opens with breathtaking scope on an Earth dominated for a thousand years by an alien invader—and man is an endangered species. From the handful of surviving humans, a courageous leader emerges— Jonnie Goodboy Tyler—who challenges the invincible might of the alien empire in an exciting battle of epic scale, danger and intrigue, with the fate of Earth and of the universe in the tenuous balance.

A perennial and international bestseller with nearly 8 million copies sold, *Battlefield Earth* has been voted among the top three of the best one hundred English novels of the twentieth century in the Random House Modern Library Readers Poll, and has won worldwide critical acclaim.

TO ORDER THIS GRIPPING TALE

Call toll free: 1-877-8GALAXY or visit www.battlefieldearth.com

U.S. $7.99, CAN $11.99

Mail in your order to:
Galaxy Press, L.L.C.
7051 Hollywood Blvd., Suite 200, Hollywood, CA 90028

FINAL BLACKOUT

A DYNAMIC AND POWERFUL BATTLE FOR FREEDOM

As the great World War grinds to a halt, a force more sinister than Hitler's Nazis has seized control of Europe and is systematically destroying every adversary—except one. In the heart of France, a crack unit of soldiers survives, overcoming all opposition under the leadership of a hardened military strategist trained in every method of combat and known only as "The Lieutenant."

Ordered to return to headquarters, the Lieutenant is torn between obeying the politicians in London or doing what he knows is right for his country, regardless of the price.

Many novels have envisioned the consequences of a future war, but few have read with such sustained tension and riveting suspense as L. Ron Hubbard's fast-paced tale.

"As perfect a piece of science fiction as has ever been written."
—Robert Heinlein

GET YOUR COPY TODAY!

Paperback: U.S. $6.99, CAN $8.99
Audio: U.S. $15.95, CAN $18.95 (2 cassettes, 3 hours)
Narrated by Roddy McDowall
Call toll free: 1-877-8GALAXY or visit www.galaxypress.com

Mail your order to:

Galaxy Press, L.L.C.
7051 Hollywood Blvd., Suite 200, Hollywood, CA 90028

Mission Earth
BY L. RON HUBBARD

The ten-volume action-packed intergalactic spy adventure

"A superbly imaginative, intricately plotted invasion of Earth."
—*Chicago Tribune*

An entertaining narrative told from the eyes of alien invaders, *Mission Earth* is packed with captivating suspense and adventure.

Heller, a Royal Combat Engineer, has been sent on a desperate mission to halt the self-destruction of Earth—wholly unaware that a secret branch of his own government (the Coordinated Information Apparatus) has dispatched its own agent, whose sole purpose is to sabotage him at all costs, as part of its clandestine operation.

With a cast of dynamic characters, biting satire and plenty of twists, action and emotion, Heller is pitted against incredible odds in this intergalactic game where the future of Earth hangs in the balance.

"If you don't force yourself to set it down and talk to your family from time to time, you may be looking for a new place to live." — Orson Scott Card

". . . all the entertainment anybody could ask for."
— *New York Newsday*

Each Volume a *New York Times* Bestseller:

Available in paperback for $7.99 or audio for $18.00 each

Vol. 1. The Invaders Plan
Vol. 2. Black Genesis
Vol. 3. The Enemy Within
Vol. 4. An Alien Affair
Vol. 5. Fortune of Fear

Vol. 6. Death Quest
Vol. 7. Voyage of Vengeance
Vol. 8. Disaster
Vol. 9. Villainy Victorious
Vol. 10. The Doomed Planet

Buy Your Copies Today!

Call toll free: 1-877-8GALAXY or visit www.galaxypress.com
Mail your order to:
Galaxy Press, L.L.C.
7051 Hollywood Blvd., Suite 200
Hollywood, CA 90028

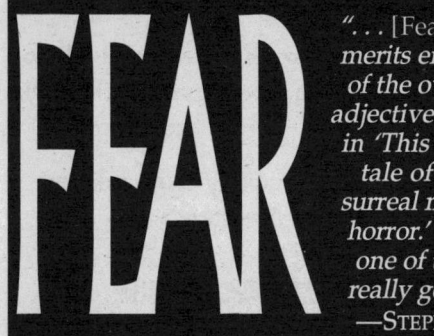

"...[Fear] actually merits employment of the overworked adjective 'classic,' as in 'This is a classic tale of creeping, surreal menace and horror.'... This is one of the really, really good ones."
—STEPHEN KING

A CHILLING NOVEL OF SUSPENSE

Professor James Lowry doesn't believe in spirits, or witches, or demons. Not until one gentle spring evening when his hat disappears, along with four hours of his life. Now the quiet university town of Atworthy is changing—just slightly at first, then faster and more frighteningly each time he tries to remember. Lowry is pursued by a dark, secret evil that is turning his whole world against him while it whispers a warning from the shadows

If you find your hat you'll find your four hours. If you find your four hours then you will die....

L. Ron Hubbard has carved out a masterful tale filled with biting twists and chilling turns that will make your heart beat faster as the tension mounts through each line of the story—while he takes a very ordinary man, in a very ordinary circumstance and descends him into a completely plausible and terrifyingly real hell.

Why is *Fear* so powerful? Because it really could happen.

Paperback: U.S. $7.99, CAN $11.99
Audio: U.S. $15.95, CAN $18.95 (2 cassettes, 3 hours)
Narrated by Roddy McDowall
Call toll free: 1-877-8GALAXY or visit www.galaxypress.com

Mail your order to:

Galaxy Press, L.L.C.
7051 Hollywood Blvd., Suite 200, Hollywood, CA 90028